___The Noble Souls: Book I___

NIGHTBREAKER

Adam Booth

NIGHTBREAKER

Cover art by Tom Lopez.
https://www.artstation.com/artist/tomlopez

Tomlopez.art@gmail.com

Cover design by Jenny Webb.
www.jennywebbedits.com

Printed by CreateSpace. Available for order from Amazon.com and CreateSpace.com.

ISBN-13: 978-0692494714
ISBN-10: 0692494715

First Edition: 2016

For more information about The Noble Souls series, please visit:

www.thenoblesouls.com

For my wife, Erin Rebecca,
who loved Valerie first.

Prologue

Marshall set the phone down, his hands steady. He was going to die—that much was sure—but he had faced this threat before. Except now, he did not feel the fear, the dread of things undone. Now, he felt fire in his chest, his soul rising.

The fight, he thought, remembering the sage words of his first teacher, *it is a long one. And there is only one victory...*

Marshall rose from his small chair, taking two steps to the window of his shanty trailer. Splitting the blinds with his fingers, he peered out in the desert. The shadow of night crept over the orange dust where gnarled weeds and ancient rocks stood solitary in the arid gloom. They were out there, the enemy. He did not need to use his darksight to be sure. They had come, as he always expected they would.

Inevitable, yes, and unfortunate.

"Marty," Warren's recording had said, "I wouldn't call if it wasn't worth the risk. I've found another." There had been a pause then, as Warren seemed to choose his next words carefully. "She's ready. More than...the others. We need to start now. No more waiting. I can bring her to you, but I have to know where. Trust me on this one."

Marshall smiled, despite his encroaching doom. Warren had sounded so confident, so sure. A welcome change. He was sure Warren was right, and more than anything, Marshall wanted to know which of the girls it was. Was it young Daphne? Or was it Valerie?

They must be how old now? he wondered, but the numbers were lost in the haze of passing years in exile. He could reach out through his dreams to answer the mystery, but he was certain darker powers would be watching, waiting to catch a glimpse of his mind.

And they had been. Marshall had returned one message, encoded, carrying his longitude and latitude, along with a single word: BRAZIL. Again, Marshall smiled. *That'll get Warren's spirits riled,* he thought. A target, a destination, a place to focus his efforts. An exciting leap out of limbo.

Of course, that single message, while a boon to Warren, came at great cost to Marshall. The enemy had been vigilant, and once the message had been sent through the billions of data-streams, they intercepted it and used it find him here.

Surviving the small gesture of sending a message was always a long shot, Marshall knew. But it was worth it. Warren would come. He would discover Marshall's dead body—probably mutilated—and then, once Warren allowed himself a moment to recover, he would find Marshall's treasure of knowledge. He was going to need all of it, as would those he trained.

Valerie, Marshall thought, remembering only glimpses of a small child from old dreams. *It's her. Has to be.*

How he wished to meet her. He wished he could complete the circle. To make things right. To atone for all the evil he had done. In his heart, however, he knew he was not deserving of such an end. What was coming—*who* was coming—was his true legacy, and he deserved to meet his end at those hands.

He heard the crunch of footsteps grinding grains of sand beneath hard soles. The woman approaching his trailer made no attempt at stealth. There was something to the rhythm of her steps, the graceful yet unstable gait that pronounced her presence. *Ismena.* The one he should have never taken, his greatest failure and mistake, had come back to him. It was only fitting.

"Excuse me," her voice called out. "Can I borrow a cup of sugar? I'm baking a cake, and, well, I'm fresh out."

She isn't scared of me, he thought, uncomfortable with the sudden implications of this. Mena had always been...disturbed. But also insecure, quick to cower beneath her betters. A renewed confidence in her signaled something bad, something unexpected. This all gave rise to so many questions, the first and most important being, *how did she get free?* It was too late to wonder now. She was here. That was all he could contend with.

Best to keep a cool head, he told himself.

Unlatching the deadbolt catch, Marshall opened the door and flicked it aside. He stood at the threshold, bare and unprotected. He would not enliven his power. Tonight, he would be a man like any other. He gazed out onto the faint ring of light his small trailer cast, searching for her.

"Ismena, there's no reason to be rude—"

The woman burst from the dark, barreling into him. His vision swirled in doubles as a red swell of pain crackled in the back of his head. Last of all, he realized he could not breathe with her forearm crushing his throat. Looking in her eyes, he saw the hate, the eagerness to get revenge for all his crimes against her, real and imagined. He did not resist.

But his submission to this fate was not enough for her, it seemed. She dislodged her arm from his windpipe then gripped his throat, not squeezing to cut off his breath. Gasping, Marshall coughed and heaved air, his face flushing hot while blood rushed into it.

"S'matter?" she purred. "Not going to fight back?" Her eyes combed his face, looking for the Marshall she had known. She snarled, perhaps disappointed to find only fragments of that man.

She smiled suddenly. "I gotta say. You really let yourself go." She poked his nose with a finger and winked. "I won't though. Promise."

Then he felt her fingers dig into his hair and scalp. She raised his head then slammed it into the floor. With the first strike, it was either the floorboards or his skull that cracked. The second time, he was sure it was his skull.

Marshall rose out of a bad dream where he had been killed, his head bashed on the floor of his small home. As his vision focused out of a blur, he gathered that he had neither died, nor had it been a dream. Despite the throbbing pain in the back of his head, his wits were returning to him. He ventured to move an arm, but couldn't. A coil of electrical cords bound him to a chair, his arms pinned behind his back, his ankles fastened together. The binds were a make-shift mess: the plug from his blender and microwave and two or three extension cords all coiled tightly around his bare body. She had removed his shirt and pants, leaving him embarrassingly exposed in his boxers only. He studied the pale, freckled skin, sagging now after years of isolation.

You know, he thought, *I really did let myself go.*

"That a grin on your face, geezer?" she asked. She rose from his cushioned armchair. She was a beautiful woman, insanity aside. Her own skin was pale, but not flawed with freckles. It was porcelain smooth, encased in a gleam of chestnut hair, pulled back in a tight bun. Her blue eyes sparkled, concealing the monster she truly was within. Though thin, she was fit, strengthened by years in the Fighting Pits. *Yes,* Marshall thought. *She is a monster. One I created.*

Looking away from her, he noticed now that she had trashed his small trailer. Furniture had been knocked over, cabinet doors were left open, and drawers had been ransacked of their contents. Cutlery lay strewn about his feet, along with the clutter of plastic plates and cups. A bottle of detergent was dripping the last of its contents into a large green puddle that now nipped at his big toe.

He sighed, leaving the grin on his face. "I see you've made yourself at home."

In a flash, she had him by the throat, the edge of his long kitchen knife ready to cut. "Listen to me, you old, pathetic..." Pausing, she searched for the right insult. She scowled suddenly, while looking at his body. "Ew. You look like a...like an old marshmallow." She grimaced thoughtfully. "Marshmallow. That's perfect."

She hasn't changed, he thought. *She's just...grown stronger.* Within, Marshall felt a flicker of his old fire, the need to fight, the responsibility to combat monstrosity to spare others its malice. But he was old now, and even with his strength, he wasn't sure he would be able to overpower her.

Not now. She had risen, and he was in decline. His thoughts went suddenly to the mission at hand: ensure that she didn't discover all his work, the notes, the literature, the clues... The answer to the riddle. Warren and his new protégé were going to need it.

He felt his stomach twist then. *I would like to have seen her,* he thought, feebly. *I would like to have spoken with her, looked her in the eyes. To see what was inside, that woman from long ago...*

Ismena smacked him across the cheek. "Hey," she said, snapping her fingers at his nose. "Stay with me, okay?"

He took in a breath and sighed, ignoring the heat in his cheek and the fresh throbbing in his head. Lifting his chin, he looked her in the eyes.

"Awe," she moaned, frowning. "Are you getting all misty on me?" She snatched him, two-handed, by the ears and yanked his face to hers, their noses touching. "Are you sorry?" she growled. "Hm? Is that what you want to say, Marshmallow? That you're sorry for what you did to me?"

Searching his eyes, she snarled, her upper lip twitching with bridled rage. Standing back, she threw his head aside, breathing deeply to control her smoldering emotions. "Well, it's too late, get it?" She held her arms out wide and grinned. "This is what I am. And you know what? Thank you, Marshmallow. Yeah, thank you, for helping me see the truth. About what it takes to be strong. When you threw me into the darkness, I was a stupid, pathetic little girl who didn't understand power. But now I do. So, thank you."

Marshall swallowed, gazing at the floor. Now he felt the weight of his sins, each one, piling on his shoulders. Old ghosts lining up behind him, old memories breaking their silence after so many years. Their faces, their names—ones he could not utter even in thought—returned to him. All they had sacrificed, all they had given, all while he stood aside and did nothing, a coward. *Perhaps,* he thought. *Perhaps in this I can make it all worth something.*

"What?" Mena said, grasping that she had been ignored. "No, 'You're welcome, Mena'? Nothing? After all that closure, you've got nothing to say?" She rushed at him, knife at his throat. "Say it!" she screamed. "Say it, 'You're welcome, Mena.' Say it!"

His eyes snapped to hers. "That isn't why you came here, Ismena." He matched her gaze, whose ferocity calmed by the second. "Focus. Remember the task at hand."

Suddenly, her chin quivered, her mouth arched down trembling, and tears welled up in her eyes. She pulled away and stomped her feet, trying her best to subdue the sudden fit. Waving her arms wildly, she opened her mouth to speak many times, but the words couldn't come out. Finally, she stomped hard, rage breaking through the despair. "No!" she screamed, pointing the knife at him. The tears dribbled from her eyes, sparkling in the half-light. "No, no. NO! You don't get to do that! Not anymore!"

She hiked her chin up proudly, pointing the knife at her chest. "I'm free from you now. I know what I'm here for!" Again she rushed at him, tilting his head back to expose the neck. Setting the blade there, she pressed until a little trickle of blood leaked out. She panted, reigning in her rage with controlled breathing. "I just thought..." she whispered, calm washing over her. "I thought I'd give you a minute to..." Again, she paused, searching his eyes. "You know what? You're right." Rising, she stood before him, arms slack her side. "The past is the past, right? I'm here about the future."

She set the point of the knife on the saggy flesh of his right breast. "All your records, your notes and stuff," she said, easing the point in. Marshall ignored the sting and burn of its edge biting his skin. He could call up his power and make his skin like stone, but today, he was just a man. "Where are they? I know they're somewhere around here, hidden. Tell me where they are, and..." she sighed, "...and I'll cut you up after."

Ismena swallowed. "Get it? Tell me and I'll take your head off first then I'll cut you up, okay? Deal?"

Marshall wanted to look away from her, but he needed to see her. He needed to keep her face in his sight. This was a part of it, his atonement, the need to not spare himself the full extent of the horror. With a flick of her wrist, the knife burned down his right breast, cutting meat and skin. Blood poured out, slow, oozing, and warm.

"Tell me," she said, setting the blade at a new point.

When he said nothing, she slashed again, this time in a curving pattern. "Tell me," she repeated. Her voice gathering heat. "What's in Brazil, huh? What did that mean? Tell me that."

He stared, his jaw gnashed tightly to bear the pain. She cut him again, a long deep gash. More blood spilled out, and though he did not see it, he felt its scarlet color crawling over the stinging flesh.

Did they feel this, their own life slipping away? he wondered. *Hannah,* he remembered. *Cassandra and William.* All those who died fighting. *Remelle,* he thought, suddenly, wanting to find a way to convince her that they had all been wrong. Remelle was still alive, or so he believed; there was still hope for her. Perhaps with time, she would see. Maybe they all would.

And even this one, he thought. *Perhaps there's even hope for her.*

She was screaming now, cutting sloppily into his flesh with more erratic strokes. His silence fed her rage, until she could no longer sate herself with the small damage to his body. Raising the knife to his neck, she paused ready to deal the final cut.

"Talk," she whispered, scowling.

He felt his mouth crack open. "No."

Then the blur of motion, a sweeping hand with the sudden bite of ice. Then there was a warm wind. It tossed his hair as he coasted into darkness, where he would sleep—but not forever.

__Chapter I_____

Blue eyes peered over the brim of the cards, emotions constrained by indecision. Though Valerie couldn't see Pam's mouth, she knew—just knew—that she was biting her bottom lip. Like throwing down a DRAW FOUR card was actually something worthy of concern.

"You know I have school in the morning, right?" Valerie said. "Come on. I'm a big girl. I can take it."

Pam grinned bashfully, apologizing. "I hate doing this." A muffled groan escaped her throat as she lowered the card. Valerie was already sliding the cards off the deck.

Pam winced. "I'm sorry."

"They're cards, Pam."

"I know," she demurred. "It's just that..." And then she started rambling.

Her foster mother got like this sometimes. Antsy, timid. Though Pam was sheepish by nature, she could descend many levels further down the passive spectrum on occasion. And if Valerie were going to take this one to Vegas, she would bet that Pam's sudden spell of insecurity was on account of one thing: she had met a guy.

While Valerie knew traditional norms required her to be happy for Pam, Valerie felt justified in her own dread at realizing the news. Her sentiments could easily be summed up in the single thought that came to her.

Here we go again.

Valerie situated her cards in her hand, ignoring their specifics on account of strategizing her words and not her play.

"So who is he?" Direct, yes. A verbal DRAW FOUR card. Pam owed her.

Knowing this, Pam paled as she beamed over the rim of her hand. She wanted to deny it. So badly. She gazed at Valerie half-pleading in a shy smile that she be given a pass, but Valerie gave the dead-eye with a single relaxed blink.

Exhaling, Pam dropped her head, burying her face in her cards. "Is it that obvious?"

Valerie dropped a REVERSE then a SKIP followed by a WILD card. "Blue."

Pam sighed deeply, looked at her cards then dropped a blue 5. "Someone I met while I was out with Shannon the other night."

The other night. Like, there were others. Pam went out maybe twice every six months. Her flaky friend Shannon was a total drunk though, helpless in her attraction for dive-joints populated by seedy males who, in their prime, couldn't attract a female or lacked the tact to keep one.

Valerie had always felt strange in her lack of pity for people in general, but she always felt something deep and sorry in her gut whenever Pam went through this. The meet, the hope, the excuses, the crash, and the recovery. Happened every time.

Valerie really didn't want to know, but, "Does he got a name?" She laid down a yellow 5.

When Pam looked up to answer, her phone suddenly blared. Viper-quick, Pam grasped her phone and shot up from the couch. A smile brightened her face when she checked the screen. After tapping it, she held the phone to her ear and scurried off to the kitchen. She probably hadn't noticed that she had spilled her cards all over the carpet.

Game over, Valerie thought. At least there was some silver lining in that. Grabbing the remote, Valerie mashed the UNMUTE to the TV, mostly to mask Pam's sweet-toned voice as she whispered into the phone. But the image on the screen begged to be heard also. The local news was reporting the day's harvest of shocking events, the greatest of which seemed to be the discovery of new evidence in a spree of local murders.

"—two weeks since the last body, that of Southwick native Marilyn Hubbard, was discovered in an abandoned building on the lower Eastside. Authorities are still asking for the public to come forward with information that could help with the investigation. Sources within Southwick PD admit that little headway has been made." A montage of weeks old footage played in a loop of the police guiding out white-shrouded gurneys from different dilapidated structures around Southwick. The anchor's voiceover continued. "They have neither a murder weapon, nor a possible suspect. What makes this a troubling case, they assert, is that Miss Hubbard is the third such murder, which many have begun to call the work of the Southwick Psycho."

After mashing the power-button, the screen faded to black, and Valerie tried to ignore the crawling sense of dread rising within her. She had read the pattern in the case. The victims were all women over thirty and single. Probably naive and trusting. Just like...

Pam pumped her legs excitedly as she pranced into the room, her hands clutching the phone to her chest. Grinning wide, she sucked in her breath and twirled in a circle.

Looking away, Valerie tried her best to play along. "You gonna have this guy's baby?"

Pam halted, her eyes wide. "No!"

Valerie glared at her, her brow downcast. "The fact that you feel the need to deny it says a lot. S'all I'm saying."

"Stop," Pam pleaded, some of her excitement fading to shame.

There you go, Val. Be an ass. "Sorry. Um..." Valerie rubbed her forehead. "So, was that him? Are you guys going out?"

A bit of her brightness flared back in her eyes. She winked at Valerie. "It was his *driver.*"

Valerie felt her brow furrow. Now that was interesting. "Wait, so, his driver asked you out?"

Pam shrugged, her smile steady and vibrant. "Yeah." She cringed then shook her head. "No, not like that. He was super tied up in a meeting, so his driver called to let me know he would swing by and pick me up for dinner."

Valerie eyed the clock above the TV. Half-past nine. "Dinner and what else?" Valerie cocked her eyebrow to drive the point home.

Pam slumped her shoulders. "Come on, Valerie."

Surrendering, Valerie threw up her hands. "Fine. That's cool. I'm just, you know…" Valerie wouldn't finish, and she hoped Pam wouldn't catch it.

She did. A grin slowly grew on Pam's mouth, spreading her cheeks to form faint dimples. She tilted her head. "You're worried about me."

And we're done, Valerie thought.

Pam's face softened like she had just seen a puppy. "That's so sweet." She even held her hands over her heart.

"It's not that," Valerie stammered, not sure why she insisted on lying. She fiddled her hands at the TV. "It's all this Psycho stuff, you know."

Pam's eyes flashed. "Oh! That reminds me. I want to show you something. Where's your phone?"

Valerie motioned at the charger. Pam sauntered to it, collecting the device then held hers alongside it. "There's this new app called Tetherping. Heard of it?"

"Tetherping?" Valerie echoed, skeptical. Easily the stupidest name ever, but Valerie didn't want to throw out anymore negativity.

"Yeah," she answered, approaching. She plopped down next to Valerie, rubbing shoulders with her. She mashed and swiped until there was a GPS map screen on both their phones. "It allows people to see the locations of friends and family in real time, anytime. If you want, you can get an instant route to get to them. Even calculates time by distance and traffic."

"Sounds big brother," Valerie commented.

"I knew you were going to say that," Pam murmured. "You can set yours to password permission only. So, like, if I have you in my tether-network, when I try to ping you, you get a notification. If you approve it with your password, then I can tether you." She shrugged and smiled. "So we can see each other, where we are, you know?"

Valerie glanced at her phone then back at Pam. She honestly didn't care, but, "Still sounds big brother."

Sighing, Pam gave a deadpan glare, one that was born of the little aggression Pam managed. "This is important to me."

Valerie shrugged. "It's fine by me, but if I don't ping you all the time don't be hurt. You know I don't do all this..." Valerie fiddled a hand vaguely at the phones, "...stuff."

Straightening herself, Pam seemed satisfied. "I set your password for you."

"What is it?"

Pam cocked an eyebrow. "Stuff." Dropping the phone in Valerie's lap, she patted her leg and rose from the couch. "I have a date," she announced. "But you have school in the morning. How is that going by the way?"

"I'm gonna graduate," Valerie said, once again reminded of an uncertain future ahead. Even after Pam was gone, Valerie sat on the couch brooding in front of the black TV screen, wondering what her life was going to look like two months from now. She would be newly graduated and freshly re-born as a bona-fide 18-year-old adult. Aging out had been a dream when she was younger, a fantasy that she would be free to do as she pleased.

Valerie knew better now, though. Freedom was not the license to do whatever. It was a person's capacity to navigate the obstacles of their lives. Whatever were the perceived constraints to that freedom were not constraints at all, but merely obstacles themselves. And though Child Services had a strangle-hold on where Valerie went, whom she lived with and for how long, once Valerie was free of that power, she knew that life had a few restrictions of its own—all of which eagerly awaited her once she was loose.

When Valerie plopped down on her bed, eyes staring at the white ceiling, she considered, again, the obvious alternative.

Stay with Pam for a while. Pay rent. Be roommates. It was a kid's dream and she knew it. It would never work out.

Besides, Valerie owed her foster mother more than that. Pam had put her life on pause for two years now. Two years with no boyfriends allowed in the apartment, not while a young teenage girl was living here. Two years without friends over for an alcohol-happy get together.

For Valerie, it had been two years without a single sweaty night locked up in juvy over a fist fight with someone who had it coming. Two years without shop-lifting, or even the feeling that something like that was her best option. After two years of sailing straight with the law and everything else, Valerie knew she had Pam to thank for the longest streak of calm waters she had ever known in her life.

So, Pam deserved to have her life back. And it was about time Valerie made something of her own.

None of this had managed to calm Valerie's smoldering anxiety. It clawed at her when the air got quiet, when she was alone like now. The feeling reminded her of the months she spent in the orphanages and the years in less-than-agreeable foster homes. It was the sensation that even the walls were bearing down, waiting to pounce at any moment.

With some embarrassment, Valerie had researched meditation and how that might cure the sudden rise of anxiety within. She surprised herself when she found a form that worked. It involved rhythmic breathing and a discipline to keep her eyes open and focused one thing. She chose a yellow circle, which she had painted on a piece of canvas and pinned to her ceiling. Focusing on the yellow circle calmed her. She neither knew why, nor cared to know why. All that mattered was keeping a cool head. So, there she lay, staring into the yellow circle, and when she woke the next morning, she had no recollection of when she finally nodded off.

It was after she exited the shower that Valerie noticed the quiet in the house. By no means were mornings normally robust with motion and sound, but the staleness of the air was a noticeable change. Fluffing her wet hair, Valerie stared at Pam's door, listening for a hint of motion within. Hearing nothing, she glanced at the clock—7:37. Coffee should be boiling. Waffles toasting, maybe an egg crackling in a pan.

Approaching Pam's door, Valerie knocked. Seconds passed and nothing. She turned the knob and cracked the door. "Hey Pam," she called out, and paused. Then she peeked her head in, seeing a dark room with a made bed.

Exhaling, Valerie grinned despite herself. *Good for you,* Valerie thought. Pam was a plain-Jane so a little adventure was due her way. Closing the door, Valerie finished her routine, understanding that soon this might be her life.

Wilson P. High was allegedly one of the best high schools in the state. Valerie had been to a few, and all she could really speak to was the paint job and the cleaner-than-normal bathrooms. Everything else was pretty much the same. Most days, Valerie went about in a haze.

She was a senior, and like many in her cohort, she regarded each task with the nonchalance of a napping cat. She did all that was asked; she made her A's and B's and passed all of her tests. She even pretended to listen to all of the hype about the big, bad world she was about to enter.

"Let's practice our mnemonic devices, guys," Mr. Kurtweller called out. "Entropy."

"End Trophy," the class repeated.

"Definition?"

Fred Decker raised his hand. "A tendency towards randomness."

Mr. Kurtweller nodded and shrugged his shoulders. "Chaos, in other words. Right. Okay, now: Syntropy."

"Sync Trophy," the class droned.

"Good," said Mr. Kurtweller. "A Sync Trophy is what a team gets when it works together, so syntropy must mean...what?"

Hands flew up. Kurtweller pointed at Donna.

"Tendency toward order?" she offered.

"Eh," Mr. Kurtweller cringed emphatically, teeter-tottered his hand, conveying as so many teachers did, that the response was wrong, but that she shouldn't feel bad about it. "That's kind of it, but I don't want you to view these two concepts as opposites. Jan, what've you got?"

"Tendency toward conformity," she offered.

"Yes, better," Kurtweller affirmed, nodding multiple times. "These two concepts are present not just in thermodynamics, but in biology and evolution. Heck, it even exists in theology: the idea that there are chaotic forces bent on rending the sanctity and purity of society, people, or the world they create together by combined effort and agreement. Go out in that big world and observe, guys." Mr. Kurtweller spread his arms out wide. "Watch these two forces in action, how they are behind what we see and—"

"Excuse me, Mr. Kurtweller," said Ms. Sandly. She was peeking around the classroom door—a shock of wild auburn hair and thick glasses.

Mr. Kurtweller chuckled and sighed.

Ms. Sandly paled. "What? I'm sorry if it's a bad time."

"No, no," he replied graciously. "Do you see, class? I had you all wrapped up and conformed. A single tribe. Me, an agent of syntropy, and in comes Ms. Sandly to stir up the bees, an unwitting agent of chaos."

Fred Decker, who couldn't let a joke be a joke at the expense of intellectual pursuits, shot his arm up and piped, "But what if her actions were actually a part of a larger system. Then she is merely acting according to pattern, and therefore an agent of syntropy."

Mr. Kurtweller sighed and said dryly, "Well yes, Fred, I guess you would be right."

Through all of that, Ms. Sandly found Valerie's gaze and beckoned with a finger. Valerie gathered up her notebook, zipped up her bag and lugged it across her shoulders. She waded through the desks and bodies as Kurtweller resettled the class to continue the lesson.

Fred was right. It was all a part of a big system. A machine whose creator had installed his long-departed soul into a small, hidden chamber where it turned and turned a mighty crank, which gave life to the infernal gears—gears whose terrible grinding music was heard everywhere.

It was dreaded as much as it was unnoticed. And this woman, this guidance counselor was certainly an unwitting agent of the machine: the high heels, the dress skirt and blouse, the manila file folders, and the turbulent need strut quickly. All of this was to assure herself that all her present actions were as meaningful as she needed to believe they were.

She was taking Valerie to her guidance counselor office, where she would attempt to give direction to another youth who already knew her options. It was just a matter of coercing her into one of the designed tracks as quickly as possible.

Valerie sat herself in one of the two vacant seats in front of Ms. Sandly's paper-laden desk. Sandly sighed and sat down in her gigantic black leather office chair. Swallowed by it, Sandly now seemed reintroduced to her habitat, surrounded by pictures of herself and her family all smiling and jubilant.

"Hi, Valerie," she said and smiled brightly. "It's that time."

Whatever that means, Valerie thought, offering a terse nod and a compliant smirk.

"Okay..." Sandly started, foraging in one of her towering stacks for the right file folder. "Here we go." She yanked out a thick one.

Sandly opened it, glancing over the pages within. "So, have you thought about what you're gonna do?"

Valerie squinted. "Do when?"

"After school, sweetie. Hello graduation! It's right around the corner. What's Miss Valerie Zeta doing day zero-one? Do you know yet? Have you thought about it?"

Valerie had thought about it. To her growing shame, she thought about it nearly every minute of every day. *What's the plan, Val?* Keep up the routine like usual? Work at Free Radical stocking shelves—all while painfully shrugging off the fantasy of what she really wanted to do: Spelunking. Cave-diving. Mountain-climbing. If any of that was a career, then that was what she wanted to do. But Valerie understood that you couldn't say these kinds of things to people, especially not guidance counselors whose job it was to guide you down more productive and promising paths.

But it was Friday, so what the heck. "Spelunking," Valerie answered. "Cave-diving. Mountain climbing. That sort of thing."

It took Sandly a whole two seconds to realize it wasn't a joke. She curbed her laughter, waxed on a straight face—remembering that the dreams of all children were precious—and started in with the script.

"Well, that sounds like...fun," she said, still grinning. "Uh, well, have you, uh, do you know a good school, like a college that teaches that sort of thing, or do you already know someone—?"

"I was going to buy some ropes and whatever." Valerie waved her hand vaguely outside. "Then go find a cave and get started."

Sandly couldn't help herself now. The mirth exploded from her. "Oh, you *are* joking!" She tapered off the fit with a sigh. "Wow. But really. You're a smart girl, Valerie. You liked volleyball. The girls wanted you to be captain. Maybe you would like to play in college. Is there anything you'd like to study?"

Valerie cringed. This woman meant well. She was a good person. She actually cared. But she was really starting to annoy.

Ms. Sandly shrugged. "In college, I mean."

Valerie glanced down at the form lying flat under Sandly's pen hand. This was paper work. A little section dedicated to documenting a graduating senior's hopes and plans. Valerie shuddered and felt the inching of an unnamable fear as she considered how such a piece of information could be of any use to anyone in the future.

"Nursing," Valerie lied. "I'm interested in that."

"Oh that's such a great career," Sandly replied, awash with sudden relief. "Such steady demand, too. You'll always have a job. Hours are a little funky sometimes, but the pay is great. Lots of school for that though." Sandly started filling in the form. "Where are you headed to study?"

"Uh," Valerie stammered. "Santa Cruz, maybe. Or Richmond."

"Oh, great schools to get started. Especially when you can't get into a four-year right off the bat." Sandly polished off a line of a scrawl and looked up with a radiant grin. "That's it, lady. How are things at home?"

"Good."

"You and Pamela getting along well?"

"Pam's great."

"I am so glad that's working out for you," Sandly said, gushing with sympathy. "And her. She is such a great lady. And, if I can say, she's lucky to have you."

Valerie felt a rush of warmth in her chest. It made her feel…*uncomfortable*, especially as she felt her cheeks blushing. Normally, scripted flattery only irritated Valerie, but Sandly meant it. She was a good person. The world was filled with them—good people who meant well and did well. Like Pam. Like Mr. Kurtweller. Like Sandly. And like Alice, Valerie's would-be best friend if Valerie would only allow such a thing.

"Hey Val-pal." Alice's bright face accosted Valerie at her locker. Alice Celwyn was the living embodiment of positivity and goodness. Quite contrary to the stereotype for the most beautiful, affluent, and popular girl in school, Alice was neither stuck up nor cruel. Alice had always been the friendliest and caring when Valerie first moved to Wilson P. She recruited Valerie to the volleyball team and taught her how to play. Also, despite Valerie's sarcastic and crass nature at times, Alice stuck with her—which was enough for Valerie to overlook the 'Val-pal' thing.

"Let me guess there's a big party you want me to go to?" Valerie turned from her locker and grimaced. Alice beamed, nodding rapidly. She took Valerie by the arm, escorting her to the parking lot. "Tonight at Brady McKnight's house. Please come."

Valerie groaned. "You know that's not really my thing."

"Oh, come on!" Alice begged. "You know how to read people, Val. Remember that creep, Toby? You totally called it. I almost let myself fall into that mess, but you saved me."

"His name was Toby," Valerie deadpanned. "It should have been obvious."

Alice tapped the air in front of her. "But it wasn't obvious. Not to me. See? I need you. And now there's this psycho guy out there. Plus, I don't mean to make a girl cry, but we're almost through here." She made pouty lips and blinked dourly. "Look at this face. You'll miss this. I don't mean to be racist either, but you're also like the only Spanish chick here." Alice tapped the air again. "We need some diversity."

Valerie tilted her head. "That *is* racist, and I'm only half-and-half, so..."

Alice stamped her foot and whined. "Come on, Val."

"I work tonight. Sorry."

"What time does Free Radical close? Like ten?"

"Uh—"

"Great!" Alice chirped. "Nothing really gets started till then anyway. Are we solid?"

With a sigh, Valerie relented. "Fine. I'll have to stop by the apartment first."

Alice squinted. "Why?"

Valerie shrugged uncomfortably. "Uh...Pam...didn't come home last night. I should check on her. Whatever."

A sly smirk crept on Alice's cheeks. "Valerie Zeta has a heart. I knew it."

"Relax," Valerie deadpanned. "It's the car I need."

"So, why don't you just call her?"

Valerie shrugged, her discomfort mounting. "She's out with a guy. I don't wanna... I don't know, ruin it or whatever."

Alice pointed suddenly. "Hey, have you heard of Tetherping?" Before Valerie could roll her eyes and nod, Alice was already conjuring her own phone. "It's this app that..."

"I've heard of it."

Alice shrugged. "Oh, cool. Add me then. I'll just send you a ping and you can find your way to Brady's house that way." Alice stared, waiting. She held her hand out. "Want me to do it?"

Rolling her eyes, Valerie sighed relinquishing her phone into Alice's care.

When Alice was finished fiddling, she handed the phone back. "Ping me, all right?"

Tucking the phone into her back pocket, Valerie offered a thumbs-up. "Got it."

Free Radical was the same as school. A haze of motion punctuated at times by some random act that seemed to disrupt the normal ebb and flow. Video game nerds came in, browsed their potential devices of escapism and bought according to their means.

Valerie liked it there since the usual clientele were awkward and easy to intimidate. The boys passed furtive glances at her body, but were easy to scare off with sharp movements, like turning around suddenly, or staring at them for long periods of time without smiling.

Valerie heard the stories about other girls who worked in department stores. They were always telling tales about the advances of persistent blowhards who were on a mission. In that light, Valerie liked her nerd-world just fine, especially since she had finally learned enough of the geek-speak to keep up.

"Hey, uh, is this a good game?"

It always took Valerie a moment to realize someone had worked up the nerve to talk to her. Valerie got the treatment, too, sometimes. She ignored the first attempt, but knew well who it was—a twenty-something surrounded by his pack, and he had something to prove.

They did a poor job of subduing their giggling.

"So, is this, is this a good game, Vagrant Wind?"

Valerie shrugged, not awarding his attempt with a glance his way. "If you're into that sort of thing."

The guys burst out laughing.

"Shut up, fags." He shoved them then recomposed himself. "So what's your name? I'm…"

"I'm not interested," Valerie cut in. She drew herself up and looked him in the face. He was an attractive guy: dark hair, fit, light eyes, and a smile that could sell chlorine to algae. He was also a grade A chump who was motivated only in gratifying his urges without enough intelligence to understand what they were.

"What? I'm not your type?" A petulant smirk curled the lines of his face.

Ignore him, Valerie commanded. But she knew it wouldn't work. Not with this guy. She shook her head and stalked off. "Look, man, just find what you want and go."

"Right," he said. "You've got important things to do. Stacking shelves."

The boys answered his dig with a collective "Oooooh..."

And this was how it always started. Some punk with a huge ego—be it male or female—would lock on to her rage button and push and push and push until violence occurred. Then, when the smoke settled, she would find herself sitting in some counselor's office encircled by all-knowing adults who would discuss ways to help her be more successful. The best way, they always seemed to figure, was to pass her on to someone else, somewhere else.

Valerie was determined to be done with all that, even though the warm and fuzzy feeling she was supposed to get when she took the high road never surfaced. She always felt like a coward. She always felt like a victim. Most insulting were hours after that she stewed even more in the infernal thoughts that chumps like that, people like him, *they* were in control somehow. If they felt like having a laugh at your expense that day, then you just had to deal with it.

The very injustice of this would feed her rage for days. In the past, her attempts to bury her anger for the sake of keeping straight with society only led her to greater violence at some unknown moment, at some inopportune time, on an innocent person who usually never deserved the full extent of her wrath.

Valerie's new resolution was to settle her problems right then, right there, with the jerk who made her angry. Or let it go entirely, which is the course she took in this case. Losing her good standing at a decent job was not worth demonstrating the value of good manners.

The guys laughed a little more, but Valerie was in tunnel vision. Currently she was stacking a used copy of *Lord of the Rings* whose cover showed a burning golden circle. *Yellow circle. Focus on the yellow circle.* The calming effect took seconds. The rage and anger drained out of her, and she almost laughed at how stupidly effective her little trick worked.

Her shift ended, and with her positive vibes in full rise, she felt something like excitement for tonight's party. Maybe she could kick back a little. Maybe she could just relax and let people like Alice be a friend to her. Maybe Valerie could be just like everybody else, laughing in brittle ignorance of the harshness closing in on them. Just for tonight at least. These two years had built themselves into something good. It had taken time, but it was worth it. Valerie was about to go to a party driving the car of a foster mom who trusted her, when all others would not. All things considered, it was a big step up.

When Valerie turned the corner to their block of apartments, she already sensed no life in their place. The windows were dark. Pam's car was parked out in front, unmoved from its position. Despite the signs, Valerie swung the door open to the darkened apartment. "Hey Pam-bam," she called out. Silence answered.

When Valerie entered, she sensed that apartment had remained untouched. Lights off, cushions on the couch just as Valerie left them. Dishes piled in the sink, uncharacteristically ignored. Even the air carried a sterile scent that hinted at the lack of human habitation. Valerie felt empty, suddenly, and cold. She didn't like it. More than anything, she wanted to call out for Pam, but Valerie did not want to face the silence again.

The answer then seemed obvious. Valerie pulled her phone from her back pocket and pressed the photo of Pam making ducky lips. The phone trilled seven times before voicemail picked it up. Again, she didn't want to speak into a void, so she cancelled it. Swearing under her breath, she thought to wait a moment for a call back.

Don't have to, Valerie suddenly remembered. She tapped the icon for Tetherping, and navigated all its features. With a final tap, she sent out a ping and within seconds a red pulsing dot appeared within a grid of GPS roads and buildings. An approximate address appeared.

1064 Marshburn Avenue, Building #6

Valerie cringed. That was the old industrial park, abandoned for many years now. The only thing over there were blocks upon blocks of boarded up buildings, empty parking lots and badly maintained street lamps. Closest thing to a ghost town Valerie had ever known.

Pam mentioned the guy had a driver. Maybe he was some rich developer buying up the properties because he knew something others didn't. He could have taken Pam over there to show it all off, an empire in waiting. Maybe he even had his own bachelor pad...

Valerie caught herself grasping at anything to release her from the responsibility of facing the grim alternative. If anybody wanted to do something shady and get away with it, it was places like the old industrial park they chose.

Once more she tried to shrug it off; she tried not to assume the worst. Normal people would wait another night, see how it all panned out. Or they would call the police.

Valerie thought a moment, knowing how that would play out. The second she told the dispatcher that Pam had gone out on a date, they'd tell her to wait another night and call back in the morning. She might expect the authorities to take this seriously because of the murders, but it was this reality that had probably led to a spike in these types of calls from equally concerned loved-ones. Their dismissal of Valerie's concerns would be as practiced as it was easily forgotten in a sea of others.

In the here and now, Valerie knew she couldn't rely someone else, and she wasn't going to sit around and wait, so…

Reaching out, Valerie plucked the keys from the hook and headed to the car. When she was strapped behind the wheel and the engine was growling, Valerie tapped an icon and a second later she had a route.

Though Friday night traffic hampered her progress, Valerie arrived at the industrial park an hour before midnight. She had clicked off her head beams two signs back, using only the dim yellow street lamps to guide her in. Creeping into the parking lot of Building 6, Valerie felt an unnamable chill as she coasted slowly behind a giant dumpster that sat slowly rusting in an otherwise vacant parking lot. After killing the engine, Valerie sat in the car a minute wondering what to do next. Leaving was one option. This whole idea was sketchy from the beginning. But there was something about the pulsing of the red dot on her phone…

And then her phone rumbled, her screen consumed by a single message: *Pam just pinged you! Allow tether?*

There was a password prompt. Valerie could not put words to why her heart suddenly began to race, why her blood pumped hot and fierce in her veins. Shouldn't she feel relief? Shouldn't she be suddenly glad that everything was all right?

Any other person might have felt that way, but Valerie had seen things others hadn't. It had been years since the orphanages, years even from the bad homes she had survived, but she would never forget one important thing. When the lights were off, you had to keep one eye opened.

The clarity of what needed to be done came to her in half-thoughts born of instinct and street logic. Fingers shaking, she carefully typed out her password: STUFF. A second later the red dot and a new blue dot were now bound by a green line. A notification brightened her screen. *You've been tethered!*

Quietly, Valerie rose from the car and locked the door. Closing the door with care, Valerie sidled to the corner of the dumpster and peeked her head around to view the face of Building 6. All was dark inside except for the faintest glow of light within.

She waited, eyes on the big entrance where the once boarded up doors were now free of the boards. Then, quiet as a mouse, a man pushed the door open and stepped from its blackness. So many meters away, Valerie could not get a good look at him. He wasn't very big, smallish for a man, dressed in slacks and a white button up with the collar spread open. The white shirt glowed suddenly as the man tapped the phone in his hand. After studying the screen a moment, his eyes jerked upward, his gaze intent on the dumpster—or what was behind it.

Valerie had already ducked her head back around, grimly aware of what was happening. She didn't want to believe it. Still, in her heart, she wanted this to be some sort of misunderstanding. This guy was the driver, surely. And he had Pam's phone for some reason, a good reason, of course. But Valerie was deluding herself, and she knew it. She needed to accept, right now, that either something terrible had happened to Pam, or that something was about to.

The strategy came to her clearly. She pinged Pam's phone again, and she could hear the friendly chirp echo from Pam's phone meters away, in the hands of that man. With that done, she closed the app and dialed 911. Lowering herself, Valerie slid the phone as far as she could under the dumpster, and then sidled to the opposite edge. When she reached the corner, she could now hear the slow footsteps of the man approaching at the other corner, intent on finding the phone that had so mysteriously interrupted the dark and the quiet.

Here I go, she thought, her heart thudding in her chest. She dashed for the door, careful to keep her footsteps muffled. The door had been left opened, so Valerie slipped through the frame, her eyes darting around the empty atrium for a sign of where she should start looking. She didn't know how long the diversion would work, so she flew to the first set of stairs leading up to a higher floor. By the time she arrived at the landing, the dark was so thick, she was now reaching out blindly at the void, eager for some sense of direction.

Her fingers touched-down on the cold flat of a door, and then, after coasting down, to a handle which she pulled. The door opened with ease, revealing a large room, gutted of all furniture but for a tattered mattress, a desk and a lantern. Its soft glow revealed the emptiness of the space.

Not totally empty. There, tucked in a corner was a mound of dirt with a shovel propped on the wall to the side. The mound's shape filled Valerie with that same unnamable chill. The mound was oval, long, and thick enough to house a body.

Her motions were not her own anymore. They came from somewhere she did not know existed. Creeping to the pile of dark earth, she saw the pale skin of Pam's arm, the soft edge of her shoulder and the curving line of her neck as it led to her head. The eyes were closed, but her mouth hung open, as though released from agony or ecstasy. The rest of her body lay encased in the dry mound of grey dirt and sand.

"Pam," Valerie muttered then clasped her mouth with her hand. Suddenly, from outside there was a sickening yelp. It was the sudden and pleading cry of a man sensing his end. The outburst was then muffled and Valerie thought she sensed motion, a scuffle somewhere out in the dark.

The time for thinking and fear were over. Valerie dashed to Pam's side, clawing the earth away, throwing its dry substance off in clumps. It was all taking too long, so she grabbed Pam's stiff arms—cold, so cold!—and tried to yank her free. Her first two attempts nearly sent her into despair, when suddenly, from some place calm within herself, Valerie felt strength rising within her. It came with a flush of blood, red and angry. Her skin riled with heat, her muscles empowered by something above adrenaline.

And then, all at once, a terrible throbbing rose in the back of her skull. It drummed and pounded until she thought her head might explode. Staggering back a step, Valerie tried to steady her herself, but her balance was lost in her sudden break of tension. Pam's body burst out of the dirt cocoon, and when Valerie toppled back on the tile floor, the body plopped in her lap, rigid and freezing. Pam was naked, pale and dusted with a film of grainy sand. Tendrils of her blonde hair carried flakes of encrusted earth.

Part of Valerie wanted to banish it from her. The other part of her felt the irrational need to cradle Pam, to hold her close—to save her. Gathering her up, Valerie stood, clutching the body to her, her eyes searching the dark for another exit. Again, the throbbing in her head seized her, like a dull boom of thunder threatening to blast her skull open.

Moaning, Valerie nearly toppled again, staggering back many steps until she caught herself against the cool glass of panning window. When the spell wore thin, and she could think again, she was aware of the presence of someone else within the room. It was to her right, emerging from the dark in slow graceful steps. No, not the man she had seen outside. This was someone else. Tall and fit, naked but for a robe draped around his body, the man glided to the edge of the dark and the light, his blue eyes burning like little stars in the shadows.

"You've strayed far from your home, girl," a voice said. The voice was calming, the resonance of it, like the soothing note drawn from a cello. He remained just out of the lantern's glow, on the edge of the dark. He motioned at Pam. "Have you come for this? Was she your friend?"

Valerie snarled. She tried to make her voice strong and intimidating. "Get out of my way."

His head tilted. "Your light…it is so different." Advancing, he passed into the light now, a pale specter of a man, bald, hairless. Inhuman.

Valerie knew how this ended. If she showed weakness, if she hoped for mercy, she would not survive. Gathering herself, she prepared to barrel through him.

The contact was sudden. Valerie flew backward, feeling glass shatter all around her, and then she was dangling in open space, unfurled from gravity with the tinkling of shards floating all around. Then the shock of impact on asphalt, rude and abrupt. Glass rained down, splattering around her like hail. When all was quiet, Valerie felt herself moving, her arms reaching out, squirming in a bid to rise. For a moment, while she was still numb, she raised her head, searching for Pam.

There was a pale body splayed on the concrete close by, still and cold, but no blood. It was then that Valerie saw the wound on Pam's neck, the tangle of flesh where some beast had mauled her. Her eyes. Pam's dead eyes were open and staring.

"Get up…" Valerie rasped, unsure if she were speaking to herself or to the body next to her. Then she saw something floating in the dark above her. The man—the thing—glided down from the second floor, out of the window's black hole and down to the asphalt next to Valerie. Even as pain crackled through her, Valerie conjured the strength to rise.

Sensing the audacity of a recovery, the thing approached and knelt over her. She locked eyes with it, rage twisted her face, "What did you do?"

"Be still," he commanded, his own face contorted with impatience.

Valerie connected one good punch across his chin, quick and even. One of her best. And it would've thrown any man back for a moment, might have bought her a second or two to rise and run. But this one... He rolled his head back and clinched his jaw tight. His eyes glowed, spectral and livid—like two eerie blue nebulas, strangely rimmed in violet. Then he was upon her. He forced her chin up and clamped the wide gap of his mouth over her shoulder and neck where he gnashed his teeth into her flesh.

Darkness took her, and while she spiraled within it, she heard a convoluted score of noises and voices: a man was gagging, coughing, and vomiting. The shadow of the thing released her suddenly, scampering off into the dark like a wounded animal. Then there was another shadow over her, a man whose hands pressed into her neck, stemming the tide of bulging blood.

"—at 1064 Marshburn Avenue, Building #6. No! Not an ambulance, life-fight. Now!" the voice was shouting. "She has wounds to the neck..."

And there was motion and sound, like floating through the drainpipes of her own mind. Then it was quiet again, only a steady, shrill beeping to keep her company.

She dreamed of things, things she would not remember wholly. She dreamed of people standing over her grave, of people talking about her as she lay on a slab at the morgue. They talked about her life like it was a tragic history. They must have been writing a book about her. There was a man writing on a pad of paper while looking her over. Pam came, too. She was dressed as a nurse. Valerie watched her kind eyes gaze into her own, and the woman stared for a while with the level of compassion that only good people knew.

"I pinged you," Valerie whispered, and then the shadows wrapped her up again. The beeping in the dark continued for a long time.

__Chapter 2

Valerie awoke Sunday morning to the sight of a man sitting in the cushioned chair opposite her bed. He was a stocky guy in his early forties, weathered and worn in the face like a jaded cop. He had blond, thinning hair, cut short in a buzz. There was nothing extraordinary about him. He wasn't conspicuously dressed: no badge, no uniform.

The police had come and asked their questions when she finally awoke Saturday. Two or three journalists had stopped by to ask questions. Valerie tried not to think about the headlines. Her one comfort was that she was a minor, so they couldn't print her name. Valerie didn't want to be known forever by this insanity; knowing she would have to face everybody at school was already crazy enough.

Speaking of crazy, the guy just stared at her.

"What d'you want?" Valerie murmured, clearing her throat.

"I want to ask you some questions, Valerie."

"You a cop?"

"No, I'm not a cop."

"A reporter?"

"I'm a," he hesitated, "...an investigator."

Valerie felt a sharp prickle in her neck when she cringed. "Is that different from a cop?"

"Yes, but that's not important right now," he answered. "My name is Warren Brant."

She stared at him a moment. He stared back, unflinching—no scripted smile or nervous gestures to pass the scrutiny. He was a rock, stoic, expressionless, and...mysterious even. Whatever this man had been through, the process had rubbed the pretense of pleasantness from him entirely.

It was refreshing to see in a person.

Valerie cleared her throat. "Go ahead." She expected him to go for his phone or at least a pad of paper, but he didn't. He leaned forward, resting his elbows on his knees.

"When he attacked you," he started, paused then restarted. "When he *bit* you, what happened?"

"I don't really remember," Valerie replied. "I blacked out."

"Can you try for me?" he asked. "Please."

We've been through all this, Valerie thought, sourly. When the other guys came, they asked her to try, too, but the memory of what happened was all just flashes and explosions of sound. But there was something about how this guy stared at her. Something that promised her effort wouldn't be a waste of time.

"Fine." She relented. "He uh, he grabbed me by the hair..." The images flashed and sparked in her memory. "Uh...he...he yanked my head back. He was strong. Fast, too, I never really saw him coming. I couldn't react. When he...bit me, it was all just...it was nothing. But, I think I heard him gagging at some point. Yeah, I think I heard him coughing up something, like he had been drowning or vomiting. It was weird. That's all I remember from that point."

"Thank you," Warren said. "I understand this might be hard for you."

It wasn't, strangely. Valerie had learned not to hope. One way or another something was always going to swoop in and break her life apart. Right when she had it good, the pendulum of good and evil, right and wrong, swung back by and shattered everything. Mourning Pam had taken some time, but Valerie had worked her way through the emotions. She did this mostly at night during the small hours where she could cry and not be seen.

"How about before that," he asked. "What did you see?"

How could she explain it and not sound insane? She kept it vague for the investigators, not wanting them to think she had lost her mind.

"He had an accomplice. I know that," she said, remembering. "His driver. The guy had Pam's phone."

Then she recalled the way the killer looked that night, white and spectral, half-concealed in the shadows. And the way he floated out of the window, gliding down gracefully next to her…

"After that I…I don't know what I saw," she murmured.

Valerie was relieved when he didn't press the issue. Warren sat back into the chair, relaxing again. After a few quiet seconds, he titled his head and squinted with curiosity. "What do you think of all this?"

Valerie didn't understand the question. No one had asked her, nor had Valerie ever expected anyone to, and yet, it was the single most important question that could have been asked. The answer that came was simple and dark.

"Did they catch him?" she asked. "Did they catch his driver?"

There was something sly in his eyes when he answered, "They didn't."

He knows something, Valerie thought. "Then," she said, grinding her jaw hard. "I think someone needs to die." Valerie thought she spied a carefully veiled smirk on the man's face, but couldn't be sure.

He sighed. "Were you close to Pamela?"

Valerie shifted a little, which aggravated the tight stitching of her wound. Unbidden, she remembered the blue of Pam's eyes gazing over the brim of her cards a few nights ago. "Yeah," Valerie admitted. "We were close, I guess. She was good to me."

Then, in an instant, she remembered that first Christmas when they traveled to Pam's parents' house, where everybody there brought a present for Valerie. It was all stuff Valerie had vaguely shown interest in that year, things Valerie *wanted* but trained herself to do without. Pam had paid attention. Pam had told her family what Valerie liked. Thinking of it, Valerie felt sudden shame for the sheepish *thank you* she had given in return.

Valerie sniffed, feeling heat in her chest. "She was a good person all round."

"Her funeral is in two days," he said, and passed a furtive glance at the guard left stationed outside Valerie's door. "Now that the autopsies are complete, they've released her remains to her family. They plan to take her back to Connecticut with them."

Valerie nodded numbly. Connecticut was far away.

"I imagine you'll want to say goodbye," he added. "And if I'm right about you, I assume that funerals are not really your scene, so..."

He stopped short, for no obvious reason.

"So what?"

"Well," he went on, clearly uncomfortable in his own clothes at the moment. "Maybe there's another way."

"Another way for what?"

"To pay your respects, Valerie."

I owe her that, Valerie thought, sullenly. She looked off and nodded.

"Your doctor is planning to release you this evening. I checked. Now, out of respect to Pamela's friends here in Southwick, her family has taken the remains to a local funeral home for a public viewing tonight. In the morning they plan to take her with them."

Valerie then shook her head. "No crowds. I'm not standing around a bunch of crying people I don't even know."

Warren gestured in offering. "Well, I happen to know the director of the funeral home. Mister Lastrick is an understanding man, and if you would like to view the...*her*...after everyone else has left, then I could arrange that for you."

Valerie chewed her lip. The deal started to take shape, and it seemed solid. She got a ticket out of the hospital and a ride to say goodbye to someone who meant something to her. Later, Valerie could collect her stuff from the apartment and hit the road before Child Services could get its mother-eagle claws around her again. She was done with all that. She was done with everything.

"Sounds good," she answered.

He rose. "This is my number." He stepped forward and handed her a card. "When they're about to release you, and you still wish to pay her a visit, call me then."

"I will," she said, flipping the card over twice. His phone number was handwritten on the otherwise blank card.

He walked out, thanking the police officer as he went.

They all stood outside her room, a little huddle of people discussing what to do with Valerie. There was a Child Service's rep, a police chief, a social worker, her school's principal, and Ms. Sandly. The talk was all about how to do the right thing for Valerie. Conflicting arguments abounded about how to ensure she graduated on time from her current school, where she could live until graduation, and who would be willing to take her considering all Valerie's history—this incident especially.

The social worker was a squat and plump woman with pink cheeks, who used her chubby hands too much when she spoke. "They haven't caught the killer yet," she said, gesturing nervously. "Some families might be afraid this psycho will come after her again. It isn't unheard of."

The police chief was a skinny old man, who looked more librarian than cop. He scoffed, "That ain't very likely."

Ms. Sandly piped up. "She said the families would be afraid, not that they would actually be in danger."

Seeing them distracted, Valerie slipped off to the only pay phone left on planet Earth. She put the change into the machine, dialed the number on the card and waited. One ring trilled and Warren answered. Valerie kept her eyes on the busy huddle as she whispered into the phone. "I'm ready. It's gotta be now though."

"I'll be right in—"

"Wait. I'll meet you outside. Parking lot A."

After hanging up the phone, she returned to the group. Valerie put on a weary face, tapped Sandly on the arm and said, "Hey, I might be in the bathroom for a minute, all right?"

Sympathy beamed from Sandly's face. "Oh, you take your time, sweetie. We'll be here."

Valerie felt a swell of guilt for a second or so. Sandly had always meant well. But Valerie didn't have time for anybody's feelings but her own. Slipping past the bathrooms, she rounded the corner to the main lobby, glided past the front desk and through the glass doors.

The air felt good. It didn't smell of anti-septics and meds, and it was open and full. It was also night, so the growing dark made her feel concealed, hidden, and safe.

Time felt like it was running out, though. With Valerie being wounded and Sandly super-concerned, she could see Sandly creeping into the bathroom to check on her.

Valerie swore under her breath, immediately regretting using lot A. Even at night it was full of vehicles, and she had no idea what this guy's car looked like. She heard an engine start from her left, followed by lights beaming into life. A gray Buick slowed to a stop next to her, and the window slid down. Warren's face stared out at her.

"I've got a feeling this isn't exactly square with your caregivers," he said.

Valerie kept her mouth shut and stared. Warren glared at her for a while more then gazed forward. "If you were planning on going to your apartment after all this, they'll be there."

Valerie swore under her breath. He was right, and she hadn't thought of that.

"Are you sure this is what you want, Valerie?" He wasn't looking at her, just staring off.

"Yes," she said gravely. "I'm not going back." She felt small suddenly. "I can't get tossed around anymore."

The man chewed his cheek and thought for a moment. "What's the plan?"

"To the apartment first," she said, already moving to the other side of the car. She opened the door, slipped in, cringing a little as she over-extended the stitching on her neck and shoulder. "Then the funeral home. I don't think they'll expect me there."

Warren nodded, released the brake, and glided out of the parking lot. Valerie could feel the tension of her plight tighten around her as they pulled out from the parking lot and onto the freeway. As more road passed under them and trailed behind, that tension broke and she felt a rising sense of freedom—and fear. *What's the plan, Val?* What exactly was she going to do with her freedom? Escaping wasn't a plan, not one that would keep her alive.

Whatever. She would figure it out. All she had to do was get away from those people. Good as they were, they couldn't help her anymore. She had to figure things out on her own terms, even if it meant she would go hungry, homeless and lost. At least it would be on her terms. After all, she had followed the plan the authorities gave her, and danger and death found her all the same.

When she arrived, the apartment was dark and still. Praying her key still worked, Valerie felt relief when the lock gave an approving click. Creeping inside, her nerves and anxiety to get in and out clouded any dark nostalgia for the horror that had occurred days ago. She fumbled around her drawers for underwear, a few sets of clothing, hair ties, two pairs of shoes and lots of socks. She changed, agonizing as it was, into more fitting clothes. Finally, she searched under her end table for a small box housing a hefty savings. She yanked the lid off and pulled the roll of bills out, stuffed them in her pocket and rose up.

Arm stretched to the door, Valerie paused and let her arm fall slack to her side. *My room,* she thought, studying the walls.

In all her life she had never felt so strongly that she had belonged to a place. Oddly, there were no significant memories she could reminisce. Just small moments. Pam leaning in her door-frame, commenting on how bare Valerie's walls were, how few things her foster-daughter kept.

Have you thought about being a monk? she mused once.

Looking above, Valerie stared at the canvas pinned to the ceiling and its yellow circle. It seemed right to reach out and take it, but she stared a moment more then turned. It had all taken seconds only.

She slipped back into the car, throwing her stuffed bag into the back seat. She couldn't look at Warren. The emotions were welling up despite her attempts to keep them buried. She didn't want anyone to read them.

He stared at her grimly. "Think about what you're doing, Valerie."

"Drive."

The car moved forward with purpose.

The streetlights streaked past as the trip took them into parts of Southwick City Valerie had not seen before. She was surprised at how much she enjoyed the freedom of that. *So far, so good.* Now, she just needed to be ready should this guy turn creep and try something with her. Valerie was aware of the possibility, and she wasn't letting her guard down. Not openly anyway.

"So, this guy Mister Lastrick, how do you know him?"

"He's a recent acquaintance," he answered.

"Meet a lot of people, doing what you do?"

A shadow passed over his face as he said, "Something like that, yeah."

She was fairly sure he wasn't a creep when they pulled into the Lastrick and Sons Funeral Home. They glided into the drive, got out and approached a back door. Valerie noticed Warren was carrying a small, black duffel bag with him. The contents clanged and jingled as he moved, like tools were inside.

The place was a typical funeral home: square building, church-like model, red brick and white mortar. Before Warren could ring the yellow-lit bell, a man flung the door wide. He was white in the face, with worry clearly flooding in his eyes.

For an undertaker, he looked passably normal, despite the hunch and his pale skin. "Where have you been, Warren?" he seethed, then his eyes widened on Valerie. "Who is this?"

Warren turned to her calmly. "This is Valerie." Then looked back at Lastrick. "I told you about her. She's going to assist me."

Assist? Valerie thought.

That seemed to put the man's heart at ease. "Come in, then," he murmured, paddling his hand for them to enter. They crossed through a narrow, faintly lit hall whose walls were decorated with old grayscale family pictures.

"Where is it?" Warren called out to Mister Lastrick.

The man was shuffling forward, his steps heated and nervous. "Storage," he answered, while his hands fumbled a set of giant keys. "I bolted it in."

"I told you it would be fine, Garry."

"You were running late, and I wasn't taking any chances. Not after last time."

Valerie cut in, "Last time?"

Warren whispered out of the side of his mouth. "Long story. Ask me about it when we're done."

Lastrick lead them to a storage room that was bolt locked on the outside. Hands shaking, Lastrick fiddled with the lock until it clicked. He cracked the door open and stepped away.

"There," he murmured and sighed with some relief.

"You can go if you want," Warren said to Mister Lastrick.

"Okay, right," he stammered, backing away. "And please, try to keep it clean. I have to have everything ready for the family by morning."

"We'll do our best." Warren didn't sound like he cared. "I'll call up when we're finished."

Alright, that does it, Valerie thought. Warren motioned Valerie inside, but she didn't move. "What's going on?"

He stared at her a moment, probably knowing that she was well within her rights to be wary of what was happening. He blinked softly. "It's something you need to see." He nodded his head inward before entering.

Something? she thought, wondering if she had made a mistake. *Only one way to be sure.* She stepped in, following cautiously.

As she might expect, the storage room was a poorly lit chamber with only two hanging bulbs. Stock caskets lined the walls on high shelves making the room look something like a mausoleum. At the extreme end, a single mahogany casket was set on a gurney. As they approached it, Warren brought his bag around and unzipped it. He drew out what looked like a key. He stood over the casket, set the key inside a small lock, and clicked it open with a twist. Putting the key away, Warren tossed his bag to the side and turned to Valerie.

She approached at a slow and cautious pace. The poor lighting, the casket lined walls, the lone coffin set at the far end of the room set her nerves on edge, though she tried not to show it.

Warren stood to the side, gripped a handle on the lid of the casket and lifted it open. Valerie steeled herself for what she would see. Nausea gripped her, but she would not look away; she would not falter and be weak. She drove forward slowly and approached the coffin.

Pam looked good. At peace, as though she were asleep—though it was hard to ignore that her chest did not move. The figure before Valerie didn't seem like the remains of a person. The body seemed more like a wax version of the woman she had once been. She was beautified with subtle shades and tints of makeup and a nice array of little flower ornaments in her hair. It wasn't too much either, all the decorative stuff. Pam looked angelic without looking inhuman, and it all suited her nicely.

Valerie breathed, feeling sudden warmth in her chest, a fire rising from her core through her skin and limbs. She was so tired. Tired of losing. Exhausted by the feeling of *this*, the pain of emotion even when she tried to wall herself off. She looked away from Warren, wiping her nose. She couldn't let anyone see, couldn't let anyone know that there was weakness deep down. Not even here, standing over the body of someone she cared about, a good person, who cared also.

Her head thrummed with congestion, the blood pumping in pounding beats. Mourning racked soul and body, and here…

Wait, Valerie thought, cringing suddenly. She had felt this before, her skin flushed with heat, blood throbbing in her brain—and this migraine… Unbidden the memories of that night flooded her mind. The eyes…and the thing that had stood half-concealed in the shadows, pale, inhuman.

A hand rested on her shoulder. Its touch felt like ice, and she slapped it away, flinging Warren back. Bracing himself on a casket behind him, Warren saved himself from a tumble. He recovered quickly, swinging the bag around to his chest and unzipping it in one motion.

In the fog of pain and the echo-chamber that was her head, Valerie heard herself try to explain, hands held up. They were trembling. "I…didn't mean…"

The sudden strike was not his concern. He looked at her severely, speaking slowly. "Valerie, you'll need to listen to me."

His voice was a low warble, clarity fading in and out. She saw that he was motioning at the casket. Turning, she saw it— the eyes twitching. She was…Pam…was *alive*?

"No, Valerie," Warren's voice said. "That is not your foster mother. This thing… She is *undead*."

The word rang in her head, echoing, mixing with another, *inhuman…undead.* Valerie's head flared with red pain. Wincing, she gripped the edge of the casket to steady herself. She had felt all this—she knew what this was; it was what happened that night when that…creature had found her. *The eyes…*

Pam's eyes opened.

They had been blue in life, but this… It was not a color, but a glow, a spectral neon, rimmed in a violet halo. Haunted and cold, they were eyes that saw so much more than the physical. They combed the room, observing at first then searching. Falling on Valerie, they locked in place and stared. Frozen, Valerie gazed back in horror.

Pam? She almost whispered the word, mouthing it silently. The thing under her made no movement, examining Valerie's face only.

"This is not Pam," Warren said, his voice still echoing in her skull. "She has been transformed into this. Against her will. And if we let it, she will grow into a monster."

Bearing a fresh swell of pain, Valerie turned to the man next to her, managing a word. "What?"

She saw budding panic tax his cool. "Do as I say. All right? Hold her down. Hold her still. Look away if you have to."

Dropping the bag, he drew out two tools. One was a rubber mallet. The other was a long wood stake, finely polished and tipped with sliver that glimmered in the half-light. Valerie felt her face twist, her thoughts pounding the walls of her resolve to stay standing.

"What the hell is this?"

He was trembling, though he still managed to keep his composure. Motioning at the body, he said, "Look, Valerie. This is what you saw that night. That man, that creature, he has done this. We have to stop it."

Valerie looked. And, yes, she saw it again. The eyes that night, they were now Pam's. How could…?

The casket shook, the limbs within urging to break free.

"For God's sake, Valerie," he growled. "Hold her down. Please."

Instinct took over. Valerie rushed in, hands reaching in to grip the writhing limbs. She caught the wrists and urged them down. Pam was cold and stiff to the touch, but the force behind her motions was unreal.

"Hold fast," Warren ordered. "Use your strength, Valerie. Don't pull away from it."

She felt that now, too. Power. Raw and violent, stored within, begging to burst out. If she unleashed it, if she let go...

No, Valerie thought, shaking her head. She had to keep herself even. She could not let the rage within go unleashed. Reaching into that well of strength, Valerie called upon only what was necessary. When the cold limbs fought against her, employing more force, Valerie matched it and more.

Warren took up his mallet and stake. The blue-violet eyes of the creature locked on the instruments, face recoiling in disgust. A languid and desperate groan—like the murmur of cat poised to strike—slivered out from some part of the darkness stirring within the body.

This was not Pam. Valerie could see it now. Pam would never have let such...violence consume her. It was some monster within her hungry to break free. Warren placed the stake over the heart and raised the mallet.

"Hold fast now," he whispered.

Valerie held it, fighting against the sudden bursts of motion. The thing groaned, suddenly locking eyes with Valerie. She was certain there was something of Pam left within. The creature paused, gazing into Valerie's eyes, searching for the meaning of the young woman standing over her. And then a jolt ran through the corpse. The chest heaved up then came to a gentle rest. The shimmering of Pam's eyes shrunk into darkness, her gaze now vacant.

Valerie shuddered and drew in a staggering breath. She released her hold as she felt the strength drain out of her.

"We're not finished," he murmured. "There are precautions we have to take."

Valerie backed away. He could take whatever precautions he wanted. She was done. One look at the blunted head of the stake protruding from Pam's breast was enough for her.

Warren did not try to stop her as she stepped away. Valerie watched him draw a knife from his bag. It was a gigantic boomerang shaped blade that flashed in the half-light. Warren stood over the casket, raised the knife, and struck down hard across the neck. The thud and squish made Valerie's stomach boil.

She hadn't looked away as it all happened. For some reason she felt compelled to watch the motion of his arm—the rise and strike. Maybe it would all make sense later. Retracting the knife, Warren sheathed it in its leather casing and placed it into his bag. As he shut the coffin lid, a weary sigh escaped his body.

Valerie stood still, her arms fallen slack at her sides, her wits and body numb.

"Valerie," he murmured. "Valerie, listen."

Valerie found his eyes in the haze of a living nightmare.

Warren stared at her, saying nothing. He read the shock, and probably figured it was too much at the moment. He collected his bag and left, brushing by her as he went.

Valerie stood for many minutes while her wits returned to her. Eventually, she was able to recompose herself enough to move and to think. Her first compulsion was to turn and leave, but she halted.

I have to see it, she thought. Once more, she had to look on the body with her awakened and thinking mind to know that it was real.

Hand shaking, she lifted the lid to the coffin. As the light spilled in, it revealed a torso pinned down by a wooden stake just above the left breast. The blunted end delved into the clothing and flesh like a pin into a cushion. The neck had been hacked through cleanly, and the severed head was tilted askew. Pam's eyes were still open and staring. They were dark now, vacant and dead.

How? Valerie begged. Even now, even in this—death—nothing was sacred. Pam had not deserved this. This world was known for its blind cruelty at times, taking lives that had earned mercy and leaving those that deserved justice. Nascent rage, tinged with despair twisted Valerie's face.

Pam had been *good!* Valerie saw the body again, mutilated, defaced...desecrated. Was no brand of innocence spared?

She had been a girl when she had last asked these questions. Like then, there was no answer when she offered them up to sky and silence. Though the caged anger remained, she no longer resented the truth that there was no reply, nor would there be. She had stopped asking when she was young because she learned that nothing was coming to save the day, and she didn't have the power to do anything either...

That was then, though, Valerie thought, remembering the strength she had felt within.

Balancing her smoldering emotions, Valerie closed the casket and turned away from the remains. The few minutes it took for her to show herself out gave her time to line up some pointed questions for the man named Warren. As she passed through the backdoor and out into the drive ramp, she thought she would start with the most important one.

The car door opened for her, pushed open by an expectant Warren; she sat herself and buckled her seat belt.

"The one who did this, the monster," she asked, "where is he?"

"Destroyed," Warren said, putting the car into gear. The car glided forward, out into the night. Valerie didn't care where they were headed either.

"Did you do it?"

"Yes."

Valerie wanted to feel justice. Wanted to feel like something had been made right. But the coals of her flagging anger lingered still. "And he…he was one of these…things?"

"Undead," he murmured.

Closing her eyes, she took a breath and tried to process that. As she accepted it, as the truth settled in, she felt calm cooling her emotions. "So this is what you do?" she asked, wearily. "You track down these…monsters and destroy them?"

"When I can. I usually just play clean up, like tonight."

"The other murders," Valerie said, suddenly. "It was him?"

He nodded. "The Southwick Psycho." After a moment, Warren continued. "I had been tracking this one down for a while. With the first two murders I was able to narrow down where he was hiding, but he and his familiar escaped and found new places to hide." He paused here, like he was weighing the value of his next words. "I was there, Friday night." Again, he paused, allowing Valerie a moment to process that.

So much echoed out of the dark now. The driver, the sound of a man crying out before she broke Pam free. As Valerie was trying to put it all together he continued.

"I was farther off. I saw you lure his familiar—" He stopped and re-started. "I saw you lure his accomplice away. I didn't know what you were planning, but the accomplice saw you run into the building. When he turned to chase you, I intervened."

"Did you kill him?" The words shot out of her, a dark hope waiting to be satisfied.

He stared a moment. "He…resisted. And I couldn't risk leaving him as a possible threat."

Why he felt a need to justify his actions, Valerie had no idea. A man who deserved to die was dead. That was enough. Then Valerie remembered the hands pressing on her neck that oozed blood, the voice calling for help.

"It was you, wasn't it?" she asked. "After he attacked me. You called for help. You…saved me."

He nodded once. "The police were already on their way," he said. "But I called in the ambulance. So, yes."

Valerie knew what she was supposed to say, but for some reason she couldn't bring herself to utter the words. Not while she still had questions. "Why didn't you go in?" she asked. "You knew where this thing was, that Pam was in there. Why didn't you *do* something about it?"

Nodding lightly, he seemed to understand this question was coming. "It was night," he answered. "That's when they are at their strongest."

Valerie winced. "But you let *me* go in?"

He tilted his head. "If I had tried, would you have let me stop you?"

Good point, she admitted. But still, "You didn't answer my question."

"I was waiting for daylight, the heat of the day," he explained. "That's when they're at their weakest. Lethargic, almost immobile while resting. But in this case, after it attacked you, I didn't have to wait."

Valerie felt her brow tighten. "What do you mean?"

He cleared his throat. "Something pushed him off you. After the creature attacked you, he was weakened. Once the paramedics loaded you into the helicopter, I tracked him into a small wooded area near the lot. He…" he paused, eyes glazed in memory. "He was too weak to resist me."

Valerie stared into the dark of the night, the light of street lamps lapping over her face as they passed into nothing.

Something pushed him off you…

What did that mean? Valerie then remembered the gagging and the vomiting and how it scampered off like a wounded animal.

"He was choking," Valerie murmured, image and sound flashing in her memory. She turned to Warren. "Why me? Why me and not Pam and the others?"

He looked at her then took a deep breath. "There are people," he started, "people who can resist their evil. You're born with it. A natural counter-balance to their power." He shrugged. "Honestly, there are only theories about people like you."

She stared a moment more. *Like me?* "Give me the one that makes the most sense."

"Well," he said, and tilted his head. "The undead, however they came to be, they are unnatural. Or so it's assumed."

"What do *you* assume?"

He sighed. "I don't know. I look at the world and I see balance. I can't say where it comes from, or why. All I know is that there is a natural order as far as life goes."

"I get it, Mufasa, just spit it out."

Warren chuckled. "All right, well, people like you, nightbreakers, you're the world's reaction to the threat of the undead." He shrugged. "Nature's response to their corruption. A way to deal with their un-naturality, maybe." He tilted his head thoughtfully. "Take, for example, the fact that the undead feed from the blood of the living, their life-energy. It rejuvenates them, fuels them with power. Your life-energy, however, is poisonous to them. That's what threw him off of you that night. And that is just one of your gifts. In presence of the undead, you are filled with heightened senses, great physical strength and a hardened durability. These powers…they grow with time, as you mature. These are all the traits necessary to hunt them, combat them, and destroy them. With the correct study and training, none of their power can prevail against you."

Great physical strength…a hardened durability. Valerie had thought it was adrenaline that night; she thought it was just luck that she managed to walk away from a thirty-foot fall through a glass window onto hard asphalt with only a few bruises and scratches to show for it.

"Nightbreaker, huh?" Valerie commented. "Who came up with that?"

"It goes back, I think."

"Was that reason this guy came after me and Pam? Because of…" She paused, lowering her voice. "…of what I am?"

Warren shook his head. "I don't think so. As freak-accident as it sounds, I think it was a matter of chance. Given everything I've seen, I'm not sure this one even understood *what* you are. If he had, he probably would have run. Also, nightbreakers are very rare; your emergence can't be traced to any type of DNA or bloodline. Your birth is random, and because of that, small-timers like this guy probably never saw this coming. All he saw was a vulnerable girl."

"That guy was a small timer?"

"A weakling by comparison, actually," he answered. "This may sound strange, but as an undead, he was something akin to a teenager. All of his behaviors, anything that passed as 'adult-like' was mimicry of what he observed in his prey. Like a child, most of the time, he may have been acting on impulse alone."

Valerie leaned forward and rested her face in her palms, letting her forehead nip the dashboard. She breathed in slowly and exhaled.

"I understand this is all difficult to take in," Warren said.

Valerie nodded. "Yeah. Is that why you took me there to see her?" She sat up again and looked at Warren. "You wanted me to see it first?"

"Yes," he admitted. His tone was genuinely apologetic. "I'm sorry it had to be that way. If experience has taught me anything thing, it's that this conversation goes over a lot easier if someone has seen it first. Not just seen it, but—"

"Got their hands in it," Valerie finished. Morally, it seemed wrong what he had done, taking her into a dangerous situation, a deeply emotional one, without any knowledge of the disgusting scene to unfold. *Then again, what could he have said to warn me?* Valerie thought. *To convince me?*

There was only one pointed question from here. "Where are we going?"

Warren shrugged. "Long or short term?"

Good question, Valerie thought. "Short term."

"I have a place, a cabin outside the city," he answered. "I've only used it a couple of times; it's probably old and musty, but it has running water and place to sleep for the night. You might not get a lot, but I think you should try."

"Sounds good," she muttered. Her head was swimming, and the sticky pain of her stitched wound prickled at her neck. She nudged the bandage with a finger hoping to re-position it in such a way that it might not bother her. She winced at the crackle of pain that followed.

"Is that bothering you?"

Valerie let out an exhausted sigh. "No," she murmured, and then, "Yes, it's getting worse."

"I've got some bandages to keep that clean," he said. "I don't have meds, though. I'll have to go back into town to get them."

Valerie leaned her head against the cool glass of the window. Outside, the world scrolled by in dark patches, all silent and pregnant with unknowns. Valerie should have felt something like fear or dread, but she didn't. She felt empty, which was oddly relieving. For so long, she sat by idly as wiser people stuffed her mind to bursting with…well, stuff. So, empty was an improvement. She felt herself nodding off, and she did not fight it.

The darkness parted back opening to more darkness. Gingerly, she rolled over, careful not to agitate her wound, which prickled like fire under her skin.

Valerie rose from a strange bed, her head throbbing and beading with sweat. She did not recognize the room. The walls were log-stacked, bound by lines of gray mortar. Though her head was swimming, Valerie surmised that she was in the cabin Warren had mentioned. She vaguely remembered struggling from the car into the abode, then nestling into the bed hours ago.

She crept down a narrow hallway into a cavernous living space filled with a few pieces of furniture: an armchair, a small sofa, and a cushioned footstool. To her left there was a high bar with some wicker bar stools standing under it. Along the wall there was a small gas stove and some cabinets. A refrigerator stood off from the group, but she got the distinct impression that there was no power in the cabin. She was comforted by the idea of it. A dark place within a dark place was as good a hiding place as any.

By now, the concerned party responsible for Project Valerie was probably busy tracking her last movements. At this point, they would have gone over the hospital security footage and questioned all the relevant people. They would have already gone to the apartment. They would have noticed that she had rummaged through her things, taken some and left most, and if they had any brains they would have come to the conclusion that she ran away of her own choosing. They could imagine whatever motives they wanted; she didn't care, as long as they could not track her here.

Outside she saw a shadow slide past the window. She slipped into the deeper shadows of the quarter and waited with balled fists. Keys jingled at the lock, the door squeaked open, and Warren stepped through with a plastic bag dangling in his hand. In one motion he set down the bag, pulled a long match from a drawer, struck it and lit a small lantern held within a wall sconce. Yellow light spread over the once gray and black forms.

"I got some meds for the pain," he said without turning around to see where the light had revealed her standing against the wall. He turned, reached into the bag, pulled out a white bottle and tossed it at her. The pill bottle hit her in the face before she could catch it.

"Dude," she said rubbing her nose and forehead.

"We might have to work on your response time," he said with a smirk. "Those are antibiotics. You'll need to do the directions there or that wound will get infected."

After lifting the bottle from the floor, she approached the bar and sat herself in one of the chairs. She studied the dosage directions on the bottle. It was a legitimate prescription for her wound, only it was written under a fake name: Sarah Connor.

"Nice," she said. "So, you got a pharmacist friend, too?"

"I do," he said, putting a few things away in drawers and lighting one more lantern on a wall sconce. "It's good to keep contacts. Bribery also works."

Valerie filled a palm with water from the faucet, which drew a pointed correction from Warren. "I wouldn't drink that," he said. "Water bottles up here." He pointed at a cabinet.

She took his advice. With pills in mouth, she hiked her head back and took a swig from a bottle.

"How long have you been doing this?" It was a dangerous question, but one that might tell her a lot of things—things about a man she might have started to like, but still did not trust very much.

At first she thought he would ignore the question, since he fiddled with a few more things and stayed silent. Maybe he was hoping she would drop it, but she kept a steady gaze on him and his movements.

"Uh, wow," he said, finally. "I'm what, forty-two now? So, about 16, 17 years or so. Yeah, about that long." He looked at her, offering a very generic smirk. He turned away quickly, clearly uninterested in telling his origin story, which could have meant a few things. But Valerie put her money on the most likely tale: young man Warren in his late twenties is thrown into this mess against his will or by mistake. He is forced to either sacrifice any hope of a normal life, or the more tragic version, he has to leave a young family behind.

Valerie thought better of asking if he had any family since either answer was bound to be painful to admit after all this time.

Warren sighed. "You should try to sleep again," he said. "The pain meds might make you drowsy, so that'll help."

They stared at each other for a moment. When nothing was said, he forced a smile then started for his room.

"Wait," Valerie said.

He straightened. "What is it?"

She thought a moment, then asked, "So...what? Are you, like, recruiting me?"

There was real conflict in his face, a range of emotions that she had not expected. There was regret in the shadows under his eyes. There was doubt at corners of his mouth as he grimaced. There was even a small coat of shame lining the folds of his brow. Eventually, determination broke through them all. "You have a choice, Valerie," he said. "Everyone should have a choice." His face softened. "It isn't one you have to make now, though."

She stared at him a moment more, saying nothing.

At length, Warren nodded. "Good night." He passed into the hall and on to the far bedroom where he shut the door behind him.

Valerie wasn't sure she would be able to sleep. She peered through the window, out into the darkness not knowing what time it was. Probably two or three in the morning. Though they were likely far from civilization, she could grab her stuff, take Warren's generous gift of medicine and painkillers, then hit the trail and never look back. Warren didn't seem like the type to follow after her.

Unbidden, the image of Pam's blue-violet eyes glaring up at her flashed in her memory. There had been something there, not just the evil brimming within, but something of Pam stirring inside. Her memories, maybe—or shards of her consciousness whose rest was suddenly and inexplicably interrupted. Valerie only now had the words for the question that swirled in her mind since: How could something so evil happen to someone so good?

Wasn't there anyone to stop it?

Valerie knew the answer. She took the meds, knowing that it might be awhile before she had another chance at a good night's rest.

With her black wet hair bundled above her exposed shoulders and her body wrapped up in a green towel, Valerie foraged the pantry for food. A clawing hunger ravaged the inside of her stomach. She found canned beans and vegetables, but little else. *So,* she thought. *This is the down side of roughing it.*

Warren emerged from the hall and plundered the pantry for a few cans. He went fast into the work of cutting them open, rinsing their contents in the sink then throwing them in a pan. He reached within a drawer Valerie hadn't searched and pulled out some eggs from the plastic bag he brought in earlier that morning. Valerie sat at the bar, comfortable in letting him make breakfast.

As their egg and veggie omelets crackled in the big pan, he approached the bar across from Valerie and leaned into it casually.

"What do you know about Brazil?" he asked. He hadn't looked at her yet. Maybe he thought it improper to glance at a newly showered girl wrapped in a towel. Whether it was appropriate or not for her to sit this way was irrelevant. They were bunking together and he would have to get used to it.

"It's full of Brazilians," she said.

He ventured a glance at her, appraising her exposed wound for a second. "Yeah, you're right about the Brazilians thing," he murmured absently. He went back to the eggs. "Anything less obvious?"

"It's the largest country in South America," she replied. "Uh, they also don't speak some form of Spanish like all other

South American countries. They speak Portuguese, I think, right?"

Warren gave a cursory nod. "That's as good as I could hope for, I guess."

"Wilson P. had Brazilian exchange students," she added. "I didn't know them though."

Warren picked out some ceramic plates, set them down on the bar, and served up the omelets. Unable to wait any longer, Valerie tore a slip off and put it in her mouth. Warren gave her an amused, albeit reproving look as he handed her a fork. She took it and gladly dug in.

"Is that where we're headed?" she asked, chewing. She looked at him. "Long term, I mean?"

Warren didn't answer immediately. He swallowed, paused a moment and stared off.

Valerie stopped short. "What?"

Warren locked eyes with her, his gaze severe. "Are you sure this is what you want?" he asked, and put up a hand to stop the immediate and insistent response he expected. "Before you say anything, you need to understand that your life will be in danger. But that's the good part, right? The adventure."

He shoved his finger into the counter top. "Now here's the other part. If you come with me, you will also not know what a normal life is anymore.

"I don't care how burnt out you are on the world, Valerie. The day will come, especially as young as you are, when you will find yourself so far on the outside looking in, that you will question whether your life ever really happened.

"The time might come when you'll watch a mother holding hands with her kids as they approach a swing set, when you'll watch her braid their hair into bows, laugh and play with them. You will stare at them and wonder if you had just walked out, right here, at this moment, that you could have had that life. One full of...goodness."

He pointed at her. "That's what you're giving up, Valerie. If you walk down this path, none of that will be available to you. Neither during, nor after. If there even *is* an after."

She had been ready to dismiss all this warning talk, but his words struck her. She could see herself there with the daughters or sons she still did not have and had never thought about having—until this moment. She saw that future for her, and only now did she even think that it was possible.

Valerie blinked softly and stared for a moment. In her mind's eye she watched herself play with the children she might have one day, watched herself and them—and turned away. The fantasy was a good one, but it was only that for Valerie.

What was it worth, she thought grimly, *when it can all be taken away in an instant?*

"I understand," she murmured. The severity of her tone seemed acceptable to Warren. He nodded, let a cloud of remorse rise and pass over his face, and then it was back to business.

"Depending on how much time it takes to get our things in order, and if I'm right about a few things, yes, we're headed to Brazil," he said. "We have to make a few stops. There's someone you need to meet. I'm hoping no more than three days, though. On the move. Hope you didn't get too attached to the cabin."

"Who are we going to meet?" Valerie said, gobbling down the last bit of her omelet.

"A friend," he said. "He's much more...knowledgeable, let's say."

Warren gathered up their plates and set them in the sink. While he ran water over them, he rummaged through another drawer before pulling out a Polaroid digital camera. "Here," he said, pointing to a plain white wall. "Stand over here."

She backed up to it, standing straight.

"Let your hair down."

Valerie pulled the pin out and tossed her head, letting the wet mess fall about her shoulders.

"Good," he said, and squinted through the camera. He clicked two pictures, reviewed them on the back screen, and pressed a button. A little photo printer on the bar coughed up two pocket-sized snapshots. He handed one of them to Valerie, "There you go, Sarah Connor."

Valerie took the photo. It was a good shot, all things considered. But somehow the image didn't seem like *her* anymore: black curly hair, caramel skin, light hazel eyes, smooth aquiline nose and full lips. The person in the picture was a typical face in the crowd, any other young woman.

It was a fake, though, a phony. The face in the picture was a front for what lived beneath. Her true-self. Valerie grinned, remembering the name.

The Nightbreaker.

Chapter 4

The next two days moved very quickly. Warren laid out the plans that morning. The photo was for a to-be-forged passport, which they would use at an airport yet-to-be-known. Wrapping up everything in the cabin had been easy. Valerie had packed light, and it looked like Warren lived out of his car, so they were out the door and on the road again in less than an hour.

From there it was a blur of road travel and supply gathering, which usually brought them to quaint towns where they shopped for essentials. Warren never talked about cost. Though she didn't think it was smart, he used cards to pay for their expenses. There didn't seem to be a limit, either. Warren even made small-talk with the shop keepers.

He was a conundrum that was for sure. Maintaining a low profile seemed like the best strategy, yet he seemed so unconcerned about those little details, while minding the big ones, like avoiding cities. She wouldn't question him about his actions; instead she decided to watch him and study his methods. In the event that she were ever on her own, she would then have an idea of how to get by.

It was day two while navigating a secluded maze of wooded back roads when she awoke from an unintended nap. "My parents," she asked. "Do you know anything about them?"

"I guess you mean your birth-parents," he said, without looking at her. His lowered tone suggested that this was a topic he knew would come up and was not looking forward to.

He relented. "Look. If you were counting on their absence from your life having something to do with all this, with your abilities, and why that might make you—or them—a target, then I'll tell you flat out, that's probably not the case."

"I get it," Valerie deadpanned. "Voldemort didn't kill my parents."

Warren passed a glance at her again, saw that her glare was unflinching, and continued. "Your father's name is Alejandro Zeta-Nacimento."

"Is?" she asked.

"He's alive, yes. He's currently in prison for first-degree murder, armed robbery, and contributing to the delinquency of a minor."

For whatever reason, it was that last count that bothered Valerie most. Perhaps because it almost sounded like the delinquent minor in question was... *her*. She brushed it off.

"And my mom?"

Warren inhaled and exhaled slowly. "Her name was Melinda Caldwell. Her ashes were spread over the Suwannee River in Florida."

Valerie knew she shouldn't ask, but... "How did she die?"

"Meth overdose," he answered, bluntly. "She and a friend of hers were discovered in the bathroom of your home after being missing for two days. You were two at the time. They found you in the home sleeping outside the bathroom door, which had been locked from the inside. You were dehydrated and weak, but they were able to nurse you back to health with no damage done."

Unbidden, Valerie felt a sudden heat rush into her cheeks. She forced it down, burying it with resentment, anger, and a bit of spite. She might have lamented for the girl, abandoned, hungry, and scared. She didn't, though. All she felt was bitterness for the two people whose highest calling was to protect her from what came after.

From there, the foster home bouncing had begun. First it was the orphanage where she suffered at the hands of girls much bigger than she. A place where the angels were rumored to perform miracles, but were sparing in their mercy in her direst moments. Then it was the foster homes where she contended with people who mistook her sullen silence as weakness, or as an invitation to mold her.

All her life she had felt like a prisoner without a prison, or a traveler without a road. She survived it by calculated suspicion and threat. She defeated it by keeping her pride at the expense of her hope.

Hope could cut, she had learned, as much as it was rumored to heal. This case confirmed the truth of it. The small part of Valerie's brain in charge of fantasy often mused that perhaps her parents' absence from her life was a result some loving sacrifice to preserve hers. The truth turned out to be blunt and coarse and much worse than she imagined.

Valerie had so many questions, but after that, she fell silent and watched the road pan by for hours. Eventually they stopped off on the side of the road to eat, stretch their legs, and relieve themselves. Valerie suspected that they were lost, but Warren gave no hint of it. They parked in the shade of a leaning willow as they munched on sandwiches and drank from water bottles.

Warren always finished first. He would then stick the phone to his ear, talk to an unseen somebody—not always in English—then return with a freshly chiseled sternness in his expression. This time, though, he crumbled up his wrapper, tucked it into the trash bag and stood still for a moment. Normally, she might have asked what had been the matter, but Valerie didn't want any more surprises.

"There's something I want to give you," he said, finally. He strolled to the trunk, opened it, and plundered for a moment. He closed the trunk and returned with an object wrapped up in cloth. After peeling off the layers, he handed her a sheathed dagger. It was beautiful in that it was very simple, subtle, and sleek. Taking it, she appraised the knife with mounting enthusiasm.

"Go ahead," he said.

Valerie unsheathed it. Its blade was thinner and longer than the standard slashing knife. It was also peculiar in that reflected her face back at her.

"Notice anything?" he asked.

She beamed at him. "It's made of silver."

"That's right." He smiled big. "Silver burns and stems their ability to heal, an important asset when fighting them—albeit expensive. It's a fine weapon. They used this model stiletto in the second World War for tight-quarter combat. A Fairbairn-Sykes fighting knife. Its blade is wider and shorter than your standard stiletto, but it can still penetrate a ribcage. You can slash with it, but it's designed mainly for thrusting. Quick, small, easy to handle."

She sheathed it and searched for a place on her body to stash the casing. Warren chuckled. "It's got a belt attachment. Just run it through after you go potty. We're back at it in ten."

"Warren," Valerie said, carefully shoving the sheathed blade into the back of her pants at the small of her back. He turned to her, his brow lifted.

She folded her arms, propped them under her chest, and stared off into the foliage. "How did you know all that stuff about my parents?" Valerie then turned and glared at him pointedly.

Warren inhaled through his nostrils and sighed. "You were out for a while in the hospital. I had time to do some homework on you."

Valerie gazed into the forest that lined the road. "So you didn't know about me before all this?"

"No, I didn't."

She stood a moment more before she relented. "Okay," she said. "Ten minutes?"

"Yeah," he said, and stalked off into the woods for privacy.

Once they were back on the road, perhaps twenty minutes of silence passed before Warren spoke. "It's deadly, especially for a regular man like me, to engage the undead at night. They're far more powerful and eager. That's why I hunt them during the day, following leads, whatever little bits of evidence of their passing I can find.

"This one in Southwick got sloppy. He didn't just feed from his victims, he courted them, and...*turned* them, which probably meant he wanted to settle down."

Valerie remembered the mound of dirt, how Pam had been half-buried in it. "Like...take a wife?"

"In a manner of speaking, yes. And that he attacked you also probably means—"

Valerie cringed. "That's sick."

"The best way to deal with them is to track them to their lair. After a feeding, the undead will return to their mortal earth. They carry that with them always, as it is the source of their power and their health as an undead. Usually, they will establish their lair, an earth chamber, protected from sunlight and far from any disturbances. Noises disrupt their peace, so seclusion is preferable. They will rest in an earth chamber during the day..."

"Does sunlight kill them?" Valerie interrupted.

Warren shook his head. "Exposure to it weakens them, drains their strength and power. Those that are powerful enough can roam during certain portions of the day, but they avoid this whenever possible."

"Certain parts of the day?"

"Morning and dusk," Warren said. "*The cool of the day*, they're called, when the sun is rising or in decline. During the midday hours, *the heat of the day*, they are the most vulnerable."

He took a breath and continued. "By night, they seek out their victims, drain them and then return to their earth chamber for a prolonged rest to rejuvenate themselves. If they are allowed to do this fully, then their youth and power are restored to them for longer periods of time."

"How much time between attacks?"

Warren grimaced. "Depends of course, on a lot of things. Months, one or two years, sometimes."

Valerie nodded. "So that's why you had to be cautious."

"Yes," he confirmed. "Tracking even a lesser undead takes time and patience."

"Lesser?"

"There is an echelon," Warren said. "Some are greater than others."

Valerie was quiet for a while. At times, especially after awakening from a nap, she felt the strangeness of all this. It felt like her life before was this mirage shrinking in the distance. Memories like walking through a high school hallway, kids talking and laughing, bells ringing, homework, and social melodrama seemed like a naive and even morbid perversion of the reality she now knew. She shook her head and cringed in the effort of reconciling the two worlds.

"Warren," she started. "How is this possible?"

"What do you mean?"

"I mean, how is this possible?"

"Well," he said, scratching his chin thoughtfully. "Largely we view our world as one that can be measured and defined by our science. This is true; it can be and is. For the material nature of it, at any rate. But our current science, and the tools and instruments that we use to define and measure our universe are not designed to probe into other aspects of our reality. Those systems that make remarkable discoveries and drive important questions for the physical world—while great and useful as tools to that end—are also blind and deaf to other matters, and so..."

"We don't know about them." Valerie finished.

"Right. Or when hear about it—or even *see* it—we call it the paranormal. Maybe even insanity."

"And what are these things that we can't detect?"

"Matters of the soul," Warren said. "The ethereal. The astral. Matters defining the worlds within worlds, the space within space, and in some cases the absence of it." He glanced at her again.

"Go on." she said, her eyes long-gazing into the space rushing toward them.

"A soul," he continued. "Try to view it as the combination of two major elements: energy and intelligence. Now, where does the physical body come from? It is produced within the womb, which is nourished and formed by energy and matter through the consumption of other life. All life, all bodies, come from the process of consuming other material things and transforming it into energy for those things to continue living. The plant transforms sun energy into its own life energy. The plant draws nutrients from the earth to grow strong and healthy. Birth, life, creation and destruction are all a part of a great system of energy transforming itself."

"Okay, I get it," she deadpanned. "Spare me the Buddhist crap, please."

"Context is important, Valerie," he insisted, his tone impatient. "You asked."

"Fine."

He was quiet for a moment, out of frustration or having lost his place in the lecture, Valerie could not tell. She decided to help him out regardless. "Birth, life, creation and destruction are all a part of a system of energy transforming itself."

"Once you understand this, the rest is easier to grasp," he continued. "Now, the natural order is that when the body fails, death occurs. The connection between the material body and the soul is severed. The body decays, and all its remaining material energy is then absorbed into the physical realm to be reused. Our current science can attest to this and does. But what our science, on the whole, neither explains nor even recognizes is what happens to the soul, when its time with the body is over. In fact, it remains unproven by our current science whether or not there even is such a thing."

"Is there?" Valerie asked. "I mean, do you believe it? Souls and all that?"

"Honestly, I try not to think about it too much."

Valerie cocked an eyebrow. "Kind of sounds like you have."

Warren exhaled, perhaps resigning himself to the truth of that. "Maybe one day we'll have the instruments to explore it all. I don't know, but the things that I have seen all point to this."

"So when we die…" Valerie prompted.

Warren finished. "After death, like the body, the soul returns to its origins, where, theoretically, its energy will be re-used."

Valerie rolled her eyes playfully. "Kind of like… *reincarnation*."

Warren groaned. "That's not what I said. When an elephant dies, its remains rot and become fertilizer for plants to use as food. I would hardly call that a reincarnation of the elephant. What I mean is that, the soul—the spirit, the mind, whatever— they return to their own realms, which, I believe work in conjunction with our own. I believe that the powers and forces of the material and the spiritual realms interchangeably influence the other. Like spinning circles whose edges connect or overlap at certain points."

Valerie was nodding lightly, taking in the information. "And the undead," she said, after a pause. "When they first die, when their soul leaves their body and goes back to…to wherever…it comes back from that place to their corpse; it comes back, doesn't it?"

Warren nodded once slowly. "Yes."

Again, Valerie was quiet a moment. She remembered Pam's eyes, seeing her in there, along with…something else. "But when that soul comes back, it doesn't come…*alone*, does it?"

Holding a prolonged glance at Valerie, he shook his head. "No, it doesn't."

Valerie drew her legs up to her chest and rested her chin on her knees. None of this had really answered her question in depth. How did this happen? Was there a process that had to be done? It all implied that magic or something equally fantastic was involved. Valerie didn't want to go there at the moment, and she was glad that Warren had gathered as much.

They had graduated into a long stretch of desert as they roared through back roads trudging up a billowing yellow dust in their wake. With dusk approaching, they turned into a narrow avenue of sunbaked earth. At either side, the world lay out flat and barren. In the distance, a range of mountains was about to absorb the sinking sun.

This had been a day of driving, so Valerie was hoping they were finally getting to a place where they could hold down for the night. One look at Warren's baggy eyes and sagging, pale cheeks would tell anyone he could use some good sleep.

A small, shanty trailer grew on the horizon. It was a mess, easy to see, even from a distance. Caked in the tawny mist of the bounding desert, the trailer fit in perfectly with every in-the-middle-of-nowhere, hermit hole stereotype. Corrupted patch-work clung doggedly to the outer walls: anything from slate tin to actual wood. Propane gas tanks were strewn about, and a generator thrummed steadily nearby. There was even a rusty satellite spiking at the sky.

Warren parked the car a way off, leaving a gap of caution between the trailer and them. Shutting off the car, he dropped his hands from the ignition and studied the trailer for a moment. There was a light on inside and what looked like the silhouette of a person sitting at the window. A blue light waved in and out somewhere within, which was probably the T.V.

"I want you to wait here," he said, without taking his eyes from the trailer. He was unbuckling himself and opening the door.

"Oh come on," she said. "Do you even watch horror movies? That's always how you get killed."

Warren paused and stared at her pointedly. After reading his frustration, she reigned in the sarcasm. "Okay, go ahead," she said, throwing her hands up. "I did warn you, though."

Satisfied, Warren got out of the car and started a slow and cautious trek to the trailer. Valerie watched, huffing indignantly as he sauntered off alone. In the failing orange and pink light of sunset, his silhouette was difficult to follow. Approaching the flimsy door, he knocked and took a step back. He waited maybe fifteen seconds before pounding on it. When nothing happened, she watched him turn in a circle, searching for a sign of life out in the desolation. Finding no one, he opened the door to the trailer and entered.

"Idiot," she whispered, and sat up straight. Her hand clasped the door latch, before she stopped herself. She took her own advice. In horror movies, it was equally deadly to ignore the order of an elder or a sagacious guide. Especially for girls. Unspeakable for minorities. Double-checked, she sat back and waited, but not calmly.

Since the sky was darkening and they had been speaking of otherworldly things for much of the day, she felt a little on edge. This was the reason she could not dismiss the sudden hint of motion in the stretching shadow of the distant hills. There it went again—something moving in the growing shadows, a sliver of something scampering in the desert.

Valerie burst from the car, racing toward the trailer. In seconds, she was up the rickety steps and through the door, slamming it behind her.

"Warren!" she rasped. "There's—" She recoiled, aghast at the sight in front of her.

Blood and gore painted the walls of the kitchenette, where, in the center, an old man's body had been tied to a chair with electrical cords. The body was naked but for a pair of boxers. Headless, his entire body was red, painted with his own blood, except on his chest where someone had carved out the word BROKEN. Warren spun around, reaching behind him for something.

Swearing, he held out a stabbing finger. "I told you to wait in the car!"

"There's something out there," she gasped, pointing. The body was difficult to look away from, but poisonous to look at. Valerie shook her head and turned away, her anxiety mounting as she considered the body and what might be lurking outside.

Warren swore again, put his hands in his hips and dropped his head to think.

"Yeah, I say we get in the car and go. Like, now!" Valerie insisted, her stomach feeling queasy with the pungent odor she only now let herself smell.

"We're out of daylight," Warren murmured. "No."

Valerie screwed up her face. "What, we're going to stay here? The night?" She shook her head fiercely. "Not happening. That's insane." She knifed a hand at the body. "With that? No, no!"

Warren was shaking his head. "If you want to try your luck outside, Valerie, go ahead, but I should warn you that while you are a nightbreaker, you are not immortal."

"We could take our chances," she insisted, holding her arms wide. It was then that Valerie felt a cold malaise wash over her. The word on this man's chest. BROKEN. The coincidence of the word suddenly made sense to her. Valerie's arms fell slack at her sides. "Wait, was he a...?"

Warren lifted his head. "Yes, he was like you."

__Chapter 5_____

The small trailer had been trashed. Home debris lay strewn in haphazard piles organized to the liking of a mini-tornado. Warren had to step over the clutter to gaze through the window facing the falling sun. He split the blinds with his fingers and peered through for a minute.

"I don't see anything," he murmured.

"Yeah, well I did."

"I'm sure of it," he said, still looking out into the red and orange wasteland. "There's a little light left." He snapped the blinds shut, backed away from the window, and looked at her. "Valerie, go get our things from the car."

Valerie didn't argue, though she wanted to. She plunged out into the open and dashed for the car, at least relieved at breathing the fresh air. She made it a point not to look into the growing darkness under the far hills. Swinging the passenger side door open, she dived into the car, grabbed their two bags from the backseat, and then rocketed out in the reverse. She slammed the door shut and sprinted back, bags jostling in her grasp.

A throaty bellow called out from somewhere in the shadow of the hills. Valerie halted, staring into the creeping dark. Though she could not see them, she could feel them out there—like bugs crawling over her skin. She shivered, feeling their presence crackle through her.

It's happening, she realized. She studied her palms, flexing her fingers in and out of a fist. Strength flooded into every part of her, hastening her pulse, fortifying her bones and muscles, quickening her senses. The world moved slower around her, light hazed, colors glowed, and sound warbled.

"Valerie!" Warren's voice was calling out to her. When she looked his way, he was waving into the trailer, his motions slow and ponderous, like a man caught underwater. "Valerie, get inside!"

Awakening, she breathed in deep and rushed for the trailer. Valerie launched the bags at him then climbed in, slamming the door behind her. Warren tossed the bags into the corner and was at the window, peering through the blinds.

Valerie braced herself against the wall as a sudden pain swelled in her skull. The migraine rose like a cloud from the base of her neck. The lights were too bright, the noises were too loud, and the smells too strong. Staggering back, she thrust the heels of her palms into her ears. She clinched her eyes shut, and shook her head all in a feeble effort to ward off the terror gripping her.

"Valerie," Warren's voice said. "Breathe. Slowly."

She steadied herself, pacing her breaths.

"Your senses are over-stimulated," Warren said. "You have to make everything empty. Keep your eyes closed. Steady, Valerie. That's it. Breathe."

She felt herself floating down to her knees. There she rested, engulfed in the dark of her own mind. There was space to the darkness now, depth and height. Each of her breaths swelled the edges of it, expanding its boundaries like a newly born universe.

"Now," Warren's voice said. "Try to focus on something, something familiar. Use it to draw in all your senses. Make them one."

Valerie thought of the yellow circle. She imagined it hanging out in the burgeoning space before her. Breathing slowly, she focused everything into the circle: sound, smell, and sight.

Tiny gray stars flickered in the dark now, lines formed from their light, connecting into geometric patterns. The beading light grew until the outline of the trailer formed around her like a gray ghost. All the clutter was bathed in gray, shimmering light, back dropped in dark, empty space.

Something orange and fiery knelt in front of her—a man made of gaseous tangerine light. Flinching, Valerie's eyes flew open, and she thrust out her hand to shield herself from it. It was Warren kneeling there, his eyes staring into hers. She must have shown her surprise.

"It's me," he said, consolingly.

A sudden crackle of pain crawled up Valerie's skull. Wincing, she planted the heel of her palm on her forehead. "I could see," she murmured. "I could see something…"

"That's your darksight," he explained. "Once you focus your senses, hone them into one, you can see into the dark, through barriers and space. The pain will ease once you have it. Try again. This time, find the edges, press them out and expand the field."

Closing her eyes, she concentrated, reining everything into the yellow circle. It happened again. The gray light melted into view, tiny shimmering beads of light running the outline of the solid things around her. The light glittered in the edges, sparkling at the seams. Warren was not gray like everything else; he looked like a molten orange ghost, whose light burned.

The colors mean something, she thought.

As she explored the field all around her, she noticed the horizon of her sight darkened at the edges of the trailer. She tried to feel the edges with her mind, like invisible hands pushing against them. The dark curtain expanded, beyond the walls and out into the surrounding desert. Forms appeared, the outlines of the deranged clutter, the rocks and the gnarled shrubs all beaded with gray light.

There was something else out there, creatures made of dull silver light. Deformed men, hunched, spider walking freaks that scampered about mindlessly. *Goblins,* Valerie thought. Their little forms gyrated madly in the dark. There were three of them, each working together as a single pack-mind. They circled the outer walls of the trailer, impatient and eager...and out in the dark, there was another form, a man made of bright sliver light flecked with gold sparks.

"Valerie," Warren said. "Open your eyes."

Valerie obeyed, taking in a breath. She flinched as light flooded her eyes, sound boomed in her ears, and the remnant stench soured her nostrils. Warren was crouched in front of her, his hand resting on her shoulder.

"There are three of them," she said as she rose to her feet. "And something else. A man, far off."

"What color were they?"

Valerie looked at him, then answered. "Silver, dull, but the one out there was brighter…"

"Don't worry about that one. Focus on the small ones, the revenants. Where are they?"

Valerie could sense them outside, like slugs squirming through oil. "They're circling the trailer. I think they're looking for a way in."

"I don't think so," Warren said. "They have to be allowed in. If they come in without permission, then they lose a great deal of their power. Revenants are savages, but they understand their weaknesses. We'll be safe here, for the night."

Raising her hands to her head, she grasped it for a moment trying to ease the pain of the headache. "I don't think I'll be able to sleep. Not with…all that out there. Will they leave?"

"Unlikely," he replied. "Your headache is result of the over-stimulus, mixed, I assume, with your fear. It will go away with time, I think."

"You *think*?" she said, wincing.

Warren began clearing away some of the clutter. "Obviously, I've never experienced it myself. So, I'm only going by the book here." He shrugged. "Just what I was told."

Valerie steadied herself as she turned over a chair and sat in it. She leaned forward, rested her elbows on her knees, and nested her head in her hands. "So, what, I just sit here and meditate?"

"Yeah," Warren huffed while lifting a turned-over kitchenette table. "But you might have had too much Buddhist crap for one day, right?" She felt his hand rest on her shoulder. "Just take it easy. We're safe inside. By dawn, they'll be gone."

She inspected the room, realizing that the body was no longer on display—for which she was grateful.

"Where did you put…it?" she asked.

He sighed heavily and gestured vaguely at a small door by the kitchenette. "Bathroom," he murmured. "I cracked the windows for the…smell."

Valerie remembered that Warren had called him a friend. She proceeded carefully. "Was he who we were coming to see?"

Warren didn't answer immediately. Paused by regret, he said, "He was preparing something for us. There was, uh—we had a plan." He stared at nothing for a long moment, lost in veiled regret. Eventually, he shook his head and started rummaging through the clutter. "We can improvise, though."

"What are you looking for?" she asked.

"I'm not entirely sure yet," he said. "Could be books. A hard-drive maybe."

The pain swelled in her head again as he collected some spilt cutlery on the floor. The metal clinking felt like fireworks bursting in her skull. Moaning, she closed her eyes, leaned forward and massaged the throbbing in her temples. It was going to be a long night.

Warren had finally cleared the kitchenette area. The room was still a mess, but it at least now the area carried some semblance of order. Resting his hands on his hips, he surveyed the area.

"All right, Marshall, where'd you put it?" he murmured.

Immediately, he knew his work to clear the kitchenette area first had been a waste. Whoever had done this had already scraped the area bare. There were no spare corners, no hidden partitions within the cabinets.

Fortunate in the small space, Warren only had two other places to search. He took three steps to his left and entered the bedroom. Compact and less spacious, it seemed like the best place to have a secret compartment. All the more reason to assume that the perpetrators would have scoured the place and found it already. Plus, the room was covered in the white foam of mattress and pillow stuffing, which Warren didn't feel like cleaning at the moment.

That left the living area, where there had been only two cushioned lounge chairs, a rickety stand and a small color TV. Valerie was seated in one of the chairs, her eyes closed, her fingers rubbing her temples rhythmically.

She was a remarkable young lady, already a hardened survivor. Her training would take much less time. Warren tried not to think about how eager Marshall must have been to meet her. Enough to risk it all, it seemed.

Not wishing to disturb her, Warren surveyed the room, tossed debris into the kitchenette area only feet away and tried to picture his friend Marshall roaming about the trailer. *I'm Marshall,* Warren thought, *where do I hide something that I want no other to find?*

The best bet would be to strip the thin walls. *No,* he thought. *Too obvious.* It would also take a lot of time to do. Stripping the walls would be a final resort. The cushioning in the chairs had been gouged and searched all ready, so that was out.

Warren went for the TV. He lifted it up and set it on its stand. Examining it, he found a corner where a screw seemed loose. Drawing out a pocket Swiss Army knife, he cracked into the TV and began stripping its innards. Finding nothing, he dropped his hands with disappointment.

A moan rose and fell. The direction of its source was impossible to detect since the sounds crawled up the walls. Then the whispering started. Warren's guts churned, knowing what came next. He wasn't going to be getting any sleep tonight either…

Valerie had done it, for the most part. The headache melted away as the sounds and smells and sights merged together as a single awareness. She could see Warren's ghost moving in the darkness, a splash of orange fire. The revenants outside were a blur of dull silver light.

There's something to that, Valerie knew. *An aura, maybe?* The obvious distinction being that Warren was alive, and those things outside were not. Excited by her discovery, she noticed that as Warren spoke to himself, even in whispers, it was not sound she *heard* but light she saw manifesting as gaseous puffs of blue.

A sudden moan broke her concentration. It had not come from any of the three creatures prowling outside. Flustered, Valerie struggled to maintain her concentration. The beading light frizzled, losing stability.

"Here kitty, kitty," a girl's voice sang. She knew the voice, though it had been ages since she heard it. In a second, Valerie was back in the confines of Saint Vincent's Home for Girls. She was so small, then. She missed her mother and her bedroom. She had to share one now with eight other strangers. They were not always nice. The older girls, especially.

They knew how to get extra food, though. And Valerie always felt empty in her tummy. She asked them once if she could have some of their food. They laughed. "Sure," Amy said. She was the big fat one. She gave Valerie food that tasted slimy and smelled terrible. "It's good for you, kitty. Eat up." The other two girls laughed as Valerie was forced to eat it, even after she spit some of it out.

After that, Valerie ran from those girls. Hid from them, especially at night when the lights were out. "Here kitty, kitty," the fat one would sing. "Dinner time."

Valerie tried to resist once. She clawed, and slashed, and bit, but that only made them laugh more. "Kitty bites," Amy chuckled. Then Valerie felt her head jerk aside, followed by a savage burning in her cheeks. "Bad kitty!" Amy shouted, pointing a finger at Valerie's nose. They made her eat the slimy, smelly food.

She tried hiding then. They learned about the closets, so Valerie resorted to sleeping in other's girls' trunks, among their clothing and personal things. Cramped, imprisoned, alone, she curled into a ball and listened as they prowled around the vast dorm.

"Where's she at?" they whispered. "Here kitty, kitty." And then they would scamper off at the sound of sudden footsteps dragging in the hallway.

Once they were gone, there was silence first, but soon Valerie would hear the breathing. It was the strained rasp of the ancient nun who never slept. Never seen during the day, the bent creature patrolled the halls at night, swishing ponderously in the dark like a living ghost. Even when Valerie was in her bed, she would pull her thin blankets over her head to try to dull the sound of the woman's breathing...

"Valerie?"

Her eyes shot open at the sound of Warren's voice. She had gripped the arms of the chair, her muscles seizing. To her left, Warren was tinkering with a TV, like he was trying to repair it. Currently, he was gazing at her.

"It's dread-speak," he said. "Do you hear voices?"

Valerie nodded tersely. "Bad memories."

"It's different for everyone," he explained. "It's like..." he shrugged. "Like psych-warfare, meant to rile you. The resonance of the chanting enters the mind of its victims and touches their fear. Calls out bad memories, things people work hard to forget. Even stokes phobias. By the way, do you have any?"

"Old women," Valerie said. "I think."

It took Warren a moment to reign in his laughter. "Well normally, people say heights, public-speaking, spiders, or clowns." He chuckled again, rising to his feet while fiddling with a small do-it-all knife in his hand. "Old women is a new one. But strangely understandable."

"This is going to be all night?"

Warren sighed and started to inspect the seams of the carpet along the wall. "Trust me it's going to get a lot worse. Right now they're content to keep us locked up, confined. Dread-speak is meant to rile a victim's fears, and after a while, draw out hostility. They'll hope for panic among us, maybe even infighting. When that doesn't work, I don't know, with as small as this trailer is, they might just try to turn it over to flush us out. Getting through nights like these is a lot easier in a place that can't be tipped over, I have to admit."

Warren's nonchalance comforted her. He seemed practiced in surviving situations such as these. That, or he just honestly held no great regard for survival.

"Well, what's this?" Warren murmured, and then his eyes widened. He started to peel back the carpet from the wall. "Of course, of course. Because who installs carpet in a dinky trailer when there's nothing but sand to get into it?" Warren beamed at Valerie. "Only a man trying to hide something under it."

With jolting tugs, Warren pulled up the folds of the carpet. Warren stood over the bare floor, eyes hunting for the clue he expected. They locked on a small section in the back corner of the trailer. Drawn to it, like the poisoned to an antidote, he dropped to the little patch of floor and clawed at it. His fingernails managed to dig under the line of a nearly invisible seam.

"I think maybe your knife would help," she said, watching him.

Rolling his eyes, he reached into his pocket and drew out his Swiss Army knife. With its blade, he lifted a square piece of the flooring, about the size of a standard atlas. Setting the square aside, he used a fallen lamp nearby to flood light within the hole.

"Marshall, you old nerd," Warren mumbled. "You did it. You really did it."

Warren then lifted three stacks of notebooks, two three-ring binders, and an assortment of papers sealed in plastic bags. The excitement was evident in the eyes of a man who had yet to show any in the short time he had spent with Valerie. Warren restored the piece of flooring to its place then organized the books and papers into a coherent array before him.

Valerie had been good and quiet long enough. "What is all this?"

He snapped out of it and offered a quick glance. "Christmas," he murmured.

Valerie cringed. "Cool, now I know what to get you." She paused a moment. "But really. What is all of that?"

Warren sighed and ran his fingers through his thinning, blond hair. "Hopefully, it's the last piece of the puzzle. The answer to the riddle."

Valerie had a special place in her heart for speaking in metaphor, but being overly cryptic taxed her patience. She cocked an eyebrow and soured her voice, "And what riddle is that?"

A haunted grimace overshadowed Warren's face. "How to end it. All of it."

Valerie slowly sat back in her chair, resting her head. She closed her eyes. "I don't know," she mumbled. "It just seems like nothing is ever that simple."

Warren appraised the array of literature before him. "Simple, let's hope. Easy," he held up a thick book, appraising it, "don't count on it."

"Are we gonna have to read all that?"

"If you can read old Ukrainian, Slavic dialects, and—" Warren picked up a plastic bag that contained a stack of loose-leaf paper. "—Portuguese then yeah, you can help."

"I'll stick to radar watch," she said, with her eyes still closed. Though the headache had gone, every time she closed her eyes, her darksight flickered with the movement of the revenants outside. "They're getting restless."

"They're monsters," he said. "They're always restless."

Warren reached for his bag and pulled a compact camera from it. He spent the next two hours taking photos of the pages, careful to ensure that he missed no edges or margins. The pages included lengthy text, written in foreign languages, many of which used different alphabets. Some of the pages contained diagrams of what looked like contraptions, tools, weapons maybe, and even what looked like blueprints for buildings. Meticulous in his effort, he was careful not mix the order as he worked.

Once he finished, he stacked the books and papers and went to the kitchenette in search of something. Plundering through cabinets, he found a trash bag, puffed it open, and then stuffed all the material inside it. He then plopped to the floor, drew his knees up, and breathed deep.

"I'll need to sleep," he said. "We have another day of driving tomorrow."

Outside, another moan floated over the air. It was quiet at first, and then very slowly it rose until it rattled the trailer's meager walls.

"Help me!" a woman screamed. "Oh God, please! Help me!"

Valerie perked up, nearly springing to the door. She stopped short upon looking at Warren. The plaintive glint in Valerie's eye drew a stern rebuke from Warren. "Do you really believe there's a woman outside, in the middle of the desert?"

Valerie settled back, but jolted when something pounded on the door. "Please! Oh God! Please open the door! My baby, they want my baby!"

"Warren?"

His reproving glare never faltered. "With a baby?" He closed his eyes, showing a cool confidence. "Is there a woman out there? It seems like you would know better than me."

Valerie closed her eyes, concentrating on the beading light. She searched the darkness just behind the door, but there was nothing there. The revenants, however, were anxiously waiting beneath the trailer, just under the rickety steps. And there was something else, not outside the trailer, but inside with them. Valerie could feel it breathing on her neck. The breath was cold and blistering, doggedly rasping in and out.

"Are you up after bedtime?" the old woman's voice murmured.

Paralyzed by the image of the old woman's lips nipping at her ear, Valerie's heart skipped and fear passed down her body like cracking frost.

"Oh well, you always were disrespectful," the old woman's voice whispered. Valerie knew her face. Sister Augusta from Saint Vincent's. She was a hunched old hag with browning teeth and a haunted ragged breath as she gimped along. The veins and sores of her ailing body showed through her thin paper white skin.

"Angry, child? Ferocity does not become you," she growled. "It can't save you. Only God can save you, dearest. The Lord of Hosts is your only salvation. Now," the old woman licked her pale, cracking lips. "Let's hear the Lord's Prayer. Say it. Let me hear it."

Valerie's heart froze.

"You don't know it?" the hag asked. "It is because you won't listen. You're too proud, and pride is the enemy of God. Pride is the root of all sin. Do you understand?"

The old hag's cackling was joined by the girls' taunting. "Here kitty, kitty," the fat one sang. And then came that same feral moan that had crept out of Pam's mouth...

Valerie gnashed her teeth, her molars grinding with mounting fury. She could feel it, deep down—that inner beast that had brought her nothing but trouble in her life, nothing but grief. And now its slathering rage begged for release, for just one moment out of the cage...

"You'll not survive," the hag taunted. "Don't you see?"

How long had it been? Valerie reflected. *Two years? Not bad. Not bad at all.*

Valerie's eyes burst opened as she rose from the chair in a march toward the door. Pulling her knife free, she clicked the deadbolt loose. For all Warren's know-how, he was still a slower, older guy; he was barely to his feet when Valerie pushed the door open. Dashing into the night, she braced herself, ready for the first one.

"Come on, you little freaks!" she screamed. "I wanna get some sleep tonight!"

The first one—overcome with a long-delayed desire to kill—lunged at Valerie from her left. She studied its leap and rise, throwing an arm up to block its advance. She swooped up with her right, firmly planting her knife in the creature's chest. She had expected a roar of agony in response, but there was only a sickening *gah-lump* as its body collapsed into stillness.

She yanked the knife free while tossing the limp thing to the ground. Taking greater caution, the second circled to her right, drawing her sight along with it. The third one blind-sided her from the left, rolling her onto the ground. It mauled her forearm, biting, tearing, and chewing. Crying out, Valerie flailed blindly at it, trying to gut it, but its fast and erratic movements eluded her attempts. It bit down for a third time and tore at her arm like a rapid dog.

Just as the other was creeping in to finish her, the one on her arm began gagging and choking. She kicked it from her and jolted upwards as the other leaped at her neck. Missing its target, it tumbled and recovered, but not before Valerie chased it down.

Pouncing, she wrestled into submission, pinning its pale, leathery arms down with her knees. After thrusting the blade into the neck, she ripped it out sideways, letting loose a gush of black ooze while blue and yellow flames sputtered on the flesh.

When it squirmed no more, Valerie rose. The last revenant was writhing and curling in agony, kicking up dust and scattering rocks. She sauntered over slowly. "Yeah, you drink that down."

Kneeling, Valerie put her knee into its back, pinning it to the sunbaked sand. It groaned, raging madly like a burning insect. She grasped its forehead from behind, yanking it back to expose the neck. She sunk the knife in the tender flesh and ripped it free, dislodging the head. She tossed it aside and hopped to her feet in a clumsy flourish.

"And if there's anyone else out there," she hollered at the dark. "Now's your shot!"

She stood alone, chest heaving breath in the arid gloom. She searched the deep black for a sign of movement, a hint of sound, but there was nothing. At length, her strength drained out of her, her senses dulled to normal, and the heat in her skin cooled. Shivering in the gathering chill, she was suddenly aware of her oozing wound.

Though covered in sand and sweat and stink, she felt awash with relief, her clawing rage sated. Finally.

Warren met her half-way as she stumbled back to the trailer, holding her wet arm.

"Sorry, man," she muttered. "They were really pushing my buttons."

Valerie had expected a speech from Warren. At least some kind of cautionary tale about this one time when this person acted just like Valerie but didn't end up so lucky. Whatever. Valerie didn't care. She wasn't trying to prove anything; she just wanted those things out of her head.

Maybe that was why Warren said nothing. Maybe he understood the torture she endured and understood her actions as a result. Or maybe he was just as glad that it was over and saw no wisdom in decrying her methods, regardless of how risky.

He was quiet as he bandaged her arm.

"When I get like that…" Valerie started, not sure why she felt ashamed. "It's just…it's hard to hold back."

Warren's expression remained unreadable as he taped the bandage off.

"Are you mad?"

Warren shook his head wearily. "You did well," he relented. "Reducing their number early, then letting them converge on you, making them over confident. You turned their strength into a weakness. It was clever."

Valerie grimaced, accepting the praise, even though…

"You made it up as you went along, didn't you?" he murmured.

"Winged the whole thing," she admitted. "But thanks anyway."

He was quiet again, while wrapping the bandage. She had missed something. "What's wrong?"

"There was another out there," he explained. "Watching."

"I saw it. At least I think I did. Is it going to—?"

"Probably not," Warren said, emphatically shaking his head. "Maybe it'll standby and watch, but it won't bother us after all that."

"So we scared it off?"

"I can't say," Warren said. "Maybe. But if that's the case, it's because it realizes what you are. Which I wanted to avoid for as long as possible. The element of surprise is very useful when you lack numbers."

"It wasn't like the others," she said, remembering only the vaguest glimmer of its presence far out into the darkness. "It was more like the one back in Southwick."

"I'm certain it was enthralling the revenants," Warren explained. "Controlling them."

"They can do that?"

"Undead of greater power can control, and even possess, those of lesser power."

"So, there's like a hierarchy?"

"Something like that," he said, and then plopped down in a chair. "How did the blade do?"

Valerie held it up. "We're off to a good start, I think." She liked how it felt in her hand, sleek, light, and obedient. A good friend already.

A faint smirk rose and fell in Warren's cheeks. "You know, in old stories, when a warrior fought with his weapon for the first time and was victorious, he would grant his weapon a name. Sometimes it was to honor the man, sometimes it was to commemorate the feats accomplished with it, but most of the time it was to strike fear in the heart of his enemies."

"Okay," Valerie said, amused. She didn't have think about it. "Pride."

"Pride?"

"Yeah," she said. "There was this nun at Saint Vincent's. She was so old and just…wretched. Used to creep me out. She was always saying, 'Pride is the enemy, Miss Zeta. Pride is the enemy.'" Valerie stared off at the wall. "I don't know. Even as a kid I thought there was something wrong with that."

"Well then," Warren said. "Keep your Pride close to you."

"What about you?" she asked. "What are you carrying?"

Warren's face lit up as he looked away embarrassed.

"Ah, come on, show me. It's not that dinky Swiss Army knife, I hope."

He reached around to the small of his back, lifted up the bottom hem of his jacket and pulled something loose. Unsheathing it, he presented a silver bladed knife. The blade was about a foot long. The spine of the weapon bent forward, making it look something like a boomerang.

Valerie remembered the weapon from the night at the funeral home. He had used it to ensure that... She stopped herself, not wanting to allow grim thoughts spoil a well-deserved moment of levity. Valerie nodded, grimacing. "Well, okay."

"It's a smaller version of the Napalese kukri blade," Warren said. "Mostly for hacking."

"Yeah," she replied. "It looks like it hacks things. Did you name it?"

Shaking his head, Warren lifted up his jacket and returned the blade to its case. "No, I try to avoid battles and all. That's not really how I operate. So, I guess I haven't really deserved the honor." He shrugged suddenly. "Listen, you should keep up with the antibiotics, and if you want, take something for the pain. We've still got the meds."

Admittedly, her arm had begun to throb. "Maybe I will."

"All right," he said, and rose from his seat. "I need to sleep. You should, too, or try at least."

"Shouldn't we trade watch duty, or something?"

Warren shook his head wearily. "No, I think we'll be fine. But if you're feeling peppy, go ahead." He dragged himself into the bedroom, where she heard him moving objects around, clearing an area for him to lie down.

Though her body felt weary, her mind was wired and awake. She reasoned it was probably on account of napping intermittently in the car for the last two days. Clearing away her own area, she made a little pallet for herself, using all the strewn cushioning and a tablecloth from the kitchenette. She popped back her pills, drank a bottle of water and lay down on her makeshift mat.

From the moment she settled, she knew it wasn't going to work; with the lights on, two days' worth of naps, and a steady stream of gruesome flashbacks, she knew she would never be able to willfully slip into sleep.

Valerie sat up and spied the stack of books and papers in the trash bag. Her eyes glanced toward the bedroom and then back at the bag. *Nothing like a little reading to put me to sleep,* she thought. She bent down over the collection; she had never been much of a reader, but she had seen that there were pictures, which might prove mildly fascinating.

Gingerly, she untied the knot. Pulling out the three ring binders, she set them aside and started in on the loose-leaf papers. They were written in foreign languages and in cursive. The books had the same problem, even though the script was pretty, and the illustrations were interesting, albeit macabre. Lots of pictures of bodies cut open.

She resigned herself to the binders. Opening the first, she leafed through the pages and was happy to see most of it was typed in English. She turned back to the first page, and skimmed over the words. Before long, she found herself reading the pages in depth.

I've decided to write the commentary after all, so here it is (you're welcome, Warren). Originally, I thought I'd just make an appendix and leave footnotes to accompany the originals, but since the literature lacks cohesion, no amount of footnotes or tag lines is going to piece the knowledge together. I have a few books that have attempted to do this, but have ended up being as limited at the primary source documents. I'll try to keep everything as concise and short as possible. Warren wanted an outline, but that alone might take months. So, I'll make a formal bridgework of all the literature and not waste time on shortcuts.

Please note that, while I have taken the liberty of scanning many of the old illustrations and embedding them in this analysis, I have kept the originals as evidence that I didn't just draw the stuff up myself. I have since, however, destroyed all electronic copies upon printing all this for fear of unwanted exposure.

I suppose it's best to start not at the beginning, but with context. The study of the undead actually is centered on the idea of living forever, or at the very least having one's eternal life assured. And not in the cryptic religious sense (i.e. in some barely definable paradise), but in the mortal sense of living here on Earth, or in the material realm forever. Most people think Alchemy, viewed largely as the proto-science to our modern sciences, held this to be its primary goal. But that is only partially true.

Alchemy was more about the ascension into *perfection.* For base metals, their perfect state was gold. For humans, their perfected state was *immortality.* The pursuit of eternal perfection remains the primary goal of the Alchemist. While many alchemists viewed this endeavor with a religious fervor, most of them were probably just slippery men who wanted to live forever, and live rich while they were at it.

I never met any of those people, so I, like everybody else, can only speculate on the writing they passed down through the ages. The sincerity of their intentions is also irrelevant. Relevant to our study of the undead, however, are their *methods.* Observe figure 1.1.

This is probably the most detailed illustration of the alchemical apparatus used for the Magnum Opus: the creation of the Philosopher's Stone. Note how closely the apparatus resembles the human digestive system.

Whether this was symbolic or systematic, I cannot tell, as nothing is written to affirm either.

However, I ask myself the question, "How does one go about becoming undead?" This graphic offers an interesting insight to the matter when compared with a piece of literature called the *Epic of Tyranny*. The work was a verse epic written by Goran Velius in the 16th century, which told the story of his protagonist Dusan (soul) whose spirit is guided in a dream by an evil necromancer—a solomanar to be exact—who called himself the Son of Frost. This necromancer then escorted Dusan's spirit over vast stretches of wilderness into a treacherous range of mountains until they arrived at a stronghold built into the side of rocks.

The Son of Frost reveals that this place is the Scholomance (the devil's personal school for black magic) and then gives Dusan a magic cloak so he would be invisible and unnoticed among the evil lurking within. Once inside, the narrative moves along much like *The Divine Comedy*. The Son of Frost shows Dusan all the many aspects (the 10 pillars) of the school, all of which I will not comment on here, except for the revelation given to Dusan in the Ninth Pillar.

It is there that the Son of Frost shows Dusan the apparatus that creates the Philosopher's Stone (which is eerily on point with figure 1.1). The Son of Frost then explains that one of the ten students had broken the apparatus, claiming that it was flawed and that nothing imperfect or flawed could create perfection. This student, referred to as the Son of Decay, had instead discovered a way to transform the human body into the apparatus, thus empowering him to create immortality with his own body.

This is interesting in the discussion of the undead and its connection to Alchemy. Creating the Elixir of Life with the Philosopher's Stone was one of Alchemy's great aims. But creating the Philosopher's Stone required extremely rare materials, often referred to as Prima Materia. Such limitations would no doubt frustrate seekers of eternal life, and the pursuit of other methods would no doubt follow.

The ending of the Ninth Pillar of the *Epic of Tyranny* has the Son of Frost reveal to Dusan that the Son of Decay had successfully changed his own body into the tool that would transmute the life-energy found in the blood of living beings into life-energy for himself. And having done so, he graduated from the Son of Decay to the Son of the Dragon, and for his great act he was then promoted by the Devil to be his representative on Earth.

Only a few copies were ever made of the *Epic of Tyranny*, and I am fortunate to say that I have the greater portion of what might be the only surviving copy. Goran Velius, the author of the epic, claimed that the writing was inspired by the true of events of a dream he himself had. Such wild claims were probably the cause of its being banned by the Church. That, and it seemed to mock the style and overall message of *The Divine Comedy*. Also, he was Romanian, which didn't earn him any points among Italian publishers of the day.

What is to be taken away from all this? Let's assume that this account has some truth to it. Then it explains the need for the undead to feed on living blood directly drawn from the host. We see that this is the case in how they feed. Standing blood will not do, nor will the blood of the dead, as such blood would have lost the fleeting charge of life-energy stored within it.

The undead, therefore, do not "drink" blood as much they "draw it out" from their victims and take it into their corpse body which is now both their vessel connecting them to this material world and the apparatus which transmutes life-energy into their power. Much like a plant transforms sunlight to energy for itself. Or how humans metabolize their varieties of food-stuff into energy for their bodies. Taking this as a truth, we can better understand how the undead replenish their strength, rejuvenate themselves, and augment their power over the elements.

Valerie rubbed her eyes. Sleep was catching on, and she was glad. Even so, she continued reading. The text was very dense, wordy, and outright boring, but she read on with a growing chill up her spine. From the start of this, she understood that her greatest limitation was her lack of knowledge. Valerie was determined to iron out that wrinkle as soon as possible. She read on until Warren woke her with a shake at the shoulder.

"Hey," he said, his blurry face hovering above her. And then, all at once, pain, ache, and discomfort flushed through her. Her back muscles felt like stones grinding together; her arm, while no longer throbbing, maintained a tender soreness. Having slept for much of the night with her head drooped to the extreme, her neck wound prickled and itched terribly.

Inhaling deeply and blinking her eyes, she stretched out her body, which caused all the papers and books to topple over.

Warren set about the task of reorganizing them. "No offense, but you didn't strike me as a reader."

Valerie was still blinking, taking a minute to awaken herself. "I'm not," she mumbled. "I wasn't really tired, and I thought it'd put me to sleep."

"Looks like it worked."

"Yeah," she replied. "Looks like." She perked up and started grasping at things to help clean the mess.

Warren knelt down, picking at the clutter to organize it. "Just, let me get this. Go pack up the bags. We're out in ten."

Bearing the aches and pains, Valerie stood and started to pack up. After taking her dosage, she stuffed the bottles into her bag, finishing about the time Warren gathered up all the literature.

"No breakfast?" she asked.

Warren glanced at the ceiling and seemed to think about it for a moment. "Watsonville is twenty miles west of here. We'll grab something there."

"What I need is a shower," she moaned. "I don't even want to know the kind of funk I have all over me."

Outside, the sun had just broken the eastern rim. Long shadows stretched from little rocks and skeletal tumble-weed littered across the plain. The bodies of the three revenants had changed into mummified husks over night; their once pale, leathery skin was now cracking-dry and hugging the bones beneath. Had they been men once? Would this have been Pam's fate if Warren had not prevented it?

When they arrived at the car and threw their bags into the backseat, Warren asked, "You don't want a trophy?" He nodded his head in the direction of the ill-fated monsters.

Valerie screwed up her face and shook her head wildly. "That's sick." She descended into the car.

Laughing, he got in, started up the old Buick, and circled away. They drove for maybe a hundred yards before Warren abruptly stopped the car. He leaned down and hit the trigger to pop the trunk open.

"What's up?" Valerie asked.

"Viking funeral." He got out and plundered through the trunk for a moment before bringing out a long-barreled rifle with a scope. Valerie stepped out of the car and watched. Warren turned toward the rickety trailer, posted his rifle firmly to his shoulder and aimed at the fat propane tank. The firing shot and the distant blast happened at the same instant. A cloud of orange and yellow fire ballooned outward both shattering and swallowing the trailer in its mass. When the ensuing blaze relented, only the hint of the trailer's foundation remained. Bits and pieces of wood and tin shrapnel rained down over the dry waste.

After placing the rifle back into the trunk, Warren and Valerie descended into the cab.

"He was partial to Norse Mythology," Warren said.

They pulled into a small truck-stop town whose main avenue was lined with bustling gas stations and twenty-four hour diners with cheesy names. They pulled into The Sherlock Truckstop, a colorful 50's era building with a neon light fedora and magnifying glass bearing its name. Warren gassed the car up to full, and even filled up two spare fuel cans that he pulled from the trunk. Valerie got out of the car and surveyed the little town in a single turn.

She watched people, men, women, mothers, fathers, children, all of them, just scurrying about with their daily business. Simple stuff, like buying food, discussing baseball, or staring aimlessly.

They had no idea. Today was just like any other, its time occupied by the chores of the moment. In none of their faces did she see a hint of dread, the evidence that they knew that they were prey, a flock of sheep ignorant of the monsters prowling just outside the halo of their light. Monsters that were very real and so *eager*.

It awed her how these people carried on, unafraid, unknowing, and perhaps...uninterested in knowing. There, she saw a truck driver, batting his giant tires with rod to test their pressure. To her right, a man sat in his van, talking into his phone, his free hand leisurely hanging from the rolled-down window, a fuming cigarette caught in his fingers. To her left, Valerie watched a young mother wipe the ice cream off the shirt of her toddler daughter, who stood by quiet and compliant as it happened.

Why not just leave the ice cream on there? Valerie wondered. The answer was because her daughter's shirt was dirty, and it was up to the mother to keep it clean. No other would do it. The care and fate of that child rested in that mother's willing hands. Anyone else, not fueled by the love specific to that child, might overlook it; any other human was bound to get it wrong. Such a connection was vulnerable to the horrors of this world. It was soft and fragile. It needed protection.

"Go in and grab a seat," Warren said, finishing up with the last gas can. "I'll be right there."

Snapping out of it, Valerie shook her head tersely. "Want me to go ahead and order?"

"Sure. Let's eat hearty. Lots of eggs, bacon, pancakes. All that."

Valerie's mouth watered at the thought of it. The diner was as stereotypical inside as it was out. A white counter top bar with round red-topped stools greeted those who entered, and the floor staff was populated primarily by jaded old women, or young ladies who had a limited idea of their career options. Valerie chose a seat in the back corner, where they would not be overheard should they digress into private conversations on unseemly topics. An older lady with pale, leathery skin common to chain smokers approached the table. With notepad in hand, she asked, "What can I get ya'?"

Valerie grabbed a menu, spread the plastic foldable open, and consulted the colored items.

"No offense, babe, but you look like a turd rolled over," the lady grumbled, which might have been her natural speaking voice.

Meeting her gaze, Valerie replied, "Oh, do you serve that here?"

They stared at each other for a few seconds before the lady cracked open a monstrous rasping laughter. "You got me, kid. But seriously, whatcha want?"

Valerie pointed at the items. "Two number 3's. Two number 7's. One 'My Dear Watson' special, two orange juices, and a thing of coffee."

The lady scrawled it all down, turned on her heel and made off for the kitchen. Warren brushed by the waitress in passing and sat himself on the other side of the booth.

"Good spot," he said. "Out of the sun. Your arm feel okay?"

"It's fine," Valerie answered, flexing her fingers. "So, you and Marshall were friends?"

Warren passed her a slide long stare. He was fiddling with the saltshaker and chewing the side of his cheek. Valerie noticed for the first time that he had a swooping scar under his left eye.

"You must have got a lot of reading done," he said, gazing out of the long and spacious window. "I called him Marty for short."

"I hurt my brain with it, yeah," she replied.

Warren checked the room for prying eyes then asked, "What are your thoughts?"

"It's a lot more complicated than I thought," Valerie said with a sigh. "There's this whole mythology behind it. It'll be hard trying to sort out what's real."

"That's why Marshall put all that together," Warren explained. "We had this idea that we could reference what we knew to be real, with what was rumored to be true. Put it all together to figure out what everything means."

"Solve the puzzle," Valerie mumbled airily.

Warren sighed. "Or at least make the big picture clearer. Let's not talk about this now. It was easy for you to leave your life, Valerie. I was surprised by that."

Valerie shrugged. "What was so surprising about it?"

"Well, I guess in the past it's just never been that uncomplicated."

Valerie decided not to be offended, even though that stung her a little. And she wasn't sure of the reason. "How many others?"

Warren cringed at the question. "What do you mean?"

"How many other nightbreakers? Other than me, I mean."

Warren stared at her for a moment. "Others total? Or how many I know?"

Valerie squinted. "Both, I guess."

"I don't know the exact number. Thirteen, according to legend," he said. "You're the…uh…" He paused, gazing at the table with a sudden somberness. "You're the fourth I've met."

"Marshall being the first?"

Warren nodded, and then gazed out of the window showing less and less interest in the conversation. Minutes later, their food arrived and they ate without talking. Valerie filled herself to bursting, and Warren did all right for an over-forty who should probably be watching his cholesterol. Eggs, bacon, pancakes, and a gigantic specialty omelet whose selling point was to eat it and try to guess what the ever-changing daily ingredients were.

Warren paid for everything with his card. After that, as they were on their way out, he stopped by the ATM and stuffed his wallet fat with twenties. They traveled to the next town, twenty minutes away. They stopped off at a gas station and he did the same thing there, which officially set off her caution lights.

When he got back into the car, he gave Valerie a stern look and asked, "Do you have a cell phone on you?"

She shook her head.

"Any cards, anything that can be traced?"

Cringing now, she shook her head again.

"Good," he said. He then took all the cards from his wallet, bundled them with a rubber band and tossed them onto the concrete near the pumps.

"What are you doing?" Valerie asked, as he started up the engine and rolled out onto the highway.

"Smoke screen," he said. And then he turned the car back in the direction they came.

__Chapter 7_____

"There's a phone in the glove box," Warren said. "Can you get it for me?"

Valerie didn't bother asking. She handed him the phone, but he didn't take it.

"Take out the battery," he ordered.

"Okay..." She did as he asked.

"Now, throw it out the window."

Hesitating, she glared at him a moment more, which didn't seem to matter much to Warren; he drove on, his expression solid and focused on the road.

After rolling down the window, she tossed the phone and battery out. When the window was back up again, she asked, "What's all this about?"

"It's complicated," he replied.

Valerie nodded sarcastically. "Really? You wanna fill me in?"

Warren glanced at her. "No."

For a moment, Valerie felt the viral urge to let him know how messed up that was. But something about his character, his coolness, his absence of concern—a heightened indifference to the entire world around him—assured her that such an outburst would get her nowhere. Another strategy was in order.

"Is it because you don't trust me?" she asked. She balanced her tone between hurt and innocently curious.

If it worked, his stony face didn't give it away. "Yes," he answered. "But I don't expect you to trust me fully either, and I'm not an idiot, so I know you don't. But let's stick with the facts. There are aspects of all this that I can't share with you. Not yet anyway."

"Can't or won't?"

Warren rolled his eyes and rubbed his forehead. "Wow," he mumbled. "Uh, I won't do it, because I can't. And I can't do it, because I won't. Happy?"

Valerie snatched up her bag and leaned her seat back. She fluffed the bag a couple of times emphatically then drove her head into it, facing away from Warren. Valerie hadn't intended to fall asleep. She just wanted to show Warren how she felt about his little hissy fit—that it wasn't worth losing sleep over. She drove the point home by sleeping for the entire three-hour drive.

To where, exactly, was the first thing on her mind when she awoke groggy-headed and sore. They cruised into a large town whose main avenue was lined with towering light posts. Splitting ongoing and outgoing traffic, a gorgeously landscaped median with fat and lushly leafing trees stretched the entire track. The sidewalks rocked with people of all shapes, colors, and lifestyles. Here, there were places to be, things to do, and lives to be made.

Valerie's eyes glittered at the sight of it. Only now had she realized what days of wilderness and desert driving, transitioned occasionally by small musty towns had done to her. The trip had left Valerie's soul yearning for a sight of real energy and worldly life. With her gaze fixed on the sights, she could feel days of mounting anxiety ease and relax.

They turned into the Nobility Hotel Suites and parked. It was a huge building, whose outer rooms held balconies that overlooked a vast patio housing two swimming pools. Any remaining tension washed away at the sight of it.

"Please tell me we're staying here," she said, rising out of the car.

Warren smiled. "Last day in the States for a while," he said. "You should enjoy it."

Her eyes flared with excitement and relief. Valerie grabbed her bag.

"No offense though," Warren said, rising from the car as well. "Just wait here and let me get the room. You look...uh..."

Valerie responded with a playful simper conveying just how much she cared. "Fine, but man, it is hot out here, and unless you want to fish me out of the pool fully dressed, I suggest you hurry."

Warren started for the lobby entrance. "Arizona heat is legendary."

"We're in Arizona?"

Warren laughed out loud as he walked in the hotel.

Within thirty minutes, they were opening their room door. A little bummed, Valerie had hoped for a room on the upper levels with a balcony, so she could sit and watch day turn to night from up high. But Warren had insisted on a ground floor, although he did manage to get one poolside. The room was beach-themed, cozy, and it had two separate bedrooms: one presumably for parents, the other for children.

"I call master," she announced, casting her things on the big queen sized bed. Warren responded by opening the sliding door to the kids' room and tossing his things in. He could be such a pushover, which was just annoying sometimes.

"Anything you need washed?" he asked from the room.

She opened her bag, getting a hot whiff of days old sweat and body odor. She groaned.

"Let me do it," she called out. "I can take your stuff, too. Just let me shower first."

"I won't fight you on that one," he said, setting his things on his bed. "Do you know where you're going?"

"I'll figure it out."

"Here," he said, handing over three twenties and his bag of clothes. "Mind bringing back dinner while you're at it?"

She took the money and clothes. "Want anything specific?"

"Sandwiches or subs," he said. "It's not the most common food where we're going."

Valerie almost fell asleep in the shower. The experience was glorious. Every drop of water was a shard of cleanliness cutting and melting away of all the accumulated filth of the day and night previous. Refreshed and soaked, Valerie dried her body, swiped a hand over the mirror and stopped short at the sight of herself.

The wound on her neck was still healing. A few stitches remained, and the pink, discolored flesh promised a scar. Slowly, she raised her arm and examined her newest wound. The puncture and tearing marks were clean and had already begun to heal, but like the other, a lasting mark would remain. She gazed at herself, clean and naked, hair slack about her shoulders.

Valerie was not vain about her appearance, but she understood that she checked off on nearly every category of conventional standards of beauty: wavy raven hair, caramel skin, a tall hour-glass figure, full breasts, and a smooth and flowing facial design punctuated with dark eyes.

This body would take upon it more and more wounds and scars. She would maim it, age it, and wear it down. Valerie understood this from the beginning. Only now had it occurred to her that something of her might also be lost in sacrificing her physical beauty. Valerie couldn't determine what it meant, though.

She put on her last set of clean clothing, bound up her hair in a white hotel towel and left the deep-thinking for another day. Or maybe never again. Valerie had very little taste for living in a state of perpetual reflection, like Warren and others like him did. As she walked out, she glanced into his room where she saw the man sitting in a chair, his eyes deep into one of Marshall's notebooks.

Dressing her wound one-handed wasn't as difficult as she expected. With that done, she scrubbed her hair dry, brushed it straight, and let it drop about her shoulders, still damp.

"I'm out," she announced, heading for the door. He didn't respond. That man was the epitome of passive. While it was convenient for her authority issues, his degree of nonchalance was almost irresponsible.

As Valerie broke out onto sidewalk, into the energy and light of the afternoon, she felt the sudden liberty of space without walls and decided to enjoy a little freedom.

After dropping off the laundry in the hotel laundromat, Valerie made her way into the world. Within minutes of sun-exposure, Valerie swung by a convenience store and bought a bottle of water and a pair of cheap sunglasses. It wasn't long before she put her hair up to keep the heat off of her neck. She could feel the heat broiling the moisture from her hair, turning it into vapor. Her hair was dry and frizzy in minutes. That people actually chose to live in this heat befuddled her.

Valerie didn't know how long the flight was going to be, so she stopped by a little family-owned bookstore and perused the shelves. Maybe she would take up reading. As she inspected the covers, all designed to capture and appeal to the eye, she wandered what all the fuss was about.

All this stuff in books, she thought, *why not just do it in life?*

Maybe there was something to be learned from all of it. She couldn't deny that people who read seemed fundamentally wiser and more temperate than those who didn't. At the same time though, when it came to living, cracking heads with the bottom-line, people on cloud nine always seemed to have trouble when it came to making those big choices. There was always this prolonged debate and consideration for what every little thing meant. Not that that was bad, of course. But too often such deliberation was used as a coward's cop-out from making a choice and living with it.

As she left the bookstore, a shop across the street caught her attention. Maybe it was the surrendering look of the ALL STOCK 70% OFF sign pasted inside the store window. That, or that it was a weapons depot. Valerie crossed the street, expecting a big line or a crowd within the store, but the place was empty. She entered, immediately disappointed to find vacant shelves, which made it easy for the guy behind the register to spot her as she walked in.

"How ya' doing?" he called out politely. He was forty-something, dark skin, graying hair, and a few nasty scars on his face. A young man—she guessed was the man's son—had been helping him disassemble a rack stand.

"Hot day," Valerie commented.

"I know that's right," the man said, wiping his hands and mumbling something to his son. The shopkeeper left the register counter, moving to approach Valerie. All the guns were either gone, or labeled with reservation tags. Tent equipment, giant gun-safes, camping gear, and other items remained in large quantities, but the place was picked dry of anything lethal.

"Getting here kind of late," the owner said, sticking his hand out for a shake.

Valerie took it. "Looks like."

"I'm Melvin," he said. "You got here at the tail end of the feeding frenzy, I'm afraid. All's left is bones. Anything you were looking for in particular?"

"My dad and I are headed out to the Amazon," she said. "And I—"

Melvin whistled and drew back. "The Amazon, huh? Business or pleasure?"

"Business," she said, primly. "It's for medical research. Herbal remedies are the thing now, so the company is trying to get ahead of the hippies."

Melvin laughed and clapped his hands, clearly amused by the virile intonation of a young girl using man-speak. "Well, all right! How can I help you with that?"

"It's mostly gear I'm looking for," she said. "A bag for my stuff, something durable, I think."

"Good, good," he said. "Now I hope you don't mind my asking, but what's your weapon of choice?"

"Knives."

"Knives," he repeated. "Well okay, Amazon. Step over here and let's get you outfitted."

He escorted her over to a corner of the store where there was an assortment of bags, pants, shoes, and vests hung and strung on racks. "I don't think I can help you with your knifing needs…" He stopped short and turned around, dipping his head in close to her. "What kind of blades are you into?" He murmured it like it was a personal question.

"Uh," Valerie stammered, trying to remember how to pronounce the name again.

Melvin scooted forward a little closer, grinning sheepishly. He whispered out of the side of his mouth, "You got it with you?"

Reaching behind her, Valerie pulled up the back of her shirt and lifted the knife from the small of her back. She offered it to him. He stepped back, holding his palms up. "Oh no," he said, "You handle it." She drew the blade from its casing and held it up for him to examine. It was like she had turned water to wine. His eyes drank in the sight of the silver bladed weapon.

"Is that...?"

Valerie nodded.

"Young lady, you could sell that thing and take a vacation," he said. "Where'd you get that?"

"My grandfather left it to me."

"Of course," he said. "That's a Fairbairn-Sykes fighting knife, used for trench warfare. The best there is for close quarters, I think. Simple and sleek. That's a beautiful piece. But don't say that to my grandfather; he took one in the leg during the Second World War. I'm guessing your grandfather was Nam, right?"

Valerie nodded. "I think it was a parting gift from his unit."

"Well, he must have been a very loved man," Melvin said. "I have to say, that should probably be safe in a trophy display somewhere. But, that ain't my business. What *is* my business is helping you keep that safe while you use it. And Amazon, I think I've got the thing. Follow me."

They walked farther into a section showcasing combat gear. "Here we go," he murmured. "I hope I'm getting the right size." He chuckled lightly. "I don't wanna hurt a lady's feelings." Melvin picked a black vest from the rack and laid it flat on a table nearby. "All right, what you have here is a nice combat survival vest that you can customize to your liking. I see you got your knife stashed in a not-so-desirable spot.

"Look at it like this, if you're ever in a situation when you need to use a knife like that, then you're going to need it quick. With this vest, you can sew in or clip on pockets, compartments, side-arm holsters, and knife casings wherever it feels natural for you to reach for it."

Valerie rested her knife on the vest. "Where would you suggest?"

"For quick draw and return," he said, and placed the knife hilt down over the left breast. "This is where I'd put it. Plus, and I'm not trying to scare you, but if you ever take a shot to that area, right over the heart, there is that outside chance that that the knife takes the hit. But I pray that is never a concern."

She examined the layout. "I like it. What about pants and shoes?"

Melvin laughed. "You're fierce, Amazon."

They settled on form-fitting pants, and a fleet-footed, light-weight model of standard combat boots, all in black. Melvin escorted Valerie back to the counter, gabbing on about his tours around the world while in the military.

After he was finished ringing her up, he held up a finger. "Wait just a second," he said, smiling. He turned and searched a series of boxes and then asked his son if he had seen the HOLD box for miscellaneous stuff. Finding it, he opened it with a flourish, and pulled out some brass knuckles. He placed it in her bag and winked. "I was saving those for my college-going daughter, but she doesn't want them cause she just joined Green Peace." He rolled his eyes, smiling coyly, which made Valerie laugh.

Valerie hadn't had to use her own money until now, and she was never more grateful that she had it. It was already weird enough that Warren was paying for everything. After folding her things and stuffing them into her newly bought bag, Melvin wished her well.

"You take care down there," he told her as she exited. "Crazy world. People on edge these days. Which is why my shelves are empty. Two eyes open. Hear me, Amazon?"

"Yes sir. Thank you."

It was on to the sandwiches and then laundry. She strapped up her bag like a backpack, and headed for a deli she had spied a block down called The Sinker. She entered and ordered two of their *Ultimundos*.

"Whose name should we call?" the clerk asked.

Valerie shrugged. "Amazon."

The kid behind the counter cringed for second, but moved on. There were others inside, eating and waiting. She found a corner spot to do the same. Everybody was watching the deli's giant flat-screen TV with unsettling dedication. It was Pilot News, one of those 24-hour networks that bludgeoned its viewers with play-by-play breaking news alerts all of which simply could not wait—unless it was time for word from their sponsors. Though she heard the voices on the TV speaking, she hadn't really tuned into what was being said.

That changed when she observed the charred remains of a human being smoking on the screen. A red ribbon on the bottom of the display read: WARNING GRAPHIC IMAGERY. The anchor was asking a voice on the phone a series of questions about some escalating crisis in Mongolia.

"Allen, is it safe for civilians to walk about the streets?" the anchor asked. "Describe how this conflict has affected everyday life for the people there."

After a pause, a voice came back. "Well, Phil, with the civil unrest spreading city by city, it's really brought any commerce to a grinding halt. Much of the citizenry who elected not to participate in the fighting did evacuate the city, but there are so many places erupting in conflict that it is unclear exactly where those people will go. I mean, they'll be mostly caravans of women and children who will remain relatively unprotected. It's frightening, in the greater context, when you think about their welfare and how it's in jeopardy."

"Allen, what is the cause of this violence?" the anchor asked. "Has there been any word about what is the impetus for this unrest and infighting?"

The screen panned images of buildings breathing curling plumes of orange and yellow fire, of concrete chunks busted and crumbled upon the empty streets, and of the skeletal remains of smoking vehicles all in what was once a busy city avenue. Much like the one Valerie and her fellow people had walked today.

"I'm hearing reports that the violence started as a response to Mongolia's decision to join the Russians and the Chinese in their newly formed Eastern Trade Federation. Many of the Mongolians view this as a submission to those two powers, and fears have been mounting for weeks—before their leaders made the decision to join—that their homeland would merely become a puppet state, or a vassal kingdom to the Russian and Chinese led ETF."

"And just for our viewers," the anchor went on, "could you please explain the global implications of this, if any?"

Now the images were of stretching lines of refugees covered in ragged clothing, some ashy with soot and bloody with minor wounds. Women and children carried small bags and pushed wooden carts filled with clothing, food, and cooking wares.

"Well," the voice said, "many Western leaders, especially in the United States and the UK, view this as a rival organization to NATO, or possibly even to the UN. The ETF is expected at any moment to announce their formal drop of the Dollar as their trade currency. They've taken small, less open steps to this end, but they are expected to make an official announcement soon. And once that happens, uncertainty of the strength of the Dollar and the EURO could have lasting damage on Western markets. If Mongolian leaders manage to reign in the unrest, and if they stick with their decision—as I think they will—then that will leave South Korea and Japan, two historically close allies with the West, feeling very, very geopolitically isolated."

They continued to deliberate over the implications of the events unfolding. Everybody on Valerie's side watched with a mixture of horror and awe at the images. The screen now displayed two men wrestling one another savagely in the streets. One overpowered the other, threw him to the asphalt and began to stomp on his head. The victor stopped only after the other rolled over and lay still.

Did these two men know each other? Valerie wondered. They were men after all. Two human beings. What force drove these two people to clash and attempt to destroy each other? Did one threaten the life of the other, and if so, why? Over a trade agreement? Valerie squinted, thinking. So much didn't add up. Normal people ravaging each other over some agreement some guys in suits made?

Eerily, the memory of her fight with the revenants last night replayed in her mind: how they attacked her savagely, the eager grunt in their throats, the growl and hiss as the one bit and tore side-to-side like a rabid dog at her arm. Why? The memory of the figure in the darkness, shadow-clad, safely out of range from the conflict rose in her mind. It had been the will of *that* thing—controlling from the shadows.

It occurred to Valerie suddenly that her fight with the revenants was no more chaotic than the rise and burst of a storm. While it was a terrible and messy thing, there was cause, control, and purpose behind it. And this unrest across the world, there was control behind it, too. On the screen, the main tagline read: CHAOS IN THE STREETS.

No, Valerie thought. It was no more chaotic than a chessboard in mid-game. Sure, the untrained eye might look at the cluttered board—ignorant of the patterns, the rules, and the strategy—only to determine that the station of each piece was a simple product of chaos, unrest, or chance. The players knew better, though. The masters knew the cause, control, and purpose of each of piece and its movements.

Shadows in the darkness, standing aloft, unseen and unknown, but in control. Valerie felt suddenly sick inside her stomach but did not know the cause. Somewhere in her mind, pieces were flourishing and coming together. *Was anything in this world isolated?* she wondered. *No.* Not while the gears turned—and not while the people listened and moved to its grinding music. Syntropy and entropy. Life feeding from life…

"Amazon," a voice called out. Valerie snapped up and paid for the food.

Moping back to the hotel, her thoughts formed and moved quickly into patterns. By the time she made it back to their room, entered and sat down at the table, her mind was full to bursting. With a click, it all came together. After Warren sat down, grabbed his sandwich and started to eat, she glared him and said, "We need to talk."

__Chapter 8_____

Valerie's fingers trembled in restraint of her smoldering emotions. The smell of food made her stomach feel sick. What she was about to discuss was a monstrous and horrible thing to think about. Above all else, she feared that it would be true. And that Warren sat there eating a sandwich only added rancor to reproach.

Fighting to keep her voice even, Valerie glared at the table, occasionally glancing at Warren. "I'm not going to Brazil until you give it to me straight," she announced.

Warren put his sandwich down, wiped his hands and mouth, and sat still. "You have my attention."

Her lip curled faintly. "You're going to give me the truth," she said, her glare fierce. "I'll know if you're lying."

"Go ahead."

Valerie gathered her thoughts, trying to figure where to start. "Your friend Marshall's notes," she started, nodding her head at the stack of notebooks. "One section of them talked about the strengths and weakness of the undead. They're weak during the day, right? They can't change their form, and their powers aren't as potent."

Warren's brow furrowed, showing his immediate lack of understanding. "At dawn and dusk, they can, but their power is still limited." He squinted. "What's this about?"

"I'm working up to it. Bear with me," Valerie insisted. "If they want to replenish their power..." She paused a moment, remembering the reading. "They have to rest on their earth, the dirt of the place in which they experienced their rebirth. They are bound to it so... if they want to leave that place, they have to take the earth with them."

Warren nodded. The tension in his eyes eased, an indication, Valerie assumed, that he was pleased and impressed with her growing knowledge.

"Now," she said, holding up a finger. "That makes them vulnerable. Especially to people like me. Marshall said that because of this the undead are inherently cowards. If they can help it, they won't engage in outright violence for fear of being harmed or destroyed. I mean, the whole point was to live forever."

Valerie glared into the table and continued, "But that's not enough. In order to protect their immortality, they have to become powerful. They have to attract—what were they called...?" She snapped her fingers, thinking.

"Familiars."

"Right," she said, and went on. "Like the guy who had Pam's phone. But even that's not enough." She looked at Warren. "Marshall wrote that the two greatest weapons of an undead are Time and Control." Valerie observed that Warren nodded faintly each time she looked at him. "Well, there's a third, I think: Anonymity. Staying in the shadows, being hidden and unseen. I mean, it would take centuries, but let's say an undead used that time to gather power around him. Political powers. Economic powers. From the shadows, one of these things could..." Valerie paused, shaking her head, disturbed by what she was about to say. "It could control the world."

Valerie looked at Warren searching for a confirmation. The man drew in a long breath and exhaled. "Keep going, Valerie. What's the obstacle?"

She glared at the table again, her eyes searching. "Us," she said, looking back up at Warren.

Somberness gathered under his eyes. "You," he corrected. "And after one has gathered this power, after it has successfully concealed its influence, what does it do with its only threat?"

Valerie glared at him severely, her molars grinding hard against each other. "Control them."

Warren lifted his hands up and placed his palms flat on the table. He would not look at her, but stared out of the window overlooking the pool.

"When were you going to tell me?" she growled.

Visibly shaken, he sighed, searching for the right words. He wasn't moving fast enough.

"You tell me," she ordered, thrusting her finger into the table. "You work for one of *them*, don't you? You clean up after its messes. When one of its servants escapes, you track it down and destroy it, so it doesn't get people seeing the truth. And while you're out there, if you find a nightbreaker..." Valerie paused and glared at him. "What do you do, Warren? Bring them in? For what? Is that why you're taking me to Brazil?"

Warren shook his head, wincing. "No, Valerie, that's not what's happening. You've done an impressive job, so far. Think the rest of this through."

That stung her. "No," she insisted. "I don't just want clarification. I want it all."

Resigned, Warren sighed. "Her name is the Red Widow. What her worldly name is, I do not know, and expect that only a few people in the world do. I suspect Marshall did, but he never told me. Maybe he had his reasons. I don't know how long the Red Widow has reigned, but from what I've read today, she probably became undead sometime after the crusades, and began gathering her political power during the Renaissance."

"And you work for her," Valerie snarled.

"Until recently, yes," Warren said, coolly. "You're right. I'm called a Hound. And I'm not the only one. My assignment was to clean up after any undead who left messes behind. Believe it or not, there are not many undead in the world. Their numbers are tightly controlled, and many of them are thralls of the Red Widow. Recently, however, her powers of control have weakened. Something is changing in the balance of things. Her influence has been disrupted, and there has been a scramble to contain the damage.

"When a thrall goes off the leash it was my job to track it down and destroy it before it unwittingly left a trail of undead behind it. Such an outbreak would inevitably awaken the attention of the populace, which, as you pointed out, is dangerous, even for one so powerful as her."

"And where do I come in?" Valerie asked.

Warren tipped his head to the side. "Men like me," he said, pointing at himself. "While I have skills, I am no match for them. I have ways of finding them and destroying them, but not before...well, not before they claim victims. Like the women in Southwick. Like Pamela."

Warren studied Valerie's face a moment, perhaps seeking to read her mood. "But agents like me, we are not as effective," he explained. "My orders were that if I were to encounter a nightbreaker, then I was to deliver them to my superiors. I received assignments from an agent over the phone."

Valerie sat back as it all came together. The credit cards. The unlimited money. The cryptic conversations on the phone in different languages. Warren had come to Southwick to kill a rogue undead at the behest of this Red Widow. He got there too late and had to clean up the mess he left, finding Valerie in the process.

"How many have you turned over?" Valerie asked, her stomach twisting in fear of the answer. "People like me?"

"None," he insisted, vehemently. His shook his head and whispered. "Never."

Though she felt some relief, Valerie dreaded the answer to her next question. "And what does she do with...us—people like me?"

Warren was quiet a moment, his eyes misting strangely. "She..." he paused, fidgeting with his hands. "She uses them. Molds them, trains them to be her personal vanguard. They're called the Fortisan. With all their abilities, they're the most powerful enforcers in the world, the ultimate protection and weapon against any enemy, living or dead."

Feeling heavy suddenly, Valerie considered how close she had come to being one of them—a puppet, a servant to her own natural enemy. She tried to keep her thoughts level.

"If the plan wasn't to turn me in," Valerie said. "Then what was it? Back in the desert, you said you and Marshall had one."

Warren nodded wearily. "We did. We had made plans to abandon the Red Widow years ago."

"Why the wait?"

"Aspects of the plan required...time," Warren answered. His lips twitched faintly, tugged by some subdued emotion. "There were things... There were parts of the plan that would take time to develop." His mind seemed to battle with a mental phantom, like the sudden emergence of bad memory. "Parts that...still need time."

Was it pity or compassion she suddenly felt for him? Whatever it was that plagued him, she felt it was something she needed to know, but she could not bring herself to pry.

"But when you found me," Valerie proceeded. "That what? Triggered it? You decided to go ahead anyway?"

"Yes," Warren admitted. "You were unexpected, but... Valerie," Warren gazed into her eyes, begging. "From the start...you were a ray of hope. Something pure, but...hard. Proven. You were ready. You *are* ready."

Valerie was quiet for a moment. "So, you were taking me to meet him," she said at length. "But they got to him first."

Warren sighed and shook his head. "And I don't know how. Marty was always careful. Unlike me, Marshall had escaped the Red Widow years ago. He was an old man and had done her dirty work for long enough. But his many years in her service granted him intriguing insight into the workings of the undead: their lore, their beliefs, and their religion. As I said, the Red Widow's influence has weakened over the years. Marshall was able to gather information before he escaped, and when he saw his moment, he went into hiding, taking all his knowledge and experience with him."

Warren gazed out of the window. "I wanted to go with him," he continued. "He recruited me, years ago. I had to stay on, though. I have my reasons. But you came along, and I knew it was time to begin."

Valerie tilted her head. "Yeah, but if they interrogated him..."

Warren shook his head. "I don't know if that's the case. They were waiting for you and me when we got there; that much is true. But a lot of what I saw there didn't add up. I don't know." He paused for a moment, reflecting. "Some of all that slaughter just didn't seem like the Red Widow's...*style*, I guess. I was trained to be clean in my work, discreet. What we saw back there was neither.

"I'm not sure they knew about Marshall's stash of literature and notes. If they did, they would definitely want to have it. Regardless, after last night, I knew I'd been made. There was no turning back."

Valerie stared at the table, thinking. "And Brazil," she said. "Why there?"

Warren wearily lifted his eyebrows and tilted his head. "Chasing legends," he answered. "When I explain it, it will sound like a long shot, but it's all we have."

Valerie paused a moment, knowing that this was the moment. If what he was about to tell her was... Valerie didn't know what. She only knew that if what he had to say did not sit right with her, then she would walk, here and now. She glared him, expectant. "Go ahead."

"As I said, Marshall had been able to document and study various doctrines and tales of undead religion. Much like the religions of our own people, their legends also have variations, and many of them view the stories as metaphors or cautionary tales. Until now, the undead, even the Red Widow would regard such stories as fiction."

"What, like undead atheists?" Valerie asked, hoping he would see the humor. He chuckled, comfortable in the brief levity. A good sign.

He tilted his head, thoughtfully. "I never looked at it like that, but yeah." Sighing, he resumed. "Something has changed, though. Their hearts and minds have turned back to their old myths.

"Among their many legends, there is one that they revere above all others," he shrugged, "kind of like the Holy Grail of undead legend. They call it the Mantle of the Dragon. It was an artifact or a weapon that gave its bearer ultimate power…"

Warren leaned in, knitting his fingers together. "The myth starts ages ago when a powerful undead—an archon—from a distant realm comes to the Carpathians looking for refuge. Apparently, he was a ruler in his previous land, some kind of god-king, but he had been driven out by his own subjects.

"Once he's safe in the mountains, the archon seeks asylum among its people, specifically a coven of witches and warlocks. He promises them that he will teach them the secret to immortality if they protect him. These wizards, whoever they were, apparently had also been shunned by society, cast out, like him. They accepted his terms to gain power over or protection from their enemies.

"With his safety assured, the archon seeks out a dragon that was said to roost in the mountain's depths. This dragon had similarly been cast down long ago by the new gods of mortal man, gods of light. Condemned to eternal imprisonment, the dragon could never hope to rise again to revenge itself upon humanity. The archon, it seemed, provided it an opportunity.

"Long story a little shorter, the archon encounters the dragon, and he proves himself worthy after he performs a series of tasks in the dragon's service. As a reward, the archon is given the dragon's power, its Mantle, the authority to act in its name. Empowered by this, the archon rises as the Son of the Dragon."

"What does it do? The Mantle?" Valerie murmured, feeling the chill of shadows in broad daylight.

"On this all the different versions of the myth seem to agree," he replied, raising his eyebrows. "The Mantle of the Dragon gave its bearer lordship over all the creatures and all the powers rooted in darkness. By the sound of his voice, the

Son of the Dragon could conjure storms, raise and master the dead, and command legions of monsters. All creatures of darkness—living and dead—were subject to his will."

Valerie stared at him, feeling a sudden weight upon her.

"Fortunately, the legend doesn't end there," Warren offered, glancing at her. "The Son of the Dragon gathers power around him. After raising armies of the living and the dead, he conquers the land around and rules its people with predicable tyranny," he fiddled his hand, "making the people worship him as a god and demanding human sacrifices. The usual.

"But, like all tyrants, his reign comes crashing down. I mentioned that the undead viewed their myths as mere cautionary tales. Maybe this one counts. The Son of the Dragon thought he was a god, and lived like one, but the price of being a megalomaniac is that eventually another force will always challenge you."

"Dracula," Valerie murmured. "Isn't that what *Son of the Dragon* means?"

Warren nodded. "The Dracula was never one man," he explained. "Dracula was always a title granted to The Lord of the Undead, their ruler and king."

Valerie squinted, feeling suddenly small. "How did they beat him?"

"In the end, the people revolted against the Dracula. Knowing they didn't have a chance against him and his armies, they prayed to their ancestral spirits for deliverance. Their prayers were answered with the emergence of thirteen warriors—the Noble Souls. These men and women, while mortal in all other ways, were resistant to the Dracula's power, and all other undead. According to a few versions, if a Noble Soul were to fall and die, then that soul would return to the spirit world only to be reborn again in three days. And so, in and out of time, the thirteen Noble Souls would always exist to combat the darkness."

Warren looked at her. "Today, they're known as night-breakers."

Valerie felt the weight again, but with it, a rising strength. *Me?* she thought…

"*Their* story is less clear, unfortunately. It follows a variety of quests in which they hunt down and destroy the forces of the undead and their servants. All of them are certain on one thing, however. The legend ends with their leader, the Paladin, cornering the Dracula within the mountains. There the Paladin overpowers and slays him.

"Afterward, the Noble Souls dismember the body and scatter the vital organs across the Carpathians, though it isn't clear why. It is believed that in the process the Paladin also took the Mantle of the Dragon with him and has guarded it ever since so that no other could wield its evil."

Valerie gazed into the window. "And you think this warrior, the Paladin, is still alive? You think he's in Brazil, hiding with the Mantle?"

Warren nodded thoughtfully. "The Tupi, an indigenous people in that region, to this day tell an interesting story. They claim that when the first white settlers arrived—I'm assuming they're talking about Cabral's discovery of what is now Brazil—they say a man had secretly come with these settlers.

"The legend goes on to say that this mysterious traveler wished to find a safe place to remain hidden since he was protecting a sacred object from an angry god. Worried that they might stoke the wrath of such a god, the Tupi people attempted to kill the traveler. During the attempt, the traveler used the power of the angry god upon them, calling down a hurricane to drive them away. When all was settled, they could not find him. They believe that the traveler escaped into one of the many stone cities concealed in the jungle, which they believed were the places of gods and demons.

"These are not rehashed Quetzalcoatl myths. It has taken Marshall's whole life to piece together these legends and try to make sense of what they all mean.

"So, it is possible that, if these stories hold at least partial truth, that this man has passed the Mantle of the Dragon down to others, and on and on through time."

"What is it?" Valerie asked. "Physically, I mean."

"We don't know." Warren shook his head. "It's sometimes referred to as an artifact, other sources hint that it was some kind of brand. These are the stories and legends of undead lore and religion. I can't say how well those can be trusted. All I know is that the Red Widow is now after it. Whether the Mantle is real or not comes secondary to the fact that it's real enough for a very powerful creature to crave it." Here Warren leaned in closer and met eyes with Valerie. "And let's assume it is, and she were able to get it. The lordship over all undead. What do you suppose she intends to do with it?"

Valerie felt the walls of the room darken at the thought of it. If it were true, and if this witch were to get it... It wouldn't be a small patch of earth over in the Carpathian Mountains for a psycho to live out a fantasy. Domination was the aim. Always. And thirteen warriors, noble or not, wouldn't cut it against those odds.

"So what's the plan?" Valerie asked. "Go down to South America, track it down with Marshall's notes, hoping to get to it before the enemy does? And then what?"

"Well," Warren said. "Assuming we can do any of that, she'll come after us, power-hungry and desperate. It'll draw her out into the open."

"No more shadows," Valerie murmured.

Warren nodded, and paused a moment before saying, "You'll need to be trained."

Valerie chewed the side of her cheek as she stared distantly out of the window watching children scamper carelessly, laughing, all while their parents looked on, their faces bright with mirth, ignorant of the danger.

"Valerie," Warren asked plaintively. "Is it worth trying, at least?"

"Oh, believe me," Valerie said and turned to Warren, her eyes solid and focused. "I'm in."

This meant that they were wanted criminals now. If Valerie understood it all correctly, then that meant the Red Widow could have eyes anywhere. What would it be for her to put Warren on a watch list?

All this circulated through Valerie's mind as they navigated the airport, as they showed their forged passports and ID's, and as they waited in the customs line. She could tell that Warren was anxious and aware of these realities. It was the first she had ever seen his eyes so shifty and alert. It was a notable change from the relaxed shop-talker a few days previous. Now, the umbrella of power that once protected him had turned into a looming shadow.

Maybe traveling by plane had been a gamble, but it paid off. Both of them cleared the lines without trouble. The only hiccup was when the customs agent tried to speak Portuguese to Valerie, probably assuming that she was a native. Valerie had made it a point to learn the language while she was down there. Not just for survival and all, but because the next time some person asked if she spoke a Latin tongue, she could answer convincingly to the affirmative.

It was late afternoon when they finally sat themselves in the cramped tube of the 747. "I don't know how our stuff got through," Valerie whispered.

"It's good to have contacts," Warren said, leaning his head back, and then he smiled at her. "But bribery also works."

Half an hour later, Valerie felt the world break beneath her as she floated with force and purpose into the air. She had done it. The life that had been planned for her, that condemnation to servitude and blindness, with all its little perks and side-dish happy moments was rapidly vanishing below her. Valerie Zeta had broken free. The world was full now, honest, open, and good.

And it needed protection.

__Chapter 9

Learning a language wasn't something one *learned*, exactly. It was more like something that grew within the mind from a steady dose of humiliation during tentative exchanges governed by trial and error. All things considered, Valerie was picking it up well.

During her first month in Minas Gerais, Brazil, she felt overwhelmed by how crippling life could be when she could not communicate even the most basic thoughts to others. She had learned the simple phrases from online videos: *Where is the bathroom? How much is this?* and *May I have some water, please?* But her untrained tongue somehow boggled the pronunciation each time. It had to have been that, since people stared at her squinting like she was a talking cow. Hand gestures didn't cut it either, and besides, charades in public never ceased to be embarrassing.

The people were very patient and gracious, and though Valerie hated it, most of the time the women thought her jumbled speech was just down right cute. That, or they treated her with a matronly pity deserving only to the sick and hungry. But the intent was real, and Valerie had learned that slapping away a helping hand for the sake of one's pride never got anyone anywhere.

This was truer now than ever for her since Warren had left her days after settling down on the outskirts of a small city called Montes Claros. She had been put into the care of the La Paz household, a young family of five that—if they had been American—would have been your textbook suburban power family.

Adria, the mother hen of the group, was a tall, lithe, ebony-skinned woman who wore tropical colored scarves to bundle up her abundant hair. She did everything with effortless grace, and while she was a quiet woman, she was also alarmingly intimidating. From the very beginning, she had treated Valerie like one of her own: she gave Valerie chores and assignments, and was not shy about letting Valerie know if they were not done properly.

Their eldest daughter was Ester, a thirteen-year-old carbon copy of her mother in looks and spirit, only she lacked a lot of her mother's confidence. The angsty teen seemed to make it a point to avoid Valerie, who had taken up a room that had been previously promised to her.

Bruno was the middle child, a cannot-sit-still ten-year-old boy who loved to tease.

"What time is it?" he would ask Valerie, in his budding English. He did this mostly when his buddies were around to listen to her garbled responses.

After a month of actually trying to give the correct answer and bearing their giggles, she began offering more creative replies, all in English, like, "You know, one day, I'm to going to accidentally step on you." The boys always laughed at her crazy words. All of it was bearable since he rarely spent time inside.

Daniela was their four-year-old daughter. She looked a lot like her father with chestnut skin, deep hazel eyes, and a curly batch of soft, black hair. Not that anyone could tell since she was rarely clean during the day. She was a spry little matchbox, whom the people around the neighborhood had nicknamed *Tigrinha*, which meant "Little Tiger." The reasons for this were obvious. She loved to laugh and get in trouble, and more than once, Valerie had taken the blame for the girl's mischief.

One day, while Valerie was mopping the floors, Adria approached her in a flourish. She was holding up a black plastic ladle that had been broken and said, "Do you know who has done this?"

Valerie cringed and was about to do her best to explain the she had no idea what had happened, but she saw Little Tiger peek around the corner of the kitchen, her face crimson with shame. Valerie sighed. "I am sorry," she said. Valerie had learned these words very quickly. "I was...cleaning, and I broke it." Valerie then tried to offer to get a new one, but probably boggled the words.

Rounding out the family was Rodrigo Oliveria La Paz, husband and father to the household. Rodrigo worked part-time at a soda plant, stacking and packing trucks, and the other half of his days he spent teaching Jiu-jitsu and Capoeira to the local kids.

In stark contrast to his temperate wife, Rodrigo was all personality. His everyday walk home was a victory march. Kids kicked their soccer balls to him; he would juggle them with a brilliant smirk on his face then pass it to the kid who never got a turn. Women swooned at his passing—but never in Adria's line of sight. Though Rodrigo was too noble to allow such adoration to go to his head, he was not ignorant of his small town legend status.

The family was able to afford a cozy home in a nice walled neighborhood on a cobblestone street. For Valerie, Brazilian suburban life was the most fascinating part of the culture. Every home had a nine to ten footwall surrounding it and a small clay yard. Families lived around and on top of one another. When a son married, he brought his new wife to his parents' home where they would build a new addition on the flat roof of his parents' abode. As years passed, generations cycled in and out of the concrete honeycombs where days began and ended with pause-worthy horizons.

Rodrigo inherited his home from his fraternal grandfather. On the flat roof of the two-story house, Rodrigo held his training sessions.

"You must feel action here," Rodrigo was saying, as he patted his abs. "This is where your fighting mind resides."

It was another of their daily one-on-one sessions. The two of them were seated cross-legged, facing each other. The red and orange sun was setting behind a gorgeous ridge of hills on the horizon.

Rodrigo slapped her on the head. Up and out went the hand, a blur of motion that would have made a cobra jealous.

"Do you see?" he said, holding up a finger. "How was I able to strike you?"

Sometimes, she just hated this guy. "Because I wasn't focused," she deadpanned.

"Focused?" he asked, smiling coyly. "Focused where?" Again, a blur of motion toward her head. Valerie blocked it with an equally precise swipe of her arm.

"Here," she said, patting her abs.

Rodrigo laughed heartily. "You are a born fighter, Valerie."

Learning to fight with knives was more frustrating, however. They used dummy blades made of polished wood. Rodrigo seldom showed mercy, which often left Valerie bruised and simmering angrily by the end of a session.

Exhausted and drenched in sweat, Valerie lashed out hoping to catch him off balance. Rodrigo danced away.

"The blade is the tool, not the weapon," he called out. "Your body is the weapon. Use your body to defeat me. The motion of your arm, mind it."

She swept in fast and made a quick thrust. He caught the length of her arm and twisted it, straining the tendons and ligaments at her joints. Valerie cringed, dropping the knife into his waiting palm. Rodrigo caught it and spun away, advertising his new prize with a smug grin.

Valerie lunged at him fiercely. He sidestepped, danced around her, and subdued her with a leg tackle. Huffing, she kicked her legs loose and jumped to her feet. With her hands on her hips, she paced rapidly.

She hated losing. When she tried to speak, she looked like a fool. When she tried to fight, either the other students or Rodrigo beat her. She lost, and she felt lost. Every day. She *hated* it.

Warily, Rodrigo rose to his feet, his victorious, playful smirk fading to a concerned grimace.

"You are a very proud person, Valerie," he commented, as he put his shirt back on.

Valerie swiped her hand. "I don't care."

"Pride is good," Rodrigo said, and brought over two mats to the edge of his roof. "Sit with me?"

Valerie inhaled through her nose, gazed skyward, and exhaled, trying to cool her brimming anger. At length, she nodded and plopped down next to him. The red sun was dipping low into the distant range of hills as the air took up a comforting chill. For a moment, Rodrigo said nothing, but she understood that this was about to turn into a counseling session.

"Warren told me some about your life. When you were small…" he said. "Did you struggle?"

Valerie felt a legion of stones mounting themselves around her heart. She hated it when people asked her stuff like this. It was so...stupid. Did they really want to know? Did they think asking helped any? She ground her molars and looked away.

Rodrigo nodded with a sigh. "I joined the military because I wanted to kill people," he said. "I was a very young, stupid boy."

He paused and stared into the sun. At length, he shrugged and continued. "I suppose I had excuses. My father sold drugs, and my mother used them. Life was not a friend to me from very early on.

"I was a bad kid. I took what I wanted; I hurt people, though at times I did not always like it. But that was the way the world was, I thought. Eventually the law caught up with me. They locked me up, and I couldn't blame them. I was an animal. Since I was still young then, they offered me the Army instead of prison time. I didn't really improve, I have to say. Even in the military, I fought and argued and rebelled, all that.

"I was still this way when I met Adria in Kenya. I...did not always treat her well." He paused a moment. Valerie had slowly turned her face to look at him.

"She got pregnant, so we married," he said. "I loved her then as I do now, but...I felt like she slowed me down. I felt like she was a burden. I was a foolish and prideful man. But I see, even now, that without that pride, the world, the life that it gave me, it would have crushed me. I needed my pride to survive.

"There came a time though, when I had to stop surviving. When Ester was born, I held her in my hands." His face lit up as he cupped his rough hands into a bowl. "She was so small and weak. When I looked at her...I knew she had no chance at survival. This world would crush her, as it almost did me." Rodrigo looked at Valerie. "But only if I let it happen." He shook his head. "I understood then, in that moment, that I had a chance to be reborn. I could not undo what had happened to me, but I could protect this little one from all the pain I had felt. I could put a stop to the hurt. And nothing would stop me from this."

Rodrigo held up a finger and gazed at Valerie. "But I also learned another thing. I could not do this; I could not protect her with my anger for the world. I had to love her. Only love would give me the power to do everything possible. My pride had hardened me. It gave me strength. It helped me *survive*. But my friends, my children, my wife, they are what make me *live*.

"You must find this, Valerie. You have great strength. And you have the will to fight within you. But you must also have a *reason*."

Rodrigo stood up and wiped his sweaty brow. "I know why you are here," he said, without looking at her.

Valerie searched his face for a clue to how he felt about it.

"Why do this?" he asked. Rodrigo looked down at her and stared for a moment. She found herself on the wrong end of nothing to say. Perhaps noting that he had successfully driven his point home, he abruptly turned and walked away.

"Don't be too long," he called over his shoulder. "Tonight is the first night of the June Festival. Will you come?"

Valerie nodded absently.

All things considered, party planning seemed like such a mundane thing to do. But after three months, all that commotion back in the States now seemed like a shadowy nightmare that she had escaped.

It was difficult to remember the mission when Warren visited so infrequently. He had rented a small cottage from an elderly woman nearby, but he seldom stayed there. Valerie assumed he was chasing leads, or investigating possible...stuff. The truth was, Valerie didn't have a clue what he was doing. So, she was left to live a normal life, the surrogate daughter to this family. It was hard to be bitter about it, though. Warren had warned her in the beginning that it wouldn't always be high adventure.

Right now, set up for the June Festival was priority number one. It was to commemorate the harvest, or something like that. Valerie was never sure she understood the reason for any of their festivals. But she had learned quickly that these people rarely needed a good excuse to celebrate. To them, she gathered, just being alive was a great reason all its own.

When night fell, the cobblestone streets filled with people. They sat out on the bulb-lit sidewalks, eating, drinking, and hanging out. Music blared, people danced and laughed hysterically. *It's weird,* she thought while watching them, *how they all...like each other.* Valerie stood apart from the action. She found a nice spot just outside the commotion—not quite in the shadows—where she watched quietly.

While she leaned into the pillar of a local shop, she felt a little body creep up to her. Little Tiger, perhaps a bit overwhelmed by all the action and noise, sidled up to Valerie and wrapped her thin arms around Valerie's legs.

Glancing down, Valerie caught the girl's contented smirk. *Cute kid,* she thought. Valerie felt a long, curving smile spread on her face and something warm churning in her chest. She immediately felt frightened, and tried subtle motions to try and jar the girl loose. The little thing squeezed tighter. *Fine,* Valerie thought, lacking the heart to tear her off.

A trio of young men, maybe a year or two younger than Valerie, approached and asked Valerie something. They were smiling and motioning with their hands for Valerie to join them in the music. Valerie shook her head and did her best to decline without having to use words. Little Tiger then broke off from Valerie's legs and pushed at one of the young men, motioning frantically for him to leave. The boys laughed and jumped back, their hands held up as they stepped away. Valerie gave them look and shrugged. They laughed heartily and returned to the action.

At some point, after Little Tiger had again clung to Valerie's leg, Valerie's hand had found its way into the soft tufts of the four-year-old's abundant black hair. Valerie's fingers gently coursed through the curls; the sensation was electric and calming all at once.

Maybe two hours into the party, Little Tiger started to slouch sleepily against Valerie's leg. Reaching down, Valerie awkwardly gathered up the tiny thing, who wrapped up and tucked in.

Okay, she thought. *I've got a kid in my arms. What do I do now?* Another lady graciously offered Valerie a nearby chair, which she descended into.

Eventually, Adria broke from the crowd—her face alight with life—and offered to take the girl. Valerie, surprised by her own response, insisted she was fine and didn't mind. With Little Tiger pressed against her, the small body molding itself into hers, Valerie felt the same warmth as before. The night passed as a moving collage of sound and motion, all to the steady pulse of the Little Tiger's breath on her neck.

Daniela, Valerie thought, as she studied the lines of the girl's face. It was odd to see them so at rest, and not curved upward in a smile, or bouncing around in speech. *So small. Innocent. Vulnerable.* Valerie remembered what Rodrigo told her after training. How little ones stood no chance, how the world would crush them unless someone loved them enough to protect them. Valerie envied how the girl slept. Deeply, with no thought of danger. *She trusts me,* Valerie realized then shook her head, uncomfortable with the thought.

When all the residents returned to their homes, silence fell quickly on the neighborhood. It was maybe midnight when Valerie awoke in her bed feeling a clawing hunger in her stomach. She crept into the kitchen for some bread and cheese.

In the dimly lit kitchen she found Adria at the small table. She was wrapped in a colorful robe and was sipping at a steaming cup of tea. Valerie stopped short and stammered out a few words. Adria offered a vague smile and motioned for Valerie to sit at the table. Bread, butter, and a block of cheese appeared, and Adria handed Valerie a spreading knife and napkin.

Valerie thanked her and started to make a snack. She tried not to mind Adria's relentless gaze on her.

"With three children to care for and two jobs, it is difficult for Rodrigo and me to have a moment to talk anymore," Adria commented. She spoke in polished English, a rare treat for which Valerie was grateful. Valerie nodded compliantly in response, but didn't really understand what Adria was driving at. The woman stared with a strange eye of appraisal, which made Valerie feel unwelcome for the first time since she arrived.

"When Rodrigo and I first met, that was all he could do is talk," Adria continued, while offering a comforting grin. "I was the shy rich girl. In Kenya, my father was in politics, and I was studying to follow in his footsteps. I wanted to be a diplomat like him. But..." Adria beamed like a teenage girl, her range of white teeth gleaming. "I met a dashing, headstrong, rebellious Brazilian soldier who, for some reason, only had eyes for me. The situation played out much like a Disney movie. My father disapproved, we saw each other in private," Adria smiled coyly, "which led to other things."

Valerie cringed and Adria laughed out loud. "Well, Ester was a result," she said, her smile still evident at the corners of her mouth. Adria shrugged. "I don't know. All I ever wanted to do was travel the world, meet new exciting places and people. But when I felt Ester growing within me, something changed. Also, I started to grow up a little. The world..." her smile faded, "The world was not what I thought it was. I began to see that there is something dark within it. It is difficult to explain."

Adria paused a moment and stared at the table, her head titled in thought. She looked at Valerie. "When Rodrigo came, begging me to return with him to Brazil, it was not a difficult choice. And I think this shocked him. I knew we would be poor much of the time. I knew we would live in small places, far away from the world. But that's why it was so easy for me. My children, my Rodrigo, they are my life now. And it is good. What is the world, Valerie, if not one great neighborhood? When I looked at it this way, I saw that it was only a matter of choosing the scale and complexity of where you live."

Adria leaned in. "Tonight was exciting. All of the people together, mixing and connecting. It was what I wanted to be a part of from the start."

She's driving at something, Valerie knew, but wasn't sure what. She maintained a gracious, but guarded smile. Adria leaned back and placed her hands in her lap. "Now," she said. "I have shared something about me."

Valerie chewed her buttered bread and swallowed it down quickly. "Uh well," she started. *Where do I even start?*

"There's not much to tell, really." Valerie fidgeted uncomfortably under Adria's unrelenting gaze. "I haven't really been in love or anything."

Adria nodded faintly. Her smile, faltered a little. "What brings you to Brazil, Valerie?" The smile was still there, only now there was no mistaking the darker edge of Adria's words. She wanted an answer. A real one.

Though she tried to keep it alive, Valerie's own gracious smile faded by the second. *What, precisely, do I tell this woman?* After months away from Warren, even Valerie wasn't entirely sure anymore.

At length, Adria let out a sigh and spoke. "Since Rodrigo was a soldier, there would be many days—sometimes weeks—that I would not hear from him."

Grateful to be let off the hook, Valerie listened, hoping Adria was about to reveal the point.

"There came a time, however, when nearly a month passed and I had not heard from him. I received a call from an American man named Warren, who told me that Rodrigo was in a hospital nearby being treated for serious injuries. When I arrived, I met Warren, who explained to me that he had rescued Rodrigo from the jungle where his unit had been savagely ambushed. By what, Warren would not say, and has not ever since."

Adria lifted her eyes and glared at Valerie. "But that night, as I held my husband's mangled hand, listened to him moan and whisper in his sleep. I thought it was the medication and the trauma that set his mind into fantasy. But I have never been able to forget his ramblings.

"He spoke of the dead walking the earth, as though living. How they devoured the flesh and blood of his men, and how they could not be killed. Rodrigo would waken, his eyes wide with fright, all the time mumbling of these horrors."

She looked away and sighed. "It was a long night, and when he woke in the morning, he put on a smile and claimed to remember none of it."

Adria gazed at the wall for a moment. "Rodrigo was a foolish, headstrong boy before this. But since this night, he has been a saint of a man. Fiercely devoted to me and completely in love with his children. Because it was such an amazing change, I did not ask questions. We soon came here, and I have loved our life since. But..."

She shifted her eyes to Valerie. "I knew there would come a day, when the phantom ramblings of that night would return. I do not fully understand why you are here, and my husband will not tell me."

Reaching across the table, Adria gathered up Valerie's hands and held them. "Warren is a good man," she said. "He saved my husband's life. I believe that he has also helped you. But you have a choice, young lady. I took you into my home to show you that there is another future for you if you want it."

Adria patted Valerie on the hand and stood from the table. Gathering the folds of the robe around her, she smiled warmly once more and left the kitchen. Valerie remained for a while after unmoved in thought.

There is another future for you, if you want it... Valerie remembered Little Tiger's breath on her neck, and then silken feel of her soft black curls entwined in her fingers...

Suddenly weary, Valerie rose and cleaned the table then returned to her darkened room where she found that Little Tiger had crept into her bed. Sliding into the covers, careful not to wake the child, Valerie snuggled in and let Little Tiger curl into her. At some point, Valerie's hand found the girl's curls and twirled them between her fingers. The sensation kept the nightmares away.

It was on a cool Saturday, a month after his last visit that Warren showed up. Once Little Tiger finished probing him for gifts, he kissed Adria on the cheek and thanked her in advance for the meal she would offer.

When greetings were done, Warren asked after Valerie. She had intentionally isolated herself on the veranda where she was hand-cleaning her laundry, taking out a lot of her frustration on the collar of one of her shirts. When Warren found her, he said hello and stood for a moment. Was the silent treatment petty? Yes, but after a month of no contact, he deserved it. It was only on account of her lack of patience that she relented.

"Stop by to say hi?" she asked, her voice icy.

"Bad day?"

She wheeled around. "Bad day?" she barked. "Bad day? That's what you want to know?"

"Well, you just seem really angry, and—"

"Don't be dense, Warren," she scoffed. "I get it. You're out doing whatever it is you do, and yeah, you told me it wasn't always going to be exciting, but..."

"But you don't like it here," he finished, and looked away.

Valerie shook her head, and cooled a bit. "No, no. I like it here. And I understand what I'm doing. But come on, it's been four months and nothing?"

Warren titled his head to the side and was quiet.

Finally, Valerie thought, hungrily. "You've got something, don't you?"

"Something," he murmured, conveying that it was nothing to be happy about.

"Well, whatever it is," she said, ringing out her shirt and casting it over the clothesline. "I want in."

"Valerie..."

Her hand flew up. "Oh no," she insisted, shaking her finger. Her other hand was behind her untying the knot of her apron. "No, no, no. You can tell me all about it in the truck. I'm getting my things, and you're telling Adria that you need me. Ester can cook tonight."

Warren suppressed a chuckle, but quickly wiped the smirk off his face when Valerie held up her finger. "Don't say a word," she commanded, emphatically stripping off the apron. "Just don't."

A three-hour truck ride through hills, two small towns, and lots of back roads delivered them to a wide gate whose sign read: *A Fazenda Bela,* "Beautiful Farm." Once at the gate, a man stepped out of a little booth, halting the truck with a hand. After the two parleyed through the window, the guard spoke into his radio. When a crackling voice came back, the guard nodded, waving them through the rising bar.

"Farm security?" Valerie asked, one eyebrow raised.

"He's a wealthy farmer," Warren said. "Let me do the talking. Regardless of what you hear, keep your face straight."

"What's the story?"

"Officially—chupacabra," Warren answered. "At least that's what I think it is. These people think we're trappers, so let's look the part and be professional."

"A goat sucker?" Valerie asked. "What, did one of their animals get killed?" *A dead cow?* Valerie thought. *Was this his idea of something?*

Warren glanced in his rear view mirror as they coasted down the long curving drive to the farm. "Probably something more than that," he explained. "People can be very superstitious about this stuff. Chupacabras are still thought to be evil here."

"Well, they are, aren't they?" Valerie said. "They're revenants."

"Right," he said. "What else?"

Another quiz. "Uh, if an undead goes without appropriate rest or feeding, they digress into these things."

"And?"

"Revenants are the first estate of a newly born undead. They awaken confused and savage, feeding from animals. As a result, they themselves become feral since the blood of the victim is what grants the undead its level of power and consciousness. Feed on beastly life, become a beast. You are what you eat."

"Good," he said. "Keep that in mind."

"Why?"

"Because I've got a bad feeling about this one."

They pulled into a grassy, fenced-in clearing where various other trucks had parked. On the other side of the wooden gate, a long, flat-roofed rectangular farmhouse stretched to the edge of a vast woodland beyond. Twenty yards away, another building of the same design stretched off and ended with what looked like a large series of stables.

They parked the truck next to the other vehicles and approached the gate, which had a little bell. Warren was about to pull the string, when a man in a cowboy hat descended the front porch stairs toward them.

While the man opened the wooden gate, he and Warren exchanged pleasantries.

"Where's the family?" Warren asked. Somewhere in his thirties, the man was a tall and skinny guy with dark leathery skin.

"Through here," he said, pointing up the stairs through an open front door. "Senhor Marcelo is in back. This way."

There was something ominous about the expediency of his gait, about the severity of his gestures, and the somberness of his look. As they strolled through the house, the keening of women soured the air. They passed by a finely furnished living room where a group of women were gathered round each other. Some were lost in tears and whining; the others were burdened with the impossible task of consoling those who were visibly inconsolable.

The shadow returned to Valerie, one that four months of pleasant idleness had managed to dispel. They passed through the back door and descended some porch stairs onto a wide, well-kept lawn of lush grass. Beyond the wood fence boundary, a dense and dreamy woodland rose full of light, color, and shadow.

Two men locked in heated debate stood at the fence, pointing avidly beyond it into the foliage. Their guide jogged ahead to announce their arrival. As Warren and Valerie approached, the three men broke apart; two of them returned to the house, while one remained. He was a short man, dressed in a nice white button-up shirt tucked into denim jeans. He looked like a regular Texan, and that was probably the point. The man removed his cowboy hat, revealing a brown, leathery face and two dark, bloodshot eyes. He regarded Valerie and Warren each with a small bow of his head.

"Are you the trappers?" he asked.

"We are." Warren put hand on his chest. "I am Warren, and this is my companion, Valerie."

The man held a longer glance on Valerie. His look seemed to question why a girl would be involved in their line of work. She kept her face straight and stared back.

"American?" he asked.

"Yes," Warren said. "And we have experience."

"Have you tracked this type of creature before?" the man asked.

Warren stared resolutely. "I have trapped and killed many."

The man gazed at the ground for a moment. "My name is Marcelo," he murmured. "I have always known of these monsters. My father would tell stories about them. I never thought—" The man choked up. He looked up at Warren, red and watery in the eyes.

"I understand," Warren said. "Can you tell me what happened?"

"I didn't see what happened," Marcelo said, "It was my other daughter who saw." Here he held his hand out, motioning behind them. One of his male farmhands was escorting a little girl to their huddle. She was maybe three years-old with black messy hair and red puffy eyes. She whimpered with tight little jerks of her shoulders. Valerie cringed and shook her head, staving off a sudden rush of dread. For a moment, Valerie thought she saw Little Tiger. Then a sickening feeling crept into Valerie's stomach. *Other daughter,* he had said…

The farmhand presented the girl and crouched behind her in support. He whispered gentle assurances in her ear to calm her.

"Tell them, Fernanda," Marcelo said. "These are good people who are here to help. Tell the nice people what you saw."

The little girl settled herself and did her best. Yesterday, the girls had been outside as it got dark. They were pretending to be faeries, and while her older sister Louisa was twisting around, a ghost-creature came out of the forest, snatching her away into the dark. Fernanda then ran to get her father Marcelo, who had been working late in the fields.

Marcelo then cut in. He told them about how they searched all night. There had been four of them then, Marcelo and three farmhands, when they went into the woods. Only he and two others came out. It was then that they put out a call for a tracker.

Marcelo, with the look of any desperate father, took Warren by the hand, looked in his eyes, and insisted that money was no object.

"We do not work for money," Warren told him.

"My men would like to help at least."

Warren turned, appraising the farmhand with a look. This one was a portly fellow, who stood up fast and straightened his shoulders.

"Have them stay and guard the house," Warren said. "Leave this to my companion and me."

"God be with you," Marcelo said to Warren's face. He looked at Valerie. "God be with you."

Marcelo gathered up his daughter and they returned to the house as a group. Warren stood for a moment gazing into the woods. "Did you get all that?"

"Yeah," Valerie said, her voice hot with anger.

Warren turned suddenly, searching her face for the source of her ire.

She let him struggle a bit before letting him off the hook. "You don't seem so surprised."

He squinted his eyes.

"Oh don't pull that crap with me, Warren," she demanded. "You're horrified, sure. But that's not surprise on your face."

"Valerie..."

"Stop!" she shouted. "How many others, Warren? How many times has this happened and you didn't come get me? How many kids was too many?"

Warren's softened and defeated expression confirmed her worst fears. She let him stew for a bit more.

"Why?" she insisted, and jabbed a finger at him. "And don't you tell me it's because I wasn't ready."

"It wasn't that," he said, finally.

"Then what?" She glared at him, her eyebrows lifted expectantly. She knew what he was doing. He was taking the necessary abuse until her anger cooled.

"Why are revenants attacking children?" Warren asked, his voice even and tutorial.

She staved off the desire to scream his head off. Taking in a deep breath, she closed her eyes and sighed. "Because they're evil, Warren. Because that's what they do."

Warren shook his head. "No, Valerie, that isn't true," he said. "I asked you to keep what you know about revenants in mind. You can't fight something you don't understand."

Valerie cooled her raging temper and tried to think. Nothing came together. All she could think about was the image of Little Tiger being ripped from her world, screaming and flailing for help. Her blood boiled just thinking it. Valerie knew that she was already not helping. She knew she needed to have a clear head, which only made the fear and desperation mount.

"Uh," she said, her voice shaking. "They feed on animals."

"Why?" he asked pointedly.

"Because humans frighten them," she said. "Even children. They're weak and afraid so they like less threatening prey."

"Yes," Warren affirmed. "Revenants, though undead, never developed beyond their infant stages because they never learned to stalk and feed from humans. As a result, they are savage and solitary."

Valerie waved her hands. "So what does any of that have to do with what's happening here?"

"That's what I need you to figure out," Warren said. "Think, Valerie."

Valerie closed her eyes and cast her face skyward. She held up her arms in surrender. "Look, Warren, I appreciate that you're trying to help me think this through and use this as a teaching moment, but all I really want to do is find this bastard and destroy it."

"Why did we get past customs at the airport?" he asked, his voice solid and demanding. "How, Valerie? Tell me how we got past all the security when you know what's looking for us?"

Valerie dropped her hands and eyed Warren. "Contacts," she said with a shrug. "Bribery."

"Contacts I made in the Red Widow's service," he said. "And how much money can I offer that it would persuade her agents to act on my behalf at the expense of hers?"

Valerie's brow darkened. "They let us go."

Warren shrugged.

"They let us go…" she started, "…to see what we would do?"

"Possibly," he said. "If that's the case, then maybe they lost us once we got out of Belo Horizonte, and they haven't been able to find us for four months. We're off the grid, and they're getting desperate."

"So they have to draw us out," Valerie murmured.

"Precisely," Warren said. "Which means what?"

"Someone is enthralling the revenants," Valerie said, her voice catching back some of its fire. "Controlling them. They're targeting people, children, so that we would come out and chase them."

"Which we've done," Warren pointed out. "A woman and her grandmother in Riberão das Neves. A crippled man from Sete Lagoas. A teenager from Pampulha. The murders have been all around where we landed and disappeared."

And now a little girl from Januario, Valerie thought. Her inner voice felt hollow in her skull, echoing in the dark. They were losing. This wasn't how any of it was supposed to go. She looked at Warren. Slinking around, sneaking, hiding, and eluding notice. This was his way. All in the name of preparation, gathering information, like it was some great exercise in academia. Hell, he might even use what he learned to think up a strategy, but always careful and reserved. Always held back and hesitant. The body count didn't seem to matter, as long as they weren't tallied in it.

Valerie's skin flushed with heat. Turning on her heel, she stormed back to the truck, ignoring Warren's calls. Eventually she heard his steps in pursuit of her. If he dared to lay a hand on her, if he even deigned to pause her progress even in the name of strategy, she would strike hard, clean, and without mercy.

Perhaps he understood this, since he jogged behind her, keeping an even distance as they stood at the truck.

"Valerie, please," he was saying. She ignored him, his voice was a swarming mumble in the back of her mind, no more relevant than the sound clouds made when they rolled across the sky. She pulled her knife and belt from the bag and strapped it on. After removing her sneakers, she put on her combat boots and laced them up.

"You're doing exactly what they want," Warren said.

Valerie wheeled around on him, jabbing a finger into his chest. "No," she barked. "I'm doing what's necessary."

She stormed past him and shouted over her shoulder. "I'm getting out from behind old ladies and kids, and I'm facing the enemy. It was always going to be a matter of *when* we drew a line in the sand. If you're waiting for the right moment, then by all means have a seat and think about when that might be."

That was below the belt, Val, she thought, regretting the insults, but it was the best way to discourage pointless debate. Warren was characteristically unfazed by her rancor while he jogged to keep up. "This feels like a trap," he said, catching up to her stride. "We need to hold back and think this through."

Something boiling within her exploded. She wheeled around and roared, finger pointed like a dagger. "Warren, that is how everything bad happens in this world! Hold back? Hold back for what?" She stared at him, seeing the loss for words on his face. Though her temper still raged, she made her speech even. She pointed emphatically at the ground. "From now on, we go straight at them, understand?"

"That might be exactly what they want."

Her temper flared again, its fire flushing her cheeks and twisting the lines of her face as she screamed: "Does it look like I'm scared?"

She felt herself shaking, enraged, as she glared at him. Again, he stared, dumfounded. Huffing, she batted a hand at air and turned to the looming forest.

Valerie hardly broke stride as she vaulted over the fence bounding the yard and forest. Dark was setting in. It would be night soon, and the enemy would be confident. *Good,* Valerie thought. She was short on patience.

Suddenly, she felt her strength rising within her, the first time since her fight in the desert. Her senses expanded, the sounds, the smells, the colors in the dim light of dusk.

Rodrigo had asked her if she had a reason. At the time, she did not know the answer. Now she did. It was this moment, when she felt the strength to do what others could not—the power to set things right.

Valerie closed her eyes and harnessed her senses. Her darksight flooded out before her. She expanded the field into the forest beyond. There, in the hollow forms of the night, she spotted the creature's dull silver specter. Her rage enflamed within when she could not find a small orange aura of a young girl nearby.

Valerie lunged forward, caution be damned.

Warren lumbered clumsily behind her. He did his best to keep up.

__Chapter 11_____

It wasn't long before Warren was alone in the forest. Valerie was right. It was always a matter of time when they would have to start answering the threat. But that didn't mean they had to be impulsive about it.

She had too eagerly thrust off, too impatient to wait for Warren, who still could not keep up despite military experience and a body that wasn't out-of-shape. Tiring quickly, Warren made it to the top of a steep slope and rested against a tree, panting for breath. He listened for cries, screams, or shouts—evidence of a fight. There was nothing, though.

It was a beautiful night. Rays of moonlight beamed in through the canopy, making the straw laden ground glow a crisp, pale blue. Frogs were on the trombone, and crickets were on the strings: a calm and soothing music that begged him to be still. How long had it been since he just sat down and looked at something pretty? How long without having to bear the dread that came with the understanding that such a thing could be defiled? Nothing was allowed to be beautiful anymore.

Not until the fight is finished, he thought.

When Warren was younger, that kind of talk made the struggle seem worth it—it sounded heroic and meaningful. Warren couldn't quite mark when he had lost sight of that meaning though.

It might have been when Marty left. When he and Marshall worked together, things made sense. There was a plan and a reason for them to move and to speak and to act. The years since Marshall left him were not kind, however. More and more often he felt propelled only by a jaded devotion to the duty of the moment. Or maybe the meaning was lost the moment Warren had to make that first sacrifice, that first big payment in the name of the greater good. He had made his payments, and he had sacrificed plenty. At some point, though, he just stopped expecting some good to come of it.

It occurred to him suddenly that he would go no farther. Warren was tired and not just of body. The chase had run out of him, and it was time to face some unsettling truths. He was slipping. The one thing he could always count on was a cool head and a calm hand, but even those old blessings were fading. Through it all, Warren had showed the grit, guts, and wherewithal to see the mission through. Had it mattered, though? Any of it?

Warren was leaning down to sit when a low groan rippled toward him from the left. Slowly, he rose up against a tree, pressing his back against it. Reigning in his labored breathing, he listened for the worst possible news. Seconds later, a throaty grumble followed from his left, and a low branch swished faintly in the shadows. Warren could feel its eyes out in the dark, watching him, stalking him, hungry to pounce. He imagined what he looked like in the monster's vision, a tired and easy victim, helpless and worthy of some playful taunting before the inevitable kill.

It had been a while since Warren had been in an outright fight. He could win, but he was going to have to offer up a few bones to be broken. The fight was unfolding in his head when the creature's low groan rustled in the leaves a few meters in front of him. Warren could delay the attack by using the tree as a barrier, but the much quicker and much stronger revenant would eventually get around it. No, the best thing was to face it outright and get it over with.

Lifting the back of his wind-breaker, he drew out his kukri knife. He caught a ray of moonlight on the silver blade, reflecting it into the darkness in front of him. Two beady, blue-violet eyes glowed meters away. They were coming, like two little stars floating closer. The outline of its form took shape as it approached, growling and seething at the mouth now. On all fours, the revenant lowered its head, never taking its eyes from

Warren, who crouched and prepared, knife and free hand out in front.

A blur of movement slashed through the clearing. The creature was suddenly on its back, pinned to the earth, its arms and legs thrashing in the straw. Valerie had been quick, precise, and cunning. Patient, even. Warren gasped, a knot of tension breaking as he watched Valerie wrestle the creature into stillness. He imagined the smile Valerie would have brought to Marshall's face. This was the pupil he should have had.

Valerie locked the moaning wretch down and taunted it, "Yeah, who's setting traps now, huh?"

She held her blade at its throat in preparation to cut.

The revenant squirmed and cried out, "Solta!"

Warren lunged forward. "Wait! he said, one hand on Valerie's shoulder. "Wait a moment."

Valerie recoiled, holding the knife back. "Did it just...?"

"Yes," Warren said, crouching next to her.

"Warren," Valerie said. "Revies don't talk, right?"

Warren titled his head to the side. "This one does."

"Solta-me!" it groaned. The sound of its voice was a lot like a garbage disposal grinding food and gurgling water. Most disturbing was the moonlight glowing off its pale, leathery skin.

"Please tell me you're not going to ask it questions," Valerie said, grunting in the effort of holding it still. "It probably knows 'Let me go' and that's it."

"Well let's see," he said, and he reached into his pocket for something. He pulled out a pen-flashlight and a little coin made of silver. There were symbols engraved on both sides of the coin: on one there was a square, which held a triangle. On the other side there was the profile of a head with two reverse faces.

"What's that?" Valerie asked.

Warren held up the coin. "This," he said, showing her each side by the glow of the flashlight. "This is a Janus Coin."

"What does it do?"

"You'll see," he said. "Hold it still."

As Warren lowered the coin to the creature's forehead, the revenant hissed and bit and twisted its head at the sight of it. For all his efforts, Warren couldn't place it. "Try to hold it still, Valerie."

"Got it," she said. She balled a fist, vaulted her arm back, and clobbered the creature in its snarling face three times. Warren was certain he heard its nose crack. She shook her hand off and wiped her dirty knuckles on Warren's jacket. "He's all yours."

Though the creature was shaking, it no longer rejected his advance. Warren placed the coin on its forehead, where immediately faint plumes of smoke rose as the coin sizzled, embedding itself in the creature's skull. It riled upward suddenly, its back arching in agony. The revenant then fell slack, offering no more resistance.

"You can relax," Warren said. "While the coin burns, the victim is paralyzed. It's also obligated to answer any questions asked of it—and it must tell the truth or it experiences excruciating pain."

Valerie rose from the revenant and crouched beside it. "Where did you put the girl?" she growled.

Dead, Warren knew, though he could not say it. "Valerie..."

She held up an insistent palm. Again, she asked it. The creature's glittering eyes shifted from left to right, squirming as though surviving a nightmare. Its mouth twitched while piping out faint words.

Lowering her ear to its cracked lips, she listened. "Where is the girl?" she asked. She scoffed and shot up, frustrated that she couldn't understand its words.

Warren looked at Valerie. "He said, 'a casa.' Home."

Cursing, she grabbed it by the face. "Where, you freak?"

"Valerie, that girl..." he began then read the desperation in her face. *What good is it to tell her?* "All it says is 'home, home.'"

Valerie slumped back, breathless. "I checked everywhere, Warren. I couldn't find her."

"You checked everywhere in the forest," Warren pointed out. "But not under it."

Valerie perked up and glared at him, hope overwhelming despair. Warren nodded wearily, knowing that she would probably only find a desiccated body, which would haunt Valerie for years. But, she had been right. It was time to face the enemy. Every aspect of it.

"Where would this thing make its home?" he asked.

Her eyes lit up. "Underground." She darted away into the dark, where Warren was certain she would find both the missing farmhand and the girl's remains. A small part of him was glad he would not have to see Valerie weep. He set aside such thoughts for the moment, for the coin's power was fading.

"Why are you here?" Warren asked. "What was your purpose?"

"Somos...os...olhos," was the answer.

Warren cringed. *We are the eyes.* He let that process a moment. "What eyes? Whose eyes?"

"O Mestre," it whispered.

"The Master," Warren said. "What master?"

It repeated itself, "O Mestre."

Warren inhaled and closed his eyes. *Of course,* he thought. A dog wouldn't know its owner's name.

"What is your purpose?" Warren asked. "What has the Master ordered of you?"

"Torne-se forte," it said. "Seja os olhos. Seja as orelhas. Busca o poder."

Warren tried to follow it all. *Become strong. Be the eyes. Be the ears. Search for the power.*

"How will you become strong?"

The creature then met eyes with Warren. "Cevar," it hissed.

A chill crawled up Warren's spine. *Feed.* The coin had sizzled to a thin puddle. Maybe another minute remained.

While the creature sat motionless and groaning, Warren searched for other things it could tell him. It was clear that the revenant only just acquired language. Its cave-man lingo was evidence of that. But how had it even gained the power to speak in the first place?

And then the final question came to him. "Where is the Master?"

The creature gurgled in pain, trying to resist such a betrayal, but the coin boiled and hissed into its skin until it relented. "Nos sonhos."

In my dreams. Warren grimaced. Whoever was controlling this creature, it was not close by, which was troubling to ponder. Like the revenants they encountered in the desert, the enthraller had to be close in order to maintain control. Physical proximity was necessary for savage creatures like these. But if what this thing said was accurate, then it implied that something was controlling it through dreams, and was perhaps very far away.

Be the eyes, be the ears, search for the power. It all ran through Warren's brain like coiling snakes. He would need time to make sense of it.

The coin was a mere vat of steam when he drew out his kukri knife and hacked the revenant's neck. The head rolled unceremoniously to the side, leaving a black trail of fluid gurgling behind it. He cleaned the blade off on his windbreaker and pondered what he learned.

For one thing, he had been wrong. This was not some elaborate trap to lure Valerie and him out into the open, which probably meant that the other attacks also had nothing to do with them. Someone was enthralling revenants, forcing them to act against their nature and attack humans. For what, though? To become stronger? Warren killed hundreds of these things in his time, and he hadn't known that such a thing was even possible. *Could decades of feral existence be reversed or improved by absorbing the life-energy of greater prey?* He felt like he had just had a conversation with the proof of it. But one thing was certain: there was something of greater control using these creatures to seek after power. *The Mantle, possibly?* There was no greater power in the beliefs of the undead.

Warren shook his head and tried to clear his mind of his noisy and jumbled thoughts, which was difficult because he knew at some point, Valerie would be returning soon, and he was not looking forward to seeing the pain on her face.

Leaning back against the tree, he closed his eyes and waited.

"Excuse me, is your name Warren Brant?" a voice said to his left. Warren had never enjoyed the company of strangers. He liked getting to know them even less. It was also off-key that this guy would not use Warren's earned rank. There should have been a 'Captain' in there somewhere.

"I'm Warren, yeah," he replied, his head feeling woozy.

Warren didn't usually drink, but the boys wanted to take him out all weekend to celebrate. An act that was getting old on its third day, a Sunday no less, when they would have made more appropriate use of their time by getting back to the barracks early. They had to be ready for drills that next morning.

"Pleased to meet you," the man said, raising his eyebrows in request and motioning a hand at the chair in front of Warren.

"Go ahead," Warren said, and he finished off his drink.

The man sat. "Lively night," he said smiling. He was a forty something with wiry ginger hair which was pulled back in the sorriest excuse for a ponytail. His dark eyes blended in well with the patchy freckles over his face and hands.

"Celebrating?" he asked.

"They are," Warren said, vaguely waving a hand at his buddies playing billiards. "I think I tapped out yesterday."

"I'm Marshall Lentz," the man said, offering his hand.

Warren reluctantly took it and resettled himself. "How can I help you, Marshall Lentz?"

The man inhaled and sighed. "Well, I think it's more about how I can help you."

A salesman, he thought with a groan. "Okay," Warren said, waving a dismissive hand. "I'm not buying anything, all right, so just spare me the pitch."

Marshall laughed lightly. "I'm not selling anything, Mr. Brant."

Warren was never big on titles and such, but it said something about guy who didn't respect the rank of a soldier. "Look," Warren said, sitting forward. "Just come out with it. It's been a long weekend, and I'm tired, so..." He motioned with his hand for the guy spill it.

"All right," Marshall said, and then glanced over his shoulder as though to ensure that they were alone. "Three days ago you became a father, yes?"

"I did," Warren assented. He didn't want to think about that, since he had spent the last 72 hours convincing himself that he was doing the right thing by being a world away in the Middle East when he should have been with his wife and newborn twins.

"Their names are Braxton and Alma," Marshall continued. "They were born two minutes apart. Braxton—whom you named after the grandfather who raised you—came first weighing in at 7 pounds 3 ounces. He was then followed by his fraternal twin sister Alma, named by your Brazilian wife after her grandmother. She weighed 6 pounds 11 ounces, and was the first to open her eyes. Currently, your new family is staying with your wife's sister and her husband in Boston where they are helping care for the children. They are quite safe."

Warren's head had been swimming in all of the words, but it only took seconds for him to snap out of his minor-drunkenness to take it all in. He didn't know this man's game, but that the guy knew all of that and felt the need to assure Warren that his family was safe bothered him in the worst ways.

What to do about that was the larger problem. Intimidating this man would do no good, and lashing out would not help the situation. This man clearly didn't come across the world, find a way to get onto a military base, and seek out one solider among hundreds in order to be threatened and beaten. There was a game here, and it did no good to react harshly.

"Come all this way to tell me what I already knew?" Warren said sniffing.

Marshall cocked his head to the side and a smirk rose on his face, showing a disquieting sentiment of pride and pleasure. "You're cool under pressure," he said, nodding faintly.

Warren stared at him. "Get to the point."

"This is about you," Marshall said. "And most importantly, your children."

Warren's left eye twitched in restraint. His right leg pumped anxiously. *I think I'm going to kill this man,* Warren thought. It was illogical to assume this man meant harm, but all his cryptic talk left Warren to assume the worst.

"They are special," Marshall explained. "More than you realize. I told you all of that to prove that I knew about them— that I knew facts and things that only you would know, and what confidential records would be able to tell me. So, now you know that I am someone with informative and powerful connections." The man stared for a moment more before saying, "And I care very deeply about ensuring the safety of your children."

Somewhere in the desert, a straw had fallen on a camel's back—and broke it. Warren threw the table to the side, casting glass and booze over the walls and chairs. Grabbing the much skinnier man by the neck, Warren lifted him up and rushed forward. The man scampered backward, his hands desperately clinging to Warren's wrist so as not to fall and be choked. Warren's buddies stopped short and perked up.

"Hey, Captain," his friend called out, his face severe and ready for a fight. "That guy got a problem?"

Warren waved them back with his other hand as he approached the bar's back door. "Nothing I can't handle," he said. "Watch the door."

"Copy that, Cap. Take your time."

Warren kicked the backdoor open and threw the man out into the ally. Warren's friends closed the door after him. The ginger haired stranger staggered up from the sandy ground, holding his neck and gagging. Warren drew his pistol and aimed it.

"Wait," the man said, holding up his hand. "Perhaps," he gasped. "Perhaps, my approach was misleading. Listen, please."

"You have my attention," Warren said, through his teeth.

"They are not in danger," Marshall insisted.

Warren cocked the gun and steadied his hold.

"Please," Marshall begged, and stood up straight. It was disturbing how unconcerned the man was about the gun pointed at him. "Please, just let me explain."

"Look," Warren said. "I get that you're just the messenger. So we can do this two ways. I can cause you pain until you give a time and place to meet someone who actually has a dog in this fight, or—"

"I am not a messenger," Marshall said, shaking his head. "This is not ransom or extortion. I am here..." He paused, catching his breath. "My purpose is benign, I promise you."

"Then who or what is the threat to my family?"

Marshall drew in a breath and exhaled. "That is what I want to tell you. But..."

"But what?"

The man looked pained to say it. "It is unbelievable," he said. "I will need you to listen to me. Then you will have to judge whether you think I am crazed, false, or true in my words."

Warren lowered his gun slowly and holstered it. The backdoor swung open and voice called out. "You good, Captain?"

"Good here," Warren said over his shoulder. Warren noticed the man was hunching over and holding the small of his back. "Melvin," he called out. "Get me two chairs."

Seconds later, his friend brought out two bar chairs, placing them next to each other. "What's his deal?" he whispered.

"Nothing," Warren answered. "Just some old-nut who needs to clear his head."

Melvin patted Warren on the arm. "You're a better man than most. I'll be inside."

Warren motioned Marshall over to the chairs. They both sat opposite each other.

"Thank you," Marshall said, groaning as he sat.

"Let's have it," Warren ordered. "I'm tired, and I don't have time for guessing games."

Marshall nodded and began telling his unbelievable story. It was every bit of that and more. Warren listened to it all. Half way through, however, he just wanted to stop the man and tell him he was insane, or drunk, or just stupid. But he listened, because—and this was the most unsettling part—the man wasn't lying. Everything about his voice and his face testified that he was telling the truth, which left Warren with two possibilities: the man honestly believed what he was saying and was crazy—or that what he was saying was true.

"I have learned a way to find these people," Marshall was saying. "I can use my dreamsight to find them out there anywhere in the world. When your children were born, I dreamed of them."

Warren eyed him warily. "What's the color of the nursery?"

"Lime green, with little bugs your wife colored," Marshall said. "Lady bug and beetle. That's their nick names."

How was this possible? Warren tried not to show his shock, and hoped that the man did not notice how paralyzed Warren was by the implications of all this.

"And," Warren relented. "This...Red Widow. She wants these children, *my* children, to be her what...her soldiers?"

Marshall nodded. "In a manner of speaking, yes."

Nightbreakers. The undead. A world conspiracy. It was lunacy in its purest. And this man...somehow he had got all that information about his family and was using it as a hook. But for what purpose? Warren shook his head and drew himself up.

"Why?" Warren asked. "Assuming you're not insane, why help me protect them? Why me? You said you've taken others and given them over to this woman in the past. Why stop now? Why turn on her?"

Marshall sighed deeply. "Six days past," he said, and licked his lips. "Two of them tried to escape her service. They were...so young, and talented nightbreakers. I was made to watch as they were executed for treason. You see, when a nightbreaker dies, his or her soul rests for three days then returns to bond with another. It is reborn. I am the only one who knows how to use my sight to find them in the world. My orders were to find them and monitor them. And when they came of age, I was to take them from their parents and induct the children to the Lady's service."

Marshall shook his head and closed his eyes to fight back sudden tears. "The fight," he said. "It is a long one. And, young man, I am tired." His chin quaked. "I've taken so many lives that..." He paused. "I've forgotten what it was to save one."

Warren hung his head and shook it. "Look, I..."

"I can show you," Marshall begged. "There is proof. Will you come with me?"

Warren looked at him. "Where?"

"Close," Marshall said, wiping his running nose. "But I would advise you to take your things with you. You will not be returning here."

Warren shook his head. "No, that isn't going to work," he said. "I need something up front, and not just some facts about my family."

"As you wish," Marshall said, and held up his hand. "Fire your weapon." Marshall pointed at his palm. "Here."

Warren winced. Marshall stared back stolidly. "It is simple," he said, resolutely. "If I am insane, then I'll have a hole in my hand, and you can report me to the authorities for stalking and threatening your family. Or you'll just kill me right here. I'm sure your friends will vouch for you. If I'm not insane, though." Marshall shrugged confidently. "Well, I'll give you your bullet back."

Warren drew his gun, held it point blank at the man's palm. One shot was worth knowing.

The echo of a gun firing startled Warren from his stupor. He had not been sleeping, but...traveling. Lately he found himself going backwards, remembering, revisiting. The years had taken their toll. Somewhere in that lake of time, the point and purpose had been lost to him. And now Warren found himself searching once again for the source of *why*. Why did he do this? What fueled his motions? Why did he even bother anymore?

There had been a time when it all made sense. Purpose was important. Reasons were important. It had been a long time since he had reminded himself what those had been. Now, as he watched this girl burn a path into her own journey, his reasons were clear again.

Warren remembered now. *My family,* he thought, his face blushing with heat. *My wife, my son, my daughter.* He also remembered why he had to bury them deep down, to spare himself the pain. To stay the course. To do what others could not, because there was no one else.

The memories were returning to him now, though. They were beautifully painful. The flash of sun in his wife's hair, the sound of her voice, as she talked incessantly about dreams and impossible futures. He remembered the laugh of his son, and the sound of his rampant footsteps at play. He remembered the caress of his daughter's little hand resting in his, fragile and trusting. Small and vulnerable, they would need him as a sword and shield against a relentless and uncaring world.

These many years, he could not think of them. It shredded him inside to be away and to know what horrors lay in wait—and the only way to ensure their protection was to work for the enemy.

They had been the source of all his movements and the reason he even bothered breathing, and it had been too long since he remembered.

Footsteps scurried toward him in the darkness. Warren struggled upward, weary of body. Valerie burst from the foliage, glistening with sweat. She had the girl cradled in her arms, a small bundle of filthy pajamas and dark hair curled up against her chest. The girl's arms were wrapped around Valerie's neck.

"We gotta go," Valerie said, her chest heaving. "She's weak."

He gaped at the fragile thing in Valerie's arms. Alive, safe now. Warren's eyes snapped wide. "Don't wait for me. Go!"

Valerie galloped down the slope and through the forest back to the farm.

My God, he thought, stupefied. *She did it.* As relentless and savage as her enemy, that young woman had plunged into the gaping mouth of evil and snatched one back.

Valerie had the fire. Warren understood now. *The fight,* Marshall had said. *It is a long one.* Only a little further, Warren knew. His final strike against the darkness he had served and hated would be to make this young woman ready.

Warren stripped his jacket off and gathered the monster's head into it. There was work to do still, but for now, a good burning was in order.

__Chapter 12_____

"Senhor Marcelo!" Valerie called out.

She could see orange and yellow bulbs peeking through the foliage while she scampered through the remainder of the forest. She cried out again, her call dropping short because of her labored breathing. Her power had drained out of her during her race back to Warren, so she was running on adrenaline alone.

Dogs barking and men shouting to one another echoed over the space between them.

"Everything's all right," Valerie whispered to the girl. "You're almost home."

The forest peeled back, and the wide stretch of lawn sprawled into view. Marcelo and Valerie met at the fence, where she dumped the girl into her father's arms. The two farmhands were half-way to them when Marcelo ordered them to awaken the mother. The men backed away, staring at Valerie with a mixture of amazement and concern. Valerie waved them away with a hand, insisting she was fine. They turned abruptly and dashed into the home where the lights were flashing on in every room.

Doubling over, Valerie gasped, catching her breath. After a moment, it occurred to her that she had to go back to find Warren. There were no other revenants out there, and there had been no one far off as there had been in the desert. Warren must have been wrong. It hadn't been a trap at all. Valerie wiped the sweat from her face and smudged it on her pants.

A woman wrapped in a blanket had come out onto the lawn. She shuffled over to Valerie, offering a glass of water. Valerie chugged it and handed the glass back.

"Come inside, girl," the woman said, holding her arms out as though to hug her. "You're tired and dirty. Come in."

After a glance back into the forest, Valerie nodded and climbed over the fence. The woman took hold of Valerie's sweaty hand and escorted her to the house, whose yellow light shining through the large plate windows looked stunning at night.

They crossed the lawn and ascended the stairs into the house where the family was frantic in the task of caring for the child. The woman, whom Valerie had assumed was the girl's aunt, led Valerie to the entrance of their large living room whose windows overlooked the forest. Only hours ago, the women were huddled together weeping and consoling one another in this room. Now, they held within their circle a little girl, barely awake and whimpering. Tears streaked their faces as they whispered words of comfort while cleaning the minor abrasions on her body.

The aunt patted Valerie on the shoulder. "You are an angel of God," the woman said, smiling. Valerie looked at her, noting the awe and reverence in her face.

"It is true. You are an angel of God," the woman repeated.

Valerie stared at her, not knowing what to say.

"We prayed," the aunt said, turning her gaze back to the small family. "We prayed for God to send help. And you came."

"I am happy that she is safe," Valerie managed.

The woman ran her palm down Valerie's arm and glared at her. "No," the aunt said, shaking her head. "You do not understand."

Valerie felt her brow furrow.

"Four men went into the darkness," the aunt explained. "Four good, strong men—men who loved that girl. But they failed. They could not bring her back." The woman looked into Valerie's eyes and flashed a glowing smile. "Only one chosen by God could do what you did. Do you see this?"

Nodding compliantly, Valerie felt her face blush. Valerie had known that fathers would often call their daughters angels. In her life, no one had ever said that about her.

The woman wrapped her arms around Valerie and squeezed tightly. When she released Valerie, she raised her hands to Valerie's face and grabbed her cheeks. She pulled gently downward and kissed Valerie on the forehead. "Thank you," she whispered and released Valerie. "Thank you for this."

The aunt went into the living room and joined the family. The girl's younger sister had just scampered out of her room, her face sleepy and puffy from crying. The little thing almost tripped as she rushed to the arms of her sister, who, though weak, smiled and cried with her.

Glancing back at the forest, Valerie saw Warren emerge from it. He struggled to get over the fence. Something was lost in him. She wasn't ready to say that he had lost it all together, but the look on his face in the woods and the eagerness to resign himself to the worst was troubling.

There was one thing that was still solid about the guy, though. He was quick up top. Calm, cool, and quick. Had the interrogation of that revenant been up to her, she would still be beating it senseless. And the girl would have withered away in a hole.

Warren wouldn't lecture her on being impulsive; he never lectured her. The only thing the guy ever did was try to get her to think, which at times, came at the expense of action. She glanced back the family once more, grinned at the sight of it then turned to meet Warren in the yard.

"Sorry I didn't go back in after you," she said. "I figured you could handle yourself. What's in the jacket?"

"Evidence," he said. "They'll want to be sure it's dead. How is the girl?"

Valerie glanced back at the house. "Nothing life-threatening. A little dehydrated, maybe."

"Valerie, I..."

"It's all right," Valerie said, holding up her hands. "We saved her. That lady in there thinks we're angels. Like, really. Not in a figurative way."

"I won't let it go to my head," Warren murmured.

Marcelo had spied them through the window. He rose from the huddle and came out unto the porch where he stood and waved them over. Valerie and Warren approached.

"There was another, my farmhand," Marcelo said to Warren, and paused.

Warren looked at Valerie. She shook her head and explained what happened. She had found a small cave, and in it she found the girl clinging to the body of the farmhand. It had been him offering himself up first that stalled the appetite of the creature. Valerie did not explain that she had beheaded the body, just to be sure.

Marcelo's eyes were cast downward as he listened to the story. "And his body?" he asked.

Valerie then turned and pointed into the forest describing in detail where he and his men could collect it.

"The creature?" Marcelo asked. "Could you find it?"

Warren held up the balled up windbreaker, which had dark stains of the creature's blood on it. "It will need to be burned," Warren said.

"Roberto!" the father called out. The skinny farmhand scurried from the living room and stood behind Marcelo. "Take this and burn it." Roberto nodded, retrieved the ball and rushed toward a large burn pit, where a small bonfire had already been smoldering.

After a moment Marcelo looked at them and said, "There is nothing I can pay you that would be enough to show my thanks. So, ask what you will of me, and I will give it to you."

Valerie looked at Warren. He was winded and weary. "We don't accept money," she said. "But we are tired and would like a place to clean ourselves and rest. Could we stay the night?"

"Clara!" he called out. One of the other women rose from the living room and approached them. "These are our guests for as long as they wish to stay. Make the spare field room ready."

"Absolutely not!" the woman objected. "They won't sleep out there. Selma and I will stay with the girls tonight. They can each have our rooms in the house. Where's your brain, man?"

"Do whatever," he barked. "Just see to their care."

Clara looked at them and smiled. "I will make you a fine dinner. Come, come."

"My home is yours. Come, please," Marcelo said, waving them in.

The excitement had finally died off sometime after midnight. The family had gone to sleep, but Marcelo had asked his two farmhands to trade shifts, watching the house during the night.

It was perhaps three or four in the morning when Valerie awoke feeling hungry. She had declined the offer of food before everyone went to bed, and was now regretting having done so.

It was rude to wander around in a stranger's house, and she really didn't want to have to deal with the awkward moment of bumping into one of the farmhands. After all, she was only wearing her underwear and a large t-shirt one of the women gave her to sleep in. Pulling the disheveled mess of her hair back, she tied it into a bun. She put on some little furry slippers that were by the bed.

She cracked the door open to her room and spied across the hall. Warren's door was open, and a faint lamplight flickered inside. Bounding across the hall on tiptoes, she peeked into his room and saw that his bed was empty. She sneaked through house, careful not make the floorboards creak. Not that it would matter; it was hard to remain undetected within such an open and well-lit home. As she strode toward the kitchen, from the corner of her eye she spied Warren on the back porch sitting at a picnic table hunched over a plate of something.

Stomach lurching, she ignored the callings for better prudence and opted not to go put some more clothing on. Gliding through the open glass doors, she shuffled over to the picnic table.

"You're naked," Warren said, chewing.

"Shut up and feed me," she said, sitting across from him.

He passed her a bowl of pão-de-quejo, little rolls of bread with cheese baked into them. They were, Valerie had now realized, the world's greatest midnight snack. She also grabbed some salt bread and painted it with swipes of butter. They ate their food in the quiet of the night, which was gorgeous, Valerie had just noticed. The thick crescent moon shone down like their own personal lamp; its brilliance highlighted the ridges of the low hanging clouds and set the flowers and grass and foliage aglow. Crickets whined and frogs croaked, and somewhere in all that darkness some animal giggled.

"We should do this more," Valerie said, at last. "Eat together, I mean. Like a date, but you know, *not*."

"Thanks, Valerie," Warren grumbled. "That makes you sitting there in your underwear all the more bearable."

Valerie shrugged. "Get over it. Just, pretend I'm your kid or something." She offered a sarcastic smirk while she studied his face. "You know, minus the hair, we kind of look alike. I could be your daughter, right?"

Warren tucked his head down and didn't look at her, offering only a compliant grin. For a while he said nothing, averting her gaze. Though he did his best to hide it on her account, a noticeable somberness shrouded him.

I've hit a nerve, she thought. *Way to be an ass, Valerie.*

Valerie didn't want to ask what was the matter. It was a similar look to the one she saw in the forest: drawn, pained, and straining to survive the moment without falling to pieces.

"Valerie..." he said at last, and paused. He was fidgeting and shifty, very unlike himself. "There is a way," he continued. "I think there is a way for you, as a nightbreaker, to find others out there in the world, and I..."

Noticeably deflated, Valerie shrunk down and groaned.

"What?" Warren asked, plaintively. He had always been a pushover and overly passive, but being humble and begging was not Warren at all. He had his own brand of stubborn pride.

"Let's just have a conversation," she begged, chewing her buttered bread. "Work can wait till in the morning, can't it?"

Warren sighed. "You're right."

"I mean don't get me wrong," she said, grabbing his hand. "I'm interested and everything, but for right now, let's have a little victory dinner. You lose sight of celebration, and it won't be long before you shrivel up and quit."

Warren stared at her for a moment, searching her eyes, which showed a renewed luminance. "Valerie," he said. "I'm glad that I met you. And yes, you could be my daughter." He pointed at his head. "Minus the hair."

She huffed. "In a few more years, you might be minus the hair anyway."

Their laughter echoed in the forest.

Morning was painful, and Valerie had almost forgot that they were in the house of strangers when she awoke. As a kid, she had done this many times. Waking up in some stranger's house, where you were supposed to feel at home; only you knew you were a guest till you had earned your keep. Her situation was probably improved since they were something like celebrities in this particular household. However, she had no intention of wearing out her welcome and was eager to jump in the truck and move on.

Finding her clothing cleaned and pressed outside her door, she dressed and headed to the porch where the cool morning breeze and sounds of animals summoned her. Warren was seated there with Marcelo and his wife Cida, whom Valerie had yet to talk to. Cida rose from her seat and rushed at Valerie swallowing her in a hug. Warren offered a petulant smirk as Valerie awkwardly hugged the much shorter woman back.

Cida pulled herself away and wiped tears. "One day," she said and sniffed. "You will be a mother. And then you will understand what you have done for me."

Unbidden, Valerie thought of Little Tiger and what she might do if something tried to harm her. Valerie smiled at Cida, and turned on her Portuguese. "Is she feeling better, Louisa?"

"Oh yes," Cida said, smiling brightly. "She is in her room resting still, but I will bring her out. She will want to see you before you go."

The family then went their separate ways. Marcelo was off with his farmhands into the forest to complete their grim task. The women busied themselves with cooking and cleaning and caring for the girls. Valerie and Warren sat at the table and helped themselves to coffee, buttered salt bread, scrambled eggs and rice.

"You're kind of a big deal here," Warren said with a smirk.

"I know, right?" she replied. "Don't be jealous. You'll always have Gollum. How did your night out with him go anyway?"

Warren chuckled. "It was revealing."

"On the first date? What a skank," she said, tearing off a piece of salt bread and eating it.

"You're terrible," he murmured. "We'll talk about it out of earshot. It's rude to speak English in front of the family, and I don't want to disturb them any more than they already are. Besides," he nodded his head in the direction behind Valerie, "I think you have a fan club to take care of."

Louisa and Fernanda dashed at Valerie, plopping down at either side of her, awash with excitement. Cida made plates for them, and they each chattered at Valerie, who couldn't contain her electric grin. She tickled them. They made fun of her sometimes-jumbled language, and they hugged her repeatedly. Warren watched with a pleasant smirk and laughed at Valerie's silliness.

Breakfast ended, and the girls hugged Valerie tightly before being ushered off. They all said their goodbyes. The women hugged and cried and wiped tears. The men shook hands and patted backs and used deep voices when they spoke. Waving, Valerie and Warren returned to the truck. It would be a long, bumpy three-hour ride back to Montes Claros.

"Hey," she said, stopping short. "Let me drive."

Warren was shaking his head and laughing.

"No, no," she begged. "Come on. Look at you. You need the rest anyway."

Warren threw his bag in the back, ignoring her.

"Warren," she said, and glared at him pointedly. "Hey, it's my turn."

Maybe it was how she said it that made Warren stop short and stare at her with a distant and searching gaze. Like she had just fulfilled a prophecy or something.

"I can handle this beast," she persisted, and appraised the big, brown box on wheels, this time with less confidence. She shrugged. "I'll figure it out."

He smiled and relented with a nod. Punching the air, Valerie skipped to the driver's seat, picking the keys from Warren's fingers as they passed each other. Starting up the engine, Valerie labored to put the hulking vehicle into gear. It took some getting used to, but before long they were on their way.

"So let's have it," she said, over the grumble of the motor. "What's the news out of freakville?"

Warren titled his head, squinting. "More confusion." He then told her everything he had learned from the creature: about the eyes and ears, about the strange transformation it underwent, and about the odd form of control it was under.

Valerie nodded and squinted with thought. "You know," she said. "Remember what you said last night about finding other nightbreakers in the world?"

"Yes."

"Well maybe," she said, glancing at him. "Maybe this dream-control works the same way. There might be something in the notes," she said, shrugging. "If you let me have those... Maybe I can figure it out."

"I'll put it all together for you."

"Hey," she said, and traded glances with him and the road, which was the best she could do for locking eyes with him to indicate she meant what she was about to say. "No more keeping me out of the loop, all right?"

Warren nodded. "Agreed."

"Okay," she said. "What's your daughter's name?"

Warren's face jerked toward her, incapable of hiding its surprise. He glared and said nothing.

"Last night," Valerie explained. "I saw it in your face. I'm sorry for saying all that, too. I didn't know."

"It's all right," he assured. "Her name is Alma. She's about a year younger than you. Just started her senior year. She and her brother, Braxton."

"Twins, I guess, right?"

"Yes."

"A wife?"

"Berenice," he said, and then smiled in reflection. "We grew up together in Boston. Call it coincidence, but her family is from here. Porto Allegre."

"How long has it been?" she asked. "Since you've seen them?"

Warren struggled to speak. It seemed like he was searching for the right way to explain a complex situation. "I've written letters. I visited them once when they were very young," he said. "But, it wasn't always safe..."

He paused. "It's complicated. I had ways of checking up on them. But seeing them...being with them. Not for many years. They do not know me."

Valerie was quiet a moment. The truck hummed along the shaved clay road. "And…" she started. She had to tread carefully here. "They're like me? Nightbreakers?"

He stared long through the windshield, saying nothing.

"Is that why you want me to learn how to search for others?" she asked. "It's okay if you say yes."

Warren's silence was confirmation enough. He stared into the road with a pale and desperate look, the expression of a man whose heart is held in another person's hands.

At the expense of watching the road, Valerie glared at Warren. "They're *not* going to be harmed," she insisted. "We'll make sure of it. I promise."

After a long bout of silence, Warren inhaled and sighed. "Valerie," he said, and paused, searching for the words. "In this work, in this life that you've chosen, there will come a time when you will have to make a sacrifice, and I hope—"

"No," she said, holding up a stern finger. "I'll compromise. I'll even negotiate from time to time. Because that means that I get something out of it. But I won't sacrifice. That's what people do for tyrants and angry gods, and it has never led to anything good except to make fat men fatter and bad men worse. I'll have no part of it."

Warren cringed at the thought of it, as though the concept was foreign to him but immediately recognized as true. Maybe he thought she was just flying off at the mouth. What did she know, after all? Valerie didn't care. She felt *good*. Never in her life had she felt as confident and sure in who she was and what she was doing.

"Call me an idealist all you want," she said. "But that's how I'm going to fight this." She smiled big, her soul gleaming. "We're going to tear a hole in this whole thing, Warren. We're going to end it. And then you're going to retire with your family. Happily ever after."

Warren chuckled. Not just at the pleasant thought of her vision, but at the playful naivety necessary to create it.

"Oh you think I'm joking?" she said, smiling and lowering her brow. "You think I'm stupid?"

"Oh no," he mused. "I know better than to stand against the almighty Zeta."

She pointed a finger at her head. "You're pretty quick up top. I'll give you that."

__Chapter 13_____

Days were always so long, plagued by an oppressive sun. Ismena felt its withering heat pushing inward, relentless as it baked the cracked, white concrete walls of their home. Only when it rolled off the world into the horizon could she stand to breathe again.

Then there was the grass and vegetation. She could almost feel them lapping up the sunrays as they spawned upward, reaching, and reaching until they would choke the life out of everything. Worst of all were the little rodents. They scurried about unchecked, harassing the silence with their little whimpers and teasing sounds. They thought they were being quiet and stealthy, but Mena could hear them. She could see them, too, skulking in the crevices of the bounding woodland.

They mocked Ismena, and she hated them. But when the night came, they would see how powerful she was and how weak they were. The grass and weeds would pale at her passing, and the rodents would blast for cover at her approach. Ismena was a princess of the night. Edgar was her prince.

Like all hot days in this wretched part of the world, Mena curled up outside Edgar's door waiting patiently for him to rise. When she did not nap, she traced the wood grains on the door with her finger and hummed little tunes, even though Edgar reprimanded her for it each time he awoke.

"The sound of it is unseemly," he would say. It was the vibrations, she knew. The disturbance of air and space, whose resonance was felt differently—more deeply—in the Highborn.

"Yes, master," she would reply, pawing at his cold hand, her face upturned in supplication. "I will learn to improve my voice."

"Do not use it at all."

She would nod many times. "Yes, of course," she would say. "Silence is the music beneath."

When she could no longer stand the crawling hunger in her stomach, she would hunt something eat. The rodents were difficult to catch, but she had learned to make traps. Mena ate them raw. That was the true way to feed. Like the Highborn did—feeding on the life-energy, raw and power-laden. Occasionally, however, she would build a fire and cook the food as a treat to herself, but always far away from Edgar so his rest would not be disturbed by the smell of seared flesh. And...she didn't want her master to be reminded of how low and wretched and *mortal* she was.

Ismena tried to prove herself with her power. When she harnessed her abilities, she could perform great feats, all in the effort to keep Edgar safe from harm. She guarded him while he rested, and she could enter human domiciles where his kind was cursed never to go unless permitted. Edgar needed her, but that was never enough.

While her power was a great blessing, it also barred her from becoming undead, like Edgar and the other Highborn. The universe at times was cruel in this way, and it tortured Mena in body and soul. Every time she felt her heart beating, or the salty formation of sweat upon her skin, or the weight of food in her belly she was reminded of how low she was. Ismena, though chosen to be Edgar's protector, was still just like all those other maggots: crawling around in the unbearable heat of the day: confused, tired, afraid, and striving for survival when death was always the end result.

Ismena began to cry as she thought of that. She was going to die. But the truth was that it wasn't death that filled her heart with dread—it was the idea of becoming old. Of aging. Of changing into a weak, elderly hag who could be of no use to Edgar. Would he discard her in favor of a new protector, one who would be younger and more beautiful? She would kill such a creature!

Mena reigned in her sorrow. She sniffed, wiping her tears away.

"Damn it!" she gasped.

She rose from the door, still wiping her tears and smudging them on her dusty pants. She went to her room. Here, most of the old furniture remained intact. Though there was no more running water or electricity in this abandoned hotel, it still provided her with some of the niceties. Two being a mirror and a big ivory tub she kept filled with water from a nearby spring. Though it would be a few more hours until Edgar rose, she still wanted to stay pretty for him. She splashed the water on her face and patted it dry with a white towel.

Staring into the mirror, she saw part horror and part beauty. Her face was still beautiful. Her pale blue eyes still glittered; her straight brown hair—which she managed with her vast array of shampoos and conditioners—still glimmered with a fine sheen. It was her skin. Though impeccable for so many years, it was now showing the first signs of age.

She had stayed away from the sun. Even when she had to be in it, she always covered her whole face in a scarf so as not to damage the thin, delicate white skin beneath. But wrinkles, faint and unnoticeable to the natural eye, had begun to slash her once perfect face.

Did Edgar notice? That was always her great concern the moment he rose from his earth. Would he give her a second look, a prolonged glance in observation of her imperfection? When would she see a curious shift of his eyes showing that he had seen it, the aging, the oldness? Did Edgar even note the passing of her mortal years? Though she claimed to have stopped noting such a triviality, she always knew it, like a deeply burned brand on her forehead open for all to see—34. She was thirty-four years old and withering by the day.

Mena felt fresh tears rising, and since she could rewash her face, she let them spill forth. She would not whimper, though. Edgar would feel the vibrations, and they would disturb his rest. She didn't want him to know that she was pathetic. No more than she already was in comparison to his perfection: the perfection of a Highborn that she could never be.

When she completed the beautification of her visage, she returned to the earth chamber, curled under its frame, and shoved as much of herself flat against the sealed door as she could.

The day was long and boring, but she knew know how important it was to stay watchful during the day. She had to stay awake. This horrible land with its horrible people and its horrible language was a threat to Edgar. They had very important work to do. They needed to be the eyes and ears for the new Master, in his search for the artifact.

Edgar was wise to follow the Master. Though Mena had not seen him, she could…sense his presence, somehow. A divine shadow looming over all things, his menace and his malice everywhere. Edgar and Mena needed to be vigilant. They watched the vago, empty-minded revenants now useful under the Master's control. In time they would gather, in time they would lead the way…

And it would be so simple if it weren't for that girl.

It was now undeniable that a rogue nightbreaker was to blame for the slaughtering of the vago. Ismena did not know everything, because only Edgar could know when to give her wisdom, but… Mena remembered the girl from the desert. Yes, it *had* to be her.

The girl had fought off and slaughtered Edgar's vago that night—*three* of them. Only a nightbreaker had that kind of strength. Watching from a distance, Ismena had desperately wanted to attack the girl and her teacher—to avenge such a blasphemy—but Edgar forbade her from doing so. Ismena would not question Edgar's wisdom either. It was not hers to question.

Still, it was a dreadful thing to ponder: a nightbreaker who battled *against* the Highborn. Such a thing was… Mena wasn't sure of the words to describe it.

It was unnatural, she thought. *Perverse.*

Did that slime not understand her true place? The thought of the girl's audacity made Mena's face hot.

Was the girl... Mena shook her head, trying to banish this reoccurring thought. *Was she...beautiful?*

If she was, Mena would carve the girl's face with red, twisted patterns. She would do it for no other reason than to serve as a projection of the hideousness concealed beneath. Then, she would present the mutilated wretch to Edgar, so he could see how weak and ugly the girl was.

Mena watched the turning pillar of light slashing through the boarded up windows. Night would come in a few hours, and the thought excited her. She wanted to be ready for Edgar when he unsealed his earth-chamber and stepped forth from the darkness.

Until that moment, though, she remained snug against the door, pretending it was his perfected form unto which she clung. Closing her eyes, she opened her darksight and found her slumbering prince beyond the sealed door. He rested within his box of mortal earth, a glorious phantom of silver and gold, unmoving, solid, immortal, and perfect. Ismena was comforted.

The council for the Betterment of Valerie Zeta was in session. Adria pulled no punches in her criticism of Warren's treatment of Valerie. Warren took the fast, verbal onslaught complete with this-is-your-last-chance finger pointing. Rodrigo, ever the temperate and understanding host, attempted to be the medium, but eventually decided to play it safe and keep his mouth shut. They were cute.

Not nearly as adorable as Little Tiger, though. Upon seeing that Valerie had finally come home, the little girl scampered headlong at Valerie and wrapped her arms around Valerie's knees. She drew back at the sight of the large bandage on Valerie's leg.

"Are you hurt?" Little Tiger asked, her eyes glittering with concern.

Valerie shook her head. "Your mommy took care of it." She forced a smile during the pain that shocked through her as she sat down in the small living room.

"Wait here," Little Tiger said, holding up a finger. "It's not done yet."

The girl bolted around the corner, entered the kitchen, rummaged in a cabinet and returned with their family's small first aid kit.

"Now hold still," Little Tiger instructed, her face emulating the expressions of the caregivers who had healed her so many times before. "This may hurt a little." Her fingers labored as they began sticking small bandages and patches of gauze over the newly dressed bandage.

"That feels so much better," Valerie gasped. "You'll make a fine nurse one day."

Little Tiger screwed up her face. "But I already am!" she insisted. Then she pointed her skinny finger and furrowed her brow hard with reprimand. "Now, no more tree-climbing. You can wait for the mangoes to grow ripe and fall from the branches from now on!"

Shaking with laughter, Valerie scooped the girl up, planting kisses all over her face. "What about *this* mango?" Valerie teased, nipping playfully at Little Tiger's cheeks. "Can I have this one? It's sooooo sweet!"

The room alighted with their giggling. Meanwhile, the debate about Valerie's health began to heat up.

"You don't have the sense to even let the old wounds heal before you take her out there to get new ones!" Adria seethed, waving a hand in Valerie's direction.

"I understand, Adria," Warren said, hanging his head. "But..."

"No buts!" she retorted, pointing her finger again. "No more of that! When will you see, Warren? When she must go to the hospital? When she nearly dies? When?"

Warren made a face and looked away, saying nothing.

"Drigo," she said to her husband. "Speak to him. Tell him. This is a young girl, Drigo. She should go to school and meet youth her age. She should live, meet someone special and have a good life. Look at her! This kind of life will ruin what God has made."

"Adria," Drigo said, not daring to look at her wide and angry eyes. "It is Valerie who decides. Warren is not lying. It is she who insists. Now," Rodrigo turned to Warren and looked at him. "Warren, Adria is right. You have a responsibility. At least let her old wounds heal before she takes more."

Valerie cradled Little Tiger in her arms and stood up. "It's bed time for this cub," she whispered. "I'll put you down, okay?"

"In your bed, with you?"

"Not tonight," Valerie said, putting on a frown. "I don't want to keep you up."

Little Tiger ran her fingers through Valerie's hair. "I wish you didn't have bad dreams."

"Me too."

Daniela nestled in, wrapping her arms around Valerie's neck. As Valerie walked away, she pretended that she hadn't understood all their talking. Adria and Rodrigo perhaps underestimated how well she understood the language. They probably also thought by speaking fast and heatedly they could conceal their conversation in babble. It was rude, after all, to speak about people in their presence.

Entering the bedroom, Valerie found Ester curled up in the bed that she and Little Tiger shared when Valerie was at home. Ester was tucked in and covered, and though her eyes were shut, Valerie knew she was awake and simply didn't want to look at Valerie.

She lowered Little Tiger into the small bed, cringing in pain as she knelt. Valerie tucked the girl in and recited their family's bedtime prayers.

"Love you," Little Tiger said, her eyes heavy as she smiled.

Kissing her on the forehead, Valerie wiped the little girl's tangled tresses of black hair behind her ears and stared. "Goodnight, and thank you for healing me."

Laboring as she rose, she felt suddenly weary. Valerie retreated to the veranda where she loved to look at their small neighborhood at night: quiet, tranquil, and safe. Little Tiger and this place are what kept her going out there. They were what fueled Valerie's desperation to strike, to retaliate.

The murders were popping up with greater frequency. She and Warren had returned from the fourth incident this month, and there was still a week to go. Summer was setting in, and the rains had started. Perhaps that drew them out. Valerie did not know why there was such a rise in revenant attacks.

They were all the same, except now the creatures were targeting men, draining and leaving their bodies in ditches. The revenants were getting stronger, smarter, and harder to bring down. She and Warren were meeting the challenge, but at the cost of good rest and health. Though she regarded all their talk as she would the rabble of children barking over a toy, there was no denying that her wounds had racked up, and perhaps, a break was in order. Just a week to let the wounds heal.

Adria was still fuming. "And how much harm has come to you, Warren?"

"Adria!" Rodrigo barked. "That is enough. Warren would never risk her health over his own. That is not fair to imply."

Warren held up his hands plaintively. "It's all right, both of you. I will...speak with her. But, if this becomes too much of a strain, Valerie and I—"

Adria roared. "You will not take her from here! That young woman needs us. We are her family!"

"Calm yourself, Adria," Rodrigo begged. "We all want what's best for her, okay? We are all partners in this."

Valerie heard it all. *Partners,* she thought. *A team. Are we?* That sounded grand, but the idea came with the inching of a nameless dread. It was the understanding that her life could not remain this way. Something was bound to swoop in and destroy it. From Valerie's beginning, that was life as she knew it.

There was silence for a moment. Valerie heard their steps slowly shuffling away from each other.

"Where did she go?" Adria murmured to them.

"She's out here," Warren said, walking out onto the veranda. He turned and looked at Adria and Rodrigo. "Could I have a moment with her before I go?"

They agreed and went to tuck the kids in. Warren sidled up next to her, placed his hands on the parapet of the veranda and gazed out on the turning night. The stars blinked in stellar rhythm. The marsh toads, empowered by the newly fallen rains, were roaring out in the darkness. Voices in the streets were fading, and all was descending into yet another beautiful and peaceful night.

"I'm sorry about all that," Warren said, speaking in English.

Shrugging, Valerie said, "Used to it."

"One of the benefits of youth," Warren commented. "Lots of people looking after you, just not at the time you want them to."

Now there's a true story, she thought. Valerie leaned into the parapet, watching a glowing light from a young boy racing to get inside his home's walls.

"Out with it," she said, at length.

Warren inhaled and sighed. "Well, Valerie, Adria is right. I have always known that the decisions were yours. I have always respected that."

"I know," Valerie said, nodding.

"Then, please," he reasoned. "Listen to them. I'm not saying stop and find yourself a man. I'm saying catch your breath and take care of yourself." Warren titled his head and shrugged. "The truth is, while I'm not as banged up as you, I could use a rest, too."

Valerie instinctively reached up and touched the bottom right bone of her jaw. It was purple and swelling where a particularly strong revenant had back-handed her. She was thankful it wasn't broken. They were right, but...

"What if one of those men were Drigo?" Valerie asked, and looked at Warren.

He drew in a breath and shook his head, knowing what she meant but still not wishing to address it. "Valerie—"

"No, Warren," she pressed. "And that lady from Diviniopolis? She had three children. Just like Adria's got. And what about—"

Warren stopped her with a hand. "I get it, Valerie."

"Good," she said and looked out at the night. "I'll let you know when I'm on the ropes. Until then, we attack. Sooner or later they'll get the message."

"So, when you've scared them all off..."

"Yeah, Warren. That's the plan. These freaks have forgotten their place, and we've got to remind them. That's how you deal with bullies and tyrants. You beat them and keep beating."

Warren was nodding, but it was a forced agreement.

"You can think whatever you want," she went on, trying to calm her rising temper. "But these aren't the cowards you said they were. They can't go around slaughtering innocent people, children, fathers, mothers. They can't do that and think they can get away with it."

"I understand, Valerie," he said. "I would like you to remember that I have never once attempted to stop you."

"Let's keep it that way." She immediately felt bad for her words and tone. She never just let him win one, even though she knew he was right.

They stood in silence for a while before Warren asked, "How are you sleeping? And tell me honestly, please."

Valerie shook her head.

"The dreams?"

"Yeah," she said. "Same ones. A woman at a door in an abandoned building, a hotel, I think. I saw its sign: The Sylvias."

"And the woman?"

"Her aura is red, not orange, like most people," Valerie explained. "Next to her is an undead, sealed in some room. An earth chamber, maybe. And it's not a revenant. It's something bigger. I think she's trying to get into it."

"What do you think it means, if anything?"

Valerie rubbed her forehead. "I don't know," she admitted. "I think she's a nightbreaker, though. It's weird. She's the only one, so far. Maybe because she is closest to us?"

Warren nodded quietly.

Valerie glared at him. "If the dreams are real, and if she's a nightbreaker, like me…" she said, her eyes begging, "…then she could help us."

Warren's eyes glazed over for a moment as he blinked slowly. "No, Valerie," he replied. "The others… Valerie they're not *evil,* but…they are not friends, either. They serve the enemy."

"Yeah, I know," she acknowledged. "But maybe it's because they don't understand. They're taken when they're young. Maybe now, you know, when they're older, they would see…"

"Valerie, please no," Warren said. "At least for now. Let's stay focused on organizing ourselves." After a moment, Warren added. "You need to rest. Not just your body either, but your," he paused and looked her, "your heart."

And what's that supposed to mean? she thought, but she knew what he was driving at. "I'm fine, really."

Warren was quiet as he seemed to study how best to put what he wanted to say. *Here it comes,* Valerie thought. *A teachable moment.* Eventually he smiled—the first in a while—and faced her.

"It's been some time since I've told you a story," he said, holding out his hands. "It's a good one I promise."

Knew it. She ticked her tongue and groaned lightly. "Go ahead."

"All right," Warren started. "Once there was a samurai whose master had ordered him to track down and do justice unto a murderer. He was guilty of murdering the master's young son. Now, because the gods frown on outright revenge, it was impossible for the master to defile himself by seeking after this murderer himself. So, he asked his most loyal and most skilled warrior to seek this murderer out and kill him.

"On top of being a murderer he was also a vagrant: he had no home or family, so he was difficult to track. Though the samurai was skilled, finding the man proved very difficult. While this murderer eluded justice, he would often taunt the samurai with notes left behind in villages and roads. Eventually, however, the people of the land had had enough and led the samurai to him. When the samurai cornered this murderer, he unsheathed his sword to deal the killing strike. But then murderer spit in the samurai's face and laughed at him.

"The samurai then sheathed his sword and returned to his master, asking that another complete the task."

Warren searched Valerie's face for her response. She thought she grasped the meaning, but wasn't sure.

"Now, the question is," Warren asked, "why would the samurai do such a thing?"

Valerie blinked. "Because it was personal then," she said. "If he had killed the guy right then, it would have been for the wrong reason. It would have been for his own revenge and not for justice."

Warren smiled, beaming with pride. "Precisely. One of the reasons you give me so much hope, Valerie, is that you always seemed to understand this. You understood that this was a calling, not a personal mission."

Valerie rose from the parapet, suddenly grasping what Warren was driving at.

"Do you see, Valerie?" he asked, searching her face. "It is good that you feel deeply about helping these people. It drives you. It thrusts you forward when all others would give in. It saves lives. But you must control your personal feelings. They will cloud your judgment and blur your target. Always keep your focus intact."

Damn him, she thought. *He always manages to be right.* Her eyes softened as she nodded lightly. "I understand."

They were quiet for a while until Valerie chuckled suddenly. "You know," she said with a grin. "For a second there I thought the whole moral was to learn how to judge between guilt and innocence."

Warren didn't laugh. His expression remained drawn and severe. It was a rare thing to see a snarl on the face of a man as temperate as he. A little scary, even. "That's unnecessary," he grumbled, his gaze reaching far into the night. He then glared at her and said, "They're all guilty."

Ismena stepped back from the sealed door. She straightened herself, squared her chin and shoulders, and put on a welcoming smile. Her skin flushed hot as Edgar rose inside his earth-chamber. She could feel the air shift, parting by the grace of his movements. She did her best to remain still, collected and magnificent. The sealed door slid to the left revealing the shadows within as deep as a moonless night.

Mena fell to one knee, dropped her head and waited. The footsteps came forward slowly, evenly measured, in perfect rhythm. Then she felt the approving touch of his hand on the back of her head. She did not look up, but remained knelt.

"What is our task this night?" she asked, her voice deep and severe, so he would know how devoted and serious she was.

A labored rasp issued from above. "She has killed again," Edgar said, his voice a gorgeous hiss. "My Mena, what are we to do with this nuisance?"

"She profanes and insults the Highborn," Ismena growled. "She must die."

A rhythmic rasp bounced and trilled from his mouth. She had made him laugh. But was it because he found her remark petulant and meager, or was he truly pleased? Mena's forehead furrowed with uncertainty.

"We have been patient, Mena," Edgar groaned. "I was wrong to spare her in the desert, and I was wrong to allow her to hunt the vago. We must set aside our efforts until she is dealt with."

"Yes," Mena said, and she could feel his grace coursing through her as he gripped her hair and pulled her up straight. The pain was good, the fire in her scalp. When she was standing, he released her, and she stood very still.

"Master, what do you wish of me?"

He drew in a breath then exhaled, the sound of it like a simmering growl. "Did you discover her name?"

Ismena had. Though it had been a loathsome chore, she spent a day visiting a family which this girl and her teacher had helped. After interrogating the father, she discovered the name. The very sound of it irked Mena, twisted her insides and made her snarl. The people, they lauded her, spoke of her like she was some kind of... Mena didn't know what to call it. She cringed, her anger brewing revulsion. Bearing this disgust, Mena gave her master the name, first and last.

"Tonight, I will find this rogue," he announced, and then he began gliding back into the shadows of his chamber. "To do this, I must dream. In the morning we will travel. You will prepare us."

A single finger, sharp with a long talon, touched her beneath the chin and raised her face level with his. She peered into his white face, gazed into his glowing, blue eyes rimmed in violet. They glided back smoothly until he was gone again. The earth-chamber door slid back into place and clamped shut.

Minutes passed in silence. Then Ismena's grateful smile bent crooked in a grimace. Her chin quivered with one-part sorrow, two parts rejection. Edgar's lips had been turned down in a scowl, his eyes fierce and angry.

It was that girl's fault!

Her interference had disrupted their designs. Her meddling with the vago—scattering them and killing them—was now more than just a nuisance to their goals. The girl was frustrating Edgar and making him angry. This made him cold and restrained in offering his affection.

Finally, Ismena felt the dark of night all around her, but there was no comfort in it. Not while such a rude and disgusting wretch existed, daring to obstruct their plans.

Thrusting herself forward, Ismena descended the three flights of old concrete stairs and burst through the doors out into the night. With a swipe of her arm, she yanked the tarp away, uncovering the large SUV. Its windows were blackened, and inside, behind the front seats, there was an empty box that needed to be lined with the mortal earth of her master.

She cracked open one of their many earth crates. Then she began the low, sweaty, and boring labor of shoveling earth from the crate to buckets, which she would then take to the box and spread evenly. There he would rest in the darkness, safe from the pains of day while she transported him.

While Mena worked, she cursed under her breath and occasionally threw her arms wildly about as though attacking an imaginary enemy. This girl would pay. Pay for all the agitation she caused between her and Edgar. And she would pay for daring to stand against the Highborn.

__Chapter 14

Marshall called it dreamsight. He had left basic instructions on how to begin the mastery of it. Unlike her strength, speed, and stamina, this power did not come to her as naturally. Mastery of it would take time, Valerie realized. In the meantime, she would have to deal with the side effects, namely, nagging dreams that strangely felt like…memories.

Her dreams troubled her now, spreading her consciousness thin during hours her mind should have been at rest. Valerie did not understand why, but they had become a stage for theater. She didn't dream about random people and strange mixtures of light and sound anymore. Now, her dreams were stories, episodic and vivid. In each, she played the part of other women, feeling the emotions of each one, experiencing their thoughts and desires.

The dreams carried a common conflict: she was embroiled in a desperate fight, or a frantic chase, always at the side of others like her. They were warriors of one sort or another, light-skinned, dark-skinned, and they spoke old, sometimes ancient languages.

In tonight's dream, she and two other warriors were in a desperate race against time. Their leader was a determined and courageous man named Yusef. He had led them through many battles, and tonight he led them in their final assault. They sought the weapon that would give them victory over their sworn enemy—the undead.

He dashed ahead of Valerie down a dark hall that stretched long in front of them. An odd fog clouded the hall's ending far off where a deep crimson light pulsed through the mist. That was their goal. After fighting for so many years, they had made it here, to the end. Groaning, shouting, and the screaming of banshees blasted from behind them. The others had sacrificed themselves to delay the enemy. Now, only the three of them remained, the last of the nightbreakers.

Wounded in the ribs, Valerie felt a debilitating malaise overcome her whole body. She halted and doubled over, hands on knees. Her chest heaved and gasped for breath. There was a woman who raced alongside her. Portia, like Valerie, was weary and fatigued from the fight. The woman halted also, sidling up close to support her.

"I will remain here," Valerie said, in some language she did not recognize. "I will delay them. Go!"

Yusef was a tall man, caramel-skinned with black curly locks. He turned and waved fiercely. "Forward!" he ordered. "It is just there!"

"This was hopeless from the start," Portia murmured.

Valerie felt the woman's hands reaching for something. It was then that Valerie felt the cold, searing bite of a blade slice from one side of her neck to the other. Warmth spilled onto her hands. By instinct, Valerie grasped her neck and tried to stall the bleeding. Her eyes flared open in shock, searching for a reason that this happened.

There was only Portia, a good friend—or so Valerie had believed—standing next to her. She held the knife out, balancing it almost playfully while it dripped blood.

"It must be this way, Yusef," Portia said. "There is no victory here."

Yusef's eyes, hard and hot with fury, glared fiercely back at her. "Why, Portia? What did the Warlocks promise you?"

"An end to all this…" Portia searched for a word. She shrugged. "Meagerness, I guess. There's a lot of talk about that New World they've just discovered across the ocean. Think about it, Yusef. We could make the trip, set ourselves up nicely." She was quiet a second, letting him consider. "You don't have to do anything. Just move aside; I will retrieve the artifact and deliver it—"

"You will earn it," Yusef growled. "You sniveling coward!"

With her killer distracted, Valerie called upon all her strength to rise. Releasing the grip from her neck, she clawed her way up the wall with one hand and drew her blade with the other. Yusef was shouting, muffling Valerie's clumsy movements.

"What did you plan to do with it, exactly?" Portia asked. "You have no idea what it even is. Besides, the Warlocks would find us eventually and take it anyway. The only end to this is to—"

"Serve them?" Yusef barked. "You have lost yourself, Portia, and it was a terrible day I called you friend."

Portia shrugged. "I can live with that," she said, smugly. "I'm going to live, see?"

Yusef seethed. "And what will that be worth in a world consumed by the living dead?"

Vision blurry and breath falling short, Valerie lunged forward and stuck her knife into Portia's neck. Falling head long, she felt a calm vibration ripple through her body as her grip on the light of the world slipped by the failing beat of her pulse.

When she thought of death and dying, she always thought that she would feel cold, but she did not. Warmth washed over her. Somewhere—it seemed like far away—she heard the sound of fierce gagging and choking. And then, all at once, she was lifted up, and there was a friendly face.

"Lynwa," Yusef whispered.

Valerie stared into the man's face, feeling warmth and relief rise within her. She wanted to speak, to tell him that it was everything she could have asked for. But she could see in his eyes that he already understood.

"We are victorious," Yusef said, through sudden tears. "We do not have the same god, Lynwa. So, you tell him. Go and tell your god that we are victorious."

She felt a slight descent into a cloudy surface, as her vision blurred into a flare of white and gray. Then she watched her friend and mentor dash into the glory of victory, into the red light where the weapon to destroy their enemy lay in wait.

The white faded to darkness, and the cloudy surface beneath her was the mattress of a hospital gurney, set low to the floor. Relieved she had not died, Valerie tried to raise her right hand to her head, which was heavy and aching. Her hand stopped short. She immediately felt the tension of restraints on her wrist. Lifting her heavy head, she peered down the length of her body, seeing the outline of padded cuffs on her wrists and ankles, which were chained to the rails of the gurney.

Panic pulsed through her. Weak and confused, she rattled each of the chains, challenging their strength against her feeble will. The room was dark and empty with only one door, which had a thin, vertical slit for a window. Blue light flickered on the other side, leaving a purple glow on all it touched within.

A bony hand, cold and white, rose over the edge of the bed and settled on Valerie's shin. And then there were the eyes, a rotting orange that appeared over the bed's rim. A shock of curly white hair encased the face of a skeletal old woman, whose cheek-bones jutted out like crags. The blue light illuminated the veins and sores, each one cracking and splotching her chalky, white skin.

"I've found you, little breaker," the old woman rasped, grinning. Her lips cracked, dripping blood. "Wherever you go, wherever you think you're safe, I will find you." The old woman's eyes coasted slowly forward. A groan issued from somewhere in the witch's throat. "You must submit. Or..." The face rose revealing two rows of brown and yellow teeth and a red tongue within the mouth. "You will never know the ease of rest again. I will haunt every dream... I will lurk in the shadow of every thought..." The hag rose over her, her face twisted in livid fury. "I will drive you mad!"

Valerie screamed, shaking the chains and binds savagely. The covers flew off of her bed in a flurry. She snapped up and held her face in her palms, resting her elbows on her knees. Her body was cold and beaded with sweat. After a few heavy breaths, she tried to swallow, but her mouth was parched and sticky.

Pam was in the kitchen frying up a midnight snack of something. Whatever it was, it stank of burning hair and spoiled broccoli. Trying her best to hold her breath as she delved into the kitchen, Valerie plundered the cabinets for the headache medicine.

"Nightmare?" Pam asked, her voice light and sweet.

Valerie nodded. "Something like that."

"It's a horror," Pam said, cheerfully. She moved to the left and drew out a long knife from the block and began dicing something on the cutting board. Valerie swallowed the pills as she glanced to see what stank so badly.

Her eyes flared open. With quick and precise slices, Pam was chopping up each of her fingers and tossing them into the frying pan. Blood spurt from the stumps, flooding the counter tops to dripping. Pam's grin was wide and bright. "It's all one great horror."

She turned to look at Valerie, her face pale and sagging, smacked with an overlay of mortician's makeup. Her neck bore a thin red line where something had cut through. A crude patchwork of stitches held the head and stump together. Pam's smirk stretched past normal limits, wider and wider until her blue lips cracked apart and bled black ooze. Her hand idly chopped at the stump of her hand.

"It is a horror, Valerie Zeta," Pam said. "Come home to me."

The glass of water in Valerie's hand dropped, shattering on the tile floor. Paralyzed once again, Valerie stared in abject terror at the contortion just feet from her. She felt shadows grow and deepen behind her. There was something in the darkness. It whispered things, and then Pam would say them.

"In the end, you're a feast for maggots, Valerie," Pam echoed the words, and deep within her sweet voice, there was another deeper voice vibrating within it. "I can feel them in me. Squirming. Eating. This is the end of us all."

The thing behind Valerie towered in the shadows, its limbs scraping at the walls. It grew confident in Valerie's mounting terror. As it expanded, the shadows crept over the walls slowly overtaking the kitchen's light. Soon, it would take everything, and when it did, Valerie knew she would not escape.

Valerie's hand shot forward, grabbed Pam by the chest, and pulled the stake from her heart. As black ooze spewed, Valerie wheeled around, thrusting the stake into shadows. The definitive vibration through her hand told her a clean and solid strike had been made. The towering creature in the shadows howled and retreated into the dark, which rolled back with it until the universe was white again.

She stood alone now, amid an ivory landscape. In the distance, a sun suddenly broke over an indistinct horizon. As its lemon-haze spilled over, a range of hills grew from the light. Then there was a valley with giant, solitary trees, rich flowing grass, and crags of stone. The sky flashed light blue, while white and gray tufts of clouds puffed into life. She was standing on an outcropping of rock, which offered an excellent view of the valley.

Something gripped her left arm lightly. She turned, facing the man next to her. She smiled at him *Yusef*, she thought. *You found me.*

Yusef, radiant and young, grinned at Valerie. "It is you who have found me. You have learned the dreamsight."

Valerie gazed out at the landscape. "Is that what this is? A dream?"

Yusef shrugged. "It is a world," he said. "This is but one. But so you can understand, yes this is a dream."

"This is how I find them, isn't it?" Valerie asked. "This is how I find the others?"

Yusef nodded. "It is how I found you in my time," he said. "When your name was Lynwa. In time you will learn to control the dreamsight better."

Valerie thought for a moment. "I have to find you in the world," she said. "The waking world, don't I?"

"You are ready," he affirmed. "There is a great responsibility that I must pass to you."

"The Mantle?"

"Yes. What you witnessed was the night that I obtained it. Our victory. You were there, young lady. Your nightbreaker soul has traveled through time since then. Now here you are, the only one of this dispensation with the strength and will to possess it."

"How will I find you?" she asked.

Yusef turned and pointed behind them. "I have come as close as I can to you. You must come to rest of the way. Follow the markers," he said. In the distance, Valerie could see the vague skyline of downtown Montes Claros. A line of hills cut into the westside.

West, Valerie thought. She could see a faint path cutting through the long stretch of terrain between the point of rock where she stood and the city.

Yusef then pointed into the northern limits where there was the vague outline of a cliff, rough and craggy. "There," Yusef said. "Finish the journey. I am waiting for you."

North, Valerie thought.

Adria did not bother Valerie that morning with talk of chores and responsibility. Everyone was committed to the plan of allowing her to recover from her mounting exhaustion and injuries. Relative to her normal time, Valerie had slept in and was glad of it. She missed the morning grind of sending the children off to school, which could be hectic and mind-numbing so early in the morning.

The extra sleep had already helped her body feel replenished. In her mind, however, there was something that nagged her, like the lingering fragments of a meaningful dream that she could not totally remember. Parts of the dream had not been pleasant, she recalled.

With the house empty, Valerie warmed a hearty breakfast of black beans and rice and a scrambled egg. As she ate, flashes of the dream came back to her: a man's face, a finger pointing into a sweeping green landscape.

West of Montes Claros, there was a grassy wilderness she had wanted to hike since she had arrived. It was a gorgeous stretch of earth, but there never seemed to be any time to explore it.

If I've got the day off, she thought. *Today was as good as any.* Once finished, she dressed and packed a bag of quick snacks and a change of bandages for her leg.

Warren's little one-bedroom hole in the wall was on the way to the bus stop. As she passed by, she noticed the truck was gone. *Off somewhere,* Valerie thought. Unable to resist, she rang the bell and waited. His landlady, a withered old woman, answered the door.

"Yes?" she asked, her tiny, wrinkled face cringing in the glare of the sun. In the many months that Valerie had lived in this neighborhood, only this woman had not been able to remember who the young American was.

"Can I leave a message for Warren?" She spoke as clearly and cleanly as possible in the hope that the woman would understand.

"Who?" the woman asked, squinting.

Valerie wanted to laugh but she held back. "Warren," she said, pointing at the small cottage at the end of the woman's property. "The American man you rent to. Can I leave a message for him?"

"Ah American," she said nodding. "Wait a moment." The woman entered her small home, and returned to Valerie with a pad of paper and a pen. She handed them to Valerie. "Go ahead."

Valerie took the pad and pen and scrawled a quick note. She tore off the slip of paper, folded it, and handed it to the lady.

"When he arrives," the landlady said. "I will give this to him."

Valerie offered to return the pad and paper, but the lady had already closed the door.

"Thank you," Valerie called out. She turned on her heel and was off.

A bus ride to the western edge of the city brought her to an outdoor tour service which specialized in taking people into the bumpy and sometimes hazardous regions of the wilderness beyond the reach of even the most remote towns and secluded farms.

She paid the guide, Daniel, who was a friend of Rodrigo's. Daniel was a man who valued the weight of money in his hand. So, for every mile she wanted to go beyond his normal limit, she paid him more. Farther and farther, they went, over rough terrain, cutting through hillsides and slopes. There finally came a point where he would go no farther, saying that it was not worth the wear to his vehicle. Valerie stepped out of the truck and thanked him.

"Wait," he called. "You have to come back with me. I can't just leave you out here."

Undaunted, Valerie gave him a smirk and answered, "You can wait if you want. But," and she turned and pointed North. "That is where I'm going."

The man cringed. "There? Why? There is nothing out there."

Valerie shrugged. "Like I said, you can wait if you like."

The man threw up his hands and ticked his tongue. "You will pay me to wait?"

"Sure," Valerie said. "If I'm not back by dark, please do not send people after me. That would be embarrassing."

"Will you be back by then?" he asked, a hint of plea in his voice.

"Should be," she said, and started for a very a familiar outcropping of stone that overlooked the valley.

Once she hiked to the top of the rocks, she observed the land. Flashes of her dream came alive. She had been here before; she could feel it. Studying the northern landscape, she could see the outline of a cliff rising out of the land. *That's it,* she thought. There was something there, waiting for her to discover. From her height, a path through the green and rocky land was easy to see. Descending the rocks, she started down what she estimated was a two or three-hour trek.

The closer she came, the more she could feel the draw of gravity toward the place. The rock formation loomed into view, a great trapezoid of dark stone, cracked and leaking water through tiny rivulets. Blossoming vegetation crawled up the rocks in some parts. Circling the mass of stone, Valerie searched for the best way to scale it. In the process, however, she found a thin slash down the rockface whose shadows promised entry. When she approached and peered within, a refreshing draft hissed outward cooling her sticky face. She drew her flashlight out of her bag, clicked it on, and squeezed through the fissure.

Valerie had no idea what she was looking for. But that all seemed secondary to the act of moving forward. The tunnel widened farther in making it easier to walk. Eventually, the tunnel opened up into a lighted cavern.

Slashes of afternoon light cut through the cavern's stony ceiling, settling on the sandy ground. A shallow pond of clear runoff water glistened in the center of the cavern, rippling with the steady drip of water from above. On the other side of the pond, a vast alcove with smooth sandstone walls towered from the ground to the ceiling. Even in the half-light, Valerie made out the hieroglyphics panning the walls. Held within the alcove, there was a stone sarcophagus whose lid was slanted open.

Though wonder fueled her movements, she remained wary of possible ambush. Valerie circled the pond, in awe yet cautious. She arrived at the alcove, whose smooth walls loomed over her.

Where do I even start? she thought, resting her hands on her hips.

The writings were not in hieroglyphics as she previously thought. It was just an array of drawings etched into the sandstone. Like a comic book, the engravings told a story from ceiling to floor, left to right, panel by panel. Considering the detail and quality, the act might have taken a team of ten men decades to accomplish.

She examined the sarcophagus. It was fashioned of a single chunk of dark rock. The interior had been hollowed out and polished like a bathtub. The lid, an easy three-ton monster, was slid to the side, angled at a slant.

She felt a sudden rush of memory. She was going to meet someone here. The matter was important. Valerie turned and surveyed the cavern, her eyes searching the darkness all round for a person. There was no one, and if there had been, he left no trace of his passing.

She decided to focus on the etchings. The pictures seemed easy enough to follow. *If only Warren were here,* Valerie thought. She reached into her bag, pulling out the pen and pad of paper. Then, by shining her light upon the wall then back to her paper, she began to summarize each panel for later study.

Panel 1: A giant imposing figure with slanted, angry-looking eyes seated on a throne (a god?). Little people lined up at the foot of the figure. Worshiping, possibly.

Panel 2: Same thing only there's a pit of fire and little people are throwing creatures into it. (Animal sacrifices? Children?)

Panel 3: A cityscape, ruined, burning and human bodies are strewn everywhere.

Panel 4: People are armed, forming up against the god, who stares on angrily.

Panel 5: The god is gone—replaced by a giant gargoyle which breathes fire.

Panel 6: The people bow under the fire; some burn, some are untouched.

Panel 7: A new group of people (warriors—13) They're formed up side-by-side, armed with spears and swords, raising them skyward.

<u>Panel 8</u>: The warriors are attacking the giant gargoyle, each taking hold of various parts of its body.

<u>Panel 9</u>: The gargoyle breaks apart. The warriors hold the body parts at the sky, while storm clouds whirl around them.

<u>Panel 10</u>: One of the warriors takes the gargoyle's head. He leaves the other warriors.

<u>Panel 11</u>: This warrior (the Paladin?) sits in some kind of temple or tomb. He is now wearing the gargoyle head like a helmet. Thin plumes of smoke rise from his body.

<u>Panel 12</u>: A traveler enters the temple. He is bowing before the warrior with the gargoyle head.

<u>Panel 13</u>: The traveler takes the gargoyle head, wearing it now like the first warrior had done. The first warrior is no longer seen.

That was all. The faint streaks of sunlight beaming in were now a murky orange. It would be dark soon. Though the thought of camping a night in an ancient and undiscovered tomb intrigued her, she decided to wrap up with the promise to come back with Warren. The look on his face alone was going to make all of this worth it.

The hike back was arduous. Her leg had begun to throb, and though she wanted to wait until she got to the truck, she stopped halfway to change her bandage. The old one had soaked a fresh stain of blood. She was already dreading having to listen to Adria complain about not taking the day to rest. Since the guy that owned the truck was a close friend of Rodrigo's, there was no way this little trek could stay a secret. Yeah, she would hear about it, but whatever. Everybody got to sit back and think about what was important. Valerie was responding in kind.

The day had been tranquil, full of air and life and peace. The world was a vast and plentiful place, slow and patient in its turning. So many people complained that there wasn't enough time. But there was plenty. The sun moved ponderously over the earth, steady and constant. The clouds flared outward, slow-motion explosions of vapor pregnant with moisture. They crackled with the first signs of a storm as the sun dipped behind the low range of hills.

How much of her drama mattered at all to the world? Considering even the monstrosities she had seen and the evil that lurked in the shadows, did any of it matter to the world? Or did it simply turn slowly like some galactic tortoise, indifferent to the battles and struggles played upon its shell?

When she got back to the truck, she found the guide eager to get back to the city.

"We'll settle up when we get back," he said, turning the engine over.

"Works for me." Valerie threw her bag in the back and settled in the passenger seat.

"Did you find anything out there?"

"No," Valerie said. "Like you said, nothing out there."

There were a lot of things Warren wished he could have back. Mostly, they were moments when he made a bad call. Tonight was one of those times. He should not have gone out on a hunt without Valerie. Day jobs were supposed to be easy, though. Revenants were easy to track, find, and kill during their hours of weakness. The job was also close by, just under an hour's drive to a ranch outside the city.

Looking back, Warren realized that he should have read the simplicity and convenience of the job as red flags. Perhaps having Valerie around these many months had dulled his sense of caution. After this failure, he would not make the same mistake.

Learning a lesson was not the biggest concern, however. Warren suspected that he was being followed, that he had fallen into a trap. He tried to convince himself that he was just being paranoid. But he had seen the same black SUV in his rear view mirror for the third time. It made sense. It had always been a matter of time. Eventually, he and Valerie were bound to attract the full attention of the enemy.

Amid his rising anxiety, one thing was certain: he was out of the game. He was sloppy and his heart was no longer in it. The tactics of the enemy had shifted, and Warren didn't have the fight in him to adapt. His pathetic struggle with the revenant was proof of that. An activity that had once been so easy for him now left him with a sprained ankle and a mauled forearm. The makeshift bandages were already soaked, and the excess blood dripped onto the floor of his truck.

The revenants were emboldened now, no longer the skittish cowards they once were. This particular one, even in the day, had leaped out of its hole and overpowered him. It would have killed him had it not been for the boom of the rancher's shotgun. That had delayed the thing's attention for the precious second Warren needed to slash the creature along its chest. Adrenaline and clever weaving among the trees had helped him lose his aggressor. But it did not help his blood-loss problem.

Warren's vision was blurry as he limped from the truck to his small cottage. Once he was inside, he limped to the bathroom where he began to clean and dress his wounds. It was a messy affair. Hands shaking, caked with dried and newly wet patches of blood, Warren washed them before setting the bandages. The dressings were as good he could expect to do himself, though he needed Adria to stitch him up later.

Through his swimming thoughts, he heard a knock at the door. Through the window, he spied the slight form of Senhora Marietta, his landlady. She was probably there to investigate what the commotion was all about. Gingerly, he hobbled to the door, put on his best face and opened it. The old woman made a very nosy inspection of the situation from the doorway, while absently handing over a little slip of paper.

"What is all this red in here?" she said, pointing a bony finger at the small flecks of blood trailing toward the bathroom. "Are you bleeding?"

"No," he said, trying to assure her. "I am painting a new bird house, Senhora. I thought a bright red would add color to the property."

"Do you think I'm stupid?" she asked, her squinted eyes glaring at him pointedly.

Warren chuckled. "I cut my arm, but I'm fine, really. I will clean it up." He held up the little slip of paper and offered an apologetic smirk. "Thank you, Senhora, good night."

He closed the door. Limping back to his kitchenette, he sat and opened the folded slip of paper that revealed Valerie's handwriting.

Hope you're not out there doing what I think you're doing. We're a team.

Damn that girl. He smiled and laughed through a sudden throb of pain. Standing, he decided he would make something to eat then sleep some to recover. As he pulled a pan down from the rack to scramble an egg, he heard ticking at the window of the bedroom. Limping, he went to investigate. As he came to the window, he heard the faint clawing of a creature scampering in a circle around his home.

Warren paled. It could be a stray dog, teasing the chickens outside. But he knew; he knew he'd been followed. He was safe as long as he stayed inside. The revenant could not come in unless—

The door burst open and the slender form of a woman stood in the frame. He wanted it to be Valerie, angry with him for going out without her. But it was not Valerie, and he stood no chance against her. As he reached for his knife, she was already within range, throwing her first punch, right to the nose. Warren staggered backwards, falling into the wall, which kept him standing. Blade out, he slashed feebly at her upper body, but her movements were a blur: she knelt and rose with a quick chop to his neck followed by a hard jab to the stomach. He toppled over and felt himself crash onto the tile floor.

He didn't want to quit. He didn't want to fail. He wanted to be in the fight, but it had been beaten out of him. Breath short and racked with pain, his body shut down and his blurred vision faded.

At first, he thought it was a nightmare—something his mind had created out of the guilt and horror he felt upon seeing Marty's end. Warren's body was tied to a chair with electrical cords. His arms were pinned behind his back, and his ankles were bound together. To free himself, his best option was to wobble until he fell over, hoping the chair might break apart. But the truth was he lacked the energy to do that even. And what would be the point?

"I've taken the liberty of reading some of your greatest hits here," a woman's voice said. There was a twisted sweetness to her tone.

A woman in her early thirties appeared from his right. She had his journal in her hands. As she absently flipped through it, she set a chair in front of him. She was a beautiful woman: well-fit, long brown hair dressed in a braid, white unblemished skin, and innocent blue eyes. The red lipstick was a bit much, though.

Plopping down in her chair, the woman's eyes never left the journal. She held up a finger and cleared her throat. "Ahem. I have to admit to myself that I'm losing my edge,'" she read with a mocking, masculine tone. She glanced at him from beneath her lowered brow then continued. "'Most of my assumptions have been wrong. That is probably because I'm basing them on outdated information.'" The woman pursed her lips. "Wait, that's not the saddest one."

She scavenged the pages until she pegged one with a finger. "Here it is. 'The possibility has crossed my mind that I could just stop. I could stop doing all of this. Valerie has already surpassed every expectation. In most cases, I feel like I am the one who is in the way, holding her back.'"

The woman giggled and stomped her feet in mockery of it. "You really are a pathetic maggot-bag."

She slapped Warren fiercely across the face with such force that his vision flashed white. "Where is she?" Her face changed so suddenly to finely chiseled contempt. "Hmm? You know, we really thought you'd bring her with you out to our ambush. But when it was just you, I thought, 'Hey, maybe they're on to us.' Then I remembered you're pathetic, so I decided that following you back to your little HQ would be just as good." She stood up, waving her hands about. "And I gotta tell ya'. You've impressed me."

She slapped him across the other cheek, an act that she seemed to enjoy more than find useful. "Will she be back soon?"

No, he hoped, grimly. *She isn't ready—not for this evil.* Warren flexed his sore jaw and blinked his eyes, which were tearing up under the crackling fire rising in his cheeks.

"I can be patient," she said, nodding and faking all the intonations of compassion. She sat down in front of him like a proper lady. "I am a patient woman, Warren." She smiled brightly. "Yeah, maybe we should get to know each other." Drawing herself up excitedly, she pointed at him. "You are Warren Brant, aren't you? I mean, I never met you before all this, but I've heard of you. You were supposed to be a big timer, even for a Hound." Her eyes combed his body as though appraising livestock. "But now that I've got a look at you, I have to say there's nothing very big about you." She brought up his knife. "Except maybe this." Examining it, she stared in feigned awe. "Do you think maybe," she leaned in close to him and squinted, "you know, you're compensating for something?" Squinting deeper, she glanced down at his crotch. "Know what I mean?"

Warren looked her in the eyes. "You must be Ismena," he croaked, then cleared his throat. "I've heard about you, too. It must be a bad day for the Red Widow if she let you out of the Fighting Pits. How was it down there, by the way, all those years?"

Ismena's face twitched under the strain of appearing empowered and unfazed, when she wasn't in fact. She managed to reign in her fury and resume her antics. "The Red Widow?" she hummed with a smirk. "Oh, you *are* slipping. Velvet Cake has seen her day, which has come," she tossed Warren's head to one side and then the other, "and gone. There's a new sheriff in town, Mister Brant. One who recognizes my many talents as being a positive contribution to the advancement of the Highborn. The Red Widow's days are nearly over."

Who? he wanted to ask, though he knew silence was best here. Warren didn't bother trying to hide his discomfort with the implications of what she said.

Ismena reveled in it. She was the type of person that rarely outsmarted someone, and when she did, it was a moment to savor.

With a self-important smirk, Ismena plopped into the chair again. "Ready to give up? No? Okay, you know what? We'll just sit here and read till your little lady gets back. What's her name, Valerie? Ugh. Tacky. Can I ask you a question? Why did you betray 'Her Lady Majesty'? I mean, she threw me in the Fighting Pits and told me I would actually like it." Her lovely simper cracked open to a scowl. "Left me there to clean up her monster problem." She grabbed Warren by the hair and yanked violently. "Just like you. Like I was some kind of dog. Took me away from Edgar, separated us."

As though catching herself slipping, she smiled wide and released Warren's hair. She wiped the grime and sweat on her pants. "But I'm over it, you know? I don't hold a grudge or anything. Edgar and I are reunited, and we are *this* close to obtaining the power necessary to put them all under control." Ismena's eyes flared wide as she slapped a hand over her mouth. "Oops," she chirped. "Have I said too much?" She giggled. "You know, I'm really disappointed. I'm used to Velvet Cake being one step ahead. Say what you want about her lack of resolve, but she's got a clever noggin. It's just sad to see that she's not putting up a fight. Kind of like you. I hope your little girl is up to the challenge."

Warren sighed wearily. "Ismena, it's always in those moments when you think you're that far ahead, that you really need to stop and think about where you've gone."

Ismena's eyes softened and stared into Warren's as though a warm revelation had come to her. "Oh my heavens," she said, and held her hand to her chest. "You really know how to break through all my barriers and just...you know...*teach* me."

She rolled off a fit of laughter and brought up his notebook. Turning the pages wildly, she pegged one and held up a finger while she read the page. "'The reason we came here was very clear in the beginning. We needed to learn more about the Mantle of the Dragon, and if at all possible, find it. But these many months have yielded very little. Based on Marshall's assumptions and my own, I was sure that we were close. What is certain, however, is that the Highborn are searching for it, but in ways that I had not expected.

"'They are enthralling revenants through what Marshall called trollskap, an ancient form of undead magic. One of their abilities is to enter the dreams of their victims, to manipulate mortals and undead alike. And if an undead's will is strong enough, it can even possess their victims. I'm now forced to assume that this can be done at long distances.

"'I can't shake the feeling that someone else is at work here, though. Either that, or the Red Widow has become so desperate as to use revenants. Using them, training them, and even empowering them is not something she would normally condone. But, I am certain that they are being used to seek out the Mantle, wherever it is hidden.

"'That of course broaches the question of *why. Why use them?* My best answer is that this strategy is something like a scorched earth approach. It is assumed that the Mantle attracts the undead unto it; it wants to be found and it wants to be in their possession. It is simple logic that if you created enough undead, all attracted to its power, that eventually its location would be discovered.'"

Ismena simpered and nodded. "You're not stupid, Warren. I'll give you that. Of course, you had a lot of help from Big Daddy Marshall." She leaned in close and squinted. "No hard feelings, right? I mean, I'm not going to lie to you. Interrogating him was uh...well it was liberating. I found out a lot about myself, how far I've come.

"I still remember the day he came for me. I was almost a teenager, not a little child like when the others were taken. Do you know what he told me when I asked him why he waited so long to take me? He said, 'I was worried this life would not suit you well, Ismena. You were not...' And he paused here, like he was looking for right word—which really irked me—then he said, 'You didn't show the same stability as the others. I thought living a normal life first might balance you.'"

Ismena gnashed her teeth and stared off a moment. "I mean, I know I should feel grateful or whatever because he looking out for me, but..." She shook her head. "Do you know what it's like living with adoptive parents? They don't *get* you. You feel like an alien everywhere you go. Understand? Anyway, he should have got me sooner. Because this…" She held her arms up. "This is where I belong."

She sighed, letting her arms plop on her lap. "I couldn't get Marshall to talk, but..." she paused and stared off for a few seconds. Then she sat back with a cool smirk rising on her face. "Beheading him...that was...my heavens, it was legendary. That was *the* Marshall Lentz. I'm not pissing you off, am I? Because if I am, we can totally change the subject."

She giggled and shifted in her chair. "How about this. Why don't you tell me where you hid all his writings? Not that we really need them anymore, but it just irks me that we let you guys get what we wanted back there. No? Fine. I can see you've had a bad day; so why don't I try to learn something from what you wrote."

She held up a finger and turned the pages of his journal. Finding a page, she continued reading. "'Valerie is starting to have the dreams. Just as Marty had. I'm afraid to tell her what they mean. I feel it best to stay out of the way, and let her find the meaning in all of it. I hold out the hope that through the dreams, the Paladin will contact her. If, of course, she is worthy to take on the burden of safe-guarding the Mantle into future generations.

"'The most horrible part of that is not knowing what that means for her. What will her life be like afterward? Whatever it is, I am convinced that Valerie is the only one capable of it. When Marty and I first began studying the Mantle's legend, we both thought it was the answer, but now I am convinced that it isn't. Valerie is.'"

Ismena snapped the book shut and faked a dry heave. "Got a little girl crush?" she asked, her face still cringing. "It's kind of creepy when you think about it."

"A bit salty considering your preferences, Ismena."

Her fist struck his nose quick and clean, throwing his head back and opening up the flood gates from his nostrils. The livid scowl on her face melted to feigned compassion. "Oh, look what I've done," she moaned. She set the journal on the kitchenette table and swiped a napkin from a small dispenser. She stemmed the bleeding by holding the napkin to his nose. "I'm so sorry about that. You've already lost so much today. Wouldn't want to kill you, now would we? You just can't go throwing me into a passion like that."

Ismena chuckled and settled in front of him again, holding the napkin to his nose. "You know, for a while we thought you were still working for the Lady when you were able to get here to this filthy piece of earth. We thought you were on assignment to find the artifact. But it turns out you betrayed her, too. Can't say that I blame you. It's kind of the thing these days, you know? So, we thought you'd be a good distraction for any of her efforts, which—I have to say—have been really pathetic next to ours. But you're guilty of murder. You can't go killing our vago and think you can get away with it."

She lifted the napkin, checked to see if the bleeding had stopped, then clogged the flow again. "This is an important time for everybody. The Lord of the Undead will be named soon. Everything's going to get sorted out then. Right now, everybody's gotta choose a side. And here you are going rogue. So it's only natural that you get cleaned out first." She looked at Warren. "Do you know what it is?"

She's stalling, he realized. *She wants Valerie to come...* Warren stared at her, knowing that he couldn't let that happen.

Ismena glared back, her awe evident in her glazed eyes. "It's the sacred birthright of the Highborn." She took the napkin away and leaned in close. "A gift from the Night Masters. The Mantle of the Dragon belongs to the Highborn. And you..." She searched his eyes. "Little wittle Warren and your skank girlfriend thought you could get in the way of that?"

Ismena drew back and sat up straight. "That's uh...what's it called?" She snapped her fingers and then pointed at Warren. "Hubris," she said suddenly. "Yeah, that's hubris. Just an idiot's pride. Well, it's time you were reminded of your place. It's time everyone learned their place. Especially your little girl. She's going to receive her education very soon. Which reminds me." She stood up. "You know, I've been patient. I kept thinking that she would come barging in here any second to save you from me, but it looks like she's out with a boy. I hope you're not jealous, you old sicko. I can see that I've worn out my welcome, so it's time we parted ways."

Ismena returned the chair to the kitchenette then stood in front of Warren, her hands lazily placed on her hips. "It's been good getting to know each other, but it seems I have another appointment. I'm taking Edgar and our new pet vago to meet a nice little family. Oh, what were their names?" she snapped her fingers, then smiled, holding her finger up. "La Paz, Le Pez, Rodrigo and Edira, Adria? I'm not entirely sure how these dirty people say it, but word on the street is that they have an American beauty living with them. I'm sure they're real sweet."

Warren would not speak, and tried not to let his sudden panic show on his face. Ismena grinned wide and skipped behind Warren's chair. She tilted it back and started to drag it to the backdoor. "I'm going to let you and our newest vago get a fresh start, and since I'm sure you won't let my little puppy in, I'm going to set everything up outside. He's just out here."

Kicking the door open, she dragged Warren through it, out onto the backyard where Warren had planted a small garden. Setting his chair down, she stood in front of him, slapped her hands on her legs and smiled excitedly. "Well, this is it, buddy. Let's have a moment of pause to let your girl jump in at the last second to save you." Mena smacked her lips and rolled on her heals, snapping and popping her hands while she waited perhaps fifteen long seconds. Behind Warren, he heard the shuffle of something approach. The telling growl confirmed Ismena's threat.

Almost there, Warren thought.

He had seen men die before. He had watched their light go inward, back to where it came from. Peace washed over him. Somewhere within, he heard the spontaneous giggle of babies. His. He saw the spray of light within the hair of a woman he loved the moment she touched him. It was all there, waiting. There was just this last thing...

"Ismena," he said, clearing his throat. She looked at him with sarcastic interest. He glared at her, so that she would understand that what he said was true. "You have this one chance, right here, get it? You walk away, and let this go then you can live whatever life you want. You'll be spared. But if you go through with this, there will be no turning back."

It was me holding Valerie back, Warren realized. *And when she sees me like this...*

"Oh, well that's sweet of you, but—"

"Shut up, I'm not done." He felt fire in his chest, hot and growing. "You're about to make a very powerful enemy for yourself. She's going to start something that no one will be able to stop. Not you. And not whoever you're working for. Everybody's got to choose a side, huh? I'd choose hers—or get the hell out of her way."

Ismena's face twitched with a cruel mixture of confusion, self-doubt, and resentment. Her hands, once playfully snapping, were now held still but for the nervous fiddling of her fingers. A scowl cracked her face. "Considering what I'm about to do to you, excuse me if I have difference of opinion." She brandished his blade, flicking the edge on his nose. She lowered the point to his chest, holding it over his skin. "I mean, where is she?"

As she began to cut into his flesh, carving out deep lines, Warren felt the revenant behind him rise up. Then there was the violent tug at his neck, teeth and jaw tearing into the meat.

Warren closed his eyes. Soon the tension and agony eased as he started his journey inward. To the place where memories lived. They came back to him, those that he had buried deep down, the ones he made himself forget. None of that was necessary now. He had won the fight. And now another would take up the fire, and with it, she would burn them all to the ground, leaving a better world than the one he now left.

__Chapter 16_____

Valerie just wanted to get back home and get clean. She was pretty sure her bandage had soaked up more sweat in the late heat of the day than any trickle of blood. Dark was setting in, but she didn't want to wait until morning to see Warren's eyes as he feasted on her amazing discovery. The truth was that she was pleased to be able to make him proud in a way that he could really appreciate.

A bus ride and a two-block stroll led her to Warren's old lady lent bachelor pad. Seeing his truck parked on the curb excited her. *Good, he's home,* she thought. Though sticky and tired, she bounced in high spirits to his door and rang the bell, hoping he would answer instead of Senhora Marietta.

When no one answered, she rang again. She hated to wake him, or the landlady, but on top of her discovery being exciting, it was also important. The Mantle was more than just a legend now. It was real, and they were close. Valerie was also certain that the Paladin was trying to reach her through her dreams, even though she could not remember everything from them. All things Warren needed to know.

Her smile vanished when she noticed a small trail of splattered blood on the concrete. The trail led inside.

Valerie climbed up and over the wall. Once inside, she dashed for the little one-bedroom cottage at the edge of the property. The lights were all on, and there were no immediate signs of struggle—until she entered the house.

The news was bad: a small pool of blood on the kitchenette floor, flecks of blood on the walls, and the pink, watered-down residue of it in the sinks. Most haunting was the crimson smear trailing to the backdoor. The door was ajar, beating lightly in a passing breeze.

Valerie's heart thumped wildly, and during it all, she told herself that the blood wasn't his. *He was a soldier,* she assured herself. *He's smart. Warren wouldn't go down so—*

She found his ragged body bent in a rickety chair, bound to it with electrical cords. His clothing shredded, his skin covered in his own blood, his body clearly sent the message the enemy wished to leave. All of it was somehow acceptable—all of it except the bite wound on the neck, and carved in the flesh of his bare chest the word BROKEN.

Her body trembled with some unbearable emotion between terror and grief. Or was it failure? She could not know. Standing over his ravaged form, she gazed with numb eyes, both searching for a sign or a hint of meaning to any of it. Some part of her imagined that his body might jerk suddenly upward, that he would awaken and offer his final words.

What would he say? she wondered

Would he beg her to keep her word: the foolish promise of a headstrong girl who assured a father that she would protect his children? Could she look him in the eye and even claim such a thing? The morbidly blunt sight of his face obscured behind the tangle of his blood-soaked hair teased her with the obvious answer.

And then she fell at his knees, weeping. Her hands were frantic to find some way to touch him, to heal him, to bring him back. But this was always the way it was going to happen. There was always going to be a moment when the enemy struck back. Inside, her rage tried to ignite, but it had been her rage that had started this. It had been her impulsiveness and eagerness to taunt the enemy. Warren had to pay the price.

I killed him, she thought.

Valerie sobbed, grasping his face. "I'm sorry," she whispered, shuddering with the sudden awareness of a son and daughter that would never know him. *Braxton,* she thought, *Alma.* Two names, two people she had never met, and yet, she had robbed them of their father. Would they forgive her? Could they?

She lifted his clinched fist and pried it open to hold his hand. Inside his fingers, she found a tightly crumbled slip of paper. Gingerly, she opened it to read her own handwriting now stained with little flecks and smears of blood.

Hope you're not out there doing what I think you're doing. We're a team.

She gnashed her teeth, biting back the swell of regret. *I never thanked him,* she realized. *Not once.* Again, she ground her jaw, swearing to sky and silence that she would make it right. Not just for what she had done, but what she had to do next. There was the neck wound…the blood…

Do it quick, she coached herself. *Don't think about it.*

She unsheathed Pride in a flourish, raised Warren's grimy head to expose the neck then drove the knife in. She sawed the blade back and forth, through muscle and bone, her agony escaping her throat in muffled cries. When the head rolled over and plopped to the red clay turf, Valerie crumbled to the ground, her body convulsing with the spasms of something beyond grief. In her tear-blurred vision the sight of the bloody knife and red-soaked note mocked her.

Gasping, she felt her body weaken at the sound of the words in her mind. *We're a team. We're a team. We're a team.* The words resonated through time, already from a past that she had never fully understood or appreciated. They had been a team. All of them.

Valerie jerked upward, flying to her feet after a sudden and unbearable thought. She struck forward savagely as the images of Little Tiger slaughtered cracked across her mind. The shrill noise of her shrieks for help echoed across the barrier of Valerie's dark imagination. Her body pressed herself forward, through doors, over walls, and across what seemed to be an impossibly vast space in order to prevent the unthinkable.

Pacing back and forth, Mena loomed over the man she had just beaten. The guy had a dojo or something outside his house, so he had to know how to fight. His skills were nothing next to her power, though. The guy didn't go down as easily as Warren, but a little challenge was always gratifying. His woman and three children had run off to what Mena assumed was a bedroom. You could never be too sure in hovels such as these.

"I'm going to ask you again, Mr. Rodrigo," she said, emphasizing each word of her English. "I know you understand me, so don't try to play the ignorant savage with me. Although, I've gotta say, you certainly look the part." As Mena spoke her next line, she made a definitive hand gesture for each word. "Where-is-the-girl? The A-mer-i-can?"

The idiot stared off, ready for the next blow to his already swollen face. Mena felt a little embarrassed. She was ineffective, and Edgar was watching.

"Okay man," Mena relented, with a sigh. She squatted in front with him. "What's it gonna take? I mean, do you really want me to get extreme, here?" She searched his eyes, which still stared off defiantly.

"Fine," she said, throwing up her hands and rising. Mena set off for the bedroom. "I would like the court to recognize that I tried to be civil. What's the order we start with, biggest to smallest, or smallest to biggest?"

Mena then heard the sudden garbled outcry of the man as she strolled into the bedroom. "Oh, it's too late for that daddy," she said. "We're on to plan B."

She barged into the bedroom. "You," she ordered, reaching out for the youngest girl. She was a squat little thing, with lovely black curls. "Your daddy wants to talk to you."

The wet-faced child curled into her mother, shivering like a puppy. The mother—a dark thing with deep proud eyes—glared at Mena with a pathetic, self-righteous scowl. There was an indistinguishable something about her that made her seem like royalty. The mother's face was solid and unflinching, projecting the unconquerable nature of her spirit. She rose, setting her pups behind her. Like it was going to make a difference. It suddenly occurred to Mena that people really did live in some kind of fairyland: a place where victims were somehow the good guys.

People needed an education about power. They needed an education about the nature of the world. The strongest ruled the weakest. Period. This idiot woman, this whole idiot family was about to receive their lesson in full. Mena could have smacked the woman with all her strength, but she settled for shoving her back and snatching the little whelp of a girl out of her reach.

The wail that escaped the woman's mouth was well worth it. Not to mention the little maggot brother who—suddenly empowered by the illusion of heroism—rose from his own fetal position and released a laughable volley of punches into Mena's stomach.

"Are you trying to hurt me?" Mena asked, laughing. She swatted him away. The mother caught him as he twisted toward the floor. Mena pointed. "I'll kill them all, right here, right now." Mena glared a second more then pointed. "Stay."

The woman's once iron-strong face melted in grief. She clutched her other two pups, resigning herself to fate. That was lesson one. She caught on quick.

Mena took the little girl by the hand, shushing her lightly while petting her black curls. "Oh, it's all right," she whispered, smiling. She tried to keep her voice sweet and gentle. "You know, I always thought I'd have a little girl just like you. I want to take you to meet someone special. Would you like that?"

The girl's eyes and nose were flowing with tears and snot, which was a shame since she had seemed...cute for a minute there. And like her father, she spoke in garbled words.

"This way, out this door here," she directed, pulling on the girl's arm as they walked by the father who was frantically yelling. "Say bye to daddy."

It was annoying to watch them all squinty-eyed and leaking all over each other. The weeping and wailing was getting old, and this was all taking much longer than Mena anticipated.

"Please," a voice said. Mena held fast and turned. Out of the back bedroom, the oldest girl emerged, her eyes red and watery. She slowly approached. "Please. You take me. Not she." The older girl pointed at her sister. "I go. She stay."

The dad cried out with an agony in his eyes that betrayed his once stalwart gaze. He shook his head savagely, moaning in long begging gasps. It was a sign that he finally understood, too. Everybody was getting the big picture, and that was progress.

Mena smiled. "Well, I think we all understand each other now!" Mena let the little girl go, who then bolted for her father, wrapping her arms around his bloody, half-naked body.

Holding out her hand, Mena said, "Everybody's going to get their turn, but volunteers are always welcome. Come here, young lady."

As Valerie rounded the corner, the terrible imaginings all swirled into a tunnel vision. Her body glided through it, balanced and focused.

The house came into view; the bottom level was dark, but upstairs, all the lights were on. She knew the situation when her powers suddenly flushed through her. In stride, she opened her darksight and found all the forms she needed to find within the home. Clinging to each other in the upstairs bedroom were the fire orange silhouettes of Bruno and Adria. Walking into the living room was the deep orange ghost of Ester. There were three others with her: the tangerine shade of Rodrigo who flashed blue and green woes of pain. The way he was bound to a chair was all too familiar. And there she was, the livid scarlet of a woman Valerie knew from her dreams—and she was tugging at Little Tiger, who whimpered green trails of fright. Valerie struggled to keep her balance within the torrent of her mounting fury.

There were other complications, though. Outside on the floor of Rodrigo's training pad stood the silver and gray outline of a bulky revenant. It peered inward through the window of the small upstairs living room, eager yet unable to enter. Behind the revenant, concealed in the shadows, there was a bright silver and gold figure, an aura Valerie had yet to encounter. It was undead, but much more powerful...and old.

The strategy came to her in images, so perfectly woven together, it was as if Warren were speaking to her. She could charge the woman inside—the woman she wanted desperately to destroy—but that was a fool's trap. If Valerie charged her, then the woman would hold Rodrigo, Ester, or Little Tiger hostage. That would leave Valerie with the conundrum of watching them be cut to death, or the other impossible choice: having to offer herself in surrender. No. No more sacrifice, no more surrender. She just needed to get the woman outside...

In stride, she leaped over the home's outer wall, rolled onto the small lawn, leaped up the first level of the house, gripped the roof and pulled herself unto its flat top. She had trained here so many times. The history of the lessons, the many hot days, sweating and exerting herself, the pain, the bruises—she summoned them to her.

Checking her last step, she leaped over the lip of the roof and tackled the revenant at the window. It was allowed a brief moment to choke before she cut and tore its head loose. A groan issued from the shadows, one that both challenged her and preached warning. Valerie answered by rolling off the headless creature and spiking its severed head on the concrete. An angry roar responded. The silver and gold outline of the thing rushed forward into the faint yellow light burning down from the bounding street lights.

Valerie remembered her studies. *The undead,* Marshall noted, *may change their forms. They may transform into a mist or a fog. They may assume the form of certain feral predators, most commonly the wolf, the serpent, the bat, or their combination—the gargoyle. While in this form, much of their sorcery will not be available to them, but they will have increased strength, speed, and a hardened defense against physical attack.*

The creature that emerged from the shadows was man in shape, erect and walking upright. All else was an abomination of lizard, bat, and wolf. Its face was a man's but with an upturned nose and stretching nostrils. The ears were long, wide and pointed; the mouth was wide and toothless, but for two long and pointed incisors. Towering at eight feet, its bulky body was top heavy, with a broad, muscled chest, long and sinewy arms, whose skin was part scaled, part hairy flesh. Above its shoulders, a set of stunted appendages, like underdeveloped wings, branched out as though to spread.

Strafing her, the thing appraised Valerie with a calm and guarded calculation. Conventional strategy might have advised her to hold back and wait for it to strike, but Valerie didn't come to play defense.

Flipping Pride's blade upward, she locked eyes with the creature and rushed toward it. Lowering its face, the thing slashed at her chest. Valerie ducked and rolled below the strike. She rose and sliced a long gash across its ribcage. The silver did its work. Along the edges of the wound, flames erupted and smoldered. The thing roared, staggered back, and slashed with the other arm.

Predictable, Valerie thought. She leaped over the sweep, redirected her motion by launching off the arm then climbed on its scaly back. To steady herself, she gripped one of the infant wings. She then drove Pride into the soft space between its shoulder blade and ribs. The ensuing howl rattled the power lines of the neighborhood.

Perhaps reveling in the cry of her enemy a second too long, she wasn't prepared when it shook its torso wildly. Jarred loose by the motion, she flew from its back to the concrete. Valerie rolled on impact and shot up to her feet just in time to meet the woman's onslaught.

She was a spry banshee, screaming promises of murder with comical fury. The woman's attacks, though rampant, were practiced and precise. Under the assault, Valerie might have let something like fear set in—had she not noticed the knife in the woman's grasp. Valerie knew the silver edge and the bent blade, and she could see the gentle hand of the man who once wielded it...

Just as quick and just as strong, the woman's second pass was a slash at the neck, which Valerie pulled back from, sending her already testy balance into a funk. Valerie stepped back to correct, but the woman had already twisted around and was sweeping around for another pass at the back of Valerie's unsteady legs.

Accepting the fall, Valerie kicked her legs up, letting the blade pass under her. Valerie landed on her back, folded herself then recoiled to her feet, easily meeting the woman's ensuing strike. Catching the woman's forearm, Valerie drew herself in close and twisted the wrist. The woman screamed when cartilage and ligament popped in her joints. The knife fell into Valerie's expectant hand. *It worked,* Valerie thought, remembering how many times Rodrigo had done it to her.

Flipping into roll, the woman freed herself and scampered toward her monstrous companion. To her credit as a fighter, she hadn't been escaping. The woman raced to the side of her master, who was bent over and groveling in pain from the knife still lodged in a spot that its sinewy arms could not reach to remove.

The woman yanked the knife loose, and in one motion, lanced it, end-over-end, at Valerie's chest. With a crisp pick, Valerie caught it and whirled it point up. Double-bladed and steady, Valerie snarled at her opponents, sending an obvious invitation for round two.

The woman's eyes betrayed the secrecy of her intent. She glanced at the now unguarded door of the home, thinking perhaps that if she took a hostage, the tables might turn. A burst of power launched Valerie's body into the air, up and over her enemies. Twisting, Valerie touched down at the doorframe, weapons drawn and ready.

A mixture of anger and awe formed on the woman's face. She eyed Valerie as a victim might regard the audacity of a thief. With all the advantages except numbers gone from them, the pair let the truth of their situation set in.

Let them go, if they run. That was what Warren would say to Valerie. *You know where they rest.* Valerie didn't want to that happen, though. She wanted to finish it here, right now while her blood was pumping hot and eager.

"Come on," Valerie growled through gnashed teeth. She had to leash herself, hold her own enraged body back from attacking. "Come on!"

Free of the silver's effect on it, the creature offered a sidelong glance at Valerie. Somewhere in those blue-violet orbs was the admission of defeat—and a promise of revenge. It then leaped away, vanishing in the shadows. Before following in tow, the woman took three casual steps back, her grimace rising into a playful smirk.

After they had gone, Valerie waited many minutes watching the dark for a sign of them. When her power phased out, she knew the danger had gone. Whirling around, she entered the home through the shattered door.

The family was now reunited. Adria was doggedly cleaning Rodrigo's wounds, all of which—while in need of stitching—were not fatal. Ester and Little Tiger were caught up in Drigo's double embrace. They sobbed and clung to their beaten father. Bruno's eyes followed Valerie as she stormed through the home to the back bedroom.

In a flourish, Valerie drew out her black bag housing all the things she bought those many months ago in Arizona. Setting out the combat vest in front of her, she went to work strapping and clipping the casings for her knives. Pride would go over her heart. She clipped it down. She clipped the casing to Warren's blade across the abdomen. As she was about to insert the blade, she stopped short upon seeing a single word inscribed on it.

Two memories came back to her. The first was the night of her first fight with the revenants in the desert. It was the night she named her weapon as Warren suggested. She remembered asking if Warren had named his, and she recalled his veiled embarrassment as he admitted to her that he probably didn't deserve to. The second memory was her eighteenth birthday she spent here in Brazil. Her present from Warren was the word PRIDE engraved on her blade. She had loved it.

Now, as she stared at his weapon, she realized that sometime during their many battles, he had named his as well. PREJUDICE. The engraving on the blade whispered his final words to her. *They're all guilty.*

She shoved the blade into the casing.

Valerie could see Bruno peeking around the corner watching her, but she did not care. His mother called after him, and he reluctantly returned to the living room where they were still avidly attending to Rodrigo.

Valerie let her hair loose, doggedly pulled it back into a ponytail, and then bound it up tighter. After peeling off her loose cargo pants, she tore off the bandage on her thigh, wiped the wound clean, and began to wrap a fresh dressing. Once finished, she stepped into her black form-fitting pants then laced up her boots. She tore her sticky shirt loose and wiped the blood, sweat and grime from her body. After wriggling into the sports bra, she slid into the combat vest. As she zipped it up, a feeling of wholeness came over her.

Rolling up the rest of her things did not take long. Casting the bag over her shoulder, she left the bedroom. In a haze, she crossed the once familiar space of the living room, where the La Paz family was gathered, whimpering and whispering words of encouragement. She was almost out of the door, when a voice called out to her.

"Valerie," Rodrigo said. Though she wanted to keep moving, her body stopped short. Ashamed, she turned to Rodrigo, her eyes downcast.

"Warren?" he asked.

Valerie shook her head. After a moment, she drew herself up and squared her shoulders. "I am sorry," she said, managing to look at Rodrigo through the glare of water in her eyes. "I'm sorry for putting your family in danger."

Gathering courage, Valerie looked at Adria, who stood among her small and beautiful family, huddled and clinging to each other, one heart and soul together. They had paused, staring at her. Was it fear in their eyes? Was it loathing? They were entitled to it all. She had brought this on them.

"Senhora," Valerie said, leaning her head in a small bow. "Thank you for sharing your home with me."

"What if they come back?" Bruno blurted, his voice tremulous.

"That," Valerie roared in English then calmed herself and made the switch. "That will not happen."

Valerie was prepared to turn and vanish, but Little Tiger broke away and dashed for Valerie's legs. She wrapped herself around Valerie's knees, squeezing. Valerie felt her eyes flare wide, filling with hot tears. More than anything, Valerie wanted to crouch down and gather the little thing into her arms. She wanted to kiss the girl's face and promise her she was safe...

But Valerie looked away, trying to keep herself straight and solid. The fingers of her right hand delved into the curls of the little girl's bountiful hair and squeezed lightly, begging for one more moment of the sensation. After a few seconds, Ester must have read the anguish on Valerie's face and reached out for her sister. Ester quietly pulled the girl away, who shuddered and ticked with weeping.

Valerie turned from the small family, exited out of the door, and immediately found her place in the night. It was where she was sworn. It was where she belonged.

__Chapter 17_____

Mena's exhaustion weighed upon her in lapping waves. She had driven all night and into morning to return to their home— if that was what they could call it. They would likely abandon this place as soon as Edgar recovered from his wounds. They were not running from danger. It was simply the procedure in situations such as these.

Edgar had not been himself after their confrontation with that girl. Mena pondered over why that was. Perhaps the Highborn were not accustomed to pain. Nor should they be, since it was her sworn mission as his fortisan to defend him. She had failed in that, and though he had not yet punished her in any form, the weight of her guilt fed her anger for the one who caused all this mess.

Yes, they had gone after her, and yes they should have been more prepared, but it was this girl's interference and meddling in their plans that caused them to act. If she could only have minded her own business.

Looking back, Mena considered that perhaps going after that family had been a bad strategy. If they had been working with the Red Widow, she would have had the local police arrest the girl on some made up charge, used the maggots to catch maggots. Then they would have dealt with her once she was caged. That was not the way of the new master, however. He was different. While the Red Widow was sneaky, the new master was powerful. He understood the value of taking what belonged to you.

The Master had rescued Mena from the Fighting Pits and reunited her with Edgar. He knew how to be merciful to those who offered him unflinching loyalty. Mena's loyalty was to Edgar alone, and whomever he served was in turn her master as well.

Right now, Mena's calling was to ensure that Edgar recovered sufficiently in his earth-chamber. Tonight when he rose, they would leave this place. Mena had made all the arrangements: she had stacked the crates of his mortal earth and prepared their vehicle. Having had no sleep the night previous, she desperately wished to bathe and to rest.

Like all days, the hours had dragged along, hot and full of unknowns. Presently, she was curled under the doorframe of Edgar's chamber, watching him in her darksight. His colors were different. His silver was still beading, but it was not as radiant. His gold had also faded, overcome by the crawling wisps of blue from his wounds. Mena was relieved to see those colors vanish as his form healed.

We're going to make it, she told herself.

They would recover then Edgar would plan how better to deal with the girl, if at all. Without her mentor, she was bound to lose her way. With time, she would cease to be a threat. The truth was the girl didn't have it in her. Her despair—which was obvious to anyone—to save a pathetic bunch of people crippled her from turning into a significant obstacle. Besides, after seeing what happened to Marshall and Warren, the girl was likely to take the hint.

Deciding there was no danger, Mena closed her eyes for a short nap. She could not know how much time had passed before she awoke with a shudder. A buzzing noise had jolted her from her slumber. The sound grew louder by the second. In their seclusion, the roar of a truck engine storming up the long solitary drive was out of place. This old hotel, years abandoned, in its own time had been a country retreat, isolated with its own road off the major highways. Edgar had chosen it for this reason. There was never any traffic or visitors. *It's her,* Mena thought. *She's found us.*

Leaping to her feat, Mena rushed to the boarded up windows and peered through the lighted cracks. The faded paint of the old brown truck that Warren had driven was unmistakable. Mena cursed under her breath for not disabling it when she had the chance. The truck thundered up the drive, scudded to a stop, and the girl, a black-clad blur, flew out of it towards the building's entrance.

Heart racing, Mena dashed back to her station at the sealed door of Edgar's earth-chamber. It was simple, really. Last night, this Valerie girl had the upper hand when they invaded her territory; she caught them off guard. But now, on foreign turf and without the element of surprise, the girl would be outmatched. It helped also—Mena noted as she snapped open a long black case—that they had a machine gun.

Did the girl like her little knives? she thought.

Lifting the gun from the case, Mena snapped in a long clip, loaded the first round in the chamber and clicked off the safety.

With no power in the building, the girl would be forced to take the stairs. Once she got to their floor, little Vally Val would face the unfortunate task of trying to close the fifty-meter distance between them while doing her best to dodge bullets from a fully automatic M-4—with no cover. If the girl managed to flee into any of the rooms, well, then she would stay there, trapped like a little mouse. Mena would then wait out the two or three hours left of daylight. When Edgar rose, they would finish the little rogue together.

What clever thing could Mena call out? Mena wanted to scare her. She wanted the girl to be the one who felt fear because that was the way it should be.

The girl was not afraid though. With her darksight, Mena watched her take the stairs in two-at-a-time strides, impatient and eager. A tremor of fear rippled through Mena then. The girl's confidence was...unsettling, and it needed to be dealt with. Mena shifted her weight from foot to foot, anxious and unsure. Had she and Edgar done something wrong?

It didn't matter anymore. The girl was winding up the last level of stairs, so it was time to act. Mena tucked the stock to her shoulder, leveling her sight on the spot where the girl was soon to turn into the long hall. Mena watched the girl's scarlet silhouette flash up the last bit of steps.

Just as the girl rounded the corner into the hall, Mena squeezed the trigger and held the weapon steady as it quaked and spit fire. Seconds later, the weapon clicked and hissed in complaint of an empty casing. Mena dropped the clip and loaded another in a breath.

The girl was not dead, but she had done what Mena had assumed all along. In her darksight, Mena saw the girl's red ghost sruggling upward inside the first empty room. She had not been wounded, but that didn't matter. Giggling, Mena reveled in the victory. She would keep the little mouse locked down, and when Edgar awoke, court would be in session.

"Here mousy, mousy," Mena called out. "This is a five-star joint Valerie, so I'm afraid a pest like you has got to go. We tried to play nice, but you just couldn't let it be—"

Mena's voice cut off at a sudden groan of thunder. It was two sharp thuds, then the grumble of stones tumbling over one another. Mena leveled her machine gun at the end of the hall, suspicious at what it meant. And again, there came the troubling beat of stone pounding on stone, followed by the crack and rumble of brick in collapse.

Tracking the girl in her darksight, Mena felt a cold shiver run down her skin. She watched the scarlet ghost breaking through the walls. Room to room, she hammered against the stone and wood with her fists and her knees, undaunted—unafraid.

Flustered, Mena leveled the weapon and squeezed the trigger. She hoped that at least one of the bullets would pierce the concrete and find a vital organ within the girl. Loading another clip, Mena watched the red phantom burst through another wall.

Panic set in, disrupting her steadiness. When Mena had fired that last time, the sound of the gun did not discourage the girl's progress. *Had the girl—so young and untrained—already learned to harden her flesh, muscle and bone? Impossible.* The stoneskin power came with instruction and experience. Mena had both and still had not been able to master it fully.

The girl was close now. One more wall and she would be in the room directly across from Edgar's chamber. Mena's fear ignited to rage. It was one thing to kill the vago, but it was another to come here to defile their home and threaten their lives. Mena leveled the weapon and unleashed a volley into the room, moving the barrel from left to right slowly spreading the line of fire. When the gun clicked and hissed, Mena yelped. Frantic to reload, she lowered the barrel just as the girl burst through the door, charging at her.

Mena tried to strike her with it, but the girl dodged the stock, snatched the weapon and tossed it away. While the girl's hands were busy, Mena swiped the knife hanging from her vest and kicked her in the stomach. Staggering, the girl recovered after a few back steps and stood still.

"Having trouble holding on to these, huh?" Mena purred, waving the blade playfully. Valerie's face was concealed in shadow, but there was something in the solidarity of her stature—the squared shoulders maybe, the confident stillness.

Valerie strolled forward, meeting Mena's slash and thrust. She caught Mena's wrist and twisted then punched Mena squarely in the nose. The audible crack stunned her more than the impact. When Mena turned—her hands cupping a freshly broken nose—she watched the shadow-shrouded girl calmly returning her knife to its case. Valerie's steps forward were casual and deliberate, as indifferent to danger as a crawling tide.

It was here that Mena realized that she had staggered beyond Edgar's door. Next to it, just a reach of the arm away, stood the firm and gorgeous figure of another woman. The sight of it enlivened Mena's insanity, one she had not felt since the Pits.

"No!" she screamed. "No, no. NO!"

Mena charged forward, unleashing a flurry of scratches, punches, and kicks—all dodged, blocked, and batted away. Mena felt the sudden loss of air after she collided with the ground. Her double-vision re-converged as she took in a gasp of air. A bolt of pain ripped through Mena's ribcage. She was certain more than one rib was broken.

The horrible part was the realization that she had flown back many feet. Mena struggled upwards, her fury still burning. Growling, she thundered forward. The girl brushed the advance aside and slogged Mena in the jaw. The force behind the punch twisted and launched Mena backward again.

What did I do wrong? she wondered.

Dizzy and confused, Mena rose from the floor, charging again. It was like battling a shadow. The girl moved too quickly, her motions too crisp and precise. Mena thrust her fist forward, ferocious and desperate to make her actions seem meaningful. Valerie caught the length of her arm and used the momentum to sling Mena into the wall, face first. Another crunch from her nose vibrated throughout her body. Mena was sure something in her face had shattered. She could feel the warmth of the blood freely flowing down her mouth and chin.

With her energy flagging, Mena tried to shake loose, but the girl curled Mena's arm up behind her back. Then Mena felt a force slam the back of her knee. Buckling, all Mena's weight went into her drop to the floor. With her arm seized, her weight and the upward jerk by her attacker cracked her arm out of its socket. The flare of pain crackled and burned from her shoulder down to her guts, where her meager meal an hour ago threatened to erupt. It could not come up for the sudden and pointed kick to her stomach. Mena felt herself slide across the floor many feet before settling.

After many seconds, she gasped and began breathing again. For a moment, she thought she had died. But the pain awakened her. She felt the dull throbbing of her dislodged arm, limp and worthless now, bent unnaturally under her head. Her chest burned inside, every breath like drinking fire. Gazing at the ceiling, she randomly convulsed with the threat of vomit that would not come out.

Mena didn't move. She did not want to provoke her assailant. *Maybe she'll go away now,* she hoped. Terror gripped her as the menacing shadow of the girl slowly panned into view. Mena wanted to say something. She felt like she should. Not beg, per se, but maybe ask Valerie why she was doing this. If the girl would just say something!

Valerie crouched down and reached for Mena's head. As the girl rose, Mena felt a crackling sting in her scalp as she was dragged across the floor by a bundle of her own hair. Waking from her stupor, Mena shook as she tried to steady herself with her one good arm. Her other lifeless arm dangled and scooted alongside her. Mena clawed along, struggling to keep up.

Mena arrived at Edgar's door. The girl had dragged her there. Was it mercy? She didn't care; she was close to Edgar. He was sure to burst open the door and destroy this girl for what she had done.

"Edgar," Mena murmured. She had wanted to sound less pathetic, but the frail and wane sound was all she could manage. "She...hurt me, Edgar."

And then she felt a sudden jerk of her hair. Mena's face was turned upward, forced to peer into the shadow-shrouded face of her attacker. The vibrant light of the girl's eyes against the darkness of her expression was something only seen in nightmares. Mena moaned.

"Your name," Valerie commanded. When Mena didn't answer immediately, she was treated to another more pointed jerk of her hair. Mena shrieked and began to weep. "Ismena!" she yelped. "My name is Mena!"

"Mena," Valerie said. Her voice seemed to play with the sound of it in her terrible mouth, measuring just how inferior it was by its very pronunciation. Then suddenly, Mena felt the cold edge of a knife along her cheek. Mena's eyes flared open. She saw a glint of light catch on the bent blade. There was a word inscribed there, but her vision was too blurry to read it.

"Mena," Valerie repeated. "You get to live."

Mena sensed an internal struggle within the girl. Her voice was low and even. Tamed. But there was an animal inside of her, raging to break loose. A snarl twitched her lips. "I want you to go back to your masters, whoever they are, and tell them what happened here. Show them."

Valerie paused, and Mena felt the knife's edge press into her flesh. *No, not my face!* she thought. *Please, not my face!*

"You tell them to find a hole and get in it," Valerie growled. Now, the blade bit deep into Mena's cheek. She shrieked long and loud as its freezing edge sliced her delicate skin, carving a red gutter from the bottom of her ear to the corner of her mouth. Mena's face flushed hot as a wave of blood poured down her cheek.

"Quiet!" Valerie barked. She yanked Mena's hair again. Mena's chin quaked in the effort of keeping silent.

"Go," she growled, and slashed the crop of Mena's tangled hair away. "Go tell them that a nightbreaker is on the loose...and that she just spent the last of her mercy on *you*."

Once released, Mena felt herself slinking off. She had managed to use her good arm to levy herself up to her feet. Struggling, she wobbled from the hall, drunk from an agony she had not known was possible.

"Run, Mena!"

The scream shocked her. Mena yelped and stumbled forward, almost losing her footing. *No,* she begged. *Stay up.* If she fell, she wasn't sure she could get back up.

It felt like years passed as she crawled down the stairs, whimpering, weeping. The SUV was waiting for her. Outside it, the crates of Edgar's mortal earth waited to be loaded. It was then that she realized the betrayal she had committed. She left her Edgar up there with that savage. *What would happen to him?* she wondered desperately. *Would he ask the girl to be his new protector? Would he think...that the girl was prettier than she was?*

Mena broke into weeping again, but quickly stifled her woes when she saw the outline of the black-clad girl standing at the entrance of the building. She was glaring at Mena with murder smoldering in her eyes. *Did she know no mercy?*

When the girl started toward her, Mena frantically stumbled into the vehicle. She fumbled with the ignition, started it and drove off. In her rear view, she watched with a wane helplessness as the girl approached the crates of mortal earth and began cracking them open. *Without those Edgar would not survive!* Mena gasped and whimpered as she swerved over the drive, barely able to keep the vehicle steady as she fled.

Valerie watched the woman limp off, whimpering. Once the woman was finally crawling down the stairs, Valerie turned her attention to the other part of all this.

Her dreams had not failed her. In an age where all things existed on the web, it was not difficult to locate the The Sylvias Hotel. While she traveled, she held on to the hope that they would not immediately flee. Her quick pursuit paid off. While they had not escaped today, she was certain they were planning to do so. The stacked earth crates outside were proof of it.

Weak, wounded, and completely vulnerable, Edgar stood no chance against Valerie during daylight hours. It would be nothing to break through the seal, open his earth-chamber and finish it. The undead inside, though lethargic, shifted and groaned with the fear of her entry.

"Edgar," Valerie called through the door. "I know you can hear me, so listen carefully. Rest. I'm not going to destroy you that way. I've got something else in mind. Your protector is gone, so if you're thinking of escaping once dusk sets in, I don't blame you, but I know you can't. Where's the source of your mortal earth? I'm guessing somewhere in Europe. How far would you have to travel without appropriate rest? You'd turn revenant before you got anywhere. That leaves me between you and your stockpile outside. If you want it back, you're going to have to earn it. So, let's have it out, Ed. Me and you, on the roof at sundown."

Valerie turned from the door in route to the stairs. There were a few hours before dusk, and she needed to prepare.

When she reached the hotel exit, she stopped short and watched the wounded woman hobble into a blacked-out SUV. When she saw Valerie, the woman scurried into the driver's seat, frantic to escape.

Alone now, Valerie went to the boxes of earth and began the laborious process of cracking open the boxes, letting all the earth spill out in piles around. If Valerie was killed in the fight, then this thing would have earned its right to gather up its precious dirt and move on. If it escaped, it would have no choice but to leave the piles here, at which point Valerie would use the fuel from the truck to poison it.

Once she was finished, Valerie began stacking the planks of wood torn from the crates into her arms. She made trips to the roof of the hotel where it was flat, open, and spacious—as good a place as any to pick a fight.

Valerie stacked the wood, organizing them into cone pyres, evenly spaced around the roof's perimeter. At night, the undead could change their form at will as long as they were concealed in shadow. Valerie's intent was to remove such an advantage. No places to slink off, and no shadowed corners to regroup and shapeshift. The outright fight was to her advantage.

Valerie watched the sun grind into the western range of trees. Its lingering red halo sunk quickly, leaving pink and lavender fire glowing on the rims of the thick clouds. Soon, even that light plunged to darkness. Valerie's fires kept the rooftop brightly illuminated.

She had come far, but now was the time to find out if she was the nightbreaker Warren thought she would become. If she was to combat them, the undead and all their forces, then she needed to step into their world and fight them on their terms.

Beneath her feet, she felt the vibration of the sealed door bursting outward. Amid the clatter of wood shrapnel, she heard the indignant groan of an awakened predator. She turned to the stairwell, setting her feet in preparation for the creature. In her darksight, she could see it moving below, prowling through the halls, a specter of molten silver flecked with gold.

When the sky was fully darkened and the stars came out, Valerie heard the first of Edgar's cries. His voice swelled in the air with an unnatural clarity. It blared outward, ignoring the concrete barriers of the building's walls. The howling continued. It was not language, but rhythmic sounds that boomed outward, convulsing, converging...

A clap of light flashed in the horizon, and seconds later came the grumble of thunder. Valerie's confidence darkened when she saw storm clouds gathering with a crazed speed above her.

Vociferations, she thought. Valerie remembered this from her studies. *When the spirit of the undead soul returns from the astral realm to its native corpse, it comes back with knowledge and with authority over the elements of the material world. Through the vibration of their voices they are able to influence the elements: the growth of plants, the turn of weather, and even the forces of gravity can all be manipulated through vociferations.*

Above her, violent black clouds roiled into a sea of flashing lights and explosions of vapor. One icy drop splattered on the dust of the roof, and then another, and another, until the clouds burst, releasing a black downpour. Within seconds, her pyres were dark, smoking heaps. The platform descended into darkness, and with it, the rain stopped abruptly. Valerie hadn't noticed the air cooling so rapidly, and though she couldn't see it, she felt the prickles of ice sickles forming on her skin. The frost settled over everything as a twinkling fog gathered thick around her.

Blinded with natural eyes, Valerie opened her darksight to see. The mist was not ordinary, though. Normally she would see through it as she did all other things, but the mist glittered with gold and silver sparks. She tried to ignore them, searching for Edgar's aura, but she could not find him. For a moment, she thought he had run, but there was something about the mist...

The particles of gold and silver floated and gusted over the platform, a fog within the fog. *He transformed himself,* she realized. He was using his own aura, expanding it into a mist that not only blinded her natural sight, but her darksight as well.

But for what purpose? she wondered.

She was confident that he could not harm her as a mist, so the danger was elsewhere. As she opened her eyes, she watched a small candlelight suddenly flicker to life meters ahead of her. Behind the candle was an ancient, hunch-backed woman with a frizz of white hair and bone-white skin. Her eyes glowed with a familiar rotten orange color.

"Out here all alone, little one?" the old woman asked, her tone pitying and mockingly friendly. "It is a terrible night to have a curse."

"I think we're past head games, Edgar," Valerie called out, not bothering to look at the apparition.

The candlelight popped, vanishing. Valerie expected the predictable old lady giggling in the darkness bit, but it did not come. Instead, she was treated to the howl of wolves. Their combined baying rose up and held the air before fading into silence. This was all getting old, and Valerie had grown impatient. Maybe the horror-show worked on some people, but Valerie was only annoyed by the delay.

Two sets of eyes flickered into life meters from her. Simmering growls followed.

Okay, the wolves are real, Valerie thought. Summoned, no doubt, from the surrounding wilderness. While she was preparing on the roof, it seemed he had been preparing, too.

To find them, she searched the darksight. Vaguely, she could make out the lemon-colored ghosts of the two wolves circling her—and a third that had sneaked behind her. The silver and gold mist made tracking them too difficult. They popped in and out of her darksight like ghosts in a field of television static.

A sliver of panic ran through her. It was enough to distract her from the sound of the wolf leaping at her. She turned a half-second too late as the wolf barreled into her stomach. As they hit the ground, its jaws caught her forearm and clamped down tight. The wolf then slung its head savagely side-to-side, slobber and blood foaming at its mouth. Pinned on her back and shaking, she didn't have time to consider the pain.

Once they saw her vulnerable, the other two dashed forward, intent on picking another of her flailing body parts. One would go for the legs and pull, and the other would go for the throat. And unlike fighting a trio of revenants, she could not count on the poisonous nature of her blood to thwart the wolves' feasting.

What she could count on was that they were animals, and that they were drunk with the idea of an easy kill. Valerie waited a second longer—waited for the other two get in close—until she drew out Pride and shoved it upward into the soft throat of the wolf mauling her forearm.

Blood spattered her face. The wolf attempted to jerk away, but the sudden motion only sliced a greater rift in its neck. It died with a whimper, and as it collapsed, Valerie set her legs into its stomach and kicked out. The body collided with the wolf now jawing her feet, sending both of the creatures into a tumble meters away. The other bit at Valerie's head, catching a sizable clump of her hair. As it snatched backwards, trying to drag her away, her scalp felt like it had caught fire.

Each of her attempts to stand ended with the beast yanking her by the hair to the ground. Desperately, she flailed at it with her knife, trying to cut the beast off of her, but it evaded and yanked. The wolf she had thrown off was by now recovering and hungry for another shot at her. At first she thought of slicing off that clump of hair, but she feared that in the chaos, she might hit her scalp and cause her own bleed-out. Instead, she twisted her body over to her hands and knees. The crackle of pain spread through her scalp and down her skin. She felt some patches of hair rip and tear, but the move worked. The wolf released its bite to avoid having its head twisted.

She heard the hungry shuffle of the other wolf's paws approaching behind her. Rolling to avoid the attack, she heard the wolf's jaws snap next to her ear. She rolled once more, and then rose to her feet. Angrily, they growled in the mist, concealed and regrouping. Valerie slowly drew out Prejudice and strengthened her footing.

Trying the darksight once more, she still could not track their auras in the roiling silver and gold mist. *I've got it wrong,* she realized. While she scuffled with them, it was sound she had used to track them. And sound had color resonance in the darksight.

Where is your fighting mind? Valerie remembered. She focused her senses into sound. The green coils rippled with each step the wolves made. It was inaudible to the human ear, but in the darksight, nothing could go unseen.

The wolves broke off and began the understandable move of each taking a side to divide her attention. Whichever one got more of it would hold back, while the other attacked her vulnerable side. She could wait for that, but...it was Friday, so what the hell.

She jerked left, faking an advancing step in its direction. As she did, the wolf to her front shimmied backward to lure her in, while the other dashed at her. Valerie stopped short, pivoted, and swung Pride up and into the soft underside the wolf's jaw. The blade point burst through the top of its skull. Raising the wolf up high, she used Prejudice to hack the neck, parting body and head from each other. The body crumbled lifelessly to the ground, spewing blood, while Valerie tossed the severed head away.

The other wolf did not hesitate, but its efforts were hopeless. She timed her attack, watching the green whips of light as it dashed at her exposed back. Valerie twisted away from its leap and hacked the thing at the base of its spine and pelvis. The vibration of her blade crunching through layers of hard bone confirmed her victory.

There was a pale whimper followed by a thud and splatter. Splayed on the concrete, the wolf's hind section was attached by a small sliver of hide, which trailed behind it as the beast fruitlessly crawled forward. Valerie did not grant it the benefit of a quick death. It anguished in the mist for many minutes before finally going silent.

Not taking the peace for granted, Valerie sheathed her blades and opened a pocket on her vest. She drew out and placed a field bandage on her wounded arm, wrapped it with a roll of gauze, then cast the rest to the side. With that finished, Valerie quickly reset her soaked and disheveled hair then stood at the ready.

"You're going to have to face me," she announced to the mist. "Or run. It's up to you. But your pets aren't going to get the job done. You're only showing me how scared you are."

The mist roiled and twisted, forming into silver and gold currents. They retreated to the far end of the roof, gathering into vortex of vapor and wind. The mist converged and rose upwards in a funnel. A figure emerged from it, not a monster, but a man. Edgar's aura was glimmering gold glinting with silver.

The pyres of wood, once extinguished by the sudden rain, exploded into life as the undead before her bellowed a string of syllables. Light covered the platform. Meters from her stood the pale and naked form of a man. Tall, lean, hairless, and chiseled, the figure was by any standard the embodiment of physical perfection. His blue-violet eyes fixed on Valerie with a cold and calculating indignation.

As Valerie began the motion to brandish her weapons, he rushed forward. In a flash, he had her by the arms, pinning them to her side. Raising her from the ground, he slammed her back into the parapet, smashing the air from her body.

The collision shock was at first a dull vibration, but soon the pain shot through her body like cracks of lightning. A gasp of agony escaped Valerie's mouth, as her assailant crushed her body into the concrete. After spending a long second in a daze, Valerie came to her senses and saw the star-lit sparkle of his eyes glaring into her. It seemed right to expect a taunting smirk on his face, but it wasn't there. A taut scowl curled his lips, revealing the white teeth within.

Valerie trembled as she felt the bones of her arms straining against the urge to snap. She drew her forearms up, gripped his elbows then kicked his knee. Growling, Edgar eased his grasp enough for Valerie to break his hold. Her hands clasped his wrists, barring his reaching hands. Their struggle became a war of inches, as Valerie battled for each one. There had been a smirk there, just for a second, but it faded when he felt himself floating away from her, forced back in a contest of strength.

Inch by inch, she pressed until his hands were free of her. Then she leaned forward, lifting her back from the concrete wall. Sensing his defeat, Edgar hissed, jerked his hand to the left, gripped her right arm then vaulted her into the air in a smooth arc. She flew a few meters before crashing into a flaming pyre, which exploded and scattered coals and flaming debris over the roof. When she rolled over the ground, a piece of wood caught her in the side. She was certain she felt a rib crack.

Using the leftover force in her tumble, she struggled upward and set her feet. She breathed in deep, recapturing lost air. Meters away, the creature belched a string of syllables and made sweeping motions with his arms. Flames from the pyres erupted, leaping high into the black, twisting in wild coils. The coils tightened into vibrant lashes that danced at his command. The first of them whipped Valerie across the shoulder, searing a band of her skin instantly. Crying out, Valerie rolled away from the second lash, feeling the pain of her cracked rib spark within her chest.

Another coil lashed her across the thigh, burning through her pants and searing a wide patch flesh beneath. She toppled to one knee, drew out Prejudice, and rolled away from another lash. Rising, she steadied her feet and took aim. She flung her knife in a sweep, just as she danced away from another lash of his flames. The blade sliced the creature across the cheek then bounced away, clattering to the ground nearby. Blue and yellow flames flared from the small wound. Edgar roared, drawing his hands to his face. With his concentration lost, the flame-lashes sputtered and faded.

Valerie drew out Pride with a jerk of her arm and dashed for him. She noted the flicker of panic in his eyes. The option for him to run was always there, and she needed to make sure that didn't happen. Valerie raised her blade high as though to deliver an over dramatic kill-stroke, hoping he would see vulnerability. Edgar advanced a step and dug in for a firm sweep of his hand. Valerie tucked down, rolled under the swing, came up behind him and thrust Pride just below the shoulder blade and ribs. Arching back in pain, he wheeled around and struck Valerie across the cheek.

Dazed, she missed the moment to dance away before he grasped her two-handed by the throat. She could feel his wrath shaking through his limbs as he squeezed. With no way to breathe, overpowering him again was unlikely. Valerie's hands clamped his wrists. Leaping up, she set her feet in his chest and kicked. The two blasted apart—Valerie to the concrete, and Edgar staggering back a few steps. From the corner of her eye, she spied Prejudice just out of reach.

Edgar was distracted in the act of pulling her other knife from his back. With growl, he tore Pride from the muscle and cast it aside.

Lurching, Valerie rose to her feet just as he charged at her again. He would expect the dance-around, so she set her feet and prepared for impact. The arms rose, hands open to grasp. Valerie saw her response, knew the motions as surely as she felt calm and steady breath in her lungs.

Catching a wrist in each hand, Valerie held him, back arching, legs bracing and absorbing the inertia of impact. She slid back, her boots skidding until they bumped the parapet behind her. Grunting, she held him, though his arms crept down, slowly toward her neck, all while he leaned in, closer, closer...

Now. Valerie lifted her back leg and planted it on the parapet wall behind, bracing herself. Lifting her other leg, she stepped onto his knee, climbing, rising, and before he could realize that she had him, she swept her bracing leg upward. Her knee struck him in the cheek, the blow empowered by their combined force.

She felt his bones crack and cave inwards. She watched his body melt and crumble, limp and haggard. Staggering as she landed, she felt his body limply crash into hers. Valerie cast him off with a sweep of her hand.

With her enemy fallen, Valerie lifted Prejudice and stood over him. As he lumbered to his knees, wriggling in agony, he reached one arm up and grasp her by the vest. She hacked the arm off at the elbow.

The proof of his suffering echoed for miles, a bitter and sorrowful howl, one telling the tragedy of defiled perfection. For good measure, Valerie swiftly brought the point of her knee to the crevice of his cheekbone, where a second crunch of bone and cartilage left a sagging mass of flesh. Edgar landed on his back, meters away.

Limping to him, Valerie picked up Pride and flipped the blade down. Spasms shook his body as black ooze leaked from the stump of his arm and the ruin of his mouth. Kneeling over him, she thrust Pride into his clavicle where it smoldered with thin plumes of blue and yellow flames licking his charred flesh.

The undead stared into the darkened sky. His blue, violet-rimmed eyes sparkled, glassy and vacant. The storm clouds now dispersed, and the once roaring flames now simmered to coals. Tranquility overtook the roof. There was only Valerie and this creature in the expanse of a starry night.

Valerie looked into his shifting eyes. His once perfect face was now a pulpy mass. His balmy flesh sagged inward at his right cheek, and only one side of his nose still protruded from his face. Within his mouth, sharp teeth were missing while others loosely hung at the gums. On his left cheek a long slice smoldered, and the skin inches above and below the wound had crisped black.

Cringing, Valerie reached into one of her vest pockets. She drew out a small silver coin and presented it to Edgar's face. His eyes locked on the coin, and any will he may have had resigned in surrender after understanding what it was.

"I'm guessing you know what this is," Valerie panted, her breath and words still a labor. "I have a few questions for you, Edgar."

His face shifted strangely. He seemed to be trying to speak, but struggled through the motions with a ruined face.

"You," he started, "You...will not...need that, nightbreaker." His voice had a strong and musical resonance to it, flowing and drawn like the deep note of a cello.

Valerie paused and read his face. She saw no guile there, only resignation.

"I would rather not bear that pain," he continued, staring off into the sky. "You," he paused, struggling to speak, "you have ravaged my form, and I am at your mercy."

"I'm fresh out of that."

"I did not mean from the destruction of this form," he clarified. "That is assured. I meant from further torture." He gagged on liquid running down his throat, and sputtered it out on his pale lips.

Certain he wasn't going anywhere, Valerie gripped Pride and tore it from his clavicle. His body jerked, and something like relief hissed from his throat. Valerie seated herself next to him, wincing as she positioned herself comfortably.

"You are a worthy warrior—"

"Save it," she growled.

She was willing to ask questions and listen without the coin. It was unexpected and welcome. While forcing the victim to speak the truth, the Janus Coin allowed the victim the luxury of being vague and only giving enough of an answer to satisfy the question. No unintended information was ever derived. Also, the effects did not last very long. Though the paralysis was also a beneficial perk, in this case, it was unnecessary. For now.

"All right, Edgar," Valerie said. "The Red Widow. Where can I find her?"

Mena tried to stay asleep. The waking world was much more horrific than any nightmare she had ever experienced. In the darkness, she could slip through time, ignoring the reality of her existence. When she woke, the pain returned, as did the truth.

She was no longer with Edgar, and though she tried to tell herself that there was some way they would find each other again, as they had before, she could not believe it. Even if Edgar survived the girl's wrath, he would detest Mena for her failure—and he would reject her because she was ugly now. Old, damaged, worn, and ugly.

A patient next to her moaned a string of nasty sounds. It was an old man, in pain, who probably needed to be put out of his misery. Mena would gladly take care of that, but she was broken, and the strength was gone from her. She was feeble, weak, and now...she was no better than the rest of the maggots that squirmed in the beds all around her.

When she first awoke in the hospital, Mena thought that perhaps Edgar had saved her. She soon realized that it had been by the hospitality of strangers that she came to this place. She had fainted at some point in her drive back to civilization and had driven her SUV into the concrete wall of a shopping center. Locals came to her rescue. That was what the translator had told her anyway.

At first they had been really nosy. They wanted to know where her passport was, what her country of origin was, and what her business in Brazil had been. Mena offered no answers. She simply turned over in her meager hospital bed, trying to sleep.

They put her in this communal haunt with invalids and psychos, all maimed and malfunctioning in their own special kind of disgusting. It was an appropriate punishment; she understood this and accepted it. But such a truth could not comfort her from the more desperate tragedy: what was Ismena to do? She was lost in this world.

After days of stillness in the bed, she could feel some of her wounds beginning to heal. She was anxious to stand and walk, but she feared what it might mean to do so. Would it mean that she was rejoining the world? If so, what part of it would she fit into? Would she be one of these...freaks? Every time she touched the long line of stitches on her left cheek she felt like she was.

Mena clasped her eyes shut and tried to make herself sleep so she didn't have to think about it. She had slept enough, though, and her body was anxious for wakefulness. The hours dripped along, hazy and dream-like. She watched the liquid dripping in her IV, she listened to the incessant beeping and pinging of unseen machines, and she could not filter out the random cough or the distant moan of her neighborly afflicted.

At some point in the haze of hours, she realized her bed was moving. She could feel one of the wheels of her gurney wiggling as it coasted through the halls. The rectangle lights panned bottom to top, bottom to top, lapping upon her consciousness. A tall, brown-skinned man dressed in blue scrubs and white latex gloves pushed the gurney leisurely. *Where is he taking me?* she wondered. She feared also what his intentions might be. Without Edgar near her, and with her body so damaged, she would be helpless against him.

The nurse spoke to someone, letting out a string of words Mena did not understand. An unseen someone answered; they shared a laugh then the nurse resumed his course. They went up an elevator and through a few more halls before he pushed her gurney into a wide and spacious quarter. The room was calmly lighted, beautifully decorated, and sparkling clean. It had its own bathroom, a television, and wide window that overlooked a vast park.

Mena's heart enlivened itself, though she was still afraid to move or show any sign of life. A female nurse entered the room stretching a pair of latex gloves on to her hands. She and the male nurse traded a few words before unstrapping the restraints on Mena's wrists and feet. Each taking a side of her, they lifted Mena's body up and set her down on her new bed. Mena felt herself sink into the comfort of the cushion. The sheets felt crisp and smelled fresh. The nurses set her IV stand, scrawled something on a clipboard then exited.

It was a miracle! As she examined her new surroundings, she tried to think about what had changed. She had spent days in abject poverty in the presence of freaks and maggots, and now here she was in a clean and private room. They had even left the restraints off.

Outside, the bright lights of the park shone like little orbs in the darkness. It was night, and it was a comfort to see that realm again. Mena sat up and stared out into the blackened landscape, her mind toying with the fantasies of what she could do now.

Maybe, she thought, *I could adopt a puppy and care for it.* They could go out at night and walk the empty roads and they could talk to each other. *What do puppies eat?* she wondered. She would also have to name it. *Baby,* she thought. Mena would name the little dog Baby.

Mena jerked suddenly when she heard someone enter her room. Then her stomach lurched suddenly and cold fear passed through her when she saw the woman.

Remelle.

Of Japanese descent, Remelle was slim in stature, lithe and fit which showed in her black fortisan uniform. Just over the Remelle's left breast, Mena spied the familiar red hourglass insignia, an honor worn only by the Red Widow's Fortisan. Remelle was somewhere in her early forties with a scarred, but pretty face topped with long, black hair tightly drawn back and highlighted with streaks of natural gray. While she was petite in form, like all fortisan she was lethal in ways that other mortals could only dream. Mena's one comfort was that Remelle was without her sword.

Maybe she doesn't mean to hurt me, Mena thought.

Remelle strode into the room, passing the bed, her eyes intent on the wide window. Once she reached it, she turned abruptly to face Mena.

Another figure entered the room, dressed also in the black uniform of the Fortisan. He was a towering young man with flawless, black skin and haunted emerald eyes. He was lean, yet well-muscled, and fashionably bald. Though he was probably in his early twenties, he projected a quiet authority in his sure and purposeful strides. The young man approached Mena's bed within feet and appraised her. Whether he was pleased or impressed, he did not show it.

"The Lady wishes to speak with you," the young man said. His voice was deep, but toneless. "Do you permit her entrance?"

Mena's chin quivered as she sought for the words to say. The nightmare just did not end. When would it stop? The Red Widow had come for her. Here. To her very room. What did it mean? Was Mena forgiven for her treason? The Red Widow was never really known for great mercy, but she was not a monster. The Red Widow detested ugliness in all its forms, and revenge and torture were ugly things. Mena decided that she would be excited. It was like her mother had come to forgive her. Relief washed over her like a calm and warming blanket.

Mena nodded rapidly and slowly lay back in her bed so that the Lady could see how badly Mena had been wounded and how badly Mena had suffered. "I permit her entrance," she whispered.

And then Mena felt it, the rise of her power. She felt the strength in her muscles and bones. In her mind, she felt the divine clarity of thought blessing her. But above all those gifts, she felt the *passion,* the will to do what others could not. For the Highborn. For—

Mena shook her head, batting away the name from her mind.

Remelle turned, opened the latch to the window and pulled the glass panel aside. A fine mesh screen with thin precautionary rods barred exit from the window. But that could not stop the shadows from rising into the room. The lights flickered and dimmed. Tendrils of shadow squirmed along the walls, spreading and reaching until they engulfed the light panels.

Once the darkness had set in, a calm and flowing fog rose through the window and spilled into the room. Soon the mist filled the floor, coursing with life. The young man positioned a large cushioned armchair in the corner of the room, farthest from the window. The fog gathered at the base of the armchair foaming and boiling into a thick mass. As it rose into the chair, the mist transformed into a woman.

Mena knew she should not look at her majesty directly, but Mena could not help herself. Her glory was a sight for meager eyes.

The Red Widow reclined with a queenly comfort. Her body was the model of feminine perfection, lithe, smooth, and unblemished. She chose to manifest herself in an elegant and simple crimson gown complete with a long cowl, which shrouded her eyes and nose. Only her bow shaped mouth and the glitter of her blue-violet eyes were visible. But it was the Lady's hands that made Mena love her. They were pale and thin, but exuded a clear and present strength. The fingers were long and manicured immaculately, void of any jewelry. As a pure being, a true Highborn, gaudiness and extravagance were unworthy of her. Those were the vain attempts of lesser mortals to garner attention when none was due.

Mena trembled, while waiting for the Red Widow to deliver justice in whatever form that seemed fitting. Why had Edgar betrayed such a grand being?

"Ismena," the Red Widow said. The motions of her mouth, and the sound that came out were a wonder to experience. "I trust you find these accommodations more suitable?"

Unsure how to answer, Mena began to weep. Mercy. The Lady was compassionate and kind. She was the one who brought Mena out of that den of invalids. She understood and knew Mena's heart. Mena felt her chin quaking, the tears streaming hot from her eyes. With a whimper, Mena nodded.

With an elegant sweep of her hand, the Red Widow said, "You have Remelle to thank for finding you." Then her hand glided to the young man. "You may not recognize Logan. He has grown since you saw last him."

The truth was, Mena had no memory of him, young or otherwise. She knew that the Red Widow had taken on new initiates years ago, but Mena had not been allowed to mingle with them. Only Marshall and Remelle had taught and trained them. She had always wanted to talk with the young ones—like having little brothers and sisters—but the Lady never permitted it.

Mena nodded her head at each of them. Neither gave a response, each staring without expression.

"It is unfortunate that any of this was necessary, Ismena," the Red Widow said. "Were you not happy in the Fighting Pits?"

Mena clinched her eyes shut, her guilt and shame evident in the piping whimper she tried to hold in. *Will she send me back there?* Mena was in no shape to return, and she hated all those people watching her. The masked faces, their eyes following her movements, their gloved hands clapping. And the monsters... the way they shuffled and growled, the way they stank... Mena wanted to be a lady. She wanted to be someone important.

"I see where I erred," the Red Widow said. "I am sorry for what I did to you."

Flaring open, Mena's eyes looked into the shaded and glorious face of the Red Widow. The feeling of warmth and belonging blossomed within her chest. The Lady had apologized...to Mena.

"My lady," Mena started, and then choked on her words.

"It's all right," the Red Widow said, her voice slivering over the air like a breeze. "This is a very confusing time for us all. Much is moving, and it is difficult for many to understand the value of loyalty—and those who are deserving of it."

Mena nodded rapidly, feeling a fresh wellspring of shame and regret. *That's right,* she thought. *I was tricked.* Mena wiped away her tears and sniffed. "Yes, my lady."

"Ismena," the Red Widow said. "Perhaps you have been confused. Among all your crimes against me, I do not fault you for that. But in the past you have proven yourself an unreliable servant to my designs. That is why I found something more fitting to your tendencies in the Fighting Pits."

The Red Widow paused and stared at Mena a moment. Mena wiped away more tears and nodded rapidly. She hated to hear the words, but she had to admit that they were true. Mena had not believed the words before; she had resented the Lady's judgment, and she had hated the Lady for taking her away from Edgar. But now, without him, now as she was all alone...Yes, Mena was a monster.

The Red Widow tilted her head thoughtfully. "Do you remember those years ago when I tried to teach you what your flaw was?"

Mena's eyes glazed in a stupor of memory. It was painful to recall, and the word hurt her heart and lips as she said it, "Hubris, my Lady. My flaw is hubris."

"Yes," the Red Widow replied. "Stubborn, unfounded, and foolish pride. It leads even the greatest of beings to their demise. History and legend try to warn us, but we always find a way to ignore the admonitions. Even myself."

Mena's soul delighted in the very thin smile the Red Widow showed her. Mena sniffed, smiled back, and said, "Yes, my lady."

"This is why I am prepared to overlook your treachery," the Red Widow continued. "But I see that you still lack the essential decency and decorum necessary to my service."

The line of the Red Widow's mouth grew tight with reproach. "I can understand why you aligned yourself with this usurper as Edgar did. By virtue of that, I can understand why you killed Marshall, though I was displeased to hear of it. I trust you did not obtain his records?"

Mena's chin quivered as fresh tears began to stream forth. "No, my lady."

"All of your actions in Edgar's service I can understand, though I find them tactless and obscene," the Red Widow said. "I can understand them. Even killing the man, Warren Brant, though it was rash and it showed your lack forethought. He seemed like an enemy, did he not?"

Well, not him, so much. It was... Mena winced, banishing the thought of *her*. She nodded rapidly.

"But even your enemies can be useful to your goals," the Red Widow explained. "Edgar, though a regrettable loss, was still useful to me. Even though his loyalties had tragically shifted, how long had he spent in my service? How well did I know him? Do you think that a connection forged over two centuries could be so easily severed?"

The Red Widow flashed a sparkling grin. "Oh yes, Ismena, I knew of his actions, and I was able to follow him. Even in his treachery, he was a servant to my ends." The smile tightened to a scowl. "And I have seen what you have done."

Mena whimpered as the shadows of the room deepened and crawled over the walls, swallowing the faint yellow light. "You have not changed, woman. Did you think that Warren and that girl were not *exactly* where I wanted them? They were perfect in their placing. I know all of my servants. I know their hearts and their minds. And even though they believe they have rebelled against me, their actions always serve my ends. But not you, Mena."

The shadows swallowed all the light of the room and even dimmed the yellow orbs of the park lights outside her window until there was nothing but darkness. The Red Widow's eyes flickered beneath her cowl. "You are erratic and beyond direction," her voice seethed.

Mena gasped, yelping, "I'm sorry, my Lady. I'm sorry. Forgive me. I beg you."

The shadows receded slowly behind the chair, and the form of the Red Widow resumed its stunning beauty. For a moment, the Red Widow stared in judgment, contemplating what to say.

"My forgiveness will be earned," she said, her voice even. "As I have said, I am prepared to accept my portion of the blame. Had I trusted you with an explanation of your banishment, perhaps you might have chosen a different course of action. Allow me to remedy that transgression."

The Red Widow tilted her head to the side. "The rumors of my failing power are misguided," she said. "You have learned that there is another Highborn rising to challenge my goals. Though his power is considerable, I have learned to deal with his brutal yet predictable methods. But a violent conflict with this usurper seems unavoidable, and I will need trustworthy warriors to defend the integrity of our dream.

"In this effort, Marshall's defection was unfortunate, but it did serve a purpose. You see, for years he has been purposefully concealing the locations of the newly born nightbreakers. I had suspected that with his age, he might begin to question our goals and consider the...morality of his actions. He was also the only one who knew how to use the dreamsight necessary to find them. His failed attempts to teach the skill to other fortisan was a deception I now see."

The Lady's eyes glittered. "Fortunately, in his absence I have discovered other methods to seek the nightbreakers. However, when you killed Marshall and failed to retrieve his carefully rendered archives, you left all that wealth of knowledge in the hands of Warren and his student."

The Red Widow paused there and stared at Mena. A fresh memory of the shadow-clad terror haunted Mena's vision. She clinched her eyes shut, shaking her head violently, trying to banish the horrifying flashbacks.

"Yes," the Red Widow said, a hint of pleasure in her voice. "It was you who created her. She is a powerful and determined young lady, this Valerie Zeta. And if she had been treated with the proper respect, there was the chance that she might have seen the value of service to me."

Impossible, Mena thought, dreadfully. Mena shook her head slowly and emphatically. "No, my Lady," Mena murmured, her chin quivering. She needed to warn the Lady, explain to her, somehow, that the girl was...

"She..." Mena stammered, her voice quavering. "She's a *monster.*"

The Red Widow growled, and Mena immediately regretted contradicting her. "I'm so sorry," Mena whispered. "I'm sorry. Forgive me."

Many seconds passed before the Widow's mouth ceased its twitching. Eventually, she recomposed herself and continued. "I do not doubt this, Ismena," the Lady said, snarling. "But she is one of your making. Not only murdering, but desecrating her teacher was your first trespass against her. And then that small family, Ismena...

"Attempting to destroy those who cared for her—those that showed her love and compassion. I see now that it is impossible for you understand how that might create unflinching enemy."

The Red Widow leaned back in her seat. "Did you know, Ismena, that Warren Brant—the man you murdered—had twin children, a son and daughter?" She paused a moment. "They are nightbreakers. They are also of an age to be taken into my service as fortisan. Marshall had hidden this from me.

"Though I did not know at the time, I understand now why Warren Brant came into my service: to watch and to ensure that his children were never taken. But once I discovered this, did I retaliate against him, a mere mortal? No." She leaned forward. "And *why,* Ismena? Because I recognize the value of loyal servants, and I know that even one so elevated as myself should be wary of violating sacred bonds."

The Lady reclined again. "Yes, Ismena, even the Highborn know and respect the laws of the material realm. It is here that we choose to exist after all. Power is not found in tyranny, but in careful and thoughtful organization. Balance. Hatred, revenge, and flights violence disrupt this balance. And though I am Highborn I notice that even mortals can bring an end to me.

"Hubris, Ismena. It is the reason this usurper will not prevail. It is the reason that Edgar is destroyed. And it is the reason you lie broken before me."

Though she tried to hold back the fit, Mena's voice cracked and whimpered at the last part.

Edgar is destroyed... Some part of her wanted to believe that Edgar had survived. Mena wanted to believe that with her new found humility, the Red Widow would see the purpose of placing them both together again. Pariahs and shamed, but together.

It was not to be. That girl... She destroyed Edgar, and it was Mena's fault.

"Your efforts are not completely wasted, however," the Red Widow said, and she waited for Mena to gather herself before going on. "Your actions were rash and violent, but as a result, they forced our enemy to play his hand in full. I believe this young woman was close to discovering the location of the artifact, a feat that I had hoped she would accomplish all along." The Red Widow snarled. "Without interruption. But when you made her presence known to our enemy, the remainder of his forces were sent to destroy her. And they would have," here she motioned at the young man next to her, "had Logan not intervened."

Mena desperately wanted to tell her that it was Edgar who made the decision, that it was Edgar who gave the command. She knew that speaking out would only stoke the Lady's anger though.

"As of yet, the girl is unaware of our involvement," the Lady continued. "But the hour is now late, and that must change. To begin to repair what you have done, you will tell Logan all you have learned during your service to the enemy. About the artifact, and about this girl."

The lights flickered and dimmed to a dull yellow. The shadows behind the chair expanded outward, swallowing the chair and the Lady seated in it. Thick tendrils of darkness crawled along the walls and over the light panels until the room was engulfed. The mist spilled upon the floor and coursed to the window where it rose, slivering out into the night. When it was gone, the shadows faded, and the lights flickered brightly into life.

Mena looked at the young man and smiled. He approached, his expression strong and professionally indifferent.

Logan asked her no questions but stood, stared, and listened. Mena told him all that she knew, and she realized through all of the telling that she could not stay on track. She babbled like a sick child. She hated talking about Valerie, and she skipped many of the details of their encounter. She summarized most of it by describing how relentless and vicious and unforgiving the girl had been. Mena knew very little about the artifact, but she felt like she was able to tell them something worth their time.

"The Mast—the Usurper—was using the vago," Mena explained. "He controlled them, I think. He...made them feed from people, to make them stronger."

"Why?" Logan asked, his voice even yet demanding.

Mena shifted. "He was using them to find the artifact because they are naturally drawn to its power. Since the vago had less complicated thoughts, the connection to its energy was clearer." Mena shifted her eyes to Remelle and then back to Logan. "We were meant to watch them—to see if the Mantle might reveal itself. Many of the vago began to gather, like a herd, and they started to migrate. We were going to follow them, but..." Mena's voice trailed off, not needing to explain the rest. "That's all I know."

Logan turned to Remelle, their eyes meeting. "Should I wait for the others?"

Remelle shook her head. "They'll not arrive in time. Besides..." she paused, considering something. "A show of force may only...*rile* her."

He did not move. "And if she resists?"

Remelle was quiet a moment, her eyes staring off.

"She was able to destroy Lord Edgar," Logan said. "*Without* proper training."

Nodding lightly, Remelle acknowledged this. She looked at him. "As unharmed as possible."

Logan turned and exited the door, a determined haste in his step. Mena stared awkwardly at Remelle who remained. The woman stared upon Mena with a stolid and emotionless gaze. Mena smiled faintly, thinking about all the forced training sessions she used to hate. Remelle hated them, too. They were never friends, but maybe now, now that things were okay, they could start over.

Perhaps, Mena thought. *I could finally become a true fortisan.*

Though there was no change in her face, Remelle had a way of making her feelings known. She detested Ismena, even now. She had always seen Ismena as a strange and volatile creature. That used to bother Ismena, but now was a new beginning.

Remelle took in a breath and exhaled. "You are healed enough to travel," she said. Remelle drew out a syringe of clear liquid. "However, the Lady insists that you rest as much as possible. This will help you sleep."

Ismena smiled. *I'm going home,* she thought. *I'll sleep all the way there. I'll sleep and dream and forget all of this.*

Suddenly, she thought of Edgar. She winced, banishing the painful memory. It was a comfort to see Remelle fix the needle into Mena's IV. Seconds after Remelle squeezed in the medicine, Mena felt very drowsy, like the end of a long day. She closed her heavy eyes, excited about tomorrow.

"Lady Vanessa," Edgar said. "That is her woken name. I, Lord Edgar, was one of her most trusted advisors. Even still, I was never shown her place of rest. She was in motion. Traveling, always. Only her protectors, her most loyal fortisan would know of her movements."

Vanessa, Valerie thought. Somehow having a name, and not some abstract title, helped smooth some of the edge of the threat.

"These fortisan," Valerie said. "They're nightbreakers? Like me?"

"Taken while very young," Edgar replied. "They are conditioned to defy their nature. Lady Vanessa saw purpose in taming the nightbreakers to serve as sword and shield against her enemies, mortal and Highborn alike. It is a clever practice, but not without its flaws. You were fortunate to avoid detection while young. Marshall's treason was no doubt the cause."

Valerie sat for a moment and let that sink in. She shook her head and resumed. "Why are you here? What were you supposed to be doing?"

"I seek the Mantle."

"Why, exactly?" she asked. "You and your lady already own half the world. Why does she want it?"

Edgar's eye glossed for a moment, and then he turned his head slightly to get a small glimpse of Valerie. "Do you know what it is?"

Valerie stared at him. "Power. Control."

"Words, merely," he gurgled. "To understand the nature of the Mantle of the Dragon you must reconsider your definition of power. Look past your star-lit world, nightbreaker. What do you see?"

Valerie couldn't help herself. She peered upward, gazed into the night sky flecked with tiny lights, but dark and empty everywhere.

"You see stars, do you not, great orbs of attraction billowing across time and space?" Edgar paused. "Your kind marvel at them. Give them names. And all the while you fail to notice the immensity of the realm in which they feebly contend for time."

Edgar shuddered as a sudden spark of fresh pain coursed through his body. After a hoarse intake of air, he continued. "Your kind is frightened and appalled by the dark. This is understandable. Your mortal frames are dependent upon your star and its light. Your rich imaginations have even given it names. You have fancied that it is your god, and that it has walked among you."

His tone blackened. "You are mistaken. The power that resides in darkness is supreme. That is why it dominates the cosmos. Your fixation on light is the reason that your scholars cannot fathom the void with the proper respect. We, the Highborn, are not superior because we are immortal or that we are stronger. We are superior because we have embraced and learned of the energies residing in darkness and shadow."

Through all the talk, Valerie's thoughts had started to swim. The pain in her arm throbbed; her ribs prickled like blinking cinders. "Well that's great, Ed. You could put that in a pamphlet and pass it out at airports." Wincing, she shifted her weight. "But what does any of that have to do with what we're talking about?"

He seemed, for a moment, to protest her petulance with silence—that or her perceived ignorance. Eventually, he sucked in a breath and continued. "The Mantle of the Dragon embodies this power, and the one who possesses it, the Dracula, is the vessel of its authority—to which all in the family of darkness must submit."

Valerie cringed, as a murky suspicion suddenly blared with clarity. "There's another," she murmured, both to herself and to Edgar. "Someone who's challenging Vanessa. That's why she wants it—to bring her enemy to heel."

"Indeed," he answered, his voice struggling. "Her feeble motive, however, exposes her weakness."

"Which is?"

"The illusion of strength. Though her power and knowledge are considerable, she has never truly embraced the darkness. She remains shackled by the vestiges of mortal consciousness. She does not understand."

Valerie felt a chill crawl down her spine, which she tried to ignore. "What do you mean?"

"Vanessa plays a careful game of managing a flock of sheep, coddling, controlling—tending to the mortals like pets." Edgar hissed, his breath strained. "The ability to manipulate a mob is nothing. True power resides in domination."

Admittedly, Valerie struggled to see the difference, which was understandable, since her exhaustion was now lapping upon her, blurring her attention. "And this…other—"

"The Master understands," Edgar replied, almost eagerly. "The Master knows our place in this world. Our right, our dominion." Here his eyes locked on her, as a snarl wiggled the dangling flesh that had been his lips. "For too long we have cowered in shadows, fearful of the footsteps of those far our inferior. No more. We rise, nightbreaker. The Age of the Immortal is upon us."

"Except…" Valerie drew in a deep breath, remembering the image of a chessboard mid-game. "It's seems like if you want to be the king, you've got to kill the queen." She paid his broken form a look. "And here you are."

"I am but one," he murmured. "Even now, the Master gathers his strength, nations of his own, pawns to throw upon Vanessa's sword. Her fortisan have proven to be her greatest strength, but the Master will soon raise his own army."

"From where?"

His eyes gazed distantly. "Ice and stone and time, where they have slumbered, forgotten—waiting for the Dracula to rise again."

Again, Valerie felt a shiver. *An army of undead?* she thought. *And all he needs is the Mantle.* Valerie tried not to show her uneasiness. "What is it, the Mantle?"

"Unknown. Our legends do not say."

Valerie cringed. "Then how do you find it? How do know it's even real and not some myth?"

"It calls to us," Edgar replied, airily. "It reaches out to the Highborn, its voice growing stronger, more eager."

Valerie laughed, dark and mirthless. "I'm getting the feeling that none of us know what the hell we're after."

Shuddering in sudden agony, Edgar growled. Valerie didn't know if she hit a nerve, or he was just suffering. Both were acceptable, since this conversation had drawn on longer than she wanted.

"My warnings to you were not enough," Edgar groaned, finally. "There is so much of our realm that you do not know, and will never be able to grasp—no more than the rat can comprehend the nature of the adder. Do you think you have demonstrated your superiority by ravaging this fragile body? You have enjoyed a victory here, but look to your teachers and the nature of their endings. Such is the fate to those who oppose the Master and his designs. You are alone. And we..." Edgar's deflated face tweaked in a grin, "We are eternal."

"Eternal, huh?" Valerie stood, balancing Prejudice in her hand. "I think you'll find my counter argument convincing."

Edgar twittered with laughter. "Do you think that this is the end of me? When our Lord, the Dracula, returns, he will call to us and raise us all. This is not my end."

Valerie paused, looming over him. At length she nodded, suddenly remembering something. "I'm curious, Edgar. Since you've been so forthcoming, help me out. What were you going to do with that family?" Valerie flushed hot, seeing Little Tiger again damp with tears. "What would you have done with the children?"

Staring at the thing, she saw his haughtiness and eagerness to brag fade away. Valerie nodded, rubbing her puffy cheek thoughtfully. "Figures." She sighed, and ticked her tongue. "You know, I can't let that pass. And all this talk about you returning has got me motivated."

Valerie reached into one of her vest pouches and pulled out a thin length of rope, intricately braided with a variety of strands of color. "Know anything about this?" She bounced the coil in her palm. "It's called an Isaac Lace. Lately, I've taken up some reading. Along with all his records, Marshall left things like this for us. Phylacteries. I guess that's one of those flaws of keeping nightbreakers as pets.

"One of the more interesting tidbits of knowledge was about how some of the undead find ways to return to the material world even after their host body has been destroyed. Maybe an annoying poltergeist or a possession of some poor conflicted victim. This," she said, uncoiling the lace. "This puts a stop to that, though. The only problem, Edgar, is that in order for me to apply it appropriately, I have to know your true name and the place where you were born in mortality."

Valerie shrugged her shoulders. "You could save us both a lot of time by just telling me." She sheathed Prejudice and drew out the Janus coin. "Not to mention yourself a lot of pain." She titled her head and grimaced. "On second thought, as far as saving my time goes…" Valerie knelt down, leaned in close to his face and snarled. "I've got plenty."

Slamming her palm into his forehead, she reveled in the sudden stiffness that possessed him. His limbs convulsed in tight spasms, his toes and fingers curled inward, while an agonizing gurgle simmered in his throat.

Valerie snarled at him. "You should not have gone to that house, you son of a bitch!" She flogged him in the chest. "What is your birth name? Tell me! Where were you born?"

Edgar's body arched as searing agony coursed through it. His voice crackled, withholding the answer. True names were sacred to the undead. By invoking the true name of the undead, mortals could resist their power, and—with the aid of other magic—control them. Edgar writhed in rejection. The pain, to him, was worth it.

Valerie watched the coin boil within his cold flesh. Steam and flames plumed upward as it sizzled into the skull beneath.

"What is your birth name?" she screamed, flogging him on the chest again. "Where is your birth place?

"Shoreland!" he shrieked, and was allowed a second's reprieve from the pain.

"Your name! Now!"

Edgar's body arched up again, convulsing. Now his eyes grew dead and distant, gazing into an unseen oblivion. The coin had melted to a meager puddle of steam. While he arched upward, Valerie ran the length of the rope around his abdomen. *Twice around the navel*, Valerie recited to herself. She ran the length across his chest. *Twice over the heart*. Then she wrapped it around the base of his neck, *Once around the throat.*

She drew out Pride and thrust it into his left shoulder, pinning down his arching body. He howled and hissed, black ooze foaming in his mouth.

"Tell me, now!" she ordered.

"Eli," he hiccupped. His body plopped to the ground, only small spasms still curling his limbs.

Valerie snatched a piece of scrap wood, charred and smoking at the point. "I bind you Eli of Shoreland," she recited, panting. "I bind you to this form in all of its changes. To this body you were born, and to it you are bound."

Vaulting her arm back, she put everything into her downward strike. The wood pierced the skin, slid between the ribs, and sunk into the heart. Edgar stiffened, his eyes glazed and gazing skyward. For good measure, Valerie hammered the end of the stake further in with the butt of Prejudice, stroke after stroke, until she felt the tip blunt on the concrete below. With one final look at her foe, Valerie raised her weapon and hacked off the head just under the chin. The head rolled lazily to the side, releasing a small trail of dark ooze as it went.

He was no more. That was clear when she felt her power fading from her body.

Suddenly weary and racked with pain, Valerie crawled to the parapet wall, propping herself against it to rest for a moment. She tried to blank her mind, but the pain and weariness of her body would not permit it. Her shoulder and leg shook, prickling with blisters from the burns. Breathing was less painful when she sat up straight, so that her cracked rib did not bear so much strain. Her mauled forearm oozed slowly into the pink soaked bandage.

Unwrapping the gauze, she considered that something had to be done about her arm. Not the immediate wound—that would heal like all the others—but something about the frequency with which that part of her suffered damaged. *A gauntlet maybe,* she thought. *A bracer of some sort.* Ideas floated in her head. She imagined a mailed glove, like she had seen once when studying gladiators in school. Who would even make something like that for her?

Warren would know, but he was gone. A sudden and unwelcome loneliness enshrouded her. There had been something there, that moment she left the hospital and got in the car with Warren. There was talk of nightbreakers and of an adventure in a foreign country. There was the dream of victory.

Though her enemies lay defeated before her—one scampering off to hell-knows-where and the other dead at her feet—she could not shake the strange notion that she had lost something. The house, that warm place with Little Tiger, Ester, Bruno, Adria, and Rodrigo called out to her. It was impossible to return, she knew. She could not wholly understand why.

Why had she started this? Why did she get in that car with Warren? Distinctly, she remembered that last afternoon in the hotel room, where Warren laid it all out for her. The Red Widow, the Mantle, and their duty to put a stop to it. Somehow it all changed, though. The image of the little girl, Louisa, dazed and shivering in a dirty hole had altered the course. The sight of Warren butchered, and the knowledge that if she had not arrived when she did, what horrors the La Paz family might have suffered.

Having recuperated sufficiently, Valerie lumbered to her feet, limping in each step. She considered the mutilated remains. She was in no condition to drag the body anywhere. Cringing at the spark in her ribs as she leaned downed, Valerie lifted the head from the ground and tossed it over the roof.

There was shelter in the hotel, many of the rooms still being partially furnished. The woman had also left supplies behind. Valerie limped gingerly to the stairwell, hungry and in pain. She hoped to be able to sleep. She hoped that she would not dream.

Though the little cottage was vacant now, Valerie still felt like she had a right to be there. One last time, at least. The tile had been cleaned, mostly. Pink shades of Warren's blood remained on the floor in small patches. Other than that, the evidence of the gruesome scene had been removed, including Warren's body.

She had entered by using Warren's spare key and was thankful that she hadn't had to break a window. Without turning on the lights, she crept through the small space to Warren's former bedroom. After lifting a loose tile-set in the floor, she reached into the secret compartment where he had put away the rest of his and Marshall's notes.

There were other items as well: trinkets, phylacteries—materials like the Janus coin and the Isaac Lace. She would have to learn more about them, what their functions were and how they worked. As she gathered all the materials, pain flickered from her wounds. She was on the mend, but she still needed medicine and rest. Both were hard to come by on her own.

Outside, someone had been watching her. She let him come in, open the door cautiously then turn on the lights. Rodrigo didn't seem startled as much as he was relieved. Valerie turned her head and vaguely nodded over her shoulder. For a moment, he stood there watching her.

"Senhora Marietta called me," he murmured. "Said there was an intruder."

Valerie huffed, smirking despite the budding sorrow in her chest.

"You are hurt," he said.

Valerie continued working. "What did they do with him, his body, I mean?"

Rodrigo was quiet for a moment. "We are having him buried here. We were able to convince the authorities that he was not a drug dealer or a fugitive."

"Did they ask a lot of questions?"

"They did," Rodrigo said, taking a few steps closer. "Even an American came. Claimed to be an investigator."

I'm called a Hound, Warren had told her, a lifetime ago. *And I'm not the only one.*

Valerie sighed and nodded, packing up the last few things. "How are you?"

"I am fine. Healing. I've got the best nurse in all of Brazil."

A genuine smile rose into Valerie's cheeks. She immediately suppressed it in order to discourage any more questions she was eager, in her heart, to ask. She zipped her bag closed and turned to face Rodrigo. He stared at her, waiting for her to speak, though she would not look at him.

"What?" she asked.

"I want to know why you won't come back."

Valerie rubbed her forehead. That was a very good question. "I can't, Drigo. You know this."

"No," he answered, shaking his head. "I don't. You removed the danger. You protected us. We want you to come back, Valerie."

There's another life for you, if you want it, Adria's voice echoed from her memory.

"It was danger that I brought," Valerie replied. "I know you're going to tell me that it's not my fault, and I believe that. It's them. It's their fault, and they should pay for it and not me. But the truth is..." Valerie paused and tried to explain what was only just clear enough for her to understand. "The truth is they are a part of me, as much as I am apart of them. Wherever I go, however far or remote, terrible things like that woman and that monster will find me. Before all this, they found me even when they weren't looking. I hate it, Rodrigo. I hate that I have to leave you. I hate that Daniela might forget my face. But as long as they are out there, they will hurt the people that I care about—and the people who care about me. And how many people have lost something precious because of that evil? That's not all." Valerie paused and stared off, remembering the cryptic warning of a fallen enemy. "The world is shaking. I don't really understand how or why, but bad things are about to happen, and someone has to challenge it. I don't know if I can do it. I'm not sure what I'm even going to do. But going after them, pushing forward, it's the only way I know that I can protect you."

Rodrigo nodded solemnly, hanging his head. After a moment he raised his eyes to her, and said, "She will never forget your face."

Lifting the bag onto her good shoulder, Valerie exited through the backdoor. Her heart pounded against the walls of her willpower. It ordered her to turn, to spend one restful night, to let Adria tend to her wounds. She knew where that path ended, though. It ended with the loss of anything that had been good within her soul.

Now she understood why Warren left his children and his wife. He did not leave just to keep them safe. He left them so that there would always be a safe place for the goodness inside him to reside. Valerie would do the same in order to preserve what small light was left within her.

It would be that, and that alone, that would make her separate from her enemy.

It was a strange thing to gaze into a hole within the earth. It was not some shallow ditch that men had dug up with machines, but a deep round pit with sheer sides and a barely perceptible bottom far below.

After three arduous days of hiking and camping, Valerie had found the hole deep in the wilderness. For direction, she had only the markers from her dreams to follow. This gaping pit was not named, and it was not listed on any of the charts that Valerie had studied. Trees and thick vegetation bounded the pit; run off water dripped steadily down the side. Valerie could hear the drops smacking lightly in unseen pools far below. Of the bottom, she could only just make out a very vague patch of yellow sand flecked with dark rocks.

Long ago, this sinkhole had probably been covered over, but centuries of seasonal rains had soaked the lighter sediment below. Eventually, the sediment washed out into underground tunnels and caves. Then, one day, the remaining rocky layers caved inward, like a brick wall suddenly stripped of its mortar.

Valerie was certain that once she was down there, she would find a vast network of tunnels where underground rivers had dried up hundreds of years ago. It was as good a place as any for someone to hide for centuries on end.

Valerie triple checked her knots, her ties and her pulleys. A two-day crash course in spelunking from a local in the nearby town was enough to make her ready for a plunge into this pit. Not entirely sure what she would find down there, Valerie hoped she would be in good enough shape to climb back out.

Down she went, a bit shaky at first, but she remembered her holds and tugs. She was able to glide down into the shadows at a steady speed. Valerie landed and unlatched herself. The faint light of afternoon beamed in directly above her, but it was only enough to let her see a few feet in any direction. Kneeling, Valerie rummaged through her bag. She placed her plastic safety glasses on her face then clicked on the lights at her temples. Surveying the area, Valerie saw much of the same: a sandy stretch of earth flecked with dark rocks large and small. After clipping on her weapons, she drew out her flashlight, clicked it on, and picked a direction.

She had been right. There were tunnels everywhere. Some were too small to crawl through, while others—though large enough—had descents that were too sheer. She directed her light on the upper arch of each of the tunnels looking for a symbol, the one the Paladin had shown her in her dreams. All of this was familiar; she could feel it inside her, the sensation of oncoming destiny.

Even before she flashed the light on the symbol, she recognized the shape of the tunnel's mouth. The symbol inscribed above the cave looked like an E drawn diagonally. Valerie did not know what the actual symbol meant, but it was clearly engraved in the rocks by human hands. She was thankful that the tunnel was wide and easy to walk through. Cautiously, she ventured into its darkness, where light from the sun had probably never touched.

It was not the dark that caused her skin to crawl. It was the silence. Smoothed out by years of water passage, the walls of a black rock swallowed light and sound, creating a dreadful silence within silence. It did not help that the air was thick and heavy, making it a chore to breathe. Even with the ample light of her glasses and her flashlight, she felt as though she were drifting in formless space. It was impossible to know how much time passed as she ventured deeper inward.

Eventually, Valerie saw light ahead, gray and faint. The tunnel widened and opened into a vast cavern, whose unstable ceiling allowed slashes of sunlight to spill through cracks in the upper sediment. Crooked roots dangled low into the chamber, dripping dirty water. On the ground, the meager remnant of an ancient river slowly crawled along. At one time, its flow might have filled the cavern, but now it was little more than a stream.

Valerie was kneeling over it to test its direction when she felt her power rising in her: the heat in her skin, the strength in her bones, and the heightened sense of everything.

Careful not to make a sound, Valerie clicked off her light and removed her glasses. She would no longer need them. Opening her darksight, she peered through walls and stone. At seventeen, Valerie stopped bothering to count them all. The dull silver auras of revenants were everywhere, skulking in the darkness, avoiding the bands of light slicing in through the roof. Many of them were content to mope about or remain still. The others were crawling over the walls, moving farther down the cavern.

It was now the cool of the day, hours that the undead could prowl before the sun vanished for the night. They had all come together, one tribe sealed in a common compulsion: they had come for the Mantle, drawn to this place by its power and its authority.

Some emotion rose inside of Valerie, warmth unrelated to her abilities. *We made it, Warren,* she thought. Here. It was real, and despite everything, despite the powers and numbers against them, she would finish what Marshall and Warren had started.

Measuring her strides, Valerie glided towards them, quick and silent. The first three revenants did not notice her blades flashing across their necks. Some took notice suddenly, as though a wind had risen, but their heads rolled off before they could explore the anomaly further. A cry rang out through the cavern. She had cut down a third of their number before they finally took notice. They found Valerie in the darkness, charging at her savagely. She cut them down as they came. Disorganized and frantic, they clattered to the ground in wriggling heaps.

Valerie paused to count: five remained. Valerie severed the leg of one leaping toward her. It reeled off as she spun and stuck another in the chest. While it wriggled, sizzling with blue flames, she hacked its head away. Contestant number three crept in low and swiped at her legs. It grunted when Valerie wheeled over it and planted her knee in its exposed back. She slashed diagonally through its clavicle cleaving a torso-splitting swath all the way below its backbone. Knocked off the body, Valerie rolled away wrestling her assailant. Once she pinned it to the ground, she unleashed a volley of punches until its skull caved in. The body twitched meagerly until she finished it with a pointed thrust to the heart.

Valerie found the legless one grunting and whimpering in a crevice. It hissed at her and swiped a claw, which she hacked off in one stroke and then its head with the next. One remained. It stalked her in the shadows, growling and seething. This one was clearly the smartest of them, understanding its chances. It frantically scampered along the rocks, desperate to find an advantageous approach. To get to her, it would have to cross a long band of light spilling upon the ground.

Valerie thought of leaving it. It was behind her after all, and if it ever tried to attack her, it would be nothing to put it down. Plus, with it around and stalking her harmlessly, her powers would be available to her. Darksight, enhanced strength and speed, and heightened senses were all going to make this trip that much easier.

A glimmer of light cut the creature in half. Its two parts crumbled limply to the ground. As Valerie's power phased out, she watched a black clad young man step into the light. Tall, fit, and armed with a sword, the Red Widow's agent stood meters from Valerie. He appraised her while sheathing his weapon over his shoulder.

Valerie cased her knives in kind and stepped into the light. "Logan, right?"

A flicker of confusion passed along his otherwise stoic expression.

"I've seen you," Valerie continued, tapping her head with a finger. "Recently my dreams have been busy. Sometimes all I want is a good night's rest, but I guess at a time like this, all the lost sleep is worth it."

Logan squared his shoulders. "The Red Widow requests—"

"Save it." Valerie shook her head. "You tell Vanessa that she can come find me. I'm not locked up and hiding like her. I'm very available. So when her ladyship wants an audience she can work up the nerve to do this face-to-face. But I imagine she knows how that's going to end."

Logan's face remained impassive. "What happened with your teacher was conducted outside of the Lady's direction."

"Don't even try it!" Valerie spat. "What about Mena and her puppet master, huh? They were created by Red Widow incorporated. If Vanessa wants to say it's not her fault when her freaks go off the leash, then she isn't half as intelligent that I've heard she is."

Logan gnashed his jaws, speaking through his teeth. "And you are as arrogant—"

"You can keep *all* that nonsense to yourself, too," Valerie snarled, pointing a damning finger. "Humility is what she loves, isn't it? That's just how she needs her sheep, head hung and weak. Well, you're just going to have get your hands dirty and beat the submission into me, *if* you ca—"

Valerie felt her body fly back and crash to the ground. Half her face felt numb. Her head swam doggedly in triple vision. Arms wobbling, Valerie struggled upward from the sand, waking from a bad dream where she had just been suddenly punched. She rose and steadied herself. Logan stood feet from her, now to her left, his hands slack and casual at his side.

Okay, how did he move so fast? she wondered.

He was a nightbreaker, but how did he keep his power without undead nearby? It was something she missed in the reading, or something Marshall had not documented. Or maybe she just hadn't got to that part in the scores of pages still not even glanced at.

"All right," Valerie chuckled. She spat out a bit of blood that formed in her mouth. "Helluva shot, Bullet Bill. But—"

He came at her again. She was only just able to brace herself for the strike that sent her reeling to the ground. Had his fist struck her shoulder any harder, he would have broken a bone—which meant he wasn't trying to kill her. He could at any moment if he wished; that much was clear. That he chose not to could only mean...

"Look," Valerie said, between breaths. She rose again and steadied herself. "I'm going to be perfectly honest with you. This is how it's all going to play out. You're going to knock me out, because I'm not going to go willingly. Then, you're going to tie me up and deliver me to her infernal majesty."

Valerie paused to catch her breath, while Logan stared on, his face expressionless.

"But," she continued, "Vanessa's at war, and she needs all the soldiers she can get. So, she'll try to find some way to uh...rehabilitate me. Eventually, though, the chance will come when I can destroy her, and Logan, I'm telling you right now, I'm going to take it. You want to know why? Because I don't save anything for the trip back. I've been this close to death since my mom locked herself in a bathroom and left me outside to starve. So," Valerie said, holding out her arms. "If you love your precious lady, then I suggest you man up and do what's necessary."

Logan's eyes shifted with conflict. *There's doubt there,* Valerie could see. Doubt that had festered for a while, buried by devotion and duty. Valerie just needed him to see, needed him to realize the nature of what his work truly was. Doggedly, he reached over his shoulder, gripping the hilt of his sword. His motions were slow and unsure, driven only by routine.

"That's right, Logan," Valerie said, nodding. "Do it. Cut me down. This is what you do. You're a murderer. Just like me. Only my enemies," she pointed at the collection of gored bodies around them. "They're the real monsters."

Logan avoided looking her in eyes as he held his sword out, descending into his stance.

"There you go," Valerie continued. "Are you feeling noble? I'm sure you've protected the Red Widow faithfully. I'm sure you're ready to die for her. But today, you're going to learn to kill for her. Just like Mena."

Trembling, Logan looked ready to scream, but he didn't seem the raging type. He was disciplined and calm, but clearly did not revel in the act of killing another. Especially when it was going to be so easy.

And maybe not. Valerie's power rushed into her, a welcome ally. Somewhere close, an undead had entered their theater. Unable to hold back, Logan broke forward and slashed. Valerie parried and spun away with equal swiftness.

Visibly confused, his brow furrowed as he appraised her again. Then he closed his eyes to search the darksight. Valerie did the same and saw it...or *him* standing far in the darkness behind them. The man's aura billowed wildly with scarlet and golden hues, like nothing Valerie had ever seen.

Opening his eyes, Logan set his sight into the shadows deeper in. Valerie sidestepped to cut him off. "We don't have to fight each other, Logan," Valerie pleaded. "We weren't meant to fight each other. We're nightbreakers! Think about what we're born to do!" She waved at the shadows behind her. "Let's face this together. The Mantle. It's going to change everything. Ask yourself if they should have it!"

"And what happens after?" he barked suddenly. "Have you thought that far? One of..." he paused, conflicted in his words, "One of *them* will take it eventually. It is better—"

"To serve them?" Valerie finished. "Logan, I know you think she's different. But she isn't. There's no gray area here. It's *us* against *them*."

He lashed out suddenly. The sword stopped short with a resonant clang that echoed through the cavern. Valerie held the blade back with her newly fashioned forearm gauntlet, thankful to all the many enemies that had mauled the idea into her mind. Frozen, Logan's face showed his sudden regret. He held there, panting, unable or unwilling to recover and strike again.

Valerie would not fight him, mostly because she knew that she couldn't beat him. This guy had likely trained for years in various forms of combat, and though Valerie had her own training it was surely slight by comparison.

Also, she needed him. She needed all of them, together. So it was a cause for disappointment when he growled and raised his blade again, doubling down on his course. A tinge of panic coursed through Valerie, who readied herself for the onslaught.

It never came. A quick and violent storm of sounds rocked the cavern. As though caught up by a phantom wind, Logan's body jolted backwards, flying through the field of light and farther into the darkness. As she watched him fly, she saw the shock in the width of his eyes. Overhead, the rocks and stones of the ceiling, already unstable and primed for a cave in, groaned and leaked thick streams of sand.

Valerie spun around, dashing farther into the tunnel, toward the scarlet and gold ghost. It stood waiting. It had been that thing that had blown Logan away, while leaving her untouched. It had chosen her.

Behind her, the tunnel imploded. Stone, rock, and sand spilled to the floor. Somewhere in all of it, she heard the crack and groan of trees as they were dragged down from above. Valerie had managed to outrun the cave-in, but only by a few meters. A thick cloud of dust swallowed her up, leaving her coughing and swiping away the particles. Trotting farther in, she used her darksight to find her way.

Ahead of her, the red-gold figure walked along calmly, leading her farther into the cavern. Slackening her pace, she strolled along setting a comfortable distance between them. Farther and farther in he led her, until she could see light ahead again. The cavern opened up to a vast chamber with stalagmite columns spiraling upward. Thin bands of sunlight slashed through the ceiling and rested on a sparkling pool of water fed by the thin stream.

Cautious in her steps, Valerie entered the chamber. As she rounded a giant stalagmite, the figure stepped out of the shadows into a column of light. She knew that she should not have been so astonished to see his face.

"Yusef," Valerie murmured. "It's you."

A bright, yet forlorn smile rose on his gaunt and balmy cheeks. Unlike the man in her dreams, this one was skeletal and worn. His hair had gone white, his eyes a pale blue, and little splotches of purple had formed under his skin. But it was him, Yusef—the Paladin.

"That was my name so long ago," he said, and motioned for her to sit next him. He rested himself the edge of a rock and smiled warmly.

Valerie didn't sit. She stood before him, many feet away, cringing. "You're..." she said, viewing him in the darksight once again. The gold in his aura; that was a color she had only seen in the undead... "You're..."

"Alive?" he said. "Yes, a little longer anyway."

"I don't understand. You're like me, but..."

"Yes," he admitted, nodding and then looked off grimly.

She immediately sensed that something was off. "Why am I here?"

Yusef sighed and looked at her with mounting grimness. "Because the time has come for another to carry this burden. Your time has come, Valerie Zeta."

"The Mantle?" she asked, and gave a cursory scan of the chamber but found nothing in the way of an artifact.

"Yes," he assented. "You are its new protector."

Valerie stared at him for a while before finally asking the question that now haunted her. "Where is it?"

Yusef hung his head for a moment then raised his eyes to her. He pointed a bony finger at his heart. "Here," he said. "It is inside me. It is...apart of me."

Valerie cringed, her thoughts racing. "Apart of you? Is that some kind of metaphor?"

"No," he answered. "It is true. The Mantle of the Dragon is a part of me. I took it upon myself so many centuries ago. It was granted unto me by its former protector, who took it from the protector before him, and back and back through time."

Valerie shook her head. "I don't understand."

"Neither did I," he admitted, with a wan smile. He stood and began pacing. "No doubt you have heard of the legend. What those tales lack is a crucial insight to the Mantle: how it was to be passed from master to master. This will sound strange, but you need to listen carefully, for our time grows short."

Valerie stared at him severely, saying nothing. Yusef bowed his head and started. "Though immortal, the undead can decay. Not their body, of course, but their mind. It takes centuries, millennia, even, but with too much time it seems their consciousness spoils. Their power weakens. If left unchecked, their minds can devolve into a state akin to insanity. To prevent this, an undead must slumber for prolonged periods of time: decades, sometimes centuries, untouched. The conundrum here is obvious. While they rest, they are vulnerable, and the promise that those who serve them remain loyal through the long years is small.

"This is an unsightly drawback of their immortality. While they are eternal, they can also become unstable, as with all things steeped in the powers of darkness."

Valerie cut him off. "How are *you* still alive?" she asked. "After all these years, centuries? How have you lived this long?"

He held up a hand. "Please, let me explain. Because of their deterioration of power, the Mantle was always meant to be passed on. But not by direct selection, as a king might to an heir. The Mantle of the Dragon is the power of domination, so it is by domination that it is passed. A challenger rises, one fresh and eager for its power. To prove his worthiness, the seeker of the Mantle must overpower its current master and destroy him.

"After his foe is dead, the Mantle—all its power and authority—then abandons its former master to fuse with the new one. And so, the Dracula rises. With each new master, the Mantle accumulates knowledge and energy unto itself, making each iteration of the Dracula stronger and more powerful than the last. Such was the design of the Night Masters. Ultimately, it was to be their revenge on the world, their revenge on *light*."

Valerie listened, repulsed by the implications. Vaguely the images on the sandstone walls of the tomb she'd discovered returned to her. The evil god, the burning people, and the thirteen warriors. But...they won.

Shaking her head, Valerie blurted. "The tomb, the walls."

Yusef nodded. "Yes, Valerie. That is where I wished to meet with you first. But a threat had infiltrated your dreams. I feared that he was able to see where I was hidden, so I was forced to move, as I have always done these many centuries. Once I felt that you had destroyed him, I knew it was safe to contact you again.

"It was wise of you to study the panels," he continued. "It tells the history of the First Paladin." He tapped his sternum with a finger. "I am the Twelfth."

Twelfth? Valerie thought, then shook her head. "But they destroyed the Dracula. They..." Valerie's breath caught in her lungs.

"Killed him?" Yusef finished. "Yes," he said, nodding. "It was the first time the nightbreakers from across the world united their strength. Their greatest warrior and leader, the first Paladin, dealt the killing strike. It is unknown how much time passed before he realized that the power of the Dracula had passed to him. This was something they had not expected. You see, the Mantle passes to the victor, undead and mortal alike."

Yusef sat himself on the rock again. "It was the First Paladin who discovered what had to be done." Yusef paused and glared at the ground grimly for a moment. Then he lifted his gaze to Valerie. "The Mantle of the Dragon must never be allowed to bind itself to another undead. The results would be disastrous. Even in bygone days, it plunged the world into darkness. The Unbroken Night, it is called. Think of your world now, Valerie, and its abundant population."

As Valerie listened, the panels flashed through her mind. *The gargoyle head,* she thought. *It was on one man's head—then the man passed it to another…*

"No!" Valerie blurted, recoiling at the thought. "This can't be the answer."

Yusef would not look at her. "It is the truth."

Valerie paled. "This is what I came here for?"

"It must be the burden of one," he answered. "And I have waited a long time."

"No," Valerie said, shaking her head, pacing. "Come with me. We can figure it out—"

Yusef shook his head wearily and held up his hand. "There is no time. I am weakening. As nightbreakers we are resistant to the taint of the undead, but we are not impervious to it. Though the Mantle grants me all the powers of the Dracula, lasting life being one, it comes at a grave cost. It has worn my body down. It has thinned my spirit."

He shook his head dolefully. "Time, Valerie. It is their weapon. And my time is nearly gone. The Mantle will not be denied, and I can no longer contain its will. It is eager for a new master. Even if I were able to hide again, it would eventually drive me mad."

"What if you…" Valerie tried to word this correctly. "What if you *die* with it?"

Yusef blinked softly and sighed. "You mean, what if I were to commit suicide?" He shook his head, resigned. "We dare not try. If liberated we fear this evil would return to its source, only to be granted to another again in time. It is our sworn duty to contain it."

"I have to kill you," Valerie murmured, crestfallen.

Yusef nodded solemnly. "Yes, and it must be soon. It rejects this exchange, as it did when I stood where you are standing now. The hour grows late, nightbreaker. There is no more running and hiding for me." Yusef stood and took a step in her direction. "You are the Thirteenth Paladin."

Valerie stepped back, her jaw clinched tightly. *No*, she thought. Her soul screamed the word, and the echo of it vibrated on the crushing walls of her own despair. She shook her head and cringed. "And then," she said, her voice faltering. "And once I have it. Once it's *in* me. I...run, hide?"

Yusef nodded. "The Mantle is domination. It will tempt you with its power. As a Noble Soul, you will be able to resist, but you must set yourself a part from the world, both to hide yourself from those who seek after it, and to hide yourself from the temptations that come with such power."

It made sense. All of it did. Valerie also understood why it had to be done. If the Red Widow, or if this Master that Edgar spoke of were to kill Yusef and become the Dracula, disaster was certain. But...Valerie's swimming thoughts couldn't shake the feeling that this was wrong. In some moral way, it was all wrong.

"And what happens when I disappear?" she asked.

Yusef looked off. "The undead will continue their struggle for supremacy. But they will be divided, and the full extent of their darkness will never wholly be focused on man. Perhaps other nightbreakers will awaken to their evil and destroy them. It is difficult to know for sure. Each dispensation is different."

The images flashed across Valerie's memory. The little girl Louisa, filthy and helpless in a dark hole. Pam a good and trusting foster-mother who was lured away and murdered, her body dumped in an abandoned building. Marshall, an intelligent and brave man, tied to a chair and beheaded in the middle of a desert. Little Tiger led by the hand of some devil, whimpering at the sight of her father beaten and bloodied. And Warren...a father who had to sacrifice his life to protect the only things he loved—only to be slaughtered and buried in a barely marked grave far from a family that would never know him.

Yusef was right. Their attention was divided. The masses were spared while they unwittingly went about their lives at the behest of hidden masters. The price? A few nameless victims—each one a sacrifice—on some random day in some insignificant middle of nowhere. A little girl here. A father there. In the great scheme of things, they were an acceptable trade off to the unthinkable alternative. Except...no, they weren't.

Valerie straightened herself. "No."

Yusef cringed, trying to grasp what she meant.

Valerie shook her head resolutely. "I said no, and I mean it."

By the second, his face softened in abject terror, as though the world were seconds away from ending. "You do not understand what you are saying."

"Yes, I do," she said, her voice rising. "I know exactly what I'm saying. I won't stand by while these things take what they want and expect the world to like it when they don't set it all on fire. I'll fight them. And I won't do it alone. You said the nightbreakers united once in the past. We'll do it again. I'll find them." She clawed at her chest, feeling fire there. "I'll *convince* them. And I don't care how long it takes..."

Yusef's eyes were side-cast, glazed and lost. "The Dracula will return."

Valerie shuddered as her next words came to her, "Maybe," she murmured, "Maybe it's time one did. Maybe it's time we *fought* again. I won't stand by though—I can't stand by— running and hiding while innocent people suffer."

Yusef stammered, trying to form words in his mouth. He reclined on a rock and stared aimlessly into the sand. Valerie understood. This was no longer a Paladin, a vessel and guardian of a terrible evil, but a man who—after so much toil—now had to face the reality that his sacrifice might have been for nothing.

Valerie took a step toward him. "Yusef, listen—"

He stopped her with an insistent hand. After a moment, he raised his worn and reddening eyes to her. "I understand," he said and smiled. Something like hope sparked in his gaze, something youthful and full of possibilities. "The fight is new in you. This is good. There was a time..." he paused and smiled broadly. "There was a time when I would charge into the dark with you, at your side. As I know you would for me. But my time is over."

Yusef turned and pointed to the pool of crystal blue water. "There is a passage out of here. Beneath this pool, there is a tunnel, which flows into a spring above ground. It is a hard swim, but it is the only way out. Once you get through, you must run. Night comes soon, and they will find me. I will not be able to hold them off for long."

They were coming. Valerie could not know who or what would come to breach the barrier the cave-in had caused. But when the dark fell on the world, the Red Widow's forces were sure to descend on this place in numbers that Valerie could not hope to survive. She trotted to the pool and glanced in.

Yusef called out to her, "Valerie Zeta, when you are victorious, and you have hunted down the Dracula, when the time comes to destroy it, what will you do?"

Valerie shook her head. "There has to be another way." She touched her chest with her hand. "I can feel it. Please, come with me. We can figure this out."

Yusef's smile was bright and good, full of memory. "You are so much like her." All the desperation and loneliness melted away, and a radiant man once again stood before her.

"I will stay," he said, and glanced at the ceiling. "I will bring this place down around me..." He paused, grinning, it seemed, in the sudden knowledge of a pleasant coincidence. "I will delay them. They will find me, but it will take time. Time you will need to escape." He looked at her again. "I pray you are victorious, Valerie Zeta."

Valerie nodded, grinning with the memory of dream she once had. "Go and tell your god that I will be."

She dived into the pool. With her strength and her darksight, she zipped through the tunnel. Stopping once along the way, she rose into a small pocket of air, gasped, and then resumed the swim out of the cavern into a small spring. Bursting through its surface, she gasped deeply and settled.

The orange sun was setting behind a range of hills and trees, sending shadows over a darkening landscape. Valerie swam for the embankment and rose, dripping sparkling drops.

The earth groaned beneath her feet. She cast her eyes at the rocky land that capped the cavern. Somewhere within, a voice boomed. The ground shuddered as a shock wave blasted outward, spraying stone and dust into the air. Trees groaned and swished, roots whined and snapped, and then a wide swath of earth collapsed inward, crushing and spilling as it settled into the once vacant space below.

Valerie could not know how long it would take anyone or anything to dig through it all to find him. Even then, she could not know what would happen. That was no longer her concern. Valerie turned from the ruin, found her direction, and started the long trek back to civilization.

___Chapter 21___

Valerie sat on the bustling patio of Southside Sandwiches. It was a nice March afternoon, and she was enjoying a gigantic American-sized sandwich.

It was strange to be back in the States; it no longer carried the feeling of home. No place did, really. Not anymore. The world was now a place to be traveled. The earth beneath her feet was one great path to tread.

She was eavesdropping on two teens a year younger than she. They were busy with a study group wrapping up a team research project on Stem Cell Applications to the Wellness Industry. They were smart, the two of them. The young woman was light skinned, thin, with dark eyes and long platinum blonde hair. She looked a lot like her father, and had his same disposition: quiet, reserved, and overly-observant. Valerie was sure the girl noticed her from a previous shadowing.

The young man was built like his father: stocky and muscled, but his face must have come from his mother. He was handsome with dark hair, dark eyes, and olive skin. He was a leader type, or tried to be. Currently he did his best to inspire everyone in the group to remain focused and on-task during the discussion. All this despite the fact that they were sitting in a sandwich shop with blaring TVs and attractive people walking around everywhere. Yeah, he was a noble Joe, and the enemy would try to use that against him.

Reclining in her seat, Valerie listened to the television, set to Pilot News. Right now, a group of pundits and experts sat around a table, debating the implications of rising tensions around the world.

"We see that the Eastern Trade Federation has emerged as the power it promised to be," said Phil Blackburn, who led the show *The Innerwire*. In the backdrop of their huddle, a montage of images faded in and out on a giant screen. The images featured armed battalions, men standing shoulder to shoulder. They showed video of missiles paraded through vast avenues. They showed heavily decorated leaders waving at marching troops from stadium booths. "Perhaps the Western nations underestimated how quickly these very diverse nations managed to unite and organize. Allen why don't you start us off with your analysis."

Pundit Allen nodded, showing a theatrical level of grimness on his face. "I think you've really said it all, Phil. Except to really spell out just how impossible this union seemed from the start. I mean, you mentioned their diversity. But that doesn't quite tell the story, Phil. In America we have diversity, but over there in the East it's a whole other ball game. We're talking about a veritable galaxy of very different cultures, languages, races, and tribes of people. And somehow, despite all these differences, they've managed to forge a trade alliance. It's almost frightening."

Phil Blackburn ticked his tongue and scoffed. "Well, it will get frightening if they follow through with their promise to form their own trade currency, especially when it comes to the global oil exchange."

Another pundit cut in. "We seem to be forgetting how all this came to be," she said. "We're just talking the economics and forgetting the humanity of it. You marvel at how quickly it happened, but you're not mentioning how they managed to do it. Not all of those nations, not all of their people wanted this union—"

"Right," another man said. "Well those people had a change of heart when their homes were burned to the ground and their fathers and husbands and sons were rounded up and shot in the back—"

"I don't think we need to be reminded of the gruesome details, Andrew," Phil said. "And Claire, I don't think anyone likes what happened, but unless we can do something about it, should we dwell on it?"

"I think so, yes!" she retorted. "Of course we should. Look, diplomatic pressure—"

The rest of the group groaned, one even laughed. Phil cut in, "Claire," he said. "You're not really suggesting that somehow the United Nations or NATO could diplomatically strong-arm the ETF. I mean, that was the point of forming—"

Allen cut in. "That's right, Phil. That was the exact point of forming the ETF. It was to tell the Western led UN and NATO organizations that the East could unite and form their own coalitions, which would, with time, rival and perhaps even *surpass* those of the West. It was to liberate themselves from long held Western powers."

"Now that interests me, Allen," Phil Blackburn said. The camera zoomed in on him as he paused for a moment, adding gravitas to what he was about to say. "I've never backed away from controversial talk on my show. That's what we do here on The Innerwire. So, Allen. The ETF—Russia, China and their vassal nations—are expected to form their own currency to rival the EURO and the Dollar. They have formed their own trade alliances complete with sanctions and perks for nations that comply. Is this, Allen," Phil Blackburn stuck a finger in his palm emphatically each time he hit a point. "Is this alliance, in economic and geo-political terms, in effect...a declaration of war?"

Valerie finished off her drink and tossed her scrap paper into the trash bin nearby. The study group had disbanded, and the last to leave were the twins who stayed back to clean up. The brother seemed overly frustrated by the mess and by the lack of effort given by the group. The sister was polishing off a drawing she had spent the last hour sketching on a scrap sheet of paper.

"Come on, Alma, help me clean this mess up," he asked, clearly frustrated. The sister ignored him and finished the shading under the left eye of a dragon.

"Alma!" he said, stamping his foot.

"What?" she murmured, and finally looked at him.

"Were you even listening? Did you get your research done?"

She squinted, rummaging through a pile of papers. "It's in here somewhere, I think, Brax. Just give me a second."

Braxton Brant sighed deeply and threw all their things into his bag haphazardly. "Just come on. We're gonna be late."

"Fine," she groaned. Alma Brant folded up her sketch. She tucked it in her bag along with her heap of papers. The twins weaved around the tables and chairs of the shop as they left, Braxton out in front and Alma tagging along.

They were soft. Valerie would have been wrong to expect otherwise, though. They had lived a good life, provided for and loved by family. The darkside was a mere myth to them, and at best a heated debate topic. That was about to change though. Whether or not that was fair was irrelevant.

It had already begun.

Coming Soon:

__The Noble Souls: Book II__
SOULSTEALER

__The Noble Souls: Book III__
WORLDEATER

__The Noble Souls: Book IV__
DAWNWALKER

__Acknowledgements_____

Contrary to popular belief, it's not all that difficult to write a book. Not when you're surrounded by such supportive family and friends as I am.

The whole process was something of a surprise journey. In fact, it was so unlikely that I haven't ruled out that this might be the best accident I've ever had happen. It started when Karen Osteen surprised me with a certain birthday present, which sparked the sudden thought that I might take up writing again. Just for fun. A hobby. Like a guy building a car in his garage. A short time after, while vacationing in the large home of JP and Gannon Valiulis, I found myself in their spacious basement with lots of time and quiet, and that spark kindled into a flame.

I wrote the first chapter. It was bad. So, so bad. But that's where supportive family and friends come in. The first of my two most dedicated readers, Heather Alice Shea, was steady with words of praise. Her commentary and chapter-by-chapter reactions were well worth the long hours spent pawing at the keyboard. The second and my most devoted reader, my wife, Erin Rebecca Booth, is perhaps the only reason (other than my busy fingers) that this series even exists. Our late night discussions patched many a glaring plot hole and solved some of the most troubling conundrums—the greatest of which being how to bring the story of Valerie Zeta to a satisfying, albeit bittersweet, finale.

With the writing finished, summoning the book into reality required the magic of others. A huge thanks to Tom Lopez for creating a fantastic cover image and for conjuring both hero and villain out of the shadows of his ink and imagination.

Then there was Jenny Webb—a true noble soul—swooping in at a moment that I had not expected help. Her practiced and professional sorcery are responsible for this book's amazingly designed cover.

Finally, I thank the other women of my life, my mother Robby Alice Booth, who gifted to me my first word processor. She was my first fan and kindred storyteller. And how could I forget my two biggest cheerleaders? I thank my daughters, Lucia Rebecca and Sophie Elizabeth, who were so patient and encouraging while I was consumed in writing.

Without any of you, none of this was possible.